WOLVES OF EDEN

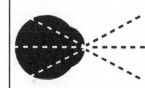

WOLVES OF EDEN

KEVIN MCCARTHY

THORNDIKE PRESS
A part of Gale, a Cengage Company

GALE
A Cengage Company

Farmington Hills, Mich • San Francisco • New York • Waterville, Maine
Meriden, Conn • Mason, Ohio • Chicago

LIBRARY OF CONGRESS CIP DATA ON FILE.
CATALOGUING IN PUBLICATION FOR THIS BOOK
IS AVAILABLE FROM THE LIBRARY OF CONGRESS

ISBN-13: 978-1-4328-6232-9 (hardcover)

Published in 2019 by arrangement with W. W. Norton & Company. Inc.

Printed in Mexico
1 2 3 4 5 6 7 2 32 22 12 01 9

To my father,
Colonel Geoffrey McCarthy MD USAF
Retired

and

To the memory of the American Indian
peoples who suffered and died
defending their homeland and the
impoverished immigrant soldiers
who suffered and died in the U.S.
government's efforts to take it from them.

CONTENTS

The Bozeman Trail and Its Forts, 1866

MONTANA TERRITORY

Missouri R.

Musselshell R.

Yellowstone R.

R O C K Y

Ft. Ellis

Bozeman

Virginia City

Ft. C. F. Smith

Powder R.

Bighorn R.

Bighorn Mts.

Ft. Phil Kearny

IDAHO

M O U N T A I N S

Ft. Reno

Snake R.

Ft. Laramie

UTAH

□ Fort

--- State/territory boundary

—— Bozeman Trail

·········· Oregon Trail

COLORAD

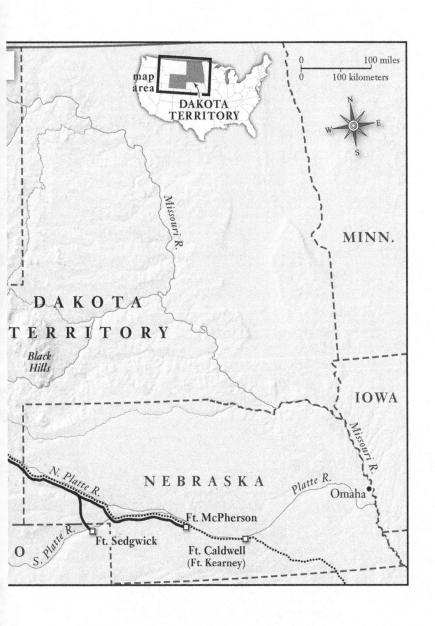

■ ■ ■ ■

I
A JOB OF WORK

■ ■ ■ ■

Something startles me where I thought I
    was safest,
I withdraw from the still woods I loved,
I will not go now on the pastures to walk,
I will not strip the clothes from my body to
    meet my lover the sea,
I will not touch my flesh to the earth as to
    other flesh to renew me.

O how can it be that the ground itself does
    not sicken?
How can you be alive you growths of
    spring?

How can you furnish health you blood of
  herbs, roots, orchards, grain?
Are they not continually putting distemper'd
  corpses within you?
Is not every continent work'd over and over
  with sour dead?

— WALT WHITMAN,
"THIS COMPOST"

1

There is a Judas hole in the heavy wooden door. Peering through it, the cavalry officer can see the prisoner sleeping under a buffalo hide rug on a rough, grass-stuffed mattress, his forage cap pulled as low as it will go against the cold. The officer tries to summon the prisoner's face from days past, from the war.

It is bitter winter and the cavalry officer can see his own breath, the dirt floor of the fort's guardhouse frozen solid under his boots. In his hand is a hardbacked quartermaster's accounts ledger belonging to the prisoner and in it is the prisoner's story. The officer cannot be certain that this story is the truth but he feels it is a kind of truth, a strain of verity.

In his account, the prisoner has written that he and the officer have met once before

13

but there is much about the war that the officer has forgotten, wishes to forget. He was drunk for much of it. Has been drunk since and is drunk again now.

A truth. There are as many truths as there are witnesses to a thing, the officer thinks. But it does not matter. Murder cannot matter. If it did, there would be little left to do in the world for men such as himself. Men such as the prisoner sleeping behind this door. For if God loves us and has put us here for a reason, then surely He means for us to do what we have found we do best? It does not matter.

2

THE TRUE TESTAMENT & CONFESSIONS OF A SOLDIER IN THE 18TH INFANTRY IN THE REGULAR ARMY OF THE UNITED STATES AT FORT PHIL KEARNY IN THE MOUNTAIN DISTRICT

— *December 18, 1866* — You will want to laugh when I tell you it was a General who did give me the idea to write down an account of my days here in the far & forlorn West. It was a General you would hardly believe it but it is True As God.

At Ft. Caldwell in the Nebraska Territories it was & I labouring for Mrs. Carrington & while packing the madam's things for transport I overheard the great General William T. Sherman himself tell Mrs. Carrington & the other officer wives that to venture so far West with their husbands in the service of the Army & not record their sentiments & observations would be pure criminal. "A crime on the historical record!" the General said & the ladies did all agree & swear blind to him they would keep account of the adventures to befall them.

Well there was I no better than an ox porting crates & bed frames as the ladies took their coffee & cakes with our beloved Uncle Billy Sherman but says I to myself that day, "Well why not you Michael?" Why do you not keep an account of your adventures & travails? Why not? You did soldier alongside boys who kept journals in the War & who did adorn them with fine drawn pictures & cartes de visits & all shades & colours of ribbons & stories cut from the papers so to record the events of battles they fought in.

One fellow I remember well he just wrote down the songs sung & stories told about the camp because he did not like to think too much on the fighting but all of them boys somehow made testament to a time in their lives when they were chucked into the roaring flames of history. So if they could do it well why not you Michael? I did wonder that day with the crates I carried for Mrs. Carrington dragging the arms near off me.

For though it is usually the Generals & Admirals who write down memories of their wars while Sailor Jack or Soldier Bill does

the dying for them it does not state anywhere in the Articles of War that a plain
fighting man such as myself <u>cannot</u> write
down his own account of what such flames
do look like from inside of history's fire.

But did I take to writing when I heard the
Great Sherman say this? Of course I did
not no more than I would of done it in the
War. Never once before this moment did I
write a single thing about myself or my
brother to spite thinking much of the notion that day at Ft. Caldwell in the Nebras-
kas. It is only now when I am <u>not</u> free at all
but instead have the time & the quiet of the
Guardhouse that I can write of how my
brother & myself come to be in such a tight
spot as we are in now with you Sir breathing down our necks like I do not know what
kind of beast in the forest.

I think it strange & sad it comes to this
but I will do it anyway & it will be an account of sorts but it will not be a diary or
story for my children to read or their
children or for myself to look back on when
I am old & grey. No. I will write it for you
Sir. For though you surely will not recall it
we met once before myself & my brother &
yourself & at that meeting you did save us
from certain harm or death indeed in a
place called the Slaughter Pen at Chicka-

17

mauga in Tennessee. I am in your debt Sir. We are in your debt & because of this you will have my record of events when a different man sent to hang us would not.

But do not expect this to be an easy record of my guilt because I have learnt that a man can be convicted of a thing by law & feel nothing about it one way or the other in his heart while guilt can eat him alive for a thing different altogether even though this may be something that the law will never know or care a thing about.

I tell you Sir things may be different altogether to how you might reckon them. Or perhaps things are exactly as you imagine them to be. It does not matter for if I have the time & lamp oil enough for it I will try to lay things out for you. As you know yourself we have a saying a shanockal as we call it in the language of home we both share which goes Ni few dada scall gan udar. I do not know how to write it properly but it means in English that a story told by a man with no knowledge of it is a worthless thing. So I say to you that while you may of heard stories about what happened that night in Sutler Kinney's shebeen well all such tales are worthless things nothing but nonsense & gossip & slander.

But I do know the story worth telling.

Perhaps it is only myself & my brother Tom who know it in full. Most of the others well they are no more of this world May God Give Them Rest. (Some of them but not all.)

So you will have the truth of things but I must first beg you Sir to forgive my poor show of letters here for I am not a learned man. Our father would only allow his children go to lessons when their labouring was done & since then I have only the back East newspapers & borrowed books for a school master so you must go easy with me.

Is it strange that I feel in my heart I should write this in the tongue I was rared up with that is <u>as gwaylga</u> or the Gaelic? I feel it is wrong that I cannot do it but the Master did not teach us to write in it while mother & father could not write anything in any language for they had no schooling. And though the Master's Irish was lovely & fine for a foreign man from Tipperary he always said that we had enough of the Rough Tongue at home & what we should acquire was the language of the conquering Crown if ever were we to get on in the World of Men. For the Gaelic is fine for songs & yarns but it will get a body nowhere at all in the Courts of Law or at Market the Master did warn us more than once. He fell down to the bloody flux in '46 or '47 so that was the end of my schooling but he gave me enough English to write this I do hope.

All of which is a fine joke because for all the <u>Bearla</u> we now speak you may see here in these pages how well my brother & myself have got on in this World of Men because for the poor man there is no language not even the Queen's Own English that will keep his neck from the noose if his betters want it in there God Help Us.

(Well God has not done <u>that</u> as you will soon see.)

3

November 12, 1866 — Dept. of the Platte HQ,
Post of Omaha, Nebraska Territory

"He drunk again, Corporal?"

"There's no *again* in it when it comes to the captain."

"He ain't no captain, neither. There be only one pumpkin rind apiece on them shoulder straps there." The young private points to the chair where the sleeping officer's uniform tunic is hanging.

"*Brevet* captain. He was knocked back in rank like all the others when the war ended. He's still a captain, though he's no longer paid as one and doesn't like being called it."

"Like Custer don't still like being called *General*?"

"You ever met Custer, Private Rawson?"

"No I have not."

"Did you fill the bath?"

21

"I filled it. And there be soap. I found some soap."

"There's a medal for that. Warm but not too warm?"

"The soap or the bath?"

Corporal Daniel Kohn turns and stares at Private Rawson, searching for sarcasm but settling on stupidity because that is mostly what one encounters in the army.

"The bath, you dunderhead. The captain's nerves don't take to too hot water on waking. You'll hear him roaring all over the goddamn post if that water's too hot."

"Well you check it then, Corp. It ain't too hot for me, but how's I supposed to know 'just right' for Captain Mucky Muck?" The young private looks down on the sleeping officer with distaste. It is a distaste his orderly, Corporal Kohn, often shares.

"Just grab an arm and aid me. By the time we wake him and get him stripped down, it should be all right." Corporal Kohn leans over the officer. "And for God's sake, don't light a match. We'd all go up like I don't know what."

Private Rawson says, "Like a goddamn cotton barn."

Kohn smiles. He had set more than one of those alight only recently. A year ago. More? It seems like yesterday.

He pats the captain's cheek lightly at first. "Captain Molloy? Captain? You need to wake up, sir."

The pats turn to slaps. A bar of sun flares through a gap in the canvas curtains and lights the officer's face. His eyes squeeze shut in response.

"Captain, you need to rouse yourself. General Cooke's summoned you, sir. You've got one hour."

The officer's eyelids flicker.

The private says, "He's right and properly fucked. He be worse than General Cooke hisself."

"He's worse than most."

Private Rawson says, with some relish, "You know Cooke can't abide a tardy man. Can't abide an early man neither. He be a crochety sonofabitch."

"I know that." *Slap.* "Captain, wake up."

The officer's eyes open, gluey lips part to speak. "I'll have you shot . . ."

"I hope not, sir, but you'll have to rouse yourself to do it."

The officer rolls over and drags a blanket across his eyes. Sour sweat and whiskey fumes in the small barracks room. Don't light a match. An empty jug on the small desk, another upturned on the floor. Belts and cavalry cutlass in a tangle in the corner.

Corporal Kohn takes up the officer's tunic and inspects it, picks at something encrusted on the dark blue wool. Dry food. Puke? A damp rag will have to do, he thinks. Damp rag and a brush to the tunic and run the britches under a hot iron. Time for it? Have to be. Rawson can give the boots and belts a wipe. Drunk again? Drunk still. Two years of it nearly. Kohn knows the day and the hour when drunk sometimes became drunk all the time.

"Take an arm, Private. We don't have all day. And then heelball his boots and belts as best you can. We can't have him meeting the General looking like he's been dragged ass backwards through a bush."

With only a scarred, paper-strewn desk between himself and the general, First Lieutenant Martin Molloy, 7th Cavalry, tries to keep himself from smiling. Poor, poor Cooke, he thinks. General Philip St. George Cooke. Bitter bastard. Bitterest bastard in the whole godforsaken army. The bitter root. You'd be bitter too if your son-in-law whipped you like a thieving house-maid in the war. And Cooke's own son even, John Rogers, another rebel Sessioner who will not speak to his father. Poor man.

I am three sheets to the breeze still, God

bless us, Molloy thinks. Coffee and brandy and a lukewarm bath. A shave and manhandled into uniform. What would I do without Daniel, my lovely, loyal Daniel Kohn? God bless and save his snipped prick. Court-martialled five times over, no doubt, but for him. He knows me. The one man in the world. Knows my ways, knows why, thank God. So, coffee and brandy, thank Daniel. And when the coffee and brandy burn off? God help me, torment surely. Terrible things to be seen behind the eyes. Nothing to smile about. Hell to pay if I sober up before we're done here. Set your face straight to bitter Cooke, Molloy tells himself. Mighty, bearded, bitter Cooke. Molloy winks at Kohn, who is standing at parade rest in front of the office door, but Kohn is inscrutable.

"Is there something you find amusing, Lieutenant Molloy?"

Lieutenant and not Brevet Captain or Captain, as is the customary address for those promoted during the war and then demoted at its end. He must have seen me smile. Don't, for the love of all that's holy, smile in the good general's presence. Though why not, by God? All of this a dusty rag, a soiled ruse, Molloy thinks. Every day passed above ground.

"No sir, not at all."

General Cooke shifts his gaze to Molloy's orderly. "Kohn . . ."

"Yessir," Corporal Kohn says.

"I knew Spiegel in the war. A good officer, Spiegel. He was a Jew."

"Yessir."

"Blown to bits at Snaggy Point. Didn't find much of him. Did you know the man?"

"No sir, I was 5th Cavalry, sir."

"With Custer?"

"Yessir. With Captain Molloy under Custer on 2nd Division staff in Texas and now in the 7th at Fort Riley, sir."

Cooke's mouth folds in on itself. "Custer. You're dismissed, Corporal."

Molloy stares at Cooke as Kohn leaves. Cooke was quick to spot Kohn for a Jew, he thinks. Everybody's on the lookout for them now, the occupied South supposedly infested with leeching bankers and postwar profiteers. Molloy had never met a single Jew man among the many leeches he met while on occupation duty in Shreveport or Austin though he'd met many who were as Christian as Christ himself. What matter is Kohn's race to Cooke? Didn't profit much from the war himself, the good general. Or Kohn. Poor Kohn got nothing but scars and horses shot out from under him from the war. And me, God love him. He got me.

Molloy keeps his face blank. I'd kill a priest for a drink, he thinks, pondering his chances in present company. Known to take a drop himself, Cooke. You'd know it to look at him. Molloy's eyes drift to the ticking clock on the wall, roman numbers reading 10:20. His hope dies with the time. Not even a frontier posted general drinks at 10:20 of a November morning. Not as a rule. Molloy lets his eyes wander to the window at Cooke's back. A large cottonwood tree with its sparse scatter of wet yellow leaves glinting in the sun. Autumn dying into winter. Jesus in heaven, where does a bloody year get to?

Cooke is speaking.

"Sir?"

"I said Custer must not like you much. I've never known a first lieutenant, a company first, exiled as you've been with only a string of ponies for an excuse to be rid of him."

Exiled? The pot and the kettle, my dear General, Molloy thinks and again tries to keep from smiling. He hears himself say, "He has good reason not to like me, sir, as I most definitely do not like him. I have requested . . ." He clears his throat. "I have requested —"

27

"I understand Custer's shunned the bottle. And ungentlemanly language." Molloy hears mockery in Cooke's words, though whether it is for himself or for Custer he does not know or care. Numb.

He hears himself continue, "I have requested a transfer out of the 7th several times, sir."

"The regiment is larger than the men in it, Lieutenant."

"And only as strong as the men who lead it, General." He feels safe enough speaking this way because he knows, without having considered it before, what Cooke thinks of Custer, the blond-locked peacock: the youngest general in army history. A glorious, bold, battlefield brevet promotion — like Molloy and so many others — now back to colonel in peacetime though still called "General" Custer in the papers back East. Meanwhile, Cooke had found himself riding a recruiting desk for much of the war and now tasked with running the North Platte or Mountain District or whatever they are calling it these days while the papers talk high political office for George Armstrong Custer. No one talks at all of St. George Cooke. Not after the whipping he took in the war. Molloy knows in his bones

Cooke despises Custer on his reputation alone.

"You be watchful of your tongue, Lieutenant," Cooke says.

"Yessir, though I feel I'd better serve the army in another regiment, General."

"The army will decide how you'll best serve it. Is that clear to you?"

"Yessir."

Molloy's hand twitches in his lap and he must focus all his attention for a moment to quell it. Sweat sheens his brow and the Nebraska light stabs at his eyes through the window. He looks away and swallows back blossoming nausea. Serve the army. Best. Last night's whiskey, this morning's brandy and coffee, all of it smoldering ash now in his belly.

Two loud raps on the door, like gunshots to Molloy, like the gallows' trap clapping open beneath a man's feet. He starts in his chair and his legs take to jigging. He tenses them and his hands resume their twitching instead. He clenches them together beneath the battered Hardee hat on his lap.

"Coffee, General." The private soldier who'd helped Kohn dress and bathe him enters with a tray. Rawson? Doesn't matter, his name. The private sets the tray down on Cooke's desk and hands a mug to Molloy.

Careful, Jesus, don't drop it. His hands shake as he takes the mug but it is only half-full, to avoid any sloshing out of the coffee. And half of that is brandy, thank God. Thank Kohn. Molloy can smell it before it makes his mouth.

Another sip and Molloy winks at the private while Cooke sugars his own mug, battered tin, a relic from his dragoon days. Bone china would work just as well for the man, Molloy thinks, the sweat cooling on his brow, the tremors stilling in his legs and hands with another sup. He smiles at his savior knowing it is Kohn's work behind it all. I would be lost without him. Must be kinder to the man lest I lose him.

"Thank you kindly, Private," he says. "It's fine coffee."

"My pleasure, Lieutenant." The soldier turns to Cooke. "Will there be anything else, General?"

Cooke blows on his coffee and waves the soldier away.

Thank God in heaven, Molloy thinks. May he bless and save Daniel Kohn, my angel of mercy, in the wings, the shadows. My guardian angel.

The coffee is warm but not too hot and the brandy is the only thing that burns.

30

■ ■ ■ ■

In the post's cookhouse Corporal Kohn says to Private Rawson, "You're certain he got the right mug?"

"Course I'm *certain* he got the right one. That boy gots the shakes like he got the malaria fevers. But one sup of the good stuff and he calmed down like we done dosed him with laud'num. Now, stump up, Corp."

"No way to talk to a man above you in rank and station, Private Rawson," Kohn says, grateful to the soldier despite something about the boy that rankles. Hardly any distance at all, Kohn knows, between a corporal and a private but some respect should be shown. It is as if the general contempt shown to Molloy has sifted down to him as his orderly. Or perhaps he himself does not command respect?

The private smiles at him. "No rank or no station gon' matter where you headed."

Kohn hands him a half-dollar coin. He will repay himself later from Molloy's purse, of which he is in charge. From his pay to his field reports to his letters home to Galway, Molloy has put it all in Kohn's hands. Kohn is honored to be so trusted, and conscientious to a fault, but wonders would

31

Molloy have made him his chargé d'affaires if he were a Catholic or Methodist. A Portugee or Swede. A Jew for your financial affairs, Molloy has said himself, in jest, yes, but half in jest, full in earnest, as the officer has also said more than once. Still, Kohn is more of a nursemaid of late than a banker or clerk and Molloy has stopped caring at all what becomes of his money or his affairs. Every morning Kohn fears what he will find when he knocks to wake him but he has stopped hiding Molloy's Remington New Model, knowing the man has chosen a slower form of suicide.

"Thank you kindly, Corp," Rawson says, making to leave.

"So where is it you think I'm going, Rawson?"

"You *and* the sot. Why you think he in there with Ol' Thunder now anyway? Only gettin' his marchin' orders."

"The Captain's transfer —"

"Transfer?" Private Rawson barks with laughter. "Hell, you boys be *transferred* north before the Sioux Injuns give y'all permanent transfer west, minus y'all's hair. Good luck and Godspeed, my friend."

Gooseflesh walks up Kohn's back. Someone stepping on his grave. He says, "Go fuck yourself, Private."

Private Rawson drags his finger across his throat. "See you in hell, Corporal Kohn."

"Feeling better, Lieutenant?"

Molloy sips his brandy-coffee and nods. Cooke knows the count, of course he does. He most probably has three parts cognac or Kentucky corn mash in his own brew. And sure what harm?

"Yessir, General."

Cooke observes Molloy for a long moment, as if reconsidering something. For good or ill.

"Fort Phil Kearny," Cooke says, picking a half-smoked cheroot from a clay bowl on his desk.

"I don't know it, sir. Forts seem to be sprouting up all over. Like . . ." He had it. Gone now. *Weeds?* Don't think the old boy would like that one. Mum's the word. *Shtum,* like Kohn says. German, the word. Yiddish? Both perhaps.

"Yes, well, it's in the Dakota Territory, Mountain District. *My* district, Lieutenant."

Cooke waits and Molloy nods obligingly, imagining he knows what is coming. Ponies. New forts want horseflesh. The general sees in me a fine drover and desires that I bring a string of them to some forlorn fort of barked logs and mud floors. And what did

33

you expect, Molloy?

Cooke says, "There's been some foul business there. Foul."

Not this. "Sir?"

"In *my* fort, *my* district, Lieutenant Molloy."

An edge around the words, Cooke's Virginia coming out in them. Glowering through cheroot smoke as if Molloy were the foul business itself. Despite the brandy, Molloy swallows and sits straighter in his chair.

"What sort of foul business, sir?"

Cooke shakes his head and flicks half an inch of ash in the direction of the clay bowl. "McCulloch. Hugh McCulloch."

Something familiar in the name. "I don't believe I've met him, sir."

"Secretary of the Treasury, Molloy. A Republican from Indiana and great friend to all the high and mighty in Washington. Particular friend to President Johnson himself and Lincoln before him."

"Now I am certain I don't know him, sir." McCulloch, the man who replaced Fessenden. He'd read about it somewhere.

Cooke cracks a smile. "No, I don't imagine you do, Lieutenant. But you're going to be working for him."

Molloy tries to link a string of cavalry

34

mounts to the Secretary of the Treasury. Cannot. He sips the dregs of his brandy-coffee. End this meeting soon, he thinks. Agree to anything to get out.

"How is that, sir?"

"His brother-in-law — McCulloch's wife's own dear brother — has the sutler's concession at Fort Phil Kearny. Had. He *had* the contract there until two weeks ago when he got himself cut to ribbons along with his wife and an assistant. Nasty, brutish business, Lieutenant, more so when you are in-law to the Secretary of the Treasury who is a fine friend to President Johnson and a finer friend to our very own Secretary of War, whence comes this order."

"Sounds dreadful, sir."

"I have the Secretary of War in my ear, Lieutenant. As he no doubt has the Secretary of the Treasury in his and the Secretary of the Treasury has his wife in his own. Justice, they seek, Molloy, I don't need to tell you, for what has befallen the good sutler."

Cooke's face shows what he thinks of such a notion. Justice? For a *sutler*? Was it in even God's power to conceive of such a thing?

Molloy stays silent.

Cooke says, "I telegraphed the man and told him that word from the fort was that

35

Indians did for all three of them but he, apparently, has had it from somebody — and God knows how word got from there to Washington so damn fast — but he has had word that it was not, in fact, Indians at all."

"Indians, sir," Molloy says, gazing down into his cup and finding it empty. He wishes he had a cheroot of his own.

"Now I do not know, nor give a sweet shit, if it was Indians or soldiers or the goddamn whirling dervishes of Ottoman Turkey who killed him, but some sonofabitch's neck is going into the noose for it in order that the Secretary of War will cease to breathe down mine. Do you see where this train is headed, Lieutenant?"

Sober, Molloy assumes he would have seen it by now. "A neck for the noose, sir?"

"Boots on the gallows. The Secretary wants them and you will bring them to me, Lieutenant."

"I don't see how —"

"Or moccasins, Molloy. I do not care a nickel fuck, but someone pays for the murder of the Secretary's wife's brother, cad and bastard though he was reputed to be. You'll move out tomorrow. Bring your orderly and speak to the quartermaster about mules and supply. My orders are here. Show them to whomever you need to

show them. Any questions, Lieutenant?"
Cooke slides a flat oilskin pouch across the
desk to Molloy.

Molloy sets his mug on the general's desk
and takes up his orders. I may wake up and
have dreamt all this, he thinks. Delirium
tremens. The Bust Head horrors. "May I
ask why I've been chosen for this, General?"
The words feel dense and slow in his mouth
but the general does not seem to notice. Or
does.

Cooke smiles. "Custer has no use for you
and I've got no one else I care to spare for
such a task. And you happen to be here,
Lieutenant." He crushes out his cheroot and
turns to a file of papers on his desk.

Where this train was heading all along, he
thinks. No good end to such a task and I
am the perfect fit for it. And Kohn. Poor
Kohn. I'll cut him loose. "What if . . ." Molloy hears himself asking. "What if it was
Indians, sir? What if —"

"A neck for the noose, Lieutenant, and
you can pick your regiment for transfer."

Careful. Be careful, Molloy thinks, what
you wish for. A drink now.

"I will need . . ." he hears himself saying.
"I will need Kohn promoted to sergeant,
sir. He deserves it and this job for you will
require it." Molloy does not know how but

37

he feels it important in some way. Sergeant's pay and the respect to go with it.

Cooke says, "Give me the orders."

Molloy hands them back and Cooke opens the flat pouch, removes the paper from within and scribbles two lines across its bottom.

"Will I begin packing, Captain?" Kohn asks.

Molloy gazes vacantly across the wide street that functions as a parade ground here at the Post of Omaha. The flagpole at the center of the ground must be a hundred feet high, the tallest thing in the Territory. The vast flag requires a stronger breeze to make it snap out proud over the plains and for now it hangs a flaccid tangle of stars and stripes.

"*Lieutenant,* Kohn, for the love of God."

"I haven't been promoted yet, sir."

"I keep you as my orderly under sufferance, Kohn. I don't keep you for your wit. And you *have* been promoted. As far as sergeant. As far as you'll go in this army I'm afraid."

"Yessir."

"Did you not hear me, Sergeant Kohn? You've been promoted. On Cooke's orders."

"Thank you, sir." Kohn looks at Molloy and decides he does not believe him.

38

"You are an ungrateful lout of a Cleveland Jew corner boy, Kohn, with no manners or grace about you."

"I will talk to the quartermaster for supplies, sir."

"Have you a cigar, Kohn? I find myself in need of the goddess tobacco's balm."

Kohn takes from inside his tunic one of the small cigars the captain likes, knowing that when Molloy begins to speak like a poorly written stage play he is nigh fully drunk and unreachable. It is as if he has let another man into his head to do the talking for him. Nothing of the captain's self in it. The drink talking. Molloy often says to him, *Don't mind me, Kohn, 'tis the drink talking.* The shores of Ireland in his words more than usual when he says it, presenting another voice to the world, this one some cap-tipping Galway peasant. Neither voice the captain's own, the one Kohn respects and admires and rarely hears anymore. He strikes a match, cups it and lights Molloy's cigar.

"I'll make for the quartermaster. And we could use another man with us, sir."

"May the strength of three men be in our journey."

"Yessir."

Molloy turns to Kohn. Life bustles about

39

them in the cool autumn air, the headquarters post in Omaha much more a part of the town than most in the army, built within the town itself so that soldiers and civilians mingle and go about their business taking little notice of each other. A platoon marching drill. Wagons. Suited bankers blustering on the capitol house steps. A rasping saw somewhere, the syncopated rapping of hammers on nails. Nails for the coffin-maker.

Molloy always thinks this when he hears hammering, sawing, though America rings with the sounds of construction, of carpentry. Always building something in this country, destroying one thing and raising up another. Homesteads, hotels, banks. Coffins. Filled my share of them, God forgive me. He always thinks this too.

"And what, pray tell, Daniel, have you heard of our journey? What scuttlebutt have you gathered? More than I have, no doubt." The cigar smoke is dry and bitter in his mouth.

"We're for the Dakotas, sir. North to some new fort. The country crawling with Injuns, sir."

"*Injuns . . .*"

"Yessir."

"Spoken like an old Indian fighter. A buffalo hunter. Have you ever killed an *Injun,*

Dan? You've butchered whole dozens of men, Kohn, but ever an *Injun*?"

Kohn's face reddens. "I'll see the quartermaster, sir. And then I'll see to the mounts and packing."

"Pack enough to get us there, Kohn, but don't fret about returning."

"Yessir."

Another man inside the captain's head and that man a son of a bitch, Kohn thinks; a meaner, simpler man able to look at the memories inside his head that Molloy himself cannot.

Molloy lets smoke leak from the corner of his mouth. Hammers. Nails. The rasping saw. A sergeant's parade ground bellow as meaningless as the singing of birds.

"And Daniel?"

"Sir?"

The distant popping of muskets at the target range outside the town. Springfields. Molloy knows the sound better than his own mother's voice and Kohn too notes the musketry and recalls that it has been some time since he has fired a gun or swung a cutlass. Molloy is not overly fond of drilling his men.

"Libations. We'll be needing libations for the journey. The road is no place for a dry

41

mouth."

"Of course not, sir."

Cooke's adjutant, Lieutenant Colonel Pearse, says to Kohn, "Take Rawson. And take care of your timepiece. And your purse. Hell, your goddamn back teeth. He's been up for theft God knows how many times and it won't be long before the men suspect that he's been at it again. I've got a report stating the same right here on my desk. And he owes a king's ransom in card debt. There's not a man here in Omaha he hasn't borrowed from and *forgotten* to pay. I'd give him the brig and the boot but Cooke won't see a 'fellow Virginian so abused.' Those are his words, not mine. The general is fond of the boy, God knows why, but the damn fool will end up with his throat cut if I don't get shot of him somehow."

Kohn could have guessed as much about Rawson. Of all the men on post. There is some justice in it, he thinks. "Begging your pardon, sir, but is there no one else?"

"Take Rawson and be happy to have him. He's not a murderer or a violator of women so far as I am aware, or no more so than any common soldier. And you can have one of Captain North's Pawnee scouts. You will have to pay him yourselves, but if you submit the paperwork on your return, I'll sign off on it and you'll get the cost back. The one called Jonathan is in from Caldwell. I just saw him yesterday and he appeared sober. He's a good man to have with you. Count yourself lucky."

Kohn did not feel lucky but he did relish the prospect of telling Rawson to load his musket and pack his haversack. *See you in hell, Corporal?* You will be seeing me before that, Private.

4

THE THING THAT MAY OF STARTED US ON THE PATH WHERE WE FIND OUR-SELVES NOW

There is no 1 single spark that sets alight a terrible thing to come in a man's life. Truly how could you point to 1 thing in a life & say it was this that caused what was to happen later? For once you decided on such a thing you would soon see another that came before it & another that led onwards from that until you came to the 1st time your mother ever set her eyes upon your father. It is that far back you could reckon a bad thing started.

But like meat tween my teeth there is a thing that sticks in my mind as what may of started us on the path to where we find ourselves now. You might say it was the War but my mind lands on a different thing altogether.

I tell you Sir it was a calf that set us on our way strange as it may sound to you a pitiful thing shunned by a 1st calving heifer with no sense at all.

A beast born to die that sonofabitch Chillicoth farmer called that calf before he left Tom & myself try our best to save it. And save it? We pure resurrected it before that farmer went welsh on his word & robbed that beast back from us when it came up good & fat with our tending.

On our mother's grave Sir I swear we brothers were given that 1/2 stillborn calf fair is fair because that farmer Harris had no knowledge nor notion how to coddle or coax it back to life or how to ruse another heifer to give it first milk. Perhaps it was because his wife & daughters were away that summer with his wife's sister or perhaps because that rummy son of his could not of reared slugs on a plate of lettuce. I do not know the reason why but he gave that animal to us brothers the way a rich man gives the rotten cut of offal from his table to the poor man & then he took it back & this I think was enough spark to catch a flame to everything I will now tell you on these pages.

For I do recall Tom at the end of a day's labouring standing up from the crate he sat

45

upon in 1/2 darkness in our digs there among the beasts on the Harris stake in Chillicoth where we took a job of work as farmhands. I tell you Sir I see it now in my mind like it was only yesterday my brother moving over the fresh hay & packed earth to where the calf was held & the calf seeing my brother shifting in his stall & gazing up at Tom with his big round calf's eyes brown as poured coffee. That innocent thing I tell you its eyes shone with love for Tom in a way that my brother's eyes no longer shone for anything since he took that minie ball in the mouth in Tennessee. (Well except for one person you will soon see.)

You could say my brother was by now recovered mostly from his bodily wounds & you would be right. He was once again tall & strong but he was a different man than he was before his wounding & things beneath the sheath of his skin were yet roiling & spoilt.

So he could be a hard man to sit with but I did for he is my brother & like that calf I loved him dearly. From my berth on a milking stool I watched Tom nuss that beast's head like a man would a beloved sheepdog & I tell you Sir that calf lowed like a fat child. You could hear in that noise a kind of joy they say that beasts cannot feel but them who listen close know they can. Them like Tom who was always such a fine man for the animals & is still to this day though not so fine a one for his fellow man betimes.

In the shadows I sensed it more than seen the calf's fat tongue curl round Tom's fingers taking the salted sweat from my brother's skin. After some time of this Tom turned & says to me, "Harris will not have this beast for his own So Help Me God."

The words were muddled & wet like the calf's breath in the near empty socket of Tom's shot through mouth but I could comprehend them & I did not like the journey my brother's thoughts were after taking. He spoke to me in English as he did more & more as if it was easier on his broken tongue. Or maybe his thinking took a turn with the bullet that carved through his gob so English came to suit it better. I am only after wondering this now for I was too much of the moment to note it at the time.

"I see no way around it Tom," says I try-ing to peacify my brother. "Sure we are owed a fortnight's wages & there is no gain in parting before we take them." I spoke to Tom in the language of our home for there was more meaning in it for me then.

But Tom went on in English. "We will take

our wages tonight by God & be done with this place but he will not have this calf. It belongs to us. It was freely given as worth nothing 1/2 in the lye pit & shunned by his mother. I will kill Harris stone dead before he ever breathes over this calf."

I stood up from the milking stool & said to him, "Listen to yourself Tom & then listen to reason. There is no gain in killing a man over a weened calf."

Says he, "There is many I kilt for far less & so have you. Fine men some of them."

"That was the war Tom when Mr. President Lincoln himself deemed it fine & proper to do it May God Keep Him." I too was speaking in English now.

Tom was silent at this & I did not like his silence. In the guttering lamplight my brother's busted visage was not visible to me but there is no cloaking in gloaming or fancy whiskers the hollows in my brother's heart or in his head. I do oft think that minie ball left inside of Tom some of its leaden venom. It is better betimes he stays in the shadows because it can put the fear of God on a man to see this come out on his face.

Says I, "Look brother. I will bring the crockery up & ask the man will he change his thinking on our calf & let us sell it as it

48

was given to us freely like you say. If he will not then I will have our wages & we will be for the road."

In truth I had no mind to ask the farmer Harris again for the calf. It was done enough already & there is no finding sense in a man's mind when greed sets in there like mortar. But I would take our wages & move us on because I did not trust my brother not to let his spleen get the better of him. It would be no good for that farmer & no good for us if it did.

Still Tom stayed quiet with the calf nussing his palm. My brother's other hand rested on the hilt of the D Bar Bowie he once took from the body of some poor dead Johnny Reb & then carried all through the war instead of swopping it as we mostly did with things we took from Sesesh prisoners or bodies. It is true I can think of nothing that knife will not carve or open but I wish Tom did not carry it at all anymore. It has too much death on it.

Says I, "Did you hear what I said Tom?"

Tom stroked & petted that calf for a long moment before he spoke. "That b_____ of a farmer is in luck I have you for a brother or he would by now have the life leaking out of him."

I could of cried I tell you.

Instead I said to him, "They would hunt us down like dogs & hang us by our necks Tom. And what a sorry way to go up that would be after living through what we have lived."

"Lived? Go away with you Michael & your lived."

"You go away yourself Tom for we did not come all the way here to America to be strung up when we could of arranged that back home in Ireland handy enough."

I did want to say it was wrong to kill a man over a calf freely given or not. I did want to remind Tom what killing that poor Sullivan boy back at home meant for us once. (I will confess this to you Sir for it surely does not matter now. Tom struck down a dirty Sullivan brother with his stick on the road from Killorglin Fair. He did not mean to strike him dead it was only their faction agin ours them waiting for us in ambush. It could of easily been one of us dead & even Father Walsh when I confessed my part in it did give me absolution.)

But still I wanted right then to ask Tom what killing a man ever won for us up to now but lonely exile & a hard labouring life here in America with one eye forever cast back over our shoulders on past sins? All this was brimmed up in me to say to my

50

brother there in the dusking barn but I did not.

I instead told him, "Look Tom I will walk over & see the man again about the calf & if he will not shift —"

Tom looked over at me & you would of not liked to see his face then it almost scared me his own brother.

I made to continue. "If he will not shift his mind then we are for the road this evening & may Harris be f_____. But it is not murder trouble we need now Tom & you know it."

Tom said nothing back to me & I did leave him there in the dark with the calf.

"It was the War made him so," says I to myself (as I oft did) crossing the yard for to rinse our two chipped dishes at the well pump.

But I wonder now does the War be excuse enough for Tom to froth up like he does? Sure I myself saw the Elephant. I myself laid down my share of poor Johnny Reb & like Tom was steeped in Sesesh blood & yet I do not think now to kill every man who crosses me. "Let it pass please God," I said to myself mounting the steps to the farmhouse.

When you kip in a barn the lamplight from

behind the window glass of a warm house does be like an insult. It makes you wonder how it comes to pass that you have no abode of your own when other lesser men do.

I knocked on the farmer's door & stood to wait. After some time the Harris boy opened it before turning back to the supper table without so much as a nod to me (fine fellow!) & I did enter & dry the plates with a kitchen rag & place them together but separate from the Harris family plates.

"Speak your mind Michael," says the farmer then with sweet pipe smoke leaking from the corners of his mouth. "Or leave us in peace. We all seen enough of each other today I think."

From force of habit I did remove my straw hat & hold it in 2 hands over my heart & I have no doubt my forehead glowed a shocking white against the sun cured hide of my face.

"The calf Mr. Harris," says I surprising myself for I did not intend to speak of it. "Only the brother & myself be wondering —"

Harris rapped his pipe down in a clay bowl on the table as if to knock it clean but more in the way of a magistrate striking sentence with his gavel.

"I have told you & that brother of yours

the calf no more belongs to you than does this house or farm or anything in it."

Harris had the stern & rosy fat face of more than one 1st Sergeant from my days in the Army. It was a fearsome face though neither father nor son saw a single ball fired in anger in the War the father paying (so it was said in Chillicoth) 300$ indulgence for men to go & fight in their place as was custom among men of means. My knuckles went white round the brim of my hat.

He went on, "And tell that brother of yours that if he wants words with me over that calf to come see me himself & do not go sending the church mouse in his place to do the barn cat's business."

Like you done in the War sending someone in your place! As I was thinking this I saw the son smile & anger flared in my heart under the straw hat that covered it. You 2 b_____ would have less mockery in you if the barn cat came in here to see you I thought & at this I did recall some words my mother oft said when her boys gave backtalk to her May God Give Her Rest for we never did. In the Gaelic the words are Iss Minic A Vrish Bale Dinna A Hrone which in English means Many Is The Time A Man's Mouth Broke His Nose as you do well know Sir. But there in that farmer's

53

kitchen my mind changed it of its own will & in my mind it went <u>Many's The Time A Man's Mouth Cut His Throat.</u>

But I pushed this terrible thinking down under the fear & prostration for both of these come fair easier to me than the rage that runs as blood in my brother's veins. I swallowed & summoned what courage I could because alongside the abject face of my God Given Nature was also a bold & stubborn aspect which in the War served me well & which <u>will</u> serve me well in life if I do ever leave this Valley with my guts still inside me & not spooled out in the buffalo grass or with my neck stretched by the rope you may wish to string round it Sir.

Says I to the farmer, "Then we will be taking our owed wages Mr. Harris."

Well that stuffed goose of a son smiled rightly at this & Harris himself made to mock the way I speak repeating my words to me so that they rung not bold but sour & ignorant a bladdery brogue like the drunken Pat in a stage play.

"<u>Then we will be taking our owed wages,</u>" the farmer Harris said looking to his son & though he did not wink his eye (the b_____!) I strongly felt it was his wish & I thought to myself right then that I would not leave that house without the wages in my pocket because if I did then something rare & horrible would befall this mean-fisted farmer & his fat soft son & I might do nothing against its coming.

Harris went on in his own Ohio voice. "You & that brother of yours are contracted to this farm until the planting is done or have you forgot that?"

Says then a voice in my head, "But if something rare & terrible did befall this f_____ of a farmer & his whelp I could hardly be to blame for it could I?"

For I will confess to you that in my mind I pictured myself stuffing that hat back upon my head & taking my leave to let Events Run Their Course as the Generals & Politicians say. Would it be wrong I did wonder to loose my brother on such men as these when the pair of us did in the War send from this world so many staunch & honest men only because they donned the grey of the Rebel Confederates & not the blue of the Union? For if it was fine & right with our Holy Father In Heaven to bayonet a man for an idea as wide & contested as setting free from chains black Africans you never met or keeping one rump of states from rending themselves off another well then surely our Holy Father would not cast angry eyes over the killing of men who would take food from your mouth or gold from your purse? Men like this yard cock farmer & his son?

I gripped tighter the brim of that suffering straw hat as if to squeeze shut a door on such notions. No there would be no gutting these two fat blaggards however much they did deserve it for I knew that I had not the stomach for it & it would fall to my poor 1/2 cracked brother The Barn Cat to do it & there would be something shameful & wrong in this.

Says I in a firm manner & to my own ears in English that sounded like the spake of a grown man, "Sir you said when we took on with you that we did be free to leave when we needed & would be paid what owed." (Pride rared its head in me I am ashamed to say.) "And we are owed a fortnight's wages for work done & wish to claim it please & we will clear off in the morning."

Perhaps the farmer noted something in my eyes because he did not mock me this time but looked away & stood up from the table setting his pipe down in the clay bowl. Was it shame perhaps or fear that made him turn his eyes away? Or did Harris see in his mind the wildness that might befall himself & his son should he shun the soft & more sensible church mouse & come to bargain

56

with the Barn Cat for his sins? Again I blinked away such speculations & waited as Harris left the kitchen for another room to return some minutes later with 9 dollars in wages 4$ & 50¢ for each of us for a fortnight's hard graft.

Well I can tell you Sir as I did put out my hand for to take the money the Devil himself made a dance across my mind his hoof steps cutting loose ill reckonings & causing me to ponder that if the farmer has 9$ so easy to hand well surely he must have much more than that about the house. I said a small prayer to myself for to chase the Devil away & in hopes that Tom did not also wonder upon this fact.

"Not in the morning. Tonight," says the farmer meeting my eyes again for the first time since he came back with our wages. "And let me tell you this Greenhorn. You will find no work round Chillicoth once the other farming men hear what I have to say."

Says I back to him, "And what have you to say? That we did not tear blisters on our hands every day for you for an honest shilling earned?"

It was then that Harris cut a quick look at the long piece hanging over the fireplace. It was an ancient thing I could see (knowing something more than most men about musketry) & a terror maybe to the fowl in the fields but not to the like of us. Sure Tom & myself would have time to brew coffee & pack a pipe in the age it would take the farmer to load that gun. I think Harris did know this too.

"Just move it out," says he looking away. "And don't darken this land again or —"

"Or what?" says I for I was bold now with the wages in my pocket. I set the hat on my head right there in the kitchen & looked over to the son who had no grin on his gob now & would no more dare meet my eyes than his father.

"Just go," says Harris.

"We will," says I.

And then to spite myself I did tip my hat. It was the habit of years of cap tipping to the Masters & Landlords back in Ireland & 4 years of Army ways being hard to shake off. At the time I was ashamed of myself for doing this because part of me believed the old ruse that in America no man is better than any other whether he was born the Queen of Sheba or in a low cottage in Timbuktoo. Of course I know now there is no truth in this.

But my shame was fleeting for as I took my leave of the Harris house there came to be a lightness in my step the same lightness

58

I felt once before when myself & Tom boarded the boat at Queenstown for a new life across the sea. It was the lightness of change I tell you the lightness of new things & of things terrible bypassed. It was a feeling like the fluttering in a man's heart when the dice still rattle in the cup or when all the cards do still be in the dealer's hand.

We took to the road that very evening walking until Chillicoth was behind us not far behind but enough so that a man might think he would never lay eyes upon it again & in the case of Tom & myself he would be right & Thank God for that.

The light of morning was just beginning to pale the sky & there we were 2 brothers passing over a covered bridge of the kind as be common in Ohio. Our footfalls rung hollow on the bridge planking in the darkness under that roofed bridge & I did say to Tom, "Is your heart still sore about that calf brother?"

Why I asked it I do not know for there are some things in the world we are better off not knowing. I tell you Sir I could feel Tom's smile in the darkness & it was not a smile you would want to of seen at all.

Says he, "Not as heartsore as that c_____

of a farmer will be when he finds it."

It took a moment for me to understand Tom's dread meaning & I stopped in the shelter of the bridge still some distance from the light outside.

"Oh Tom how could you do something the like of that? How could you?"

I spoke to him in Irish the way we did for matters of import or matters of the heart though I came to wonder betimes if my brother did still have one beating in his breast.

"I will not be taken for a fool Michael," says he. "Run off something rightfully mine because a man has a farm of land & money in his pocket. You asked me not to kill Harris & his boy you said it would be wrong —"

"Wrong!" I did cry at him. "Killing that calf was wrong Tom! Christ Wept in Heaven you loved him like a pet."

Tom spat on the bridge boards & said to me, "We rared him up for slaughter Michael so give over your crying for him. I only done what was coming to him soon enough. You may blame that f_____ Harris for it coming now & not later."

He said this to me in English & some of his words were garbled & some I missed altogether but I took the main of his meaning & it was myself who was heartsore. Heartsore for that calf surely for I had helped rare him but more for my brother & what was become of him. I did of a sudden yearn to be out of the darkness of that covered bridge & into the light of the morning so badly I had to stop myself from running.

Now that I am after writing all this I do reckon perhaps it *was* the War that was the cause of the wicked things to come. Tom was a different man after his wounding & the War made peacetime a trial for him but can this be excuse for all that I will tell you Sir? Betimes it is hard for me to think that Tom & myself share the same blood at all. I love him as he is my brother but I do also hate him May God Forgive Me for writing it.

My heart did weep for that pitiful calf though I cannot imagine why for there has been so much killing since that day & there was so much before it. But it stays in my mind all the same & I go back to it. If Harris did not thieve back that calf we rared up —

Oh I cannot write another G_____ D_____word it is too cold in this Guardhouse cell & your terrible Jew will not feed the stove for to spite me.

5

November 12, 1866 — Post of Omaha, Nebraska Territory

Like any cavalry man, he claims he can sleep in the saddle but this is a stupor more than sleep, a pale purgatory of half-consciousness and in its thrall, Molloy dreams of the boy, of a Tennessee river town that for five days would not surrender.

"Sir?"

Molloy starts and his mount feels it through the saddle, the streak of fear charging through her master, and this unsettles her and she snorts and shakes her mane. The Indian takes the mare's ear between his fingers and rubs and squeezes it until she settles. The mare eyes the Indian and wills her master to wake, her eyeballs wide in their sockets. She too dreams of the war sometimes and twitches in her stall, her legs pumping, pumping in her sleep, galloping.

Molloy's heartbeat runs hard in his chest

62

and, though he cannot remember his dream, he knows of what he has been dreaming. He dreams of nothing else.

"Kohn, Corporal Kohn." His voice is weak. He clears his throat. They have traveled only as far as the loafer camp just outside the main gates of the Post of Omaha and Molloy is shaken to discover how briefly he's been asleep. He blinks and gazes in surprise at the tipis and drying frames hung with strips of goat and buffalo meat. At dogs in the dust. An Indian woman wrapped in a shawl splintering crates for firewood. "What is it, Kohn, for the love of God?"

"Sir, this is Jonathan. He's the scout we've been recommended by the adjutant."

Molloy turns to the rider stroking his mare's ear. "An Indian scout for Indian country."

"Something like that," Kohn says.

"He's a Pawnee. A real, goddamn Wolf Pawnee," Rawson says.

"Jonathan is a queer name for a Pawnee, is it not?" Molloy says.

The Indian holds Molloy's gaze and there is perhaps the hint of a smile at his lips. His hair is shorn to a stripe down the center of his skull with the top of the stripe dyed bright red. Four black tattooed lines run from his lower lip down his chin and he wears a buttonless blue army tunic open over a breastplate of beads and bear claws. Two bandoliers of conical rifle and pistol rounds cross his chest. He sits, on a cavalry saddle that is much worn, on the back of a brown and white pony four hands shorter, at least, than Molloy's cavalry mount. He wears two Colt pistols in a sash of blue cloth tied around his waist and a Spencer repeater rests in a scabbard strapped to his saddle. Nine cured scalps hang from the buffalo hide shield strapped to his back with leather ties.

Kohn says, "He won't tell his Indian name to whites. Says we can't pronounce it properly. The adjutant told me that. I've paid him half his wages up front from your purse, sir."

Molloy waves this fact away. "Why . . ." His lips are parched and he wets them with his tongue. He pulls the cork from his canteen, drinks and winces. "Why do we need an Indian scout, pray tell, Kohn? Surely the trail north is well enough marked."

"Well, I imagine he'll be able to spot any hostiles on the trail. Ambushes and the like. The Sioux and the Cheyenne are huffy, sir, about the railroad and all the travelers passing through their lands on the way to

Virginia City. Lieutenant Colonel Pearse wouldn't recommend traveling without one, as far north as we're going."

"And has Lieutenant Colonel Pearse made the trip himself then?"

"I don't think so, sir."

"I thought not."

Kohn presses on. He wants Molloy's sanction to bring the Pawnee as a guide. He feels they will need him. "Jonathan's a temporary take-on, sir. He's got a private's rank. It's customary, apparently, to pay him half in advance from our own monies, pay him the rest when we're finished with him and claim his wages back from the paymaster later."

"Not much incentive for him to stay the course otherwise," Molloy says.

Kohn says, "Sir, he will stay on as long as we will have him. According to Pearse, Jonathan here lives to fight the Sioux and is only happy to be paid for it as well."

Molloy sips again from his canteen and this time hands it to the Indian when he is finished. "Welcome aboard our little ship, Jonathan." He turns to Kohn and begins to slide from his saddle. His mount corrects the slide from underneath him, keeping Molloy upright. "I wonder does an Indian even know what a ship is? Has Jonathan ever seen the ocean? Have you ever seen the ocean, Jonathan?"

The Indian takes a long drink and hands the canteen back to Molloy without answering.

Kohn approaches, pressing his mount close in on Molloy's. "Will I tie you on, sir?"

"You insult me, Kohn. You never cease with your bloody fretting. Sissy would never buck me, would she? Would you, girl?" He pats the mare's neck and the horse settles. She shakes her ear free from the Indian's fingers and nips at Kohn's mount.

Kohn's horse is new enough to him, a fine Louisiana quarter he won from a mustered-out Confederate major in Austin in a game of sevens some months before. There had been as much chance the rebel major would challenge Kohn to a duel as pay his debts in horseflesh but the man had come a gentleman. Kohn has been through nine or ten mounts in the three years he has been with Molloy. Most shot out from under him. Several made lame through ill- or over-use and one dead by infected water moccasin bite. Kohn has not allowed himself to become attached to this new horse and neither has Molloy's mount taken to her.

"Are you well enough to travel, sir?" Kohn says.

Molloy ignores him and takes another

66

swig from his canteen. "Lead the way, Jonathan. Time for you to earn your keep. And watch out for Indians, my good man. I'm told they are everywhere in this country."

Molloy laughs at his own joke but the others do not. Instead, they spur their mounts and move off, pack mules in tow. Kohn fears it is late in the day, late in the season, to be starting such a journey.

6

LABOURING ON ANOTHER FARM & DECIDING TO TAKE ON AGAIN UNDER UNCLE SAM'S BANNER

As you can surely tell by now Sir this is no diary like I did want to write back when the Great General Sherman gave me the notion. It is no fine memoir of my Life & Times in the West like you see so many folk reading by the by. It is something different altogether. I would not write it at all surely if it was a testament to be read by any other but yourself for there are shameful things to come that should not be shifted from the dark of the mind where they are held. These things have no right to ink & paper in regular times for regular men.

But a man's life does take some wild turns & if only so that there is a record of the life myself & my brother lived on this Earth I will go on. I will continue so that there will be some small sign that we existed on it & that we played our best with the cards we got dealt. Well only for this I will go on scratching these pages though it does make my heart ache to do it.

Later that same week after we left the Harris farm Tom & myself found work on another. I cannot recall the new farmer's name Curse of the Devil on him anyway. It was a larger holding than the Harris stake a 2 day walk from Chillicoth & for a week we laboured there in the turnip fields beside freed black men & women for 55¢ a day. And though it was a fair stretch from the 75¢ we took under Harris we did not gripe over it because beggars as we ought not be choosers & at least we took our lodging in the barn while the blacks made do on less money with no lodging at all.

A small part of me then seen this as injustice for our work did be the same black & white & I learnt off 1 of the black fellows that he & his wife & their small children (who did also labour with us in the fields) made their home under the canvas of a surplus Army wedge tent strung between branches in a nearby stand of trees in all weathers. So I did feel at least some good fortune in being among the white men of this country though as 2 poor Irish boys we were in truth little better to the farmers of Ohio than the niggers & in some ways worse because we demanded better pay.

If ever I stopped to ponder why we were sheltered with the beasts but not <u>as</u> beasts like the blacks well I reckoned that at least we had some learning for to read a seed bag or such & in my foolishness I considered that it may be this that made us deserving of finer lodging. But in truth no farmer did care if you could read the whole of the Bard Shakespeare or the Blessed Holy Bible itself. A hiring farmer checked your hands for hardened blisters to see are you used to work for that is all they gave a D_____ for. Some were good about it & did shake your hand like a fellow well met & got a rub of your palm that way while others pure ignorant did tell you outright, "Show me your hands before I hire you boy." It was the way of things then & may still be now. We were accustomed to it.

But when the rain came down over Ohio & made the fields into mud as thick as blackstrap & turned the nights damp & cool well I did wonder on them Africans under canvas their children wet & hacking with the croup & my heart swoll up some with guilt. For in truth I know that though we

70

are weathered farm boys Tom & myself & able for the work of 2 men each & that we are fine men for the animals & such well I know too that there be no bodies more fit to hard labour than them brought to this country & bought & sold on the back of it like the black Africans.

But on the other hand my heart rode the guilt only so far when I stopped to reckon that Tom took a minie ball in the mouth for to free them from terrible bondage. After all under canvas in a wood & free was better than no freedom at all & many American & foreign boys suffered a great & terrible cost to get it. So mostly I thought that what Tom & myself suffered in the name of liberty for them Africans was worth a kip with the beasts & wages 10¢ to the ripe side of their own at the very least.

In truth it was not hard to stamp out any shame I might of felt. For though the African lad labouring beside us there at that farm & living under canvas in the wood did seem a fine & decent fellow him quick to smile & proud of his wife & children & comfortable in his liberty as if like any white man he was entitled to it well in spite all this I never did call a black man a friend & likely never would because it is just not the way of things. Just as no well heeled Methodist gentleman would take the hand in friendship of a Catholic Irish man or the vicey versa. It is not done in this country & it never will be because there does be too much between us by way of hard ideas & ill feeling. Each to his own so it is said for it is hard enough understanding ourselves & those like us without having to trouble ourselves trying to know them that are so different. (This does not be always true in the Army as you know Sir but I will let it bide for here I am talking of life in the world outside it.)

So let that black fellow himself beg the farmer for a proper hay stuffed bed or better wages because it is every man for his own self in America & every man living in her wide spaces knows it or goes hungry & May You Be F_____ For Your Troubles! as the saying goes.

But sometimes when my thinking was like this I did call a halt to it & wonder was my brother's foul & fevered view on the world starting to put a warp to my own way of looking on things? The possibility of this turned me woeful & something at a slant to things myself. In truth I think a thing 1 minute & then something different the next. I knew many black whores in the war & some I did surely call <u>friend</u> if only for the short time we passed together God Forgive Me. Life is a queer thing.

Yet all the workings of my mind & my conscience were of no real matter for in the end it was the black hand & his wife & childer who did be kept on in the farmer's employ while Tom & I were for the road. It was <u>us</u> the hungry ones & I will never know if we were cut loose because Harris's slander did finally worm its way to the new farmer's ear or because the new farmer finally decided that he could work 4 blacks for the price of 2 white veteran soldiers who though hard men for the work did no doubt be hard men to look at & harder men to warm to with Tom's hollowed out face & bitter eyes.

So the road for us & I well recall it stopping 1/2 way from hell to nowhere wondering what would become of us with 13$ between us & only our haversacks for a home.

"So where now brother?" says Tom to me after us walking half the day going where only God knows. He was squatting on the roadside sharpening that Bowie with a whetstone by way of a habit he has when one of his angers is after stirring inside him. It is like men who when vexed do smoke more or chaw at their nails. It is the same with Tom sharpening that knife but you would not care to see it.

And as I stood there with fields of corn shifting in the wind to either side of the road & with a grey sky above us & the waning heat of September upon our shoulders I felt tears rising in my eyes & I did rub at them with scabbed knuckles. For though I knew it was not all Tom's fault that the 2nd farmer gave us marching orders with no blessing for the trail well some small mean part of me blamed the ugly roasted head of Tom & the way his eyes never just looked upon a thing but instead hunted it my brother's eyes like them on a falcon instead of a regular man of the world. I tell you them eyes would put the fear of God in any farmer with sense on him. So while 1 part of me did blame Tom for this another part felt guilt for the blaming & as if to rid my heart of such feelings a rage as pure & dark as one of Tom's rages did brew up inside me & I tell you I could of wept with it. Black notions filled me like soured milk in a pail bubbling & rotten.

"May this whole country & all in it be f_____," says I to myself for what it done on us. May it be f_____ for what it done on the nice packet we saved in the war & put aside to buy a parcel of land for to live on. May it be f_____ for its War

Between The States & what that War wrought on Tom & f_____ as well the Army for thinking his injuries did be not bad enough by 1/2 to warrant a proper pension. And may every one of them freed darky niggers be f_____ for taking our labouring jobs at slave's rates & f_____ every tight fisted farmer stuffed to the guts with the greed of a land agent's fattest daughter. And f_____ the Sullivan boy them years back for the soft head of him & for dying under a blow that would not of felled my sweet mother God Be With Her & driving us brothers from Ireland & off into the terrible wide world. And most of all f_____ Tom for the notion he had that no matter what the world did to him he would do to the world one worse.

Mad with pity for myself I was & for my plight. Well I could of kilt my brother stone dead there on the roadside but soon the feeling passed only for sadness to settle down in its place.

"We could take on again with the Army," says Tom in Irish with his knife back in its scabbard & the calm come on him again like a storm gone past us. Says he, "A free ride West & some savings before we skedaddle by night & claim ourselves a farm of land as we did plan all along."

Well I did want to scream at my brother then. The Army! The poxed & cursed Army? Has the pig f_____ Army not took enough off you to sate it? Have you not took enough off it to last 2 men 2 lives? But I did not holler all this & May God Forgive Me my restraint.

Instead I scinched my eyes tight closed for to staunch the tears of anger <u>hoping fierce</u> that when I opened them we might not be standing on a roadside tween cornfields in Ohio but somewhere else & better altogether.

"The Army Tom? Have you gone mad have you?" says I back to my brother.

"Sure there are worse things we might be getting on with the hard days that are in it," says he. "I cannot abide no more farmers Michael. I might just gut one of them & then where would we be?"

He did smile as he said this & I thought Well isn't it a fine thing you can laugh at what is not so much a joke at all?

"There must be something else for us if we think on it Tom," says I.

"Thinking of work does not fill a man's belly."

My face went dark. I know it did because with Tom everything does be in deadly earnest until of a sudden it becomes a joke.

You never know when & it makes life a trial with him betimes. Says I, "You do try a man's patience Tom."

"Poor Mickaleen. Hunger makes you like a vexed wife."

"It is not hunger," I said back to him. "It is you & your wild notions."

"So will it be the Army then brother?" says he still smiling like the most ugly lunatic in the asylum.

"The f_____ Army then G_____ D_____ you!" says I knowing I would say it & knowing I would regret the saying. But as you may be thinking Sir I did not know how much I would regret it.

So our decision was made just like that with little thought given to it. At least our bellies will be full I told myself more than once 100 times even! as we walked on down the road for Columbus where there was a depot where we could take on again with Uncle Sam. I tell you Sir there was no better fools than us fit for this very Army of fools.

The only thing that kept my feet going 1 foot in front of the other was knowing that the Army would surely send us West where we might with our saved wages once again aspire to buy a small farm of land. Or maybe we will just stake claim on a plot of some acres for it is said they are nearly giving land away there is so much of it west of the Mississippi & all of it in want of men to work it or beasts to graze it.

"And there is gold out West," says I to myself the earth bulging up over the seams with it so goes the scuttlebutt in taverns from Boston to Baltimore. It is said all a fellow has to do is throw a spade at the dirt in Virginia City or Silver Creek & he will be riding the pig's back his pockets bursting for the weight of gold & silver. Well every soul knows about saloon tales & I never did believe all of them but sure there it was in my head as I walked for I was searching the very air for reasons why taking on again with the Army would be good for us brothers & not as bad as it turned out the last time.

3 days we walked & the weather was fair for September in Ohio & we slept in hayricks or under trees on the roadside. On the 3rd day we bummed a lift up on a farmer's wagon. That farmer was a veteran soldier of an Ohio volunteer regiment himself the 34th I think & a man who after some time saw us for boys who like himself once met the Elephant of War & lived to tell of it Thank God. Truly he was a blessing him & his slow horse & cart.

"You are lucky boys," says he. "Taking on with Uncle again. I would up & join you if it was not for the farm & the wife & children. Course if it was not for the farm & wife & children I would have no yearning to join you."

The farmer did smile at this & tap lightly on the horse's back with his long switch & I took note that Tom was at his ease with the man riding beside him on the buck board while I sat in back on a barrel behind them. To my eyes my brother's face was calm with no madness or bitterness or bile brewing underneath it & I thought then that perhaps we made the right decision after all to sign on again for there was some comfort to be had at least with other men who knew what it was to fight for a living. There was comfort to be had from sharing a thread of understanding though that thread may be dipped & dyed in the gore of battle.

And as if to confirm my ruminations after some minutes of riding in silence with the cart bumping along in the rutted tracks of the Columbus road the farmer says to Tom, "The war was hard on you my friend. You must of taken that ball standing."

Now Sir you have to understand that others almost never spoke of Tom's face from fear of what they saw in Tom's eyes or from kindness or both maybe & I flinched a little at the farmer's words.

"I did," says Tom. "Chickamauga Tennessee in '63. Sure I was fierce pretty before that fight I was."

I repeated his words for the farmer molding the muddle from Tom's mouth into something the farmer could understand & the farmer smiled back & jigged the reins across the horse but there was sadness in that farmer's smile.

"I lost my brother at Peachtree Creek. I still think to tell him things I seen or heard in town. I right forget a good deal of the time that he aint around no more."

Tom doffed his hat & said, "We are sorry for your troubles Sir."

The farmer gave a nod. "Thank you kindly boys."

Well there was an understanding between us & we rode together on that wagon in a peace I feel was the last real peace we ever had in this life though I know there must of been other times I now forget at this late hour.

But God Bless him that farmer brung us the whole way to Columbus & paid us 25¢ each for to unload his wagon. He told us as well that he wished he could hire 2 strong veteran boys like ourselves but that his holding was small & there was scarce enough work on it for 1 man never mind 3.

"Uncle will fit you up nicely anyhow," says the farmer when we were finished. "And you might get the chance to plug an Injun or 2 in the bargain."

"Grub & kit & a wage is all we are looking for," says Tom. "I have no mind to plug any b_____ ever again for I did plug enough in the War."

I translated my brother's words (not even 1/2 believing them) & the farmer then shook our hands bidding us fine luck & good fortune.

After this we did what any boy who is to take on the next day as a soldier would do God Forgive Us & we spent our last few greenback dollars on whores & whiskey in several taverns on the lanes around the Columbus Recruit Depot.

Of course Sir you would be right to say that all our troubles which I am going to tell you of in these pages did later arise from whores & whiskey. But then I would say to you in reply that if we did not have whiskey & whores well how could we stand to live in this world at all? It is strange how things can be at once both good & bad for a body.

7

November 30, 1866 — Bozeman Trail,
Dakota Territory

Three days out of Fort Laramie — where Kohn had purchased buffalo coats and hats against the chill of autumn that had, in their previous two weeks of travel, turned to the cold of winter — and they are descending the muddy, rutted Immigrant Road for the banks of the North Platte, where they plan to cross and pick up the Bozeman Trail. They spy covered wagons in the distance. Kohn extends his field glass and puts it to his eye. Oxen teams, three, and two more of mules. Slow going, women and children walking beside the wagons to lighten their loads on the sandy North Platte banks.

Kohn says to Molloy, handing him the telescope, "Small party, sir. And late in the season. If they are heading north, they'll be held up at Fort Reno until a larger group assembles. They'll probably have to winter there. Maybe at Phil Kearny if they're lucky with the weather."

Molloy grunts and ignores Kohn's offer to look through the glass. He is conscious but only just, having passed the three days of their stay to rest the horses and mules at Fort Laramie drinking with a detachment of 4th Cavalry officers out of Texas who regaled Molloy with stories of Comanche raids, of terrible butchery and wild pursuit. He has passed much of the last three days' travel vomiting from his saddle and has dropped his flop-brimmed Hardee hat several times so that Rawson is weary of dismounting and fetching it. It is a hat unbecoming a cavalry officer, Kohn has told Molloy more than once, though Kohn supposes the tall, furred buffalo cover is no better.

The officer's face is bright red with windburn and winter sun and sickness. He wears spectacles of dark green glass against the sun which he purchased in Louisiana, these being the fashion among men of means there, and Kohn cannot see Molloy's eyes behind them. Kohn views the glasses as ridiculous, a foppish affectation, particularly when worn with the Hardee hat.

Kohn continues, "Cooke's orders. Not safe to make your way to the gold fields in groups of fewer than sixty, with twenty armed men at least. It makes for bad reading in the papers back east and ill affects the price of gold when prospectors are opened up like herring on the Bozeman and their women taken for Indian wives."

Jonathan smiles at this, though not so the bluecoats see it. And how many Pawnee women, he thinks, have been taken by white soldiers? Too many to count.

"You are talking like a Jew now, Kohn," Molloy says.

Kohn laughs. "And you reek like an Irishman, sir, but you are awake at least. Will we dismount here and make ourselves presentable before we ride up on those wagons, sir? There may be women present."

At least Molloy has been listening. Anything to bring him back. Worst I've seen him, Kohn thinks. He has eaten little more than porridge oats and brown sugar in the past how many days. And most of that left in the mud of the trailside.

"You may be right, Kohn. Rawson, Jonathan, pull up. I'd ask for my strop and razor but for lack of water."

Kohn and Rawson dismount and Kohn aids Molloy down from his saddle. The Pawnee scout stays mounted and scans the trail, the grassy hills around them. The air is cool, the sky clear blue. Autumn on the edge of winter. The month best on the plains, the scout thinks. More of the lieutenant's whiskey, if he offers, to keep the chill from my bones. Not so much though. Sioux about. Signs of unshod ponies crossing the trail half a morning behind. Fresh. Young braves or women. Close by but no danger. Still, watch, notice everything.

"We've enough," Kohn says, "for a wash of your face. And a run of the comb, sir."

"Splendid, Daniel, splendid. And a drop for my canteen too. We will water down the whiskey some. I believe it may be time to wean myself in anticipation. . . ."

He does not finish his sentence, as has been happening more and more lately, but Kohn is happy that Molloy has seen the need to taper off his consumption. It would be suicide to stop outright. The word is prominent in his thoughts lately. Suicide. Kohn has done the drying out with Molloy before. He knows the drill. A slow and steady readmittance to the slaughterhouse of sobriety, to the grim gauntlet of memory. Kohn is not without his own sorrows.

"Of course, sir. Rawson, get a cloth and basin from the mule, the lieutenant's set of combs and razor. I will make a fire and heat the water, Captain. We'll scrub up nicely, sir, and go a-visiting."

He smiles and Molloy smiles feebly back at him.

"*Lieutenant,* for all that is holy, Kohn, I've told you a thousand times how to address me."

Kohn's persistence in calling him Captain annoys Molloy as it reminds him of the war, of a time he has done his bloody best to scour from his mind with whiskey. Still, good health to him, for he does bear up well under the cross, my Daniel. Never a finer man in the whole of the world's armies, Molloy thinks. He holds your worthless life in his hands and holds it gently. As if it is worth preserving. Not like that thieving ape of an orderly in Italy. Have not thought of him in years. Took a ball in the neck on the last day of the siege of Ancona. With the Devil now, no doubt.

Molloy's service in the Irish Brigade in defence of the Papal States, only six years earlier, seems ancient to him now. A lark for a lad on the lookout for adventure; blessed escape for the youngest son of Catholic landowners, for a boy with no hope for the priesthood, no prayer of adequate inheritance. Twenty-four years old and happy to see the back of benighted Ireland — God keep her from all harm — a foreign war in need of Catholic boys then a blessing to him.

From Ancona's fall and *parole d' honneur* prisoner of the Piedmontese to the mud and blood of Virginia, Kentucky, Tennessee and Georgia. A terrible rending of a nation, a great rebellion in need of quelling, and the Union Army in need of professional soldiers, the priest from Washington had told him that fine spring day in Dublin after his release and return from Italy. Men with experience of war, of command, he'd said. And you *do* look the part, Capitano Molloy.

From capitano to lieutenant to captain to lieutenant in three different armies. Molloy had known he looked the part and had learned to play the part as well. He had succumbed to the American recruiting father's flattery along with a number of other of Pius's veterans, to bolster Union ranks in the early days of the war. His own mother had once told him he could never resist the lure of kind things said about him. You are as simple to see through as that pane of glass, my sweet Martin. He remembers his mother's face. Not so simple now, my dear mother. Filthy with the muck of my sins, the pane cloudy and opaque. God bless and keep her. He has not written to her in months or has he? He cannot remember. Quell the thirst. Barley water and cherry juice for me now. Small beer. Why now? Don't dwell on it, Molloy. There are those who depend on you.

"Sir." Rawson hands Molloy a tin basin with an inch of warm water in its bottom. Not much but enough for a wash and a shave.

"Splendid, Rawson. Good man. And a drop from your canteen into mine, young sir, if you please."

"Will I fetch another bottle from the mule, sir?" Rawson says. Molloy has given him the first draught of every bottle he has cracked since they left Fort Caldwell. He has been near as drunk as Lieutenant Molloy for much of the trip.

"You might as well," Molloy says. "Take a draught yourself, give a sup to Kohn and Jonathan and the last bit for myself. This will be all for some days, I fear. The last supper . . ." Again his words tail off to nothing. But he smiles.

Jonathan sees terrible sadness in the smile. He thinks he might be better deserting the white soldiers. Or he could kill them and report back that they were killed by Sioux while he was scouting ahead. Then he could take work with other soldiers who would

88

bring death to the Sioux and Cheyenne instead of hoping for death to come to them.

Ablutions complete, they mount and ride to meet the wagons which now have stopped and formed into a loose and porous circle into which the oxen and mule teams are being led. Early for camp, Kohn thinks. Two-thirty in the afternoon but perhaps they have been travelling longer than normal or need repairs. He glasses them again and sees why they have stopped.

"Jonathan," he says, offering the scout the field glass. "Are they Indians? Can you see them?"

"Women and children. Old folk," Jonathan says. "Maybe Sioux. Maybe not Sioux. No warriors with them. Maybe more up the trail. We will watch for them."

It is the first time any of them has heard the Pawnee speak. He prefers to listen rather than talk. Even when he is drunk on whiskey, he does not often talk. The *taakaar* — the white soldiers — are the other way around mainly. He thinks they might better understand the country they are in, the enemy they are fighting, if they talked less and listened more. Still, he thinks the curly-headed corporal named Kohn may be *piita,* a warrior. There are not many of them among the bluecoats but there are some.

89

He takes the scope from Kohn and looks through it, though he saw the Indians at the pilgrims' wagons while the others were still shaving and combing their locks. He assumes they are Sioux, or maybe Cheyenne, but he cannot be certain until he is closer. There do not appear to be any warriors among them. Some young braves perhaps but through the glass he confirms that they are mostly women and children mingling with the pilgrims. Some young boys on ponies, some travois pulled by dogs. Jonathan has heard talk of all the bands of the Lakota and Northern Cheyenne and Arapahoe meeting together in alliance to fight and drive the white soldiers from the Powder River valley. These could be a band or some families en route to such a meeting place. Perhaps the warriors are waiting further up the trail in ambush or maybe they are away hunting or on a war party, the scout thinks and wonders would the lieutenant let him take a woman or a child as a captive. His wife at home would like another child and he would like to bring her one. A girl child — for she has only sons — to help with the hides and the cooking and to keep her company when he is away. A pang of longing for his wife comes to him, a piercing arrow high in his chest. He doubts he will be

let and it will be difficult to travel and scout
with a captive in tow but then the lieutenant may well be dead before they reach the
fort where they are headed. On this he
would bet ten horses. The afterlife will not
be kind to the lieutenant; he can see it in
his face. He is destined to follow the Morning Star to the spirit village in the south. A
cold place. Dark.

Rawson takes out his rifle.

"Put it away, Rawson. Unless I tell you,"
Kohn says.

"You heard the Pawnee. They is Sioux
most likely."

"Put it away, Private," Molloy says from
behind his green spectacles. "I wouldn't
want you to hurt yourself."

Kohn smiles and urges his horse forward.

They arrive at the wagons and there is no
threat from the Indians but consternation
and ill temper among the travelers. Black
clothes and round-brim hats and beards,
the women in bonnets and plain dresses,
the pilgrims running to and fro after a group
of Indian children. One of the traveling
women swings a broom at an Indian child
who laughs and darts under the wheels of a
wagon. Kohn notes a group of sullen boys
on ponies, young, thirteen to fifteen years
old perhaps, sitting just off the trail. They

91

are speaking among themselves as if deciding on something. Kohn looks to Molloy and sees that he has noticed them as well but knows that there is little chance of him engaging them, even if they do become aggressive. There is too much about them that is similar to that day in Tennessee. Young boys acting as men.

"Good afternoon, friends," Kohn says.

Instead of returning Kohn's greeting, one of the pilgrims says, "Please, they steal from us. Drive them away from us please. They —"

The man — in his thirties with blond hair and the black clothing of an Amish or Mennonite — turns and catches an Indian boy of four or five climbing down from the back of one of the Murphy wagons with a fistful of brown sugar. The pilgrim holds tightly to the Indian boy's arm and slaps him across the face, causing the boy to cry out.

One of the pilgrim women shouts something in German at her husband or at the Indian woman who is holding her baby. Until now the white woman has been smiling and trying to take her baby back from the Indian woman, who is teasing the Mennonite mother, making to hand back the baby and then pulling it away. The

Indian woman holding the baby sees the Mennonite man slap the boy and shouts something back. She shoves the baby into its mother's arms, nearly dropping it.

Kohn can comprehend some of the German spoken by the woman to her husband. It is a dialect he is unfamiliar with — and nothing like the Silesian German spoken by his father until his father learned enough English to never speak it again, but many of the words the woman shouts are close enough to his mother's Yiddish that he can make out the admonishment in them — "Stop" and "Don't hit" — and there is much about God and something about peace and the Book, and as he scans the group of pilgrims and the Indians intermingled among them he does not sense threat but there is confusion and an atmosphere of antagonism. Indian children chase one another, oblivious, under the wagon wheels, and another of them, older than the first, climbs out of the covered back of another of the wagons holding a rag doll. One of the Mennonite children begins to cry and another mother shouts up at the soldiers.

She shouts something in German and then in accented English. "Please, make them depart! They take things from us."

Kohn answers her in a rough, simple German that is much colored with eastern Yiddish. Though his father mostly abandoned his native German soon after arriving in America, his mother raised him and his siblings with Yiddish in the home and it was much spoken in *shul.* There was a time when Kohn spoke it fluently. But like every immigrant kid on the streets around his Cleveland tenement home, he turned to English on entering school and soon was answering his mother's Yiddish — he thinks she must also have spoken Polish though he cannot remember hearing her ever do so — in a language she often only barely understood. It pains him to remember this and so he rarely does. The only time his childhood Yiddish — and the faint remaining traces of his father's German — is of any use, he thinks, is when he occasionally barks orders in pidgin German at immigrant Bills but does not think a soldier should be coddled in his own tongue when he is in the employ of an English-speaking army and so rarely does it. The words feel awkward in his mouth.

"*Seien Sie ruhig, meine Frau.*" Be calm, missus. "We will try to be rid of them." He turns in his saddle and Jonathan appears to understand what he will ask before he asks it.

The Pawnee slaps his mount with the reins and gives a whooping shout that reminds Kohn and Molloy of the rebel yell that so many times froze their blood in the war.

"Do not harm any of them, Jonathan. Not a hair on their heads, do you hear me?" Molloy shouts, as if sober. "And put that bloody rifle back in its scabbard, Rawson, or I'll plug your arsehole with it."

Kohn smiles again. Something of the old Captain in the words and the way he says them.

He turns to watch the Pawnee maneuver his pony among the wagons, whipping the Indian children with long cavalry reins, lashing out with his moccasins. The Sioux women appear to see him for what he is for the first time and begin to shout and call their children. Kohn and Molloy can hear the concern in their shouting and watch carefully as Jonathan goes among them, whipping and kicking the children, once snapping an old man across the back with his reins and saying something to him and laughing. The older Sioux shuffle away, averting their eyes from the Pawnee, and the boys on ponies gallop in among the wagons now. One of them, a chubby boy in a bright red shirt and breechcloth, his hair

95

in two long braids, swings down from the bare back of his horse, holding onto the pony's flanks with just his legs, and swoops up an Indian toddler by the arm as he rides past. Kohn smiles at the feat. Five years a dragoon and he has never seen horsemanship like it.

Another of the boys rides dangerously close to the Pawnee in a show of swagger and defiance. Jonathan laughs and rides at a small cluster of them to see if they will attempt to touch coup on him. He knows that for the Sioux boys, striking an enemy on the body with a stick carved and blessed for the purpose is as honorable an achievement as killing the enemy in battle. If they try it he will grab their coup sticks and dismount them. He cannot kill them — the bluecoats won't allow that and there are too many pilgrims who may not want him to do it either — but he is taking some pleasure in terrifying the Sioux women and the old folks. Like lice, the Sioux, he thinks. Everywhere, lording it above all other tribes. Butchering, taking slaves. Jonathan's sister was captured in a Sioux raid when she was only a girl of seven summers and every time he encounters the Sioux he looks for her though he knows he will not recognize her. There is a sore part of his heart that will never heal, for he loved his sister and watched her taken, hidden as he was in the scrub with his mother. Every day he has lived since, he remembers the shame of hiding and watching her taken by Sioux and remembers the sound of his mother's weeping when she thought she was alone.

He gives a war call and turns his horse and rushes at a group of retreating women and children, their dog following, a lodgepole travois bouncing in the rutted track behind it. A pot stolen from the pilgrims is dislodged from the travois and rolls onto the trail and Jonathan, like the boy in the red shirt, swings down from his mount at speed and collects it. The Sioux women seem to know that he would happily rape and gut them and hurl their babies into the river and they do not look him in the face. He whoops and lunges from his saddle at one of the boys whose eyes go wide with terror. He slaps the boy on the back of the head with his reins as the boy turns and flees. He prays that he will meet the boy's father, farther up the trail.

Soon it is over, dust settling, the pilgrim women repacking crates inside the wagons, folding linen. Some of the Indian women took a dress or two, a fry pan or cook pot, and the young Mennonite girl still howls for her rag doll but not much of value is missing.

"Thank you, sir," a man says, his English better than the woman's. "I am Willem Vogl and we are Vogls and Hitzelburgers. We go to Montana for farming and not gold. We are not gold-seekers."

Molloy tips his slouch hat to the man. "Lieutenant Molloy, at your service, sir. Corporal Kohn, Private Rawson. And that is Jonathan. You won't have to worry about him stealing your sugar."

"I am pleased to meet you, sir," the Mennonite man says, and he is joined now by an older man wearing a beard that covers his jawline, but no mustache. This man says something to the younger, then speaks in German to Kohn.

Molloy and Rawson look to the corporal. Kohn says, "It's Swiss. Or Schwabian or some such. I can understand some of it. He thanks us, anyway, for driving off the Indians."

The older man continues to speak to Kohn in his dialect.

Molloy says, "Well, you tell him he's very welcome and that we would be much obliged to share a meal in return for escorting their train as far as Fort Reno."

Kohn nods and speaks to the older Mennonite. His voice has taken on a harsh aspect that Molloy does not often hear from Kohn unless he is giving orders. Perhaps, Molloy thinks, it is just the language and the way it comes off the tongue.

"And tell them that we would be —"

"He wants rid of us now, sir," Kohn says. "He's saying they are pacifists and cannot abide soldiery about their camp."

"What's pacifists?" Rawson says.

"They don't believe in raising a hand in violence against another man. Or they're just damn cowards who don't mind if others do it for them."

"Admirable. Admirable . . ." Molloy says, uncorking his canteen. He hands it to Jonathan, who drinks and hands it back.

"And they cannot abide liquor either," Kohn says.

Whether Kohn is translating the old man's words or stating a known fact, Molloy is unsure. He does not care. The Mennonites have ceased to interest him. He is beginning to feel poorly again. These arrogant, grasping, pious pilgrims. Thieving, urchin Indians and their howling matrons. He could be in Dublin or Genoa. Rare, he thinks, to meet a German who won't take a drink with you. Or share a sausage. Should not have watered the whiskey down. Get Rawson to crack another bottle once we are away from these crawthumpers.

"That fella done raised his hand and slapped that Injun kid. I seen it," Rawson says.

"They're not supposed to, but of course it happens, Rawson. It's more in the way of being against warfare and fighting, I imagine. Against soldiers." There is disdain in Kohn's voice and he does nothing hide it.

Rawson says, "Well, did you tell them they wou'n't have no goddamn sugar or a stitch of goddamn cloth between them without us soldiery comin' up on them? Them Injuns was only kids and old folk and they done near cleaned 'em out without us, without Jonathan there. Did you tell them that? I have heard of ungracious —"

"Shut up, Rawson," Molloy says. He turns to Kohn. "You tell him this, Kohn. Sir, I quite understand your position. I have no time for soldiery myself. Nonetheless, we will camp somewhat up the trail in case the Indians return. For this we would only beg a gallon of water for our pot. The river is brackish, we're told, and not fit for man or beast for drinking."

Kohn translates, adding some of his own sentiments to Molloy's and the old man sends the younger off for water. "Get him a barrel, Rawson," Kohn says, "and fill it up. Least the gentle sonsofbitches can do."

Rawson dismounts, fetches a half-barrel from one of the mules and follows the man. Molloy and Kohn and Jonathan sit in silence, the old man no longer speaking to them, and wait for Rawson to return.

Kohn says, "It's common among these kind, sir. Mennonites and Hutterites and the like. Happy to avail of the protections offered by the soldiery but too good to share a meal with them all the same. And abolitionists, every damn one of them, but not an ounce of blood shed for the cause of it. Shit on them, sir, and let's be on our own goddamn way."

"No way to treat your Dutchie kinsmen, Kohn," Molloy says. He swigs from his canteen. Kohn has not told him that he suspects a further reason the old man will not share a meal with them is because he has recognized Kohn's German for the Yiddish it really is. Jews as bad as soldiers to them. Peace-loving Mennonites have their hatreds too. Kohn spits into the dust between them and the old man. If the old man notices this, he does not react.

"Now now, Kohn." Molloy spurs his mare and salutes the Mennonites. Rawson returns and stows the water barrel on the mule, climbing awkwardly onto his mount. The women and children, Molloy notes, are watching them from behind the wagons. He winks at one of the girls, who blushes under her bonnet and turns away.

A mile downriver they set up camp on a bluff above the North Platte banks and Jonathan takes the horses and mules away with him in a loose train to a watering spot he knows so they will not have to risk the brackish waters of this part of the river.

Kohn wonders is it wise to have the Indian away with all their mounts and the mule. They will be riding shank's mare if the Pawnee sees their animals as more valuable than his wages. *Vos Got tut, iz mistomeh gut.* Yiddish in his head unbidden. Speaking with the Mennonites has awakened it. If God wills it, it is good. With the captain making such slow going, they'd be as fast walking to Fort Phil Kearny anyway.

"Will I raise the dog for you, sir?" They are carrying two tents with them on the mules. They have thus far only had to use them once.

Molloy sits with his back to a rock and is writing in a journal, drinking from a fresh bottle. "I don't smell rain, do you?"

Kohn looks at the late afternoon sky.

Clear, cold blue cut with high streaks of white cloud that remind him of Spanish moss. Which reminds him of Louisiana and Texas, which in turn strikes him as far and many years away from here. He wonders how the boys in the 7th are getting on. Unlike Molloy, he does not hate the newly founded regiment though he has no love for Custer or Davidson. He considers the sky, not wanting to set up the dog tents if the weather does not demand it. On the plains it is hard to tell from one minute to the next. The weather can move in fast, as it could at sea or over the Lake Erie of his youth. His breath comes out as steam. If the temperature drops further, Kohn thinks, anything falling from the sky will likely be snow. "I don't think so, sir."

"Well then . . ."

"A letter, sir?" Kohn says, beginning to dig out a fire pit, setting stones around it. It has been years since he has written any letters of his own. He would not write his father if his father was the last living man on earth. His mother died soon after he himself joined up in '61. His brothers and sisters look upon him as a shame to the family and he feels only anger and envy when he thinks of them. He would dearly like someone, anyone, to whom to write a letter. There was a girl, once, a French Jewish girl in Cincinnati. He imagines she is married now.

"Who would I be writing, Kohn?"

"Your mother, sir. You haven't written her in a long while. And that time only because I hounded you to it."

"What would I tell her, Kohn?" Molloy asks, and there is something so sad about the way he says it that Kohn does not pursue the matter. Molloy pulls from his bottle like an orphaned lamb fed from a teat of India rubber.

"Rawson, gather buffalo chips and wood for the fire," Kohn says. To hell with it. Molloy would drive a man to drink. And Kohn wonders: does sympathy have its limits? Does love?

"Right-o, Corp, and then we can make us some of these," Rawson says, opening his haversack to Kohn and Molloy. Molloy does not rise but looks into the mouth of the pack with Kohn.

"God damn you, Rawson, did you steal those sonofabitching eggs from the pilgrims?" Kohn says, taking the haversack from him. He looks inside again and counts seven eggs.

"I did not, the man gave 'em to me. He was 'shamed he says, with the old fucker not sharing up their grub with us for chasin' off them Injuns. He gave me the eggs in thanks."

"I will put you in a hole, Rawson, you thieving scalawag bastard."

"I did *not* steal them. Sir, you got to believe me." He turns to Molloy.

Molloy smiles drunkenly at the two enlisted men. "I *believe* I would enjoy some eggs fried in bacon grease with my beans and pilot bread. I believe that, Rawson. Kohn, how many times did you liberate grub from civilians in the war?"

"Only in hungry times, sir. We have enough vittles by far to get us to where we're going. There's no need —"

"I'm assuming they'd poultry with them, Rawson. The pilgrims?" Molloy says. He has reached that place in his drunkenness where the world appears designed for his amusement alone and all others be damned.

"They did, sir. An almighty pile of laying hens in crates the back of that Murphy. They ain't gonna miss no dozen eggs."

"There's only seven here, Rawson," Kohn says.

"Some got broke, sir," Rawson says to Molloy. Then, as if he has remembered, "*And* a man don't miss what he gives away as a gift."

"True as God's word, Rawson," Molloy says, and goes back to writing in his journal. His skin is pale and sweaty even in the chill air. "Fetch fuel for that fire, Rawson. And a blanket, Kohn. I could use a rug round my shoulders while I await my eggs."

Kohn fetches the blankets from Molloy's bedroll, noting that the captain is cold even under the heavy weight of his buffalo coat. "That boy's a thief, sir."

"We are all the most frightful thieves, every one of us, Kohn. God forgive us."

Kohn does not know or care what Molloy means. The officer has moved from the world as a source of amusement to the world as a pit of vipers, a dark and fatal place where no love or kindness lives. Kohn does not need whiskey to feel the world is such a place but he resists the idea. Someone has to.

8

NEW NAMES FOR US

"Names," says I to my brother as we stepped tender headed & gut scorched from our skite through the cursed Depot gates of Ft. Thomas in Columbus. "We will be wanting a new name for ourselves Tom."

Tom hacked & spat partly in the illness of drink & partly at my notions. "A <u>new</u> name?" says he. "I can scarce think of my own name now Michael. Sure our mother's name has done us well til now why change it?"

I must confess to you Sir we did take the name Kelly spelled as such with a <u>K</u> which was our mother's maiden name when we signed the manifest on board the La Belle Poole at Queenstown harbour & left our father's name Sugru behind us in Kerry for the scouring Sullivan brothers & prowling Peelers.

Says I, "You heard that Michigan boy in the saloon when we did be speaking to him at the bar rail."

"What Michigan boy?"

"The veteran Wolverine fellow who fought at Gettysburg & all over the farm as well but then stuck his fist into some drunk officer & was had up for it. You remember Tom he finished up the war in stockade lucky not to have taken the 1 ball in 6 agin the wall for his troubles. Do you not remember him at all Tom?"

I walked on a little into the Depot & Tom followed past a gathering of men & families & some sweethearts seeing off their beaus & honeys. Once inside we stopped & stood we 2 brothers on the laid stone parade ground. The flagpole in the centre of it was topped off with Uncle Sam's banner which to spite myself I did love mostly for I had fought 3 years under it after all. Red brick barracks where we would live for the next weeks & months bordered this parade ground & in front of one of them was a lazy & drink sore line of smoking men waiting their turn for the receiving office & we would soon be among them.

Says Tom, "I dont remember him at all. I was well spiflicated by then surely."

My brother had trouble with the words he

108

chose at the best of times his scarred lump of tongue thick in his gap toothed mouth & I did oft wonder why he chose the words he did when simpler ones might have done the job just as well. But that is my brother who once could talk the stockings off the king's own whore. Old ways die hard in men & I had some pity for him.

I said to him, "Well that fellow told us & I believed him that if a boy had trouble in the War <u>any kind of trouble</u> Tom well then that boy should take on under a new name for surely there was a record somewhere in Washington or some place & it would catch you up eventually. And when that happens sure the lad is given the boot with every penny of wages owed him signing on bonus & all revoked said that Michigan fellow."

I waited to see how much of the <u>trouble</u> of which I spoke did Tom understand. This <u>trouble</u> you know well Sir (though you may not recall it) for you were there.

"Trouble?" says Tom.

Says I, "The trouble with the Provost Marshal's mob that day when —" I pointed to his face.

"Sure I remember very little of that day Michael & know of it only what you told me. I know that we are still among the living Thanks Be To God."

"Yes," says I. "But our names went down in the Provost Sergeant's book that day. God knows they may well be on a page somewhere & like that Wolverine boy says come back to haunt us brother."

Tom rummaged his pockets for the dust of tobacco he had left & rolled a needle. He put a match to it & passed it first to me as is the way with brothers with one burn between them.

Says Tom after taking his pull of smoke, "There does be very little reason I suppose, to risk 13 bucks a month & passage West for the sake of a name."

"Very little reason at all Tom & every reason to change it."

Says he, "We have given over our father's name for our mother's once before."

"We have Tom."

"So will we go with the mother's mother's name God Rest Her In Heaven?"

"No finer woman was our grandmother God Keep Her," says I. "Best pleased to meet you Thomas O'Driscoll."

My brother gave the pinch to his cigarette dropping the dog end back into the pouch waste not want not. Says he then as if trying it out in his mouth, "O'Driscoll. Thomas O'Driscoll pleased to meet you." He gave a laugh then & said, "A fine Cork name for

110

two fine Cork lads like ourselves."

Well I gave a smile back at him forgiving Tom for all the things he done. I could forgive him even killing the Sullivan boy the thing which cast us across the ocean into the bloody maw of this wide queer kip of a country & to this junction between one life with one name & another life with a different one.

Our new name decided Tom & myself did Q up with the other men & for the 2nd time in our short lives we took on with the Army of the United States this time as Thomas & Michael O'Driscoll of the County Cork & Tom cast me a wink as he scratched it in the ledger as if to say, "Imagine 2 Kerry boys like ourselves playing <u>Corkmen</u> of all people!"

To spite my misgivings I was happy that day & so I do think was Tom. There is comfort to be had in something that is familiar to a fellow like the Army was to us.

9

Darkness settles and with it cold. A million
stars and a half moon and the low licking
flames of their fire. Molloy and Rawson are
drunk. Jonathan may be but it is difficult
for Kohn to tell because he has not spoken
a word since returning from watering the
horses. Kohn takes a sip of whiskey, limit-
ing himself. He will take first guard. He has
coffee warming in a tin pot in the ashes at
the side of the fire.

Molloy sings a snatch of a Galway song
and then stops. His heart is not in it. His
mind wanders, his thoughts disconnected
and unwilled. How did I get here? A campfire with a Jew and a Pawnee and a fool of a
Virginian thief in the wastes of America. No
place for a Galway man at all. He thinks of
his mother and curses Kohn. What could I
say to her in any letter? I kill children,

112

Mother. I have killed . . . I kill. Killer. No better than the savages we revile. No better than Jonathan there across the fire.

He sings another snatch of song. *"She wore a bonnet with a ribbon on it, and around her shoulders was a Galway shawl . . ."* Again, he lets the song die and he pulls the buffalo coat tighter around his shoulders. He hands his pipe and tobacco to the Pawnee. "Fill that for me, Jonathan, would you? I fear I am unable . . . Take a draw yourself. Go on."

The Indian packs Molloy's pipe and lights it with an ember from the fire. He inhales the smoke and lets it seep from his nostrils, pulling again from it before passing it to Molloy. They are generous with their whiskey and tobacco, he thinks. Not like some. Some soldiers would have him at his own fire or standing picket all night while they slept. The lieutenant is a weak man and this is why he allows it. He wants others to share in his poison. But it makes the journey go quicker, and this is a good thing. Money for old rope, he has heard the bluecoats say, meaning easy work. This journey is money for old rope.

Kohn hands the scout the bottle. "Where did you come by your English, Jonathan?

Did you learn from the soldiers you scouted for?"

The Pawnee appears displeased at being asked to speak. He takes a pull of whiskey and some moments later, almost when Kohn has given up on an answer, says, "My father. He was scout for the bluecoats. It is not hard to learn."

Molloy says, "It's hard for the likes of Rawson, it is."

Rawson smiles. "My daddy learned me English too, goddamn it, sir. Even if I don't be a educated man, I speak as good as any dog fucking Injun."

The Pawnee ignores Rawson. Kohn says, "And do you have sons, Jonathan?"

Again, Jonathan frowns. Might as well be putting the thumbscrews to him, Kohn thinks, determined to ask him more questions, knowing now his distaste for answering.

"Four sons," the Pawnee says.

"And will they scout for us as well, Jonathan?" Molloy says, his speech so slurred that Kohn repeats the question.

"Quite right, quite right," Molloy says, taking a long drink from the bottle before handing it to Kohn. Kohn passes it to the Indian without drinking.

"So would you have them scouting for us

bluecoats as well, Jonathan?" Kohn asks.

Jonathan drinks and hands the bottle to Molloy, deliberately passing Rawson. He does not think the private worthy of the whiskey. *He* should be sitting outside the light of the fire. Though he stole the eggs, he remembers, and they had been fine to eat with flourcakes. I will give him the bottle the next time, because he took the eggs from the travelers.

He says, "They will scout for the bluecoats if they want to do it. It is good sometimes. You can buy fine things with the greenbacks of a soldier's pay. But maybe the Sioux are all dead when they are of the age to scout. And when the Sioux are gone, and the Cheyenne, then the Pawnee will have no need to scout for you."

"The enemy of my enemy becomes my closest friend," Kohn says and Jonathan does not respond.

"You hold your liquor well, Jonathan," Molloy says. His voice is loud and Kohn wonders can the pilgrims hear him in the ring of wagons a mile away. So what if they can? He hopes it keeps them from sleep, the unneighborly sons of bitches.

Molloy continues, gesturing with the bottle, and Kohn pities him. "I have been given to think that you Indians do not hold your liquor quite so well and you appear to disprove this." Molloy again raises the bottle in a toast. Kohn shakes his head.

Jonathan takes the bottle back from the officer. "And I have been told that white soldiers do not hold their liquor well. The lieutenant does not disprove this." He takes a long drink and passes the bottle to Rawson and for the first time since his harassment of the Sioux women and children, Jonathan smiles.

Kohn smiles back at him. Molloy has closed his eyes.

Just when Kohn thinks he is asleep, Molloy smiles and says, "Well done, Jonathan. Quite right, quite right."

Moments later the officer is snoring. Kohn reaches over and takes Molloy's pipe from his hand, taps the ashes from it into the fire and puts it in his own tunic pocket for when Molloy awakes and searches for it. They ran out of the cheroots he likes some days ago.

"I'll take first guard, Rawson. I'll wake you when it's your turn. Jonathan, you'll take over from Rawson."

The scout nods.

"I think we'll once again be without Captain Molloy's company standing picket this evening."

116

■ ■ ■ ■

The sound of hooves in the dirt wakes Kohn and he sees only the black silhouette of the Pawnee riding out of their camp. The fire is burned down to dim orange embers. A faint line of dawn light scores the eastern horizon. Near on six, Kohn thinks. Where is Jonathan going? His ears prick at a sound out of place on the plains, out of place in the dawn's fading darkness. The morning is cold and still, a dusting of frost on his blankets, his breath a thick, warm fog about his face. There, again, the sound. A woman screaming. And the howling, whooping shouts recalling the Confederate rebel yell but different.

He throws off his blankets, sleeping as he is in his buffalo coat and hat.

"Sir," he shakes Molloy and hears the officer groan. "Sir! The pilgrims, sir. There is something happening with them. Jonathan has gone."

Rawson wakes now. "What's that?" He leaps up and in terror looks left, right. His rifle is beside the tent canvas he has used for a pillow and he grabs it and this time no one tells him to put it away. The horses have been left loosely saddled but with their reins picketed to stakes in the ground.

"Lift up the pickets on the horses, Rawson, and tighten the saddles. Sir, wake up, sir." He shakes Molloy and the officer wakes. "Sir, there is something wrong with the pilgrims. I can hear shouting. A woman."

Molloy stares at Kohn. He understands the urgency in Kohn's voice but cannot make sense of the soldier's words. In his mind, in his dream, he is at home and speaking Irish to a woman he knows is his sister. His mother is scolding them for speaking Irish instead of English but in his dream he cannot speak anything else and he wakes to this. He tries to stand and crumbles back into his bedroll, his body locked in cramp. Cold, Jesus in heaven, cold. Bile rises in his throat and he tries to swallow it but cannot and spews some sour whiskey into the ashes of the fire.

"The horses, Rawson . . ." Kohn says,

"They're ready, goddamn it all." Rawson holds the reins to the three mounts.

"Come on, sir," Kohn says, but decides then that he will leave him. He will be no good to them.

"Fuck. Christ, I am coming, let me rise, for the love of God Almighty." He begins to rant in Irish as Kohn has heard him do when he is not fully awake.

118

He manages to get to his feet and stumbles to his mount. Even at his drunkest, on the blackest night, he can always find her. Rawson hands Molloy the reins and intertwines his hands as a bootstep for the officer. It takes two attempts for Molloy to put his boot into the private's hands. When he does, Rawson heaves upwards and Molloy swings his free leg back and kicks the private in the jaw, causing him to release the officer before he has landed in his saddle.

Kohn is lifting his rifle from beside their bedrolls when he sees, from the corner of his eye, Molloy go tumbling over the horse's back. The sound of his landing is that of a heavy barrel dropped from a wagon. Kohn knows it is a broken leg before Molloy starts swearing. "Mother of Jesus my cocksucking leg, Jesus in heaven."

Rawson is bellowing, "My jaw, my goddamn fuckin' jaw, goddammit."

Kohn decides quickly. "Rawson, get him his whiskey from the mule. Give him the bottle and wait with him till I'm back. Get one of the dogs up and put the captain inside and under all the blankets we have, is that clear?"

"Here? Wait here with him? By my lonesome?"

Kohn brings his fist back to strike Rawson

but for some reason stops himself. He mounts his horse. "Do exactly what I say, Rawson. Shoot anything that moves that isn't one of us. Is that clear?" And the way he says it so frightens Rawson that the private begins to act without questioning the order. "And picket the horses again, you shit brain, or you'll be walking the rest of the way."

Kohn spurs his mount and rides hard for the pilgrims' camp.

The Indians have left before he gets there and there is no sign of Jonathan. He rides a circuit of the loose collection of wagons. They are no longer circled, as they are routinely arranged at night for protection and as a pen for the animals. One of the wagons has its oxen yoked and harnessed while the others are in disarray, traces cut and tangled, yokes askew in the grass. Other than two tethered oxen, there is no sign of the twenty-odd animals he saw the day before. Kohn realizes the party must have begun to break camp when it was raided.

He meets the young man whom he spoke to the day before jogging out of camp with an ancient musket. He has not thought they might have a gun with them, being pacifists, but assumes it is probably a bird gun. Little good it will do him.

"What happened here? Where are you going?" He speaks in German.

"The Indians came. The older boys, from yesterday. They have taken our beasts. I must get them back. *Ich muz.*"

"I think you should stay with the others. Do you have a horse? If you had a horse we could search . . ." Kohn thinks better of this. Instead, "Is there anyone hurt?"

"*Ja,* my father is struck on the head but he will be all right. I must go."

"No." Kohn dismounts and stands beside the man. He has his Spencer carbine in his hand and he places it back in its scabbard. "Your family needs you here. It's not safe for you to go after them. Not safe. You have never fired that at a man before, have you?"

He reaches for the musket and the pilgrim hands it over. It is only now that Kohn realizes how young he must be. Eighteen at the most, with a wife and children. And I am thirty, and father only to one drunken officer. Mother to him. He remembers what has befallen Molloy and wants to get back to him. He checks the musket and sees it is not loaded.

"Have you got balls and powder? Cartridges?"

The young man looks away. He opens his

hand to show a muddle of wadding and card and loose rounds of birdshot. Kohn thinks that the man, the boy, might cry. "We must have back our beasts. We will be stranded here. Winter is coming . . ."

Kohn hears weeping from behind the wagons, shrill voices raised in fear and anger. *Der Winter ist da, mein Freund.* "Are they all right?"

"Yes. They are vexed. We cannot make Montana without our beasts."

The old man, as if summoned by the doubt shown by his son, comes over to them from the wagons. He has a bandage around his head and blood seeps down his cheek from underneath it. Kohn notes a trail of clothing and goods from the back of one of the wagons strewn out on the ground, and thinks perhaps the Indians made to steal the goods as a distraction while their brothers cut through the traces and stampeded the mule and ox teams.

"Jacob, come and help your family," the old man says.

"I will, Father." He takes the gun back from Kohn, pocketing the small parcels of birdshot. He looks ashamed.

The father notices the musket in his son's hand. "What were you going to do with that? You know the teachings. And you would be killed. Do you want to die and to die in sin? Pride, Jacob, pride. You are a fool for it."

Kohn understands some of this. He understands the words "die" and "sin" and "pride" but the rest is clear enough. The old man wipes at the blood on his cheek and checks his hand. Dawn light is leaking over the plains and Kohn can see frosted buffalo grass running east, the undulating land like rolling waves of the sea. These Murphy wagons, prairie schooners folk call them, like lost, demasted ships, Kohn thinks, having seen storm-damaged barques limp back up the Cuyahoga every winter as a boy. He considers the pilgrims' chances. One team of oxen left. They will be all right but will be going no farther, only back.

"Sir, was our Indian here?" Kohn asks, as if to distract the father from his tirade. Kohn pities the son. Sees himself in him. Sees his own father in this bearded Mennonite.

"Savages, savages, damned savages," the younger man says in English, as if he has heard it said before and liked it.

"There were many and it was dark," the old man says.

Kohn looks west. The land rises away from the riverbank and he can just now make out

123

the trail up into the bluffs the raiders would have taken. Jonathan too. He decides he will make his way back to Molloy and Rawson in camp.

"Will I load the gun for you?" he asks the young man. "I can give you some balls you can melt and shape for shot. You will need a heavier load than the one you have there if you are to do any good with —"

"We do not need your help," the old man says.

Kohn looks at him and rage rises in his gullet. Pride. *Pride?* The old fucker, the son of a bitch. Let the Sioux have his scalp. Let them rape and kill every goddamn one of them. Kohn thinks that he may be all used up with pity. Fathers. Every son's curse to have one.

"Suit yourselves." He ignores the old man and speaks to the youth in English. "If you can't find your animals, pack as much as you can from the other wagons into one of them and head back for Laramie. You'll have to winter there. It's too late in the season to restock and try again until spring."

"I will try to tell them this. My father, the others, but they will not listen. They say it is the Lord's will and He protects us. Where is His protecting now I ask you?"

The old man says something sharp to his

124

son, a rebuke, as if he has understood his son's words.

"Well, good luck," Kohn says. "I'm sorry we could not be of more help to you."

He rides slowly out of the jam of wagons to the sound of the old man scolding his son, of women weeping and a woman shouting, hysterical with rage. A child crying. They'll be all right, Kohn thinks. They'll be fine once they make it to Laramie.

Halfway back to camp and he can no longer hear the pilgrims and their lamentations. Instead, he hears gunshots. Two or three, perhaps one with an echo, from somewhere in the hills west of the trail. He stops and listens and some moments later hears screaming again. This time he is certain it is not a young woman but a boy.

Back in camp, just over an hour later, Kohn is about to set Molloy's leg when Jonathan rides into camp. His buffalo coat is open to the cold. Winter sunlight on hoar-frosted grass, steam rising from his pony's back. Under his open cavalry tunic the Indian wears a bright red shirt Kohn has seen before. The scout's leggings are smeared red with blood. It takes Kohn a moment to recall where he has seen the garment, his attention drawn from Molloy's injury to the brilliant red of the jersey. Yesterday. The stout Indian boy was wearing it, the one who grabbed the toddler up from the ground from horseback.

Jonathan dismounts. Two raw, fresh pelts of skin and black hair are stretched with sapling sticks and lashed to a branch that rises up from his saddle like a grim cavalry guidon. Kohn cannot look at him.

"Did you get their animals back?" Kohn asks.

"No. The Sioux killed the animals when I came to them. And I killed the Sioux. Two of them. Two others I did not see."

"They were only . . ." Kohn sees that Molloy's eyes are open and he is watching them. There is no way that he can know what has happened, what Jonathan has done, but there is terror in his eyes nonetheless.

Kohn says, "The lieutenant's leg is broke." He thinks both bones are broken but cannot be sure. The jagged shinbone has cut through the skin and Molloy screams each time Kohn attempts to examine it. It will need to be set, Kohn knows, and cleaned up and plastered or gangrene and the saw will have it. Jonathan has told them they are four days' riding from the fort. Four days from a surgeon of any sort, even an army surgeon.

126

"He ain't gonna be riding no horse," Rawson says, taking a draft from the captain's bottle.

"Give me that bottle, Rawson." And to Molloy, Kohn says, "It's all right, Captain. It's all right, now. Take a drink. Take a drink."

Jonathan squats on his haunches in the open mouth of the tent and lifts back the blankets and buffalo hide. Molloy's leg is white and frail-looking and the skin around his shin is beginning to discolor where the jagged bone has torn through.

"Do not move him," the Pawnee says, rising and mounting his horse.

"We won't be going no goddamn place today," Rawson says, eyeing the bottle.

"Shut up, Rawson," Kohn says. "Shut your mouth before I shut it for you."

The sun has risen to its highest point in the winter sky and Kohn believes it is near noon when the Pawnee returns to camp. Tied to and dragging behind his horse are several trunks of sapling trees shorn of branches. Lodgepoles, Kohn has heard them called. For making tipis. He wonders at their purpose.

Molloy is in a fitful sleep, starting awake now and again with pain or nightmares. His

127

forehead burns with fever and Kohn mops it with a damp kerchief, feeding him whiskey with a mess spoon. Rawson adds buffalo chips to the fire and watches as Jonathan dismounts and takes a leather satchel from his saddlebag. The scout crouches in the tent mouth again.

The two soldiers stand back as the Pawnee scoops a poultice of what looks like mud mixed with leaves and stems from the buffalo hide satchel. "Whiskey," he says.

"What is that you've made?" Kohn says.

Jonathan looks at him for a moment before answering. "I do not know the name in English. I need whiskey."

Kohn nods at Rawson and the private takes the bottle from beside Molloy, handing it to Jonathan.

The Pawnee takes a mouthful and, pursing his lips, sprays it over Molloy's bare leg. Molloy opens his eyes and mouth but does not scream when Jonathan begins to pat the site of the protruding shinbone with a layer of poultice. He does this several times until there is a thick layer of the stuff on the wound and then, without warning, grasps the officer's lower leg in two hands and bends roughly inwards. Molloy screams and faints and the tent is filled with the rough pop of setting bone. Jonathan does not seem to notice but rises and goes to his horse again, returning to the tent with a square cut of soft buffalo hide and several long leather strips. He covers the poultice with the hide and wraps it tightly with the strips. He then binds the officer's two legs together, inhibiting any movement.

"Will his blood not be constricted?" Kohn asks. He knows some field medicine. No more than most soldiers, less than many. Jonathan does not appear to understand and makes no effort to do so.

"We ride tomorrow," the scout says.

Kohn can't take his eyes from the bright red shirt Jonathan is wearing, or from the specks of dried blood on his face, but he is thankful for his presence. There is some comfort to be taken in the confidence the Pawnee has shown, as if he has done this many times before.

Later, Jonathan makes a travois from the lodgepoles and a buffalo skin, a stretcher of sorts to be dragged by horse or mule, and Kohn is again glad of the Indian's attendance. The journey will be hard on the captain, Kohn thinks, but he would have tied him to a horse and that would have been far worse.

"Fine work," Kohn says but the scout ignores him.

"Tomorrow," Jonathan says, wondering now, with the officer incapacitated, could he track down the band of Sioux and take one of the squaws hostage. He could tell the bluecoats he took her to nurse the captain. He looks at the sky. Too late today. "You," he says to Rawson. "You cook now."

Rawson looks to Kohn and Kohn ignores him.

Snowflakes drifting in halos of lantern light. The horses breathe heavy bolts of steam. Safe, Kohn thinks. Safe, goddamn it all. They have been led from the Fort Phil Kearny gates by infantry soldiers in thick buffalo coats and hats to the hospital barracks, a building of planed logs and a pitched sod roof. Light emanates from the few buildings that sport window glass and Kohn pictures a warm bath, a bed, a hot meal and a bottle.

It has taken six days, not four, the going slow, sleet and rain turning much of the trail to mud for a day, frozen ruts the next and the jostling, bouncing travois causing the captain to scream until his voice was but a dull rasp. They finished the whiskey dosing him. One more day would have been the death of him.

They dismount and tend to an unconscious Molloy. In the days since Molloy's injury Kohn has grown used to command but wishes now to be free of it.

"Stable the horses and mules, Rawson. And see to it they're well fed and watered. See the quartermaster if you must and if he's got a problem with your asking report back to me. Tell him we're under General Cooke's orders."

A surgeon's orderly helps Kohn lift Molloy onto a stretcher. Supervising, the surgeon orders some men to bear the officer inside by lantern light.

Jonathan watches from his horse. He will set up a tipi, using the travois poles and buffalo hides, outside the fort while he waits for the bluecoats to finish their business and return to Omaha. The lieutenant will need some weeks to recover, maybe the whole winter. He will be here for some time, he thinks.

The scout has seen the loafer Cheyenne outside the fort and he will not camp with them but may trade or pay for one of their women to keep him warm and do his cooking. He will hunt in the mountains for fur to trade with the bluecoats. If he comes across any Sioux or Northern Cheyenne, he will take more scalps and maybe a hostage. Or he could set out for home with the two scalps he took for his wife to dance with and come back here for the bluecoats in the spring. He thinks of how proud his wife is when he returns to her bearing scalps and he has a pang of longing for her. But the scalps he took on the trail are only the pelts of young braves and will be worth less to the creator of all things — *Tir a wa* — in the scalp dance or as sacrifice in the New Fire in spring. They are an excuse to return home to her but only that. He will watch the weather and then decide.

One or two of the bluecoats around the hospital barracks are staring at him. He meets their eyes and they look away. They are afraid. He can see it in them. Their scalps too would be nearly worthless.

"I will tend to the lieutenant and tell you what he'll need, how he is. You get yourself a feed and a bath and come back to me in the morning," the surgeon says to Kohn and Kohn is glad to hear it.

Molloy is sleeping, delirious and drunk, but his fever is gone and his foot beneath the bindings and poultice shows no signs of gangrene. Kohn is happy to be relieved of the burden of his charge. My turn for a bottle, he thinks, as he undresses Molloy with a surgeon's orderly, a young private

132

who does not seem to know much English or want to speak it. Italian or Greek, perhaps. Doesn't matter. As the orderly removes Molloy's tunic, a flat oilskin pouch falls onto the bed and he hands it to Kohn, who puts it inside his own tunic. Cooke's orders. He will read them later. Tomorrow. Now food, a drink. Blessed rest.

10

GAOL WITH PAY & MEETING THE MAN
WHOSE DEATH DID BRING YOU HERE

Tom and myself found much that was the same about our mustering into this Regular Army & much that was different from the Union Army of the War. Sure some of the differences we did expect for we thought (well all America thinks it!) that the men enlisting with us had a raw edge to them now. You must of noted this yourself Sir. This Army is surely different from the one we both know from the War.

Of course the Volunteer Regiments like the Ohio 10th in which myself & Tom fought did be locally drawn & made up of eager dutiful boys pals all from farms & towns & baseball clubs. The sons of doctors & school masters & mercantile men marching alongside the drovers & teamsters & labouring men of smoke belching cities &

we Irish boys were many among them then as now. And all of them (or most of them in the beginning at least) were fired by duty to the Union or fired by local pride or even by fear of being shown up a coward for not taking up arms in defence of the Unity of States.

Well we 2 brothers took on in '61 for the grub & the wage as much as anything (which is no different in truth from this 2nd take on) but we too came to be moved by the spirit of the times & by the pride in Union blue shown by the Ohio boys around us then. Our patriotic fire was lit by the band concerts & pot luck suppers held in the fields where we made drill. The fire was lit I tell you by the local girleens with their pies & cakes & ice cold jugs of buttermilk brought to us fighting boys in them early days of the War them days before we saw anything of the War itself so that we felt soon enough like local boys ourselves. Hardly a month in the country & the first stirrings came on us of what it might feel like to be right & proper American boys & no longer just off the boat Micks signed up for cannon fodder. The war did knock much of that sentiment from us but it was there at the start & though there was surely some rum eggs in the Volunteers with us well most of our comrades you would call brother. I tell you Sir they were different from this lot we would serve with now.

This time there was no sweet girleens bearing pies to the Regular Army Recruit Depot at Ft. Thomas of Columbus or to The Soup House as the local people called it. Gaol With Pay us soldiers named it & more than one lad had experience enough of both to say how true that was.

Ft. Thomas was a place full of men 1/2 broke by drink or 1/2 starved for want of work. There was Bowery toughs & former convicts & the generally work shy. They were likely not looking for it but all were given discipline & routine along with their rations of slumgullion stew or cold corn bread & white flour water gravy & coffee so bitter & thick you could trot a mouse on it. The idea was that given all this plus exercise & kit & clobber & the Army pride would follow.

Sure it had worked on us once. Tom & I learnt our 1st time in the Army to bathe once a week at least when before but once a month did us grand. I tell you in the early days of the War it seemed to us that soldiering was the best thing we could be doing with our lives. We learnt to walk tall & proud like true American born gents with our chests out like cock roosters as if we were no lesser men than any other. All this we did learn in 10th Ohios only for the War to knock it from us. We had it shot & bled out of us on the battlefields of the South & then ground out of us as labouring men afterwards tipping our caps to any farmer who would give us a start for 50¢ a day & a warm rick of hay for to stuff a burlap sack for a mattress.

That pride we once felt well we would surely not be getting any of it back in Columbus. I looked around me at this raggedy shower this higgly piggly rabble of blaggards & drunks & thieves & defilers of gentlewomen & thought that the only thing an enemy might fear from this mob of men is losing his purse.

I turned one day to say all this to Tom but as I did I saw in a flash my brother as others might see him standing there with his scars & hunting eyes & this did cause me to think that as much as this mob was different from the Volunteer Regiments who fought in The Rebellion we too were different now. We did be <u>no</u> different in many ways now to the men around us & it made me sad to see this. My own brother appeared every bit the boss of a murderous mob of brigands I could picture in my head slouching West in search of terrible mischief. (In this I was correct in thinking. As you can see Sir we here in Ft. Phil Kearny are just such a band of filthy highwaymen mostly & dangerous to gentle society but less so to the Indian I think though not for want of trying.)

But 13 bucks a month & passage West I told myself. Grub & kit & clobber. There are worse places a fellow could find himself. Not many but some.

All this is by way of telling you Sir how we made acquaintance with the man who is the cause for your coming here. That is Mr. Kinney the Sutler of course who would post West with us in the 18th & by cruel fate cross our path again May God Have Mercy On Him.

We 1st met him with the issuing of uniforms which we would be buying the fee deducted from our wages. This is standard as you know well & we did not think much of it Tom & myself until our Recruit Company 1st Sgt. there in Depot (a lump of a Cavan man by way of New York & a veteran of the War like ourselves) insisted we were to buy not 1 but 2 cleaning kits from the Depot Sutler's Store. (We thought that Cavan 1st Sgt. was rotten then but came to know him better after & he was a fine man

138

but that was later God Keep Him.)

2 kits that Sgt. made a point of saying causing Tom & myself to realise that while much may be different in this new Regular Army much was still the same. Of course you can see Sir that the 1st Sgt. & the Sutler were running a game together each scratching the other's back fine & dandy.

I can see him now that mean fisted b____ of a Sutler as he set down 2 cleaning kits before the both of us brothers on the counter in his Stores.

"We will only be needing the one," says I to him the 1st words I ever spoke to him but not the last.

That Sutler looked up at me & says, "You are to take 2 kits & you know it well."

"It was advised strongly we take 2 but not ordered," says Tom. To me in Irish Tom said, "Tell this c_____ what I said & make sure he ticks us down for only the 1 each."

I repeated Tom's words to the Sutler changing some of them but he did not answer & instead looked round for the 1st Sgt. in his employ.

Says I, "And make your mark to our names for only 1 kit each if you please. We would not want to be docked for kits we do not buy." I smiled at him when I said it & perhaps this is what riled him so.

"The guardhouse is where the clever buckos end up. You 2 boys think you are clever?"

Says Tom in Irish, "Clever enough not to buy two cleaning kits when one is all that is needed." Of course the Sutler did not understand Tom & I was glad of it.

Still smiling I said, "No Sir we are not clever at all just poor soldier Bills like all the rest."

Well there was not much the robbing Sutler could say to that so says he, "Move your stinking Mick skins out of my stores before I call the Provost Marshals in & have you up in irons."

Now Tom & myself having some experience with the Provost Marshal's men in the war did take our 1 kit each & left Kinney's Stores knowing well we had not heard the last word on it.

Sure enough it did not be 10 minutes later the 2 of us standing with some fellows smoking & waiting for the others in the Stores to finish up when that New York Ca-van b_____ of a 1st Sgt. roared to me from across the parade ground. "You Private! Stand to boy & Quick Time! And bring that ugly f_____ with you."

Well we quick timed it over to him & I took a look at Tom for to judge how rough were his eyes because Tom does not care for being called ugly & more than a few fellows have paid dues for it in the past. But I knew what was coming from the Sgt. & so did Tom & his face Thank God had the cast of only squally weather & not a storm like it could take on when the climate was right for it.

Says I sweet as sugared rum, "Yes Sergeant?"

Well let me tell you that fellow did loom as much as stand over you a bigger man than even Tom & not afraid at all of the likes of my brother or of his face or the grim things brewing in his eyes. For like Tom 1st Sgt. Nevin had that shard of madness lodged in the back of his own eyes too though it did be tempered (we learnt later) by the good humour & kindness that makes for a fine leader of fighting men. Of course along side the madness there was a sharp mind too. He was in cahoots with the Sutler after all. (Sure for such reward who would not be?)

Says I to myself, "Tread lightly around this b_____. There are no flies on him."

"1 cleaning kit is all you smart boys reckon you will be needing is it?" says the Sgt. a glop of tobacco juice spat onto my boots as if to mark his words like shit from a gull bearing bad luck instead of good. He did not bother staring me down but held his eyes to Tom's & Tom being Tom held the Sgt.'s & did not look away.

I will tell you I was afraid then though I had no regret in not buying a 2nd kit & have no regrets now & never will for any soldier with a day's dust from the road on him can spot fixed Faro & has the right not to fall for a ruse once he has rumbled it. But I was afraid more for what might happen if that Sgt. did turn Tom the wrong way in his head.

I weighed my words with some care while the big men eyeballed each other like 2 bulls in a pen with 1 heifer. I weighed also the music of my words as I spoke them the very tone & pitch of them.

Says I, "We reckon 1 kit each will do us fine Sergeant." I held up the leather cleaning bag. "1 <u>each</u> mind you making it <u>2</u> bought between us which will be more than enough we reckon. Or can you tell us why we might be needing <u>2 each</u>?"

The big man turned to me now & he smiled in an innocent way that was as far from innocent as dear Ireland is from Kingdom Come & I did think, "Oh no good will come of this for the sake of a dollar saved." I gave a smile back to him with no challenge in it. The 1st Sgt. stared me out & I could see he was reckoning if the price of 2 kits was worth troubling the like of us for. 2 cleaning kits my arse! A master of arithmetic could only reckon what that Sgt.'s cut off the Sutler was for <u>200</u> cleaning kits sold to <u>100</u> men needing only 1. I was a small bit afeared of what may happen but a fair part of me knew the man would make little more of it for the greedy be as regular as cocks crowing the sun up in their ways. Smooth running was what he wanted & boys such as Tom & myself could only foul the wheels for him.

Says he finally, "I will be checking your leather —" He spat another tawny stream of tobaccy on my boots. "And your coats & collars specially. I will want to be able see the hairs up my f_____ nose reflected in your boots & belts I am telling you boys now." Another brown bark of spittle to mark his point. But he saw he met his match in the O'Driscoll brothers & fair play to him he did smile at us as if to say this.

He gave a nod to Tom. "And you boy where did you ship that dint in your mug?"

Says I, "It was trying to free a plough blade when a skittish whore of a draft horse spied a field rat & rared in her traces freeing the blade to shoot up into the brother's

143

gob. Terrible unlucky my brother is Sergeant."

"A plow blade."

"It was fierce freakish," says I.

Still the fellow smiled & I thought we might be all right with him in the future if we had to be. Says he, "Looks a terrible lot like the scar a minie ball might make. Straight through all the way like a dose. Which makes the 2 of ye Single Cleaning Kit Buying Chancers of Kerrymen —"

"<u>Corkmen</u> Sgt. Begging your pardon," says I.

"Making the 2 of yous seem all the more veteran fighting b_____ like myself. <u>O'Driscolls</u> are you?" He tested our name out in his mouth like a man bites a gold coin & finds the glint of tin beneath.

"We are & fresh fish to the Army like all these other boys Sgt. We are so soon off the decks of the coffin ship you can smell the sea still on us. You know yourself the strange likenesses that may occur in the world that only God Himself can explain. Like the way the cut of a plough blade might show up as a minie ball scar in the ruins of a brother's face May God Go Between Him & All Harm," I said much relieved at the course our talk was after taking.

"May He Go Between Trouble & All Of

144

Us," says the Sgt. "Can the f_____ not talk for hisself?"

"He can Sgt."

"Proper American lingo like you & me here?"

"Not proper. But he does understand it well enough."

The Sgt. gave a grunt & turnt away before turning back. Says he, "Once he understands orders Pvt. O'Driscoll I don't care a D_____ if he got that wound when your draft horse stuck his prick in his mouth but you boys are veteran Yankee Bills or veteran Johnny Rebs from the War like myself or my mother's a whore & my daddy the Devil."

But he winked at us to show there was no hard feelings between us & I thought that from then on we would be in that New York Cavan Sgt.'s good books & sure enough we were. It pains me now to think of what did happen to him later God Rest Him for oft it be the good ones who roll 7s as if there is no God at all sitting judge in the Heavens.

And well the Sutler Kinney who the good Sgt. had his deals with only outlived the Sgt. by some hours & in a way their deaths are 2 links in a chain that begun for all of us back there in Columbus.

As I write this now I think on how many other ways things could of gone. If 1st Sgt.

Nevin had not of hauled us up over the cleaning kits we would never of grown so fond of him maybe. If Kinney had been licensed a Sutlery at some other Depot or post. If a snake (a lowly cold blooded snake!) had not of crossed a mule team's path. You could go on & on. Your head would spin with all the things that might of changed what happened later.

We had little else to do with that Sutler at the Depot & 3 weeks later after having our fill of Soup House slumgullion & setting up drills Tom & myself did volunteer for an early posting with the 18th & with a mob of men deemed ready to be shipped Westward.

The good Sgt. Nevin was with us for much of the journey & he would catch us up in the Powder River country once we arrived here in Ft. Phil Kearny some time after. He did last but 3 months here in this Valley. 4 years of the Great Rebellion & scarce 3 months of this smaller one. But you know well Sir both kinds can kill you if your number comes up.

■ ■ ■ ■

II
WESTERING

■ ■ ■ ■

For West is where we all plan to go some day. It is where you go when the land gives out and the old-field pines encroach. It is where you go when you get the letter saying: Flee, all is discovered. It is where you go when you look down at the blade in your hand and the blood on it. It is where you go when you are told that you are a bubble on the tide of empire.

— ROBERT PENN WARREN,
ALL THE KING'S MEN

11

December 7, 1866 — Fort Phil Kearny,
Dakota Territory

December cold. Sleet and rain and thawing mud. Daniel Kohn crosses Fort Phil Kearny's parade ground. The flag lies heavy and limp against a towering flagpole. Rawson had woken Kohn. Told him the bastards were trying to steal their horses. Use them anyway. Like they belong to the ground-pounding, infantry sonsofbitches, he had said, Rawson forgetting he is just such an infantry soldier and no more than that himself; Rawson thinking perhaps that, like a pig among dogs, he has become a cavalryman. Still, Kohn is thankful for the kid calling the alarm.

The stables are dark and smell of freshly cut pine. The whole fort smells of pine sap, Kohn thinks. Go up like a powder keg, if you put a match to it.

"Get those saddles off our goddamn

horses, Private," Kohn says, turning to look for Rawson and finding him absent. Kohn forgives him this. Rawson has to bunk with these men most likely. Play cards, filch from them. He will not want enemies so soon into their stay.

The private halts, halfway to Molloy's horse, a standard army saddle over his forearm. Another soldier stares at him in the gloom. Shavetails, Kohn notes. No roughness in them yet, just the lazy, hopeless stupidity that might drive a boy to join the regular army now that the war is over. He knows what they will say before they say it.

"We got orders to saddle all available. And these is available," one of them says, his mate looking on, setting the saddle he lugs onto a rough barked rail, happy to do nothing until the conflict is resolved.

"Whose orders?"

"Cap'n Brown. The quartermaster. You got stink with the music, Corporal, speak to the organ grinder. We just monkeys here. No need to kick the poor goddamn monkeys."

Fair enough, Kohn thinks. Not these boys' fault. "Where will I find the quartermaster?"

"He'll be taking his breakfast. You can talk to our first shirt, you want. He's in barracks,

150

putting his toes to the fire. He was sergeant of the guard and just in now."

Kohn considers it. It is always easier dealing with another enlisted man. But a hungry one, just off picket, likely not aware of the order at all?

"I'd rather see the organ grinder, Bill," Kohn says, calling the infantryman Bill, the name any private in the army will answer to, as if to show him there is no blame attached to his actions. "These are cavalry mounts and our own, personal horses, in need of a week's rest easy. Not even the quartermaster can up and requisition the like of these."

Kohn thinks this is true. He's not certain. If Molloy were up and about there would be no question of it.

Private Bill shrugs. Not his problem. "Cap'n Brown ain't gonna like it none, you innerupt his breakfast to tell him he got three less horses for the woodtrain guard."

"It's not a question of like or not like, Bill. They're our horses."

"You ain't met the captain."

Kohn finds the quartermaster tightening the saddle on his own mount in front of the log and daub quarters he shares with several other of the fort's officers. Kohn notes that some of the quarters along the row are rough constructions of barked logs, earthen roofs and stovepipe chimneys, while others are clad with boards planed and washed white, roofed with wooden shingles. Must have rushed the construction as winter came on, Kohn thinks. He notes the head-quarters barracks nearby, with its viewing platform and a fine, white-washed building next to it. The fort commander's quarters. A doe antelope is tethered in front of it, licking at the paint.

"Sir," he says. "Captain Brown? May I have a word about our horses, sir?"

Brown looks up. "Whose horses?"

"Ours, sir. 7th Cavalry, out of Fort Riley in Kansas. I'm Corporal . . . *Sergeant* actually. Sergeant Daniel Kohn, sir." His newly elevated rank sounds odd to his own ears.

"Custer's boys?"

"Yessir."

"I met that bastard once. West Point peacock."

Kohn says nothing to this.

"Where's your stripes, Sergeant Actually?"

"I learned of my promotion only last night, sir. When I read my captain's orders. He's incapacitated, sir. I haven't had the chance to find a tailor or to visit the sutler for the stripes." As he says this, he wonders if there is any sutler to be found now on the

152

post. They are here, after all, to investigate the murder of the post's original contracted king of robber's row. He will ask later.

"Well until you do, you are a corporal to me unless you can show me orders that says different." Brown winks at two soldiers who have arrived holding their mounts by the reins. Rough men, Kohn sees, much different from the two in the stables. Fighting men. Big, the QM's special detail, their buffalo coats worn open, the heavy hide coats hooked behind Colt pistols stuffed in belts from which also hang cavalry cutlasses and Bowie knives the length of a man's forearm. There is something of the frontier in these men, something savage and untethered. He fought against rebel boys like these in the war. Tread wisely, he thinks. Still, our goddamn mounts and nobody's borrowing them or otherwise if I can help it.

"Our orders, sir." Kohn hands the oilskin wallet to the quartermaster and watches as the officer removes and reads the pages inside.

Brown hands the wallet and pages back to Kohn and says, "The good general might have sent us fresh horses and the oats to feed them in place of jumped-up NCOs, but mine is not to reason why."

Brown closes his eyes and turns his face

to the sky as if to a warm sun instead of the winter murk that hangs over the valley like a burial shroud.

In a voice more suited for recitation than conversation, the quartermaster continues, "For I would ride into the goddamn valley o' death if I had sixty horses, much less six hundred, but I've barely six that are worth riding and these three alone that can keep up with or run down any of Mr. Lo's ponies, and now you want us to leave your goddamn horses to luxuriate in our stables while my men go into battle on ill-fed asses fit for the knacker's yard, *Corporal*?"

A poem or song of some sort, Kohn reckons, bastardized by this strange captain. Is there a single officer in the whole of this army not cracked in some way or other? Brown opens his eyes and gazes with an odd ferocity at Kohn and Kohn knows better than to answer.

"Well, Corporal *Kohn*?" There is some distaste in the way the quartermaster pronounces his surname. Jew hater? Find me a Christian man in America these days who isn't. I should have been a profiteer. A banker, lending money for the Reconstruction. Fat on the spoils of war. If you are to be hated, you might as well be rich, Daniel, you no-good fool. No better than any of

154

these men. Worse in ways for you should have known better than to sign up to fight. And then stay on after the fighting is done? God damn it all to hell, Kohn, every word your father ever said against you was true.

"They are our own private mounts, sir. The captain's especially. He's had her since the early days of the war. The pack mules, and the third mount, they are army beasts, sir, and we would happily offer them up to you if they are needed."

The QM has one hand resting on the butt of his Colt. He too wears a long, open buffalo coat over his uniform which appears, from what Kohn can see of it, ill-used and stained dark in places. "Your own private mounts that you feed and stable with *my* scarce oats in *my* stables?"

Kohn meets the captain's eyes. The man is as obvious as a filthy postcard. How simple things are, sometimes, in the army. "Sir, I . . . we, Captain Molloy, sir, will pay the going rate for what we use. Once our horses are let be." He goes into his tunic once again and comes out with his billfold and removes a five-dollar note. "Perhaps you'll take this to start with, sir. I'll leave it to you to draw up a bill for Captain Molloy. He is incapacitated at the moment and I do not know how long we will require your generosity."

Brown pockets the note. "You will be informed when further payment is called for."

"Thank you, sir."

Brown jabs a boot into a stirrup and hoists himself awkwardly onto the back of his horse. The two soldiers are also infantrymen, Kohn notes with the disdain of the true dragoon, though he cannot see their uniforms clearly or any insignia. They are not cavalrymen anyway. He has seen sacks of grain tossed onto wagon beds with more grace than these men show when mounting their horses. All three are now looking down at Kohn, his boots in thick mud, lodged there as if set in tar.

Almost as an afterthought — but not quite, Kohn feels — the quartermaster says, "And what's this about a murder, Sergeant? An investigation, it says there in your orders. I thought you boys were cavalry. Is your captain there a provost marshal's man? Some kind of constable?"

"No sir. I'm not certain why Captain Molloy was sent here, only that he was. General Cooke must have had his reasons."

"Murder?" Brown shakes his head. "Do you know how many men we've had *mur-*

dered since arriving here in this valley, Corporal?"

"No sir, but I don't imagine many of them were in-laws to the Secretary of the Treasury."

Again the quartermaster looks to the two privates and back to Kohn and this time he smiles. "The same army that cannot send me the goddamn ammunition and horseflesh I need to run a war can manage to send you two bucks to investigate the murder of a shit-heel whoremaster cut down by Indians. Just when you think you've seen all the bug-fucking foolishness this army can come up with, they come up with something else."

"General Cooke seems to think that it may not have been Indians, sir."

The three men on horseback stare down at Kohn and gooseflesh peppers his back. There is something flat and dead in their eyes. It is as if he does not matter as a man to them, as if he is but an obstacle to be ridden round on their way to some place grave and dark.

"Poppycock," the quartermaster says, gathering his reins in a gloved fist. The leather has been cut from the index finger of the right glove, leaving the captain's trigger finger exposed. A man who takes shoot-

157

ing seriously, Kohn notes. And does it often.

"Poppycock and nonsense and you tell that to General Cooke back there behind his desk in Omaha. And then you tell him to send me a hundred horses and five thousand cartridges of .58. You tell him that. And get your stripes sewn on, Corporal, if you're going to be swaggering round this post as a sergeant."

"Yes, sir."

The quartermaster spurs his mount and his rough sentries do the same, steering a berth around Kohn, standing there in the mud.

12

THE 2ND TIME WE MET THAT MAN (& HIS WIFE) ON ROUTE TO LEAVEN-WORTH

Well before you give yourself over to fits of fine humour at the very notion of two veteran Bills such as ourselves volunteering for any D_____ thing in the Army (as if we would not know better!) you may well note that even in the Army there comes a time when stepping forward is better for a body than stepping back. And this was 1 such time though a fellow could argue it was the wrong thing to do knowing what would come next for us.

But sure only God could of known what was to follow that we would land here in the vast nowhere of a Valley where only bloody murder & lonely death waits for white men & God did stay <u>shtum</u> about it as the Dutchy boys say. Honestly a man might wonder what God gets on with all the days just watching over us but doing nothing to warn us from harm that He must surely know is coming? It can drive a man wild wondering on the things that lead a man to where he is come. It could make you a lunatic altogether recalling the notions that seemed grand at the time but were as far from grand as they could be.

Anyway it did suit us at the time to bid our leave to the Depot in Columbus & ship West this being our plan from the beginning. The 18th were in need of men & we were ready to roar Good Riddance! to that depot & its barking sergeants & parade drill & its pig fit vittles & calisthenics. I do not need tell you that in all them weeks of training to be soldiers we never fired 1 single musketball & nor did any other recruit. As you can see it would not be long til we would learn how remiss were our masters in leaving this ignorant scumtide of men with no means to fight or to die fighting at the very least. After all the Army is paying them as soldiers so that you might get to thinking the Army would instruct them in how to load & shoot like soldiers. But you know well Sir that would be too sensible by far for the Army. No word of a lie that Depot was more in the way of a workhouse than a

160

place where a man might learn the first thing about proper soldiering.

Tom & myself knew already more than any man needed about parade drill & we were lucky enough to know even more us about musketry so out of there we did get & onto a troop train bound for Ft. Leavenworth in Kansas.

The less said of the journey the better for the air inside the train cars was as cold as a coffin & every inch of that train was stuffed full of men in every posture of ill repose with each car choked with tobacco smoke & steam & engine ash that coated the innards of a man's nose like a whore powdering herself from the inside out no matter how tight we tried to shut them windows.

Tom & myself & a gentle Ohio boy some years younger in age to us did stay drunk for the duration on homestilled whiskey we bought at whistle stops & arrived in Kansas in no fit state to fight off so much as a head cold never mind your red savages but sure by then they were mostly peacified round Ft. Leavenworth anyway. But little did that matter for every other man on the train was drunk as well & there was a fine lot of fighting on the journey between some Dutch boys over bad cards & the way certain words be pronounced in their language. I am sad to write that one well juiced soldier God Keep Him did fall to his death trying to piss from between cars & more than one man ended that journey in the Leavenworth Guardhouse. The Provost squad on that train had its work cut out & well for them the b_____.

But never mind because as is the way of things in the Army well when we did arrive what did we do but set up waiting there. It was cool the boots I tell you for most of that bitter flat Kansas winter.

Now I may as well say here (for it be of some importance to my story) that on that journey we met for a 2nd time the Sutler Mr. Kinney whose fate we now know but could never imagine then.

You see we never once returned to his Stores at the Depot though we did purchase the odd bobbin here & there by giving our money to other Bills for to get it so as to avoid his evil eye & ill will after rumbling his & Sgt. Nevin's ruse. And though we never saw him on the train we came across him at a whistle stop somewhere West of Indiana outside the hired car (1 in front of the caboose) which he shared with his wife & all his goods & wares & which was guarded by 4 sentries with sidearms & Springfields.

We would bide time by strolling up & down the platform at whistle stops looking for a fellow with a bottle & some boiled eggs to sell as there did be more than 1 such lad at each junction. This was the 3 of us myself & Tom & the Ohio boy who had a fine way about him which endeared him to many. He was a kind & harmless thing who in the end did get a bottle stuck in his neck in a hog ranch outside Ft. Riley so I later heard tell & I always wondered who could of done such a thing. This country is chock full of terrible violent men. But that is by the by for as we did amble that snowy Indiana platform one of the days we came upon that dirty nuck of a Sutler there in his gleaming beaver coat & you will not believe it but he smiled when he saw us.

"You might of bought a 2nd cleaning kit after all boys the way you are looking now," says he & I smiled back at him but the brother did not.

"The coal ash does get in even with the windees closed," says I tipping my kepi to him but he only winked his eye & said no more turning to one of the soldiers minding him for a match for his cigar.

His fat wife gave us the onceover for a mere tick & then turned away with her hands tucked into a fox fur muff. For the like of us soldier filth did be of no interest to her but for what her bent Sutler husband could cull from us in coin. God Forgive Me for we know now what did befall the woman Lord Have Mercy On Her but that is how I felt. It is how I <u>still feel</u>. For I will tell you she had a black cruel heart bedded down under the fine fat tits of her & well what happened in the end she might of had it coming some would say.

But I only say this now after knowing her later & after that time on the wind roughed platform in Indiana we saw no more of them on the train. Nor did we see them that winter in Leavenworth & did not see that Sutler & his wife again until Ft. Caldwell in the Nebraska Territory when we set out from there on our journey to this place we call the Powder River Valley.

It is of no bearing on my testament at all but did you know Sir that this Valley is called Absaraka by the Indians who once lived here but lost these sweet lands to the terrible Savage Sioux? Absaraka means Home of the Crow. That is the tribe of Indians not the bird & that tribe might be fine allies in our fight with Red Cloud but they have no stomach for it at the moment. We do not see much of them.

I tell you it would make you laugh thinking on how the Crow got whipped by the Savage Sioux & run out rightly to the bad lands of dry grass & little game & now here are we the US Army trying to run them Sioux off just the same. It would crease you it would the joke of it. The 18th is made up nearly 1/2 of Irishmen & every Mick among us is doing to them Sioux what them Sioux did to the Crow & what the English (God Curse Them!) done to poor old Ireland. To hell or Connacht for the poor Indians only now it is us playing the b_____ Cromwell's men. It is enough to make you laugh.

I did say it before & I will say it again but it is a fierce queer f_____ world we do live in.

13

On their second full day at the fort, Molloy
awakes and asks for Kohn. The morning is
bright, the parade ground brilliant with
snow beginning to melt under the winter
sun.

Before entering the hospital barracks,
Kohn stops and looks up into a sky as bright
blue and clear as any he has ever seen. In
the distance, beyond the half-mile surround
of the log palisade, the Big Horn range rises
up, snow-capped, glorious. Fifteen odd
miles away, he has heard, and in the clear
winter air the mountains look close enough
to touch. This is the first time the weather
has lifted, allowing him to see them. Something rare and wonderful about this place.
Even he can see it, a Cleveland Jew with no
more mind to open spaces than a tick in a
sow's ear. Still, a cavalryman for the better

166

part of five years, Kohn can spot good grass as well as any man, knows the value of icy streams that run all summer long with snow melt.

A sergeant bunking in with Kohn has told him it is the best grazing he has ever seen in the most beautiful valley on earth and he had been around his share in the war. A great, good and pretty as punch place, all right, and Adam and Eve's beasts didn't graze half as goddamn good as they would here, the sergeant told him, if it wasn't for the mob of red-skinned sons of bitches trying to give you a barbering every chance they got. Another NCO, a Marylander, had told Kohn he would burn the entire valley to a cinder. The whole goat-fucking place, like Sherman did on his march to the sea, and that would take care of the goddamn Injuns once and for goddamn all.

Molloy gives Kohn a faint smile from his bed when he sees him. "My Daniel," he says, his voice deep and furred with sleep.

"Captain, how are you feeling, sir?"

"How do I look?"

"Like a shit left out in the rain, sir."

"And there's your answer . . ." He pauses, noticing Kohn's uniform tunic, cleaner, sharper than usual. He remembers asking Cooke for Kohn's promotion, amazed that

167

he does. "Look at you, Daniel, all striped up and polished nicely. You look like bait for a rich widow, *Sergeant* Kohn. A fine thing for your army career, Danny my chum, coming to this terrible place."

Kohn smiles back at him. "My last promotion, sir. I am throwing in the towel when my take-on ends. You watch me."

"Kohn, you will be heelballing my belt and boots long into decrepitude."

The surgeon joins them at the bedside. He is a balding man in his thirties, with mustaches hanging below his chin, spectacles at the end of a nose surprisingly free of gin blossoms for an army doctor.

He says, "Well, it appears you will live, Captain Molloy. And we shall wait another day but, with the help of the gods, you may keep that leg. Whatever it was your scout put on the wound, it appears to prevent infection from bedding in. The set was rough and you may limp some if you keep it but there are worse ways of getting from one place to another."

"Limping preferable to hopping, surely," Molloy says, distracted, looking about his bedside.

The surgeon sees this. "I'll dose you with more tincture of laudanum and you may have a bottle of stout for your lunch, but I am afraid you will be having no more whiskey while fighting for Company Q, Captain."

Molloy's face darkens. Get myself out of Company Q soon enough, off the sick list and back with . . . with whom? He has only Kohn and no proper company of men, no regiment. He remembers now why they have been sent to this distant fort. God help us, it's bloody Pinkertons we've become. Cooke in want of a head on a plate for the Secretary's wife.

"And when will the captain be up and about to start his work here, Doctor? If his leg takes to healing?" Kohn asks.

"A number of weeks, I would imagine, Sergeant, all going well. His work will have to wait, I'm afraid. And after that I cannot see him traveling back south until the winter has relented. You are in for a stay of some length. I do hope you enjoy the place." The surgeon smiles, amused but without rancor.

"Thank you, sir," Kohn says. "Can I bring the captain his grub, sir, or is he fed here?"

"We will feed him for the time being, until we see there is no infection. And under no circumstances are you to bring him whiskey. That's an order, Sergeant, and if it is disobeyed you will be court-martialled, is that clear?"

"Yessir."

Kohn is happy that this has been said in front of the captain for he knows that as soon as they are alone, he will be asked to bring libations. A wee dram. A drop. The surgeon's orders will make his refusal easier.

The surgeon goes away and returns with a small glass vial of claret-colored liquid. "Drink this, Captain. Into the arms of Morpheus for you, sir."

Molloy drinks and savors the taste of the laudanum. Mostly alcohol, he thinks, thanks be to God. Do the work of whiskey for now. Odd dreams it gives a man. Odder than the ones I have without it? Hardly possible. Odder? Blacker. Darkness hedges against his consciousness. He feels it, prays the laudanum will keep it at bay the way whiskey sometimes fails to do.

"Well then, Daniel, tell us what mischief you've been making since we arrived. And what of the young Virginian? And our Indian . . ."

"Jonathan, sir. He's set up a bivo outside the stockade with the other Indians. Near them anyhow. And he's found himself a winter wife, lucky fellow."

Molloy smiles. "Surely there must be an establishment for you to find one for an evening at least, Daniel. Even here. Where there are Bills and Jacks there are surely Jills about the place and a soft patch to lie down in."

Kohn smiles back. "The only such place for two hundred miles was the one run by the man who was killed and the cause of our being here. Alongside his sutler's store, on post, he ran a hog ranch outside. A musket shot away, I'm told. I have seen it from the wall but was waiting for you to go down and take a closer look. It's been burned out."

"By whom?"

"Everyone I've mentioned it to says it was Indians. They killed him and his wife and, some days later, put a torch to the place. Mr. Lo, they call them, the Indians, God only knows why. *Ah, that goddamn robber got skinned by Mr. Lo. Murder? Bad luck, more like and now there ain't no whores for a sojur to pass a time with.*"

Molloy's speech is somewhat slower, the rasp in his throat eased by the tincture. "You are a mimic of the highest, highest . . . the stage, Kohn. You should be on the stage. I saw *The Colleen Bawn* in New York five, seven times. In Dublin . . ." The officer's eyes close and soon he is snoring lightly.

Kohn finds the surgeon behind a curtain at the back of the barracks tending to a civilian contractor who crushed his hand felling timber. He waits while the surgeon doses the timberman. Seems to be the potion of choice, Kohn thinks. Will have to do for the captain as I am not bringing him one goddamn drop of whiskey no matter how hard he implores me to bring it.

"I wanted to thank you for looking after Captain Molloy, Doctor," Kohn says when the surgeon comes out from behind the curtain.

"No need for it. You were fortunate to have that Indian with you. I tried to ask him what he used in his concoction but he only grunted and said he did not know the names of the things in English."

"He said the same to me, Doc."

"A fortune a man could make, if it was indeed the poultice that prevented infection. Of course, your captain could just be in possession of a strong constitution."

"Well, he is strong enough in body all right," Kohn says.

The surgeon says nothing for a moment. Then, "You served under him in the war?"

"Yessir."

"Then you know maybe why he drinks. He is not the only man to come out of that affair with such an affliction."

"I know officers who spent the entire war

drunk, sir. I wonder do they remember a single ball fired. But the captain . . ."

Sensing his reluctance, the surgeon says, "You are here, I understand, to investigate the killing of our sutler."

"Yessir. The captain is."

"It will be some time before he is able for it."

"Yessir."

"And by then memories will have been scrubbed free of the detail you may need by the passing of time. It has already been a month since I submitted my report on the deaths to Colonel Carrington."

"Report, sir?"

"Of course. It was I who examined the bodies. Declared the deaths. I have done it forty-nine times since arriving here in July, both soldier and civilian."

Kohn offers the doctor a cigar from a box he purchased in the new sutler's store when he bought his sergeant's stripes. The doctor accepts it and lights a piece of kindling through the open stove door. He puts it to both cigars.

"And those forty-nine, sir — they were all killed by Indians?"

The doctor puffs his cigar until its tip is red with heat. He inhales and speaks on the exhalation. "All but four. One crushed by a

173

falling tree, one broken neck from a fall from a horse. One a suicide, one a presumed suicide; there are questions I would ask of that one but no one else would as the deceased was a lowly and thus expendable private and an unpopular one at that. It is difficult to beat oneself to death before shooting oneself in the head but that is the way of things here."

Kohn thinks for a moment. "Can I read your report, sir? On the deaths?"

"You could if I had it. But I gave it to Colonel Carrington, who of course forwarded it to General Cooke because that is what any officer would do when faced with the brutal killings of civilian employees under his command."

"You don't believe he sent your report? How did Cooke come to hear of the killings then? How did it come to be assumed that there was more to the deaths than an Indian attack?"

The surgeon puffs at his cigar, then says, "Well that I do not know, but there are five hundred-odd people, soldiers and civilians, attached to Fort Phil Kearny and every one of them knows that it was no more Indians who killed the sutler and his wife and the other fellow than the man on the moon."

"And do any of the five hundred know

who did it if it wasn't Indians?"

"Only those who did it know for certain, Sergeant, but there is talk."

"And what does that talk say?"

The surgeon washes his hands in a tub of soapy water atop the wood stove, his cigar clamped between his teeth. When he has dried his hands, he says, "That you will have to discover yourself. I will not be a party to men hanged on hearsay. I am aware of Mr. Kinney's familial links to certain parties back East and know that is the only reason you and Lieutenant Molloy are here, Sergeant. I don't doubt your honesty . . . or the lieutenant's, but as a man of science I will not trade in rumors."

"Of course, sir."

"I can, however, show you pictures of the death scene and of the bodies. Come with me."

The surgeon leads Kohn past a row of beds to the back of the barracks where he has hung a sheet weighted with lead shot to cordon off an office for himself. He unlocks a strongbox under the sturdy desk which would not be out of place in a grain merchant's store and Kohn wonders how the doctor has come to have it; did he transport it all the way into this wilderness? The doctor lays out a series of photographs on the desk.

"You made these, sir?"

"Of course not. We have the good fortune to have on hand the services of one Ridgeway Glover, a professional photographer from Philadelphia. I asked him to make these pictures. He was not pleased to be asked but he did a fine job of it nonetheless, don't you think?"

Kohn nods. The photographs are clear in their composition and terrible to look at. He can understand why the poor picturemaker would have balked at the job. Kohn has seen as much death as the devil and yet there is something about seeing it preserved in the utter stillness of the pictograph that adds to the horror. Like insects or fish frozen in the ice of a winter pond, the victims laid out for all eternity in the posture of their violent deaths. What value are these? He feels sordid, ashamed almost, to be staring at them.

"I had to get some of the men to tear away the roof to let enough light into the tavern for the pictures to be made. The camera's eye requires more light than you would find in such a hovel."

Kohn moves on to the pictures of the bodies laid out on the operating table he has seen at the far end of the barracks. Cleaned of blood, naked as God brought them into the world, the wounds like gaping mouths, so many in the woman's body you couldn't hope to count them all. A bullet wound, two, in the torso of the bigger, younger man. His scalp and hair gone, leaving only skull bone showing. One wound only, to the back of the head of the older man. Kinney. The sutler. The man we've been sent to avenge, Kohn thinks. He knows the type of wound.

"This younger man is scalped, sir. Surely . . ."

"Our soldiers also take scalps. It is a fact not widely disseminated in the Eastern papers but the habits of one side in a war are often enough adopted by the other. I will grant you, the younger male — no one seems to know his name — was scalped in such a way as to suggest that Indians had killed him. Perhaps they did, but . . ." The surgeon points to the two bullet wounds in the photograph with his cigar.

"But?" Kohn says.

"But I took two balls from these wounds. Curiosity, you see. A theory of mine. His death was not caused by scalping. I have tended to men who have been scalped and then lived on, God knows how."

177

"But the Indians have guns, Doctor. Why does his getting shot rule out Indians?"

"It doesn't. You are correct. A goodly number of Indians have taken to the gun. Our own government, in its wisdom, has traded rifles and ammunition to them, as do all the private traders in the West. Would you care to see the bullets that killed this man?"

Kohn shrugs.

Again into the strongbox, the surgeon removes an envelope and from it tips two spent, deformed ingots of lead into Kohn's palm. Kohn studies the rounds. They are damaged from their fatal transit within the victim's body, but recognizable. He says, "Colt pistol rounds. .36 caliber?"

"Correct. And that is not to say that the Sioux does not carry the odd handpiece, but if you ask any of the men about the camp who have encountered them in battle, they seem to rarely use them. Ammunition is hard to source and expensive. The bow and arrow is equally, if not more, effective at close range and there is a lifetime's habit of use in it for an Indian brave."

Kohn looks up at the surgeon.

The surgeon continues, "Which proves nothing, of course. But it does leave one thinking."

Kohn is silent for a long moment. Then, "Can you advise me where I might begin with . . ." He nods at the pictures. ". . . with all this?"

The surgeon sits down at his desk and looks up at the rough ceiling boards. "I have to live here, Sergeant. And work here. My work is valued and needed in such a place."

"I don't doubt that, sir. But if I could make a start of it. For the captain. . . ."

The surgeon smokes in silence for some moments. Then, "There are the Irish to think of certainly. You might start with them though if you are possessed of any sense of self-preservation you might not. Hatred of the informer and the constable extends beyond the shores of Ireland, but in present times one might take into consideration that the men of Erin consider any attempt to even so much as impose common army discipline upon them as a Masonic or English conspiracy. They do tend to react badly to things and . . . Well, you serve the lieutenant in the bed there, Sergeant, so surely you have some idea what they are like. You are not a Mason, Sergeant, are you? An Englishman?"

"No sir." Kohn smiles. "I'm a half-Polish, Silesian Dutchie Jew. An American, I suppose."

The surgeon smiles back at him. "Then you are only at minor, rather than major, risk of the knife or bludgeon."

Kohn has not thought of this. Molloy may be of some help with the Irish when he is fit for it. Until then, I am on my own. I could sit and do nothing, he thinks. I should, perhaps, do nothing.

"Now, as an officer, it would be my duty," the surgeon says, "to ask have you presented your orders to the officer commanding? To Colonel Carrington, as commander of this post and the Mountain District? Have you done this?"

"No sir."

"I thought not. Well you should do it, and in doing this you may cast your eyes upon an Indian girl in the employ of the colonel's wife as a housemaid. A striking girl — you cannot miss her."

"Yessir."

"She has not been in Mrs. Carrington's employ for long, Sergeant."

"Sir?"

"Well, you might begin your 'investigations' by asking about her time working for Mr. Kinney before she began to work for the colonel's wife. And while you are there, you might ask the colonel to give you the freedom of the post and a letter

180

compelling his officers and men to answer your queries regarding the sad end of the sutler. There are, I am told, logbooks and such, detailing who posted guard at which gates on a given night; company musters which may or may not detail men absent from quarters without leave. There are also the sutler's account books, of course. A record more soured by bad credit and docked wages you will not find outside of a debtors' prison. I've heard this new regular army of ours called just that, Sergeant. A big, blue debtors' prison."

Kohn says, "Thank you, sir. I —"

"Don't thank me, Sergeant. You have heard nothing from me. Not a thing. And if I find that you have brought whiskey to my patient, I will be a witness at your court martial." The surgeon smiles.

"Yessir."

"The Indian girl. You cannot miss her."

"Yessir."

14

TOM & HIS MEXICAN GAL

So at Ft. Leavenworth in Kansas we waited & as you well know Sir waiting in the Army means the usual run of dog's work for a soldier thought up by officers who themselves are most of the time neck deep in whiskey because there is never a truer notion than <u>The Devil makes work for idle hands</u>!

There is some truth to this for the enlisted man as well because at Leavenworth (it being a jumping off & transit stop for any Army heading West) there be any number of Hog Ranches outside the gates stuffed to the gills with whores & brimful of beer & trade whiskey in which a Bill might indulge himself once his wages caught him up & card debts are paid & expenses incurred for kit & caboodle back in Depot are taken out. Work for idle hands & then work for the sawbones with his mercury cure.

There is only so much daylight & so much labour so what is a Bill to do with the acres of time he has once the work is done & there is nothing but flat hard frosted prairie grass around you & rumours of red men stalking every blade of it? Well Faro & Stud & Chuckaluck of course for they be all fine ways to pass the time though they do little for you in bitter winter when you are in need of a body in the bed beside you & maybe this is why Tom took such a shine to the one the soldiers at Ft. Leavenworth called the Mexican Gal. May She Go With God.

Now before you think otherwise that Mexican Gal was no whore not in the way of the normal whores in the hog ranches off post. No for she was a wedded woman married to a Corporal from I Company who was a long time at Leavenworth & not one to cross so it was said though I never saw him in a fit of anger. But saying she was no proper whore is not to put her in a higher place than the hog ranch girls or the hog ranch girls in a lower one for we are all low creatures in God's eyes & there is no lower on this earth some say than the immigrant dog face soldier in the Regular Army of the United States.

But others such as myself would say that the lowest dog in a kepi cap & sky blue britches does in his heart be no different than the finest gentleman & the needs of his heart (& other parts of him God Forgive Me) are surely the same. A kind word from a woman or a smile even if bought & paid for. The soft stroke of a woman's hand on your own or the press of a warm body against you of a cold night. I ask you where is the man on God's earth who is not in need of such things?

I tell you there is <u>no such man</u> & Tom well he does need it too maybe more than other men because he once had a world of women all for his taking so handsome & fine with words was he before the war. I reckon that poor Tom had a fear he would never get such comforts from a wife him being both of ruined face & Irish & a Regular Army soldier which are 3 terrible things in this country. He must of thought, "Who would have such a man for a husband but a whore?"

But the lure of the cards was so strong on Tom that there was scarce a penny left for so much as a sniff of a whore at one of the ranches outside the walls of Leavenworth after paying his debts & for whiskey & what we all in the Company did kick in for extra grub. I thought then & I do think now that this is why Tom took his sweet shine to the Mexican Gal. She was free with her favours while asking little more than kindness in return I am told.

As well as this she was a fine fair thing to look at with skin so brown you could feel the glow of the Mexican sun from it like there did be a coal stoked fire alight inside her & with a nose turned up & thick black curls a fellow could lose himself in & with brown shining eyes the colour & heat of bricks warmed in the sun. And though she was sparse & thin upstairs well a grand soft girl she was under her bustle with an arse like a lady's pony I tell you.

But no matter all this. It is of no matter that she was a camp laundress of the kind known for sharing her wares round the post as them in that trade is known throughout the Army & no matter she was the wife of that Cpl. in I Company a hard man from the shores of New Jersey & a veteran of the War like us brothers. No matter the way she had with delivering the babes of the wives on post into the world safe & sound with her mind full of potions & poultices & herbs collected from the plains about the Ft. for to stop the bleeding & soothe a wound. No matter still how she was known by all on post from Colonel's wife to drunken Bill for selling the sweetest wild cherry pies for a fair price & for turning sheets white enough to blind a circling hawk & crisp enough to cut tin. No matter all this there did be something off about the girl. Something not quite right I tell you something as God Is My Witness & I did say this to Tom when I saw how sweet he got on her.

"Nothing good will come of it," says I to the brother. "With you mooning about her every free moment & lugging tubs of sodden sheets & smalls from laundry to line in the way of a gentleman suitor when she does be well made for hauling herself sure. Her man is one to watch Tom even for you."

I do not need tell you what Tom thought of the husband being one for him to watch. He laughed at me & clapped me on the back & in the Gaelic said back to me as we swung picks into the frozen earth for to dig yet another latrine sink, "Jealous Mickaleen. I can see it in you. Your eyes are gone green with it."

"Oh you are right Tom of course. Jealous as the brother with no peppermint stick."

Tom gave a laugh & went on with his digging leaving me again to think, "Nothing good will come of it" & nothing did but it does get me thinking (now if not then) that

186

the <u>off part of her was what drawn him to the girl</u>. She was a Mex so she was an exile from her home place like Tom but it was something more than this something broken or bent inside her that Tom did sense like a horse can sense a rider's fear or a dog a master's sadness. Something askew much like his face was askewed & the thoughts in his head were at odds with all things peaceful & good in the world. And maybe I do not mean to say <u>off</u> but that she was <u>different</u>. She had a peaceable & warm way to her that was so at odds to Tom. It was so at odds to all the rough souls in the camp. Maybe it was this that made Tom love her & seek her out each day.

This makes some sense to me now because at the time of his intoxication for the Mexican Gal Tom was a well settled boy in camp with the storms in his head becalmed the D Bar Bowie knife firm in its scabbard. His hands that were fists more than fingers mostly were loose & still in his lap when he sat & smoked his pipe like any other Bill. There were none of Tom's usual brutal contests behind the barracks & no harsh words over cards or grim & terrible stares that caused me to pat his back & tell him to leave off that the man on the other end of his eyes had meant no harm in asking an innocent question. No my brother was as sweet & calm that short spell of winter & spring as the calf we rared up back in Ohio. It was like that Mexican did share some of her goodness & peace with my brother & he was for a time willing to take it.

So though I <u>was</u> sure that no good would come of Tom's passion for her (she having a husband who did appear to be fierce fond of his wife himself) I was happy to let things roll on as they did for it made my life a sight easier altogether.

But I knew this could not go on for it was too good to be true by 1/2.

What could be wrong with her you ask Sir? More than you might think altogether for it came to be the strangest thing I did ever hear. You see not long after Tom begun to spark with her the poor girl fell down with the cholera that betimes does besiege a camp or town & in her sickness is how her secret was discovered.

Now the other women at Ft. Leavenworth (the officer's wives even for she did help them birth their babbies & sew them up after so they did not tear easy the next time or so it was said round the Ft.) well the women of the camp did be fierce fond of the Mexican Gal & when she took ill with the cholera they nursed her & it being the cholera they minded to bath the poor girleen & what do you think they found? Forgive Me Sir but didn't they find she was no darling girl at all but a fellow a proper born man like yourself or myself with the prick & balls of any bull you might see in a field?

Well there is some strange things in the world Sir & I am telling you I did look upon some of them but this? Surely it was stranger to me because my brother was sweet on her but I tell you she did make for a fine woman & though I sensed there was something off about her well this is the last thing I did reckon. I do not even think I had it in me to imagine it at all but there you are. God has wrought this mad world & all in it so He must have good reason for the things he does. I am no priest or scholar & so I do not question it. She was a kind girl after all & May She Sit With God Who Made Her.

But let me tell you Sir news of this did not take a long day to reach every ear in Leavenworth & so a fierce wild scandal was born in the camp & perhaps showing His mercy our Lord took her to Him later that night sparing the shame & banishment that was surely coming to her.

Now a fellow could ask did the women tending to her refuse her care that might of

189

saved her once her secret was discovered? For as bad as the cholera was that spring it was worse other times before & there is now medicine for it I am told. If I remember rightly she was the only one to die that time at Leavenworth though many fell ill & were cast to the hells of puking fluxing sickness.

But a part of me also did wonder was it not a mercy her passing for maybe in the comfort of Heaven the Mexican Gal could not see how her loving husband did rise up from the depths of his wild mortification at the ragging & joking of his pals & one evening some days later did step out the livestock gates of the Ft. & into the long spring prairie grass for to put a Colt Navy to his head & spread his brains all over Kansas.

I can tell you them I Company boys took it hard & decided it must be a broken heart he died of for he took the ragging well like a man should do it being only fair in the circumstances that your pals might have a laugh at such a thing. But to all who would listen they would say that <u>shame</u> did not come into it. It was <u>grief</u> spurred him to take the life that God once gave him & not the shame of wedding a Molly & not knowing it. Them I Company boys told us it was his love for that Mexican Gal no matter

190

what hung tween her legs that sent him away in the head so that he put a bullet in it May God Rest Him. For love can drive a man to all sorts Sir it can.

Of course I did not know the New Jersey Corporal himself & came to know him more in death than life so for me it is not here nor there at all. But Tom was fierce quiet about the whole thing & I never again did talk of his mooning round after her with his hair combed & tunic brushed nor did I talk of the gentle favours she shared with him among the sheets behind the sluice house.

Well in quick time his mood blackened & Tom began again to pass long hours on his bunk with his arms behind his head & eyes staring wide at nothing on the ceiling while the barracks rumbled on round him & when he did rise from his mattress his D Bar would again slip its scabbard & even after the lamps were snuffed & The Taps sounded & men snored in their racks you could hear that knife running up an edge on the whetstone & could see if you looked my brother's eyes shining with dead light in the darkness.

You may wonder Sir what good is this to my testament & you would be right to ask it perhaps but I would answer that I write of it because it opens a window for to see the state of my brother's heart back then. It was like an engine always running on damp coal & rank steam. I write of it so that you might know of Tom's condition when he 1st made acquaintance with the one who would become his True Love on the long march to this Valley of the Powder River. She is a part of this story maybe a bigger part than you would reckon though likely it was as much her misfortune to meet my brother as it was his to meet her.

15

*December 9, 1866 — Fort Phil Kearny,
Dakota Territory*

The staff officer, a young captain, eyes
Kohn with disdain. He says, "A *sergeant,*
here to present orders to a *colonel?*"

"Yessir."

Kohn stands at parade rest in an office
inside the largest structure in Fort Phil
Kearny. The headquarters barracks is constructed of planed logs and painted white
both inside and out, unlike most of the hastily erected buildings. Rising from its roof is
a lookout platform, allowing a view of the
fort entire as well as of the surrounding valley and hills.

"This is most goddamned unusual, Sergeant," the staff officer says.

"Yessir. My captain is incapacitated, sir.
Captain Molloy, 7th Cavalry, sir. On the
blue list, under surgeon's orders. His leg
was broken on the journey. We were sent

193

here on General Cooke's orders, sir."

Suspicion casts up on the captain's face. "General Cooke's orders, Sergeant? Why, you hand them over right this minute. How can —"

"I would prefer to present them to the Colonel himself, sir."

"Are you giving me guff, Sergeant? Goddamn guff, are you?"

"No sir."

"Then you present me with those orders or you'll be had up for insubordination faster than you can shit grease."

"Yessir. But I don't imagine General Cooke would want our investigations . . . thwarted, sir, as he has ordered them. I thought the colonel should be aware of them. As a courtesy, sir. . . ."

"Thwarted? Investigations?" Now there is more than anger or suspicion in the officer's voice. A desk man, elevated by his distance from the musket ball and his proximity to power. Nothing like an investigation to pique interest, Kohn thinks, or inspire fear. Investigations linked always to inspections, promotions. Demotions or drummings out of the army. *The inspection discovered poor performance of assigned duties . . . recommends dismissal.* "What investigations are you talking about?"

194

"The death of the sutler, Mr. Kinney, and his wife, sir. General Cooke seemed to feel it of great import."

The officer stares at Kohn in an attempt to detect mockery in his words.

"And why would Cooke want something like that *investigated*?"

"I don't know, sir. Only that I was told to present these orders to the colonel."

The officer stares at Kohn for a long minute and Kohn stares at the whitewashed office wall. He can stay here as long as the officer wants him to. He will eventually see the colonel and the officer knows it.

"Wait here, goddamn it all," the officer says.

Kohn can hear voices from behind the door, deep, muffled and rising with some urgency. After some minutes of this, the door opens and the adjutant says only, "In."

Colonel Carrington — late forties, black-bearded, thin, small, academical — is seated behind a desk not unlike the surgeon's, thick and polished oak and conspicuously grand for an outpost such as this. The colonel appears to Kohn to be a man used to sitting at desks, and from men around the fort he has heard that this impression is not far from wrong. A recruiter during the war, Carrington never lifted so much as a feather duster against the rebels, yet here he is, in command of a fighting fort at the edge of nowhere. A paper colonel given the stage when the lights have dimmed and the big show is over. It's the way of things in the army. Political connections mean as much as competence. Mean more, most likely.

The one thing the men Kohn has spoken to will concede is that Carrington can build Uncle Sam a grand fort for his money. The men call him Carpenter Carrington. There is little affection in it. Fighting men will love or hate a fighting officer. Indifference is the best they will do for desk dragoons.

"Sir —" Kohn begins. He notes the desk is strewn with official missives, orders, quartermaster's reports, draughtsman's drawings. A map labeled "Mountain District and the Dakota Territories" is pinned to the wall.

"Orders, Sergeant. What is this about orders? From Cooke? Cooke sent you?"

The colonel's voice is nervous, pitched high and clipped, dry-mouthed. He looks away from Kohn and down at the papers on the desk, moving the drawings in front of him, squaring them off amid the clutter of other paperwork. How different from Cooke's office, Kohn thinks.

"Yessir. And a letter, addressed to you, sir.

196

The orders were issued to my captain but he is —"

"I know that, Sergeant. I've been told that. But *you* have these orders. And you are to fulfil them? An enlisted man? An investigation? Cooke wants an investigation into the death of our sutler? I simply . . ." The colonel looks up again at Kohn and appears to study him.

"Yessir, and his wife. As you must know, sir, Mr. Kinney was brother-in-law to Mr. McCulloch, the Secretary of the Treasury. General Cooke —"

"I know who McCulloch is. Kinney never let us forget the connection. And Cooke . . . Cooke. God d—" Carrington swallows down the oath as if it were a draught of poison. "Blast that man. What else did he say? Tell me, Sergeant. I simply don't believe he sent you for the sole reason of determining that the sutler and his unfortunate wife were killed by Indians."

"I have been told it was not Indians who killed them, sir. General Cooke himself said this to Captain Molloy."

"And who told *you* this, Sergeant?"

"I understand it is taken for a given among the men of the fort, sir."

"You would do better than listen to the idle speculation of the enlisted soldier,

Sergeant," the adjutant says.

"Of course, sir. Though I believe there was a medical report. A report of death, sir, which stated as much, based on the surgeon's examination of the bodies."

"Speculations merely," Carrington says. "God blast it, Sergeant, do you think I do not have enough to manage without such nonsense as that godless surgeon's speculations? I forwarded that report to Omaha and thence, I would imagine, it was forwarded to Washington but it can be taken as nothing more than the . . . the assumptions of a surgeon. An army surgeon, I need not remind you, Sergeant."

Kohn is uncertain as to whether or not he should defend his impressions of the surgeon. Army surgeon he may be but the man seemed sober and learnèd to Kohn. Unusually sane for an army sawbones. He remains silent. From outside he can hear wagons and the suck of hooves in the thawing mud. Skinners' calls and barking sergeants. Carrington hears them too and stands from his desk.

"Your orders, Sergeant, and the letter."

He takes them from Kohn and first reads the orders, then opens the letter from Cooke. Without looking at Kohn, the colonel turns and opens a door behind his desk

198

to reveal rough stairs ascending. He mounts them and is followed by his adjutant. Kohn waits for a moment before following the officers up onto the viewing platform he saw from outside. The colonel and the captain stand at a railing and overlook a body of mounted soldiers in buffalo coats gathered around a number of box wagons hauled by mule teams. Civilian drivers and timbermen smoke pipes and cradle repeater rifles. Some of the box wagons have raised sides and behind them sit more soldiers with muskets and crates of ammunition, all manner of saws and axes. Kohn stands behind Carrington at the railing.

"Captain Brown, you do not appear to have a full complement, sir," Carrington shouts down and Kohn recognizes the quartermaster he met some days before.

"We are short horses, sir," the quartermaster, Captain Brown, shouts back to Carrington. "We will have to make do unless you can impress upon the good general to send us more men and beasts. And bullets, sir."

Brown smiles and Kohn sees derision in it. A fighting man to a writing commander.

"Do your best, Captain. And under no circumstances are you to pursue any Indians in case of ambush. Defend the woodtrain and return to post, sir."

"Yessir," Brown says, spurring his mount and saluting. There is no respect in the gesture. The fort's gates are opened and the wagons begin to move out, followed by the mounted infantry and a smattering of cavalrymen. One of the two pretorians who was with Brown when Kohn met him stares up at Kohn and Kohn meets his gaze. The big man turns his horse and follows the wagons, his buffalo coat making him look somehow less than human. A mounted bear, a minotaur.

Kohn watches the wagons stretch out across the plain and Carrington points. He raises a spyglass. "There, Captain."

The adjutant extends his own glass and directs its lens on the hills across the valley and Kohn sees them now himself, tiny silhouettes on a rolling ridge line roughly half a mile away across the valley, east of the hilltop road where the wagon train will pass.

Kohn speaks, "Do the men spot them, sir?"

Carrington claps shut the spyglass. "Spot them! Why they expect them, Sergeant. They are there every day the woodtrain goes out. They are there most nights as well, looking down at us and our activity. Let them have the howitzer, Captain. The gun that shoots twice, as our Sioux friends have named it."

The adjutant crosses the viewing platform and bellows orders to a cannon crew on a bastion built into the stockade wall. The gun is small, likely a twelve-pounder Kohn reckons, and known as a mountain howitzer. Kohn watches as the men go to work, sighting along the barrel, adjusting the range, loading, ramming. Setting and lighting the fuse.

Detonation rips the still winter air and smoke and flame spit from the cannon's barrel. The Indians on the hilltop wrench their mounts to the ground by the neck and use them for cover. Kohn follows the arc of the shot, as experienced men can do, by the warp and disturbance of air. He loses it as it falls to the hilltop and then watches it explode, showering the hillside with scorched shrapnel. Moments later one of the Indians pulls his horse to its feet and remounts, shaking his spear at the fort as if willing another shot. Kohn can just make out the sound of the Indian's shouting and whooping. A second Indian appears to be preoccupied with his horse, still on the ground, and Kohn wonders if the beast has been struck by shrapnel. The Indian kneels to the horse and then stands and leaps up onto the back of his friend's mount. They leave as the howitzer fires for a second time and the shell explodes over the dying horse and the hilltop empty of Indians.

"That will be enough for today, Captain," Carrington says.

The adjutant bellows to the gun team to cease firing and his order is repeated.

"You may perform your investigations, Sergeant," Carrington says, turning to Kohn and handing him back the oilskin wallet containing his and Molloy's orders. "But let me warn you not to interfere with the mission of the fort. I will not tolerate it."

"Yessir."

"And you are to report your findings to me, Sergeant, is that clear? Any prosecutions to be carried out will be sanctioned by myself alone. No suspect leaves this fort without my being informed or you will be subject to court martial proceedings, Sergeant."

"Yessir," Kohn says, noting that he has been threatened with court martial more times in the past three days than he was in the whole four years of the war.

Carrington turns back to watching the woodtrain as it begins its climb from the valley floor to the road that runs atop the hills. If I were an Indian, Kohn thinks, that is where I would attack. Maybe the howitzer discourages them. Maybe there is a better ambush site on the descent. Kohn shrugs away the speculation. He wonders if he should ask Carrington if he can interview his wife's serving maid, the Indian girl the surgeon had mentioned. He decides against this and will find another way to do it. Or perhaps he will return to his quarters, lie down on his bunk with a bottle and do nothing at all until Molloy recovers.

"You are dismissed, Sergeant," Carrington says.

Kohn comes to attention and snaps out a salute. The colonel and his adjutant ignore him, watching the woodtrain.

16

HOW WE GOT UP AS HORSE SOLDIERS & TOM BROKE CAPT. BROWN'S MOUNT

From Ft. Leavenworth in Kansas we did shift kit & caboodle in the spring to Ft. Caldwell in the Nebraska Territory. (This was where I did overhear Gen. Sherman tell the ladies to keep account of their journeys West & had the notion to do it myself.)

Here the soldiers detailed to the 18th Infantry Regiment began to arrive forming 8 skeleton companies of the 2nd Battalion. Most of these boys arriving were fresh as new baked bread on a windowsill with but a few veterans of the War like ourselves mixed in. We were thin on the ground I can tell you.

You would not believe it Sir (or maybe you would because you know how the Army works!) but the detachment of Cavalry promised to us got shanghaied & sent somewhere else altogether. This being the case a plan was made by the bigwigs to fit some of us infantry Bills out as Mounted Infantry which does sound like a fine plan until you learn how little time most of the new take ons had around horses. Sure they are city mice most of them & about as easy with a beast as they are with a rifle. Afraid of the horses 1/2 the lot while the other 1/2 knows not which end is the arse & which the eyes. But my brother & I did know a thing or 2 at least about them & soon for the price of $1.50 each paid to Sgt. Nevin we did find ourselves mounted & saving mightily on bootleather.

I write of this because it was detailed to the Battalion's horses that we came to meet Capt. Frederick Brown who is also called Mad Fred by the men of the 18th. He is called this out of respect & awe & not mockery if you can reckon it. For though he is the Quartermaster here at Ft. Phil Kearny he is also the most terrible harrier of the Sioux & Cheyanne you would ever like to meet.

But surely you have already met him yourself Sir. Did he show you his collection of scalps? They are on fine display tacked to the logs above his bed & in the blockhouse in the Pinery so that he may work & dream to his soovaneers of butchered red men. He at first did string them from his saddle like Mr. Lo does himself but The Carpenter noted this & ordered him to take them down that it was not right & proper for a soldier (an officer & Quartermaster no less!) to be gallivanting himself across the plains of America kitted out much like the savages he is fighting. Carrington did not order him to stop the scalping mind you only to take them pelts down from where they could be seen by the women & civilians about the fort & Mad Fred did as he was ordered all the while with a smirk at his lips that any fool could see. For like all others he obeys Carrington's orders out of duty & not love but that is another story.

Our Capt. Brown is undaunted as they come. He is as fearless as my brother & you might say it does be madness in him & not courage at all that makes him such a man for the Hurly Burly but I am not one to say it for though he did ride myself & Tom into a fair few bloody scraps he also got us out of them Thanks Be To God.

I will describe our meeting him because there is something in my mind that tells me if we did not come to his attentions well then I may rightly not of come to the tight spot where I do now find myself.

But meet Mad Fred we did coming out for to select a horse for breaking one morning himself & Lt. Bisbee. We came upon them at the corral smoking cheroots & looking over the horse flesh before them.

Now you know well yourself that manys the officer does keep his own personal mount for riding but this Army after the War is a different place altogether from before & many cannot afford this nowadays. So as my brother & I forked hay & slung buckets Capt. Brown & young Lt. Bisbee wandered among the beasts & from the side of our eyes we watched them pat flanks tug lips back & lift the hooves of the more gentle of the herd. Some of the horses would start & scatter when a body came near so these horses would likely be the finer of the mounts among them sure even a fool could tell it by looking but there are fools & then there are officers. (No offence to you Sir.)

Well in fairness Lt. Bisbee did have some knowledge of horse flesh for all the good it did him. He was jumped by some of Red Cloud's Braves out on a scout shortly after we set up here in this Valley. The savages left him his prick & balls attached which was some good fortune I suppose but nothing much more of him was left alone. It is said his own mother would not of known his face if it was she that found him. God Rest Him but he was a kind soul & a good officer who did know his horses.

But that was later & that morning we watched the 2 of them as if we were not watching at all which is the way all soldiers watch their officers & come to know far more about them than any officer imagines.

So we knew from the off Tom & myself that the mount Capt. Brown finally chose though it was the fairest in appearance in the pen a big fine quarterhorse with some Indian paint mixed in & white socks well we did know that horse was in no way broken & had no mind to be. And perhaps poor Lt. Bisbee knew as well that beast was no good for a weak rider like the captain but him being of lesser rank & a softer sort of gentleman said nothing but took a coil of rope from where it hung on a post & fashioned a lasso from it.

"Give me that rope Bisbee," says Capt. Brown all full of bluster. I saw Tom smile a smidge at this & pat the muzzle of a kindly piebald. My brother then rested his elbow on that horse's bowed back & set himself to watching like he might a theatre play or music show.

In the Gaelic says I to Tom, "A dollar he

never gets that loop round her neck before Taps be drummed out."

"I would sooner hold a Loco to a dollar & watch it burn than take your wager brother."

A smile came to my lips & I ducked behind that placid pony too so no one would see it. There I set up with my brother to watch that madman lassoo just about everything in the corral except that horse. He did even manage to rope a horse nearly losing his arms from their sockets in the doing but it was not the horse he was trying for & I learnt much in the way of new oaths & curses in English. (There are many things you cannot imagine doing to a horse but Capt. Brown could imagine them & roared more than once how he would do them to that mare!)

I tell you 7 or 8 times Mad Fred flung out that rope & once he even drew his pistol in a rage & threatened to shoot the white stocking mare if she did not heave to but that mare had more things on her mind hopping & snorting to send the other horses in the pen away in a fearful whinny of horse bodies & rising dust.

"Are you certain you want that one Sir?" says Lt. Bisbee in a mannerly way that would be hard for most men to manage. There was no judgement or mockery in his voice above the water but surely it lurked beneath making his words all the more merry for the rest of us.

Well Capt. Brown's face was red & his hat cocked cattywampus. A pure state he was in & we 2 brothers & some other boys now in a gather at the fence fought hard to keep from showing the deep cut of our mirth. Truly Mad Fred & his mare did be a better show than the best motleyed harlequin in London Town or Dublin.

We did not know Brown was 1/2 mad then & only thought him too proud to admit how little he knew of horses him being a behind the lines Q.M. & an artillery man in the War & not much in the way of a Dragoon as perhaps he had a mind to make himself.

Says the Mad Capt. back, "No Bisbee I am as sure as the G_____ D_____ day is long I will have that particular one D_____ his eyes."

"<u>Her</u> eyes," says Bisbee but not so Capt. Brown can hear him & showing his kindliness & fair minded manner he cast a wink my way letting us know he was enjoying himself as much as the rest of us watching that lassoo sail through the clear blue sky at nothing time & time again while that white stocking mare pranced away with a flick of her arse like a whore meeting a man with no money.

"Sir?" says Tom of a sudden fair shocking me & putting me in mind to worry. It was a riot of a performance altogether but I feared the brother might be for showing up the Q.M. Some of the boys at the fence did see things the same way & shoved off with the look of the busy bee about them.

"Sir?" the brother said again leaving me at the sag backed pony to approach Capt. Brown.

"Not now Private G_____ D_____ it all. Not now," says Capt. Brown tossing the lassoo to catch on a fence post some feet away from the mare.

Tom did salute & say, "Only can I snare your mount for you Sir?"

Even I had trouble understanding Tom's question & so stepped forward with my heart up in my throat.

Says I, "He wants to know can he loop your horse for you Sir? Tis not something an officer need be at when there is us Bills detailed just for it. Our 1st Shirt would be sore to hear we let you rope your own Sir."

The Capt. cast an eyeball at us then & we stood the both of us to attention. Says I, "He is a fine man for the ponies Sir my brother."

For a moment there was silence causing

me to wonder would the Q.M. draw his Colt again & shoot us both down dead for interrupting his labours. The last remaining boys watching from the fence moved away for fear of catching some of that officer's rage.

Well I can tell you I wished now the brother & myself could of done the same & leave the lunatic Capt. to it for his gaze upon us was as hot as the desert sun & in them eyes of his (which I did not dare look into) there shone flickers of the terrible wild warrior he has inside him.

Even the horses put a halt to their shunting about & waited for the man to speak. Even the birds did whisht their singing in the branches is the way I remember it.

Says the Capt., "I am not sure how to take such an offer from two Paddy Bills who seem to have forgotten their place in the world. How would you take such an offer Lt. Bisbee?" He did not look over at the Lt. as he spoke but stared only upon us there in front of him with terrible venom in his eyes.

Well that Lt. Bisbee was a good man & a better officer I am telling you Sir. May God Keep Him but he did reply to Brown, "I would say there is no offence in it Sir. No Bill in this whole Army would be such a blockhead as not to know that insolence & insubordination would bring hell down upon his back. I cannot imagine these boys are so blockheaded are you boys?"

He was an educated man Lt. Bisbee & it took me a moment to reckon up what he said but I did not mistake the warning in it.

"No Sir," I said to him. "We are only meaning a good turn for an officer of the 18th as we do be detailed to the herd anyways Sir."

"And you boys are surely sober aren't you?" says he back to me.

"We are sober as Mohamedans Sir."

Now the brother put his spoke in but in such a jumble from his mouth that I cut him off in the ditch altogether. Says I, "Only that my brother is after telling me what a fine horse is that mare Sir."

In a fit of nerves I did doff my kepi & put it back on & spoke directly to Capt. Brown for the 1st time. "And only that he would be much obliged if you let him snare & break her to the gun for you Sir. For she would make a fine mount in battle or parade & it is a rare horse that does make both."

After a moment the Capt. said, "Can this brother of yours who is so G_____ D_____ good with horses not speak his own mind Pvt.?"

"He can Sir but you would be hard put understand it. His mouth is 1/2 kaput Sir."

The Capt. stepped over to us & Tom squared himself up like to be inspected by him near snapping himself up to attention again while Capt. Brown took a long gander at my brother's mug. He did this from below looking up at him as our Mad Fred is not so tall a man & this perhaps goes part the road in explaining the way he carries on for it is well known that oft times the shortest man does be the tallest bastard in a room. I have seen this to be especially true of the officer class.

Well for a time the Capt. did eye up the brother's gob & the horses began to once again shift around the pen nibbling at the hay in the racks or dipping their heads to the trough as if their work for the day was done.

Finally the Capt. spoke. "What happened to your face Pvt.? Pvt. whatever your G_____ D_____ name is."

"O'Driscoll Sir," says I.

Says he, "What happened to your face Pvt. O'Driscoll?" He did turn to me then. "And if <u>you</u> don't let this soldier answer my G_____ D_____ pig f_____ question for himself I will take the skin from

your Greenhorn back with this f_____
rope."

I said nothing to this of course.

Says he again, "What happened to your
maw Pvt.?"

"Took a minie ball Sir," says the brother.

"And where did you take it?"

"Tennessee Sir. Chickamauga."

I kept shtum at this though my heart leapt
in my breast like a hooked salmon wondering oh wondering why to God the brother
saw fit to tell the truth of his wounding for
the 1st & only time since we took on with
the Army in Columbus some 5 months past
under the name of O'Driscoll. Every man
who asked since then we told it was a horse
that did it & lying as is the way of things
becomes easier than the truth over time.
But here was my brother telling the truth to
an officer. An officer! I tell you there is no
accounting for Tom's ways.

But if I think on it now perhaps Tom saw
something in Brown that he felt to be inside
himself as well & so he could trust him. It
was like Tom smelt the same poison running in that Q.M.'s veins the way red blood
runs under yours & my own.

"Chickamauga. Well," says Brown. "You
got it in the face so that tells me you are a
fighting man at least. You can tell a great

215

deal about a man from where his wounds are. Did you know that Pvt. O'Driscoll?"

Says Tom without pause, "I have heard it said Sir. And sure my arse does be all of one piece." This did come out clear as a church bell when he said it & I closed my eyes at this & thought to myself, "Oh Tom you dunderhead. You innocent f_____ you done it now boy."

But didn't the Q.M. just laugh right at him giving a big fine bellow from his guts up. And maybe this was because Capt. Brown could see the same thing in my brother that my brother saw in him so laugh he did fairly pissing himself with the laughter. When he was after righting himself & wiping down his eyes with his kerchief he handed over the coil of rope to Tom.

"Here," says he. "Just loop that G_____ D_____ beast & be quick about it."

He laughed again & repeated my brother's words to Lt. Bisbee. "Sure, my arse does be all of one piece Sir! Where do we get them Lt.? Where do we G_____ D_____ get them?"

Well in a tick my brother lassooed that white stocking mare & in an hour he was on her back & by the next day he had a saddle on her that horse licking brown sugar from his palm like a kitten from a bowl of milk & that next very day Mad Capt. Brown came back to the pen & mounted her.

Over the weeks we broke that horse to the gun with the help of Lt. Bisbee & a cavalry Sgt. up from Texas. And though that mare never in truth settled to the Capt. for he does ride a horse like a boy riding a barrel down a river well she settled rightly enough when Tom was nearby. All it took was a soft look or tender word from that crooked gob of his a few words from him in the Gaelic that even I could not understand & she would heave to & be a show of great pride for Mad Fred to have beneath him.

And as a reward the Capt. gave us pick of the mounts for ourselves while warning the other officers off taking our new beasts from us when they saw what warhorses we made of them.

So there was reward in being the first 2 Berserkers in Mad Fred's Dragoons but it is in me now to think that we would of been better off to be mere Run of the Mill Bills instead. There is less wildness in it less of the madness that can slip from one part of your mind to the other & so direct of its own bidding the hand that holds your weapon. But there was no knowing this then.

In truth I do think life is a series of things we do without thinking leading on & on until blood is spilt & when it spills everything seems such a surprise to us God Love Us All.

17

Kohn sits on a rough log bench in front of one of the three company barracks across the parade ground from the commander's quarters. Carrington, he has surmised, shares the quarters with his wife and son. The doe antelope is again tied by a rope to a post in front of the quarters, a pet no doubt acquired on the Carringtons' travels. Sheets and clothing flap bright white in the gentle wind on a line running from the side of the quarters to a staked-out post in the grass. A good drying day despite the cold. Kohn can think of no other way to proceed with his investigations but to sit and watch and hope to catch sight of the Indian girl the surgeon mentioned. He is no Pinkerton man, no constable or sheriff. His feet ache with the cold in the mud under the bench. He has smoked all of his cheroots but is

219

afraid the hours he has spent here will be wasted should he leave for the sutler's store to purchase more. This is no kind of kosher soldiering, Kohn thinks. No kind at all.

He considers again heading to the sutler's for tobacco. It could be a place to start, he thinks. He has been there already, to buy his sergeant's chevrons and various sundries and has heard that a son of the sutler at Fort C. S. Smith now maintains the murdered Kinney's store on post. Half an idiot the lad, Kohn has heard, but just bright enough to make money in a place where the closest competitor is several hundred miles away. Greed surpassing intelligence when it comes to the running of a sutler's concession, Kohn thinks, and then wonders if the lad might be in possession of sutler Kinney's account books.

An idea stirs within him. *I could look at the books.* Discover a motive within them perhaps. Kohn sees the error of his thinking. He laughs to himself. Probably three hundred of the five hundred men in the fort owe money to the sutler's store. It is common for wilderness-posted soldiers to be almost indefinitely indebted to the baron of robber's row, his pay never full for what is docked in monies owed to the sutler. There must be another way.

He rises from the bench intent on renewing his tobacco supply and slaps his deadened thighs. As he does, as if he has summoned her, a brown-skinned woman in a cotton dress and heavy woollen sweater emerges from the Carringtons' quarters. Her hair hangs down her back in a thick black braid and Kohn watches as she takes an empty crate with her to the laundry lines and begins to remove and fold the aired sheets and clothing.

He approaches across the parade ground and as he does feels there is something amiss about the woman's appearance but cannot determine what it is until he is standing before her. Though she is aware of his presence, she continues folding sheets, ignoring him and moving down the line, removing pegs and loosely folding a shirt, setting it in the crate atop the folded sheets. Kohn sees what it is about her now and recoils slightly. The girl is missing her nose. Scar tissue rigid and welped around the nostrils. Leprosy? he wonders, never knowingly having seen it before but aware that it is common enough in the West. Syphilis? He has heard that galloping syph left long untreated may take the nose or ears. Even the eyes. He has heard many things and knows not what is true. But the woman

221

looks otherwise healthy and the colonel and his wife would hardly have a diseased woman folding their linen. An accident, perhaps. A wounding.

"Excuse me, miss," Kohn says, unsure what he will say next.

The woman glances at him but does not stop her labors. She moves to a woman's nightdress and Kohn averts his eyes so as not to be indelicate. "I was told . . . I was led to believe that you worked . . ." He does not know how to put this. ". . . that you were in the hog ranch. In the tavern?" He points in the general direction of where the brothel once stood outside the walls. "That you worked for Mr. Kinney, the sutler."

The Indian girl glances at Kohn again at the mention of the name — Kinney — and he notices that despite her disfigurement, she is beautiful. To Kohn, in his limited experience, she is tall for an Indian woman. Her eyes are caramel-colored, wide and liquid. She has full breasts and thick round hips under the sweater and cotton dress. She could be anywhere from eighteen to thirty years old and Kohn feels the stirrings of desire for her. He wonders if it is because he knows she was once a whore. Once a whore, he thinks, and regrets thinking it. He has known many wives of men he has soldiered with who had been taken from the ranks of the laundresses and upstairs girls to become solid, upright women. Whoring is no more a permanent curse than soldiering, he thinks. Once a soldier . . . He shrugs these thoughts away.

"Mr. Kinney," he says again and the woman looks away. The sun is low in the sky, resting for a moment in the nadir between two of the Big Horn mountains, setting aglow the rich brown of the woman's skin. "Do you speak English?" he asks.

"She doesn't speak much at all . . ."

Kohn turns to find a woman in her mid-thirties, a white woman he assumes to be Carrington's wife, examining the yellow stripes on his arm before continuing. Not a natural or long-time army wife or she would not have to think about it. ". . . *Sergeant.*"

Kohn tips his kepi to the woman. "I'm sorry, ma'am, I didn't know. I'm Sergeant Kohn. I spoke with your husband earlier. I'm investigating the deaths of Mr. Kinney and his wife, ma'am. I was told your serving girl might have been there when —"

"And if she was, Sergeant?" the woman says. She is stern and straight-backed and her diction denotes wealth and education to Kohn. Something else too. Kohn feels embarrassed suddenly, his task low and sullied in the presence of this gentlewoman.

"Forgive me, ma'am. I only thought that she might be able to tell me what happened. There seems to be some talk that it was not Indians who . . . did for the Kinneys, ma'am."

Mrs. Carrington holds her gaze on Kohn for a long moment. She is a handsome woman and, though stern, there is kindness there as well, Kohn feels. An understanding of things. He does not feel she despises him.

"And what makes you think that, Sergeant?"

"I was told . . . I heard from men around the camp . . ." A low and sullied business this *investigating*. He wonders how he has come to this place, this set of circumstances. ". . . that she used to work for Mr. Kinney and might be able to aid me in —"

"Work?"

"Yes, ma'am."

"General Cooke sent you, did he?"

"Yes, ma'am. He sent my officer, my company first lieutenant, actually, but he is Company Q, ma'am . . ." He catches himself. "He is injured and in the hospital barracks. I am making the best of our orders but I am not much in the way of an investigator. I hardly know how to go about things."

The Indian girl takes the last item from the laundry line, a boy's shirt by the look of it, Kohn notes, not having seen children on the post but knowing there must be some about. She folds the shirt and lifts the crate from the winter-browned grass, looking to Mrs. Carrington, who nods to her. She leaves with the crate of laundered clothes and enters the colonel's quarters. The sun begins to dip behind the mountains and Kohn and the colonel's wife are now standing in shadow. Kohn feels the cold.

"Sarah has had a hard life, Sergeant."

"I can see that, ma'am."

"She understands some English but she cannot read or write, so I do not imagine she can help you. She has been delivered from that life and is happy now."

"Yes, ma'am."

"What do you think of our fort, Sergeant?" The woman looks around her. The dying sun washes the sky winter pink behind the mountains. The flag stirs on the flagpost. The parade ground is hoof-cut mud that will freeze again overnight. Men loiter in the last of the day's light outside of barracks. A cow lows from somewhere. Sentries with cradled muskets walk the stands along the stockade walls.

"It's a good fort, ma'am. One of the better ones, I would say."

"Do you really think so? You have the look of a man who has seen many."

"I have, ma'am. And I do . . ." He feels the need to reassure this woman that it is, indeed, a fine fort. That it is safe and well-built. A beacon of civilization.

"If only General Cooke thought the same. If only he could see it," the woman says.

"Yes, ma'am."

"I don't think Sarah knows anything, Sergeant. And I don't think it matters much anyway. There are times in life, Sergeant, when we are . . . called to account for how we have treated others."

"Called to account, ma'am? By who?"

The woman smiles at Kohn and again there is kindness in the smile. Pity, perhaps. "Are you a churchgoing man, Sergeant?"

"Not especially, ma'am. It is hard enough to find a rabbi west of the Mississippi."

"Perhaps when you do find one, you might ask him who does the calling. Or perhaps you know the answer already. Good day to you, Sergeant."

Kohn tips his kepi. "Ma'am."

18

HOW WE MET YOU (THE GALWAY CAPT.) IN THE WAR

— *Dec. 19, 1866* — It is morning now though you would hardly know it so dark & cold is this Guardhouse cell. You might think that terrible Jew of yours Sir was burning his own wood for how little he will put in the stove for to heat this place but that is the Army for you. It is all Tyranny & the whims of bullies.

But I did not always hate the Army as I do now. No Sir there was a time the fine blue Army of the Union was a salvation to us. The War Between The States was blessing & boon to Tom & myself as we set our boots upon the quayside cobbles of a Philadelphia summer in '61. It was a blessing because the war was just running up to speed when we arrived from poor Ireland right in time for Uncle Sam to lift back his toasty counterpane & say "Hop into bed with me boys & I will feed you & clothe you & teach you the trade of killing Johnny Reb who wants to start up a new nation in the South & keep the poor black man in chains & in the cotton fields. And to top it all I will pay a fine wage in US Greenback Dollars for the privilege of putting the bayonet & musketball to old Seseshoner Johnny Reb!"

Not that Tom & I would of gave a tinker's f_____ for the black man's plight at the time much concerned as we were with our own & nor could we of located the Carolinas or Georgia or grand old Virginia on a map at knife point but we could see no better start on offer & both of us liked the cut of a soldier's bags with the warm dark wool of the Army tunic & the pretty duck egg blue of the kersey leggings & rakish set of a kepi cap on a soldier's head. Never mind the hunger that made our bellies think our throats were cut for as I told you we spent all of our money in quayside pubs in Queenstown & so we had hardly more than a bean to eat since 2 days into the crossing. I tell we would of signed our souls over to the Devil for a plate of eggs.

So the Army it was for us & Thank God for it but we never planned (in so much as young lads as we were then can plan anything from 1 minute to the next) to spend so much as a single hour more in the Army than it took to get a fine fat lump of saved wages together for to buy a plot for grazing or some fields for tilling.

But in the beginning soldiering suited us just fine & dandy for the best part. We mourned brothers killed in our Company to be sure same as we do now for this is the most terrible thing in a War & like all men who fought in the Rebellion we blanched now & again at the sight of Johnny Reb all lined up like some grey & venomous snake a mere musketball away & like all men who fought on the Union side we did flee in terror at the horrible screams of the Rebel Yell that Johnny gave when he came down upon you in your trench or behind your stone wall out through smoke as thick as yearling's milk. It did sound like a thousand banshee coming for you Tom said once & every Irish boy there knew well what he meant. But mostly alongside our new found brothers in Company J of the 10th Ohio Volunteers (which for reasons I still do not fathom that is where we ended up though we signed on right there on the Philadelphia quayside & you would think the Pennsylvania regiments would of been in want of men) well alongside them we mostly stood & fired & fought

& stabbed & clubbed & roared our own savage roars when we bore down on poor Johnny Reb for we did it with all the might of the Union behind us & all the savagery of men thankful for the shirts on their backs & the fried mush & saltpork in their bellies. We begun as apprentices in the trade of killing & over time came to be proficient at it & did hone our talents sharp on the whetstone of the battlefield.

I tell you Sir we thought ourselves better off in most ways than we were in Ireland to spite the bloody business of the War. Well yes we did wake betimes from terrible & bloody dreams jumping & starting at loud sounds or sudden movement. Even after the War in the frail comfort of a barn amidst the warm breathing of beasts or in the flea racked bed of a tavern or doss house this can happen as if the war did burrow itself into our skulls & lays there in wait for the times when we take rest like some mad & sinister bugler calling Revellee.

But we could not complain overmuch for we had a notion Tom & myself to pool our hoarded wages & buy a small plot. It would be nothing grand or jumped up we thought but something small to work & live on & the Army would be our way of doing it if 1 or the other of us did not lose our heads to a cannon shot or leave our guts in the southern dirt. And if <u>both</u> of us did so fall our savings would be sent home to our brothers & sisters left in Ireland with no plan of ours mattering a winking star's light in the heavens if we were dead & gone & buried.

It was the wager a boy made when he took on in Uncle Sam's big show in the South seeking a new start in the world. Never mind the racking fear we felt or the night visions or nerves that snapped like bullwhips or jangled like a jailer's keys. Never mind hands that shook & would not stop shaking so that a tin mug of coffee was hard to sip without slopping down a poor boy's tunic. Never mind all that because in truth no soldier in this world does ever think he will be the one a bullet picks to visit.

Which was why the ball that struck Tom in the mouth came as such a living shock to the both of us casting our plans in disarray & sapping our savings in powders & curatives & whiskey & eggs & rent for a warm room in which Tom could <u>recover</u> once we mustered out. I say recover but more than the plans & saved wages & the power of clear speech that minie ball through my brother's face took with it the mighty faith we had in the Army. It was a faith that if we served the Army proper & correct it would serve us the same right back.

How many times after all had we heaved ourselves over stone walls to advance on Johnny Reb the lot of us flinching white with terror but never for turning never stopping until we were upon him elbow deep in blood our ears ringing with the concussion of musket fire & whistling grape & the woeful cries of the fallen for their mammys? How many times I ask you?

But this one time when Tom took his wound & fell to the boot tramped grass of Tennessee we did stop. I tell you when that ball struck my brother he dropped down like a sack of spuds & well this time we did abandon that charge at Chickamauga & I stooped to heave poor Tom across my back big as he was & carry him to a running creek with my tunic sopped with the blood we shared as brothers. It was more ditch than any kind of coldwater stream back there behind our lines & I set down there with him washing out his wound with canteen water & whatever cornmash whiskey Tom had left in his reserve canteen after taking it some days before from the body of a dead Reb. I sat pouring them both water & mash whiskey through that hole in my brother's face which is not a thing you would ever in your life imagine doing but the War was like that as you well know Sir.

Well Tom was unconscious to this world Thank God with his head beginning to swell up like a sweet melon & I tended to him like we later tended that sickly calf shunned by its mother.

But troubles are many in a poor man's life & that day by the sluggish stream behind the lines at Chickamauga my tears did drop onto my brother's face to run in with the dirty ditch water & whiskey. Truly I did not know I had so many tears in me & as I let them run we were come upon that day at the dirt water creek by a Provost Marshal's gang & hauled up & shackled for deserting cowards.

<u>Cowards</u>! My hand trembles as I do write the word! I tell you as God Is My Witness we were no braver nor no more <u>cowards</u> than any other Bill marching under Uncle Sam's banner but we stood as hearty uncomplaining & fierce boys when the fighting started & oft praised by NCOs & Officers alike we were for our willingness to do the wet & filthy work of the War. We could shoot but were no slouches either when there was no time for the manual of arms & the musket was turned & used as a club or with the bayonet as a fighting knife in a fellow's

hand. All in the Company did know us in short as good soldiers no better nor worse than any other & we took pride in this God Forgive Us for pride as we do well know comes riding in before the fall.

So when we were shackled by the Prov. Marshals & taken up with the other gang of cowards & shirkers & malingerers & deserters I was for the 1st time since setting foot in America or since taking on with the Army forced to speak up for the pair of us brothers. And it being the 1st & such a vital time for us it did not go well for I could not separate the <u>Gaelic</u> from the <u>Bearla</u> mixing Irish talk with English in the fear & misplaced shame of our predicament so that what came out of my mouth was a babble not likely to be understood by any man.

Now I did hear since that the Union did not shoot deserters but I also heard tell that we did & I have seen men with the cursed brand of D for Deserter burnt into their skin which in some ways may be worse than shooting. But the only thing I knew then at that moment was that we were chained up as cowards when <u>we were no such thing</u>! It fills me with rage to remember it now as I write!

But God's Blessing was upon us that day & this is what I want to tell you Sir. For as we stood there with the other prisoners in the mud & my brother draped with his manacled hands over my shoulder his low pained bellows in my ears well God did send his emissary to us in the form of a brave & kindly Galway man a battlefield brevet Captain who was only <u>yourself</u> Sir who we were bound by fate's rope to meet again here in this frozen waste of a Valley.

But that is later. Then we knew you only as the Galway Captain on a white charger standing some 18 hands high its white coat swabbed with streaks of red & at that charger's tail was left only a charred stump that even in our distress was painful to look at as if it had been scorched from its rump in battle not at all docked in the proper manner. Well that horse stood there before us its hooves hopping in the dirt eyes bulging & rolling round in their sockets with the terror & hot thrill a good horse feels for battle. That beast was so vexed from the fighting that the Galway man had to hold tight to the reins while he looked upon us once over one shoulder & again over the other as the horse turned of its own will.

So it was like this that you Sir over what must of been a terrible ringing in your ears did come to hear my protestations my gabble of Irish & English words mixed together in a pitiful testimony of innocence. And hearing this you did reef your white & blood stained charger to order & look down at us. In truth I once before heard you speaking in Irish Sir & this gave me pause & comfort & some pride at the time for I did not think there was any man from Ireland's shores with the Gaelic tongue on him who was risen to officer rank at all though I never did imagine you would 1 day speak it to me Sir.

In English you did say to the Sgt. of the Provost Marshal's mob, "Why have you taken up these men Sgt.? These 2 men?"

"Which 2?" says the Sgt. his words showing not the proper respect due an officer of the Great Union Army. But that Sgt's. words & their freight of disrespect did not pass unnoticed by you Sir & Thank God for that.

"Which 2 <u>Captain</u>," you did reply drawing your sabre & tapping the charger's rump with it & yanking her reins for to turn & face the Sgt. And when you tapped that mare's haunch it did be plain to see the blood drying in the runnels of your cutlass the long curved blade much nicked & scarred by use.

Well you may not remember it Sir but that Sgt. stared up at you for a moment before correcting himself & right then looking up into your eyes I felt you would take that scut of a Sgt's. head from his shoulders with that sabre such is the way your eyes turned so fierce & dark. I reckon the Sgt. did see them turning too for he said sharpish, "<u>Captain</u>. Which 2 do you mean? These 2 Sir?" He pointed at my brother & myself.

"What do you have them up for?"

"Deserters Sir," says that b_____. "We found them here by the ditch this one sitting in his pal's lap like sweethearts Sir. And I don't even need to tell you that here is a long way from where the fighting is at."

"That man is wounded Sgt." You did point with your cutlass. "Any fool can see it."

"Yes but —"

It was said (though I never knew the truth of it) that the P.M. gangs were given quotas of cowards to fill & fill them they must or they would be sent as lowly guards to one of the back line Union prisons packed with typhus & mutinous Confederate boys. So maybe that Sgt. was thinking of his quota & what his C.O. might say while my brother moaned in my ear & begun to feel dead heavy about my own shoulders. Says he, "With all respect Sir it don't matter. Any found conscious or without mortal wound-ings behind our lines is a yellow deserter &

237

we has orders to hook them up."

I found my voice at this my English like a child's then like the thick & unschooled Greenhorn that I was with a head full of useless Gaelic.

"I am no deserter no yellowbelly at all by f_____ & nor is my brother but he is shot through the gob & didn't I bring him back here to —"

I could not think of the right word. I said, "aira tubbartdo" which I now know means to tend or care for in English & were the words I was feeling in my heart but for which I had no English. In my desperation I did look up at you & change to Irish. "Sir we are no deserters but staunch Ohio fighting men. Only for the brother is shot through the mouth we came back here. He would of died. He might still God Forbid It but he would of surely if I left him there on the field for the crows & worms & litter bearers who come in their wake."

At this Tom unhooked his shackled hands from my shoulders & bent himself double at the waist the low groan coming from him now sounding for all the world like the wind in the rigging of the ship that brought us to these shores.

"Unshackle them Sgt. & be quick about it," you did say then Sir while your blood streaked charger danced a turn & shrugged up her blackened stump of a tail & pissed a long heavy stream into the bubbling dirt.

But the Sgt. did not move & made like he was contemplating in the way of all soldiers the consequences to his own prospects should he obey one man's order at the expense of another's.

Finally he did say to his troop of 6 men in full earshot of Tom & myself but perhaps not yourself, "Unhitch these two lucky bucks & whatever we done here stays here So Help You God. If I hear tales told I will have your skin for stockings."

Your warhorse huffed & danced some as our manacles were removed & I waited for the chained snake of deserters to move off under the Prov. Marshal's guard before thanking you Sir. But now it was like your mind was on another thing altogether.

I thanked you in English but to my surprise you answered me in your Galway Gaelic which is someways different to ours but the same in most ways & all ways in the heart of it as it is spoken. You spoke to me Sir as if remembering why you stopped for us in the 1st place as if there is some comfort in the old talk of Irish for you. I think you were then a good man a kind one with a kind word for any pitiful fighting soldier & maybe this is why you stopped for us.

"Get your brother to the Dressing Station & report back to your 1st Sgt. Tell him what happened & that I sent you."

You did jig your mount's reins as if to leave but turned her again & still in Irish said to me, "And you may not be so lucky next time. If one of you falls keep fighting. No one man brother or not is more precious to any soldier than the other men he fights beside & you would do well to remember it."

I snapped a salute knowing you to be correct but yet entirely wrong & because you spoke to me in the Gaelic your reprimand was softer as if in the language we share there was an understanding of a brother's plight run up alongside the truth of soldiering as you told it. I think now it is only in Irish that I could take both such notions together the softness along with the hard truth of a thing. English as I later learnt to speak it does run much harder at a thing & much more direct at what a fellow reckons is the truth so that betimes the meaning of a thing is lost to me beneath all that truth.

"Yes Sir," said I & with nothing more to say as if saving the skins (the very souls!) of two men came as easy to you as the taking of them on the pitch of battle you did show me your charger's arse its char-docked tail & trot off with your white mare's shoes making a sucking sound in the blood soaked earth.

It was that sucking sound I recalled & your warning about the brotherly way of things when I watched you arrive here in this wintering place. I was one of the men who carried you into the hospital barracks from the cold on that Indian litter. You were 1/2 dead Sir & well wrapped up but even so I knew your face & something in my bones did tell me your coming would be the start of something for Tom & myself or the end of everything. I did not know which but I knew it would not be a good thing your coming to spite not knowing that night that you were sent to hang us. God Forgive Me I wish that I never again rested eyes upon you.

But there is no going back. You are here & you will have your account. It is because of that day at Chickamauga & the fair turn you did us on the bank of that dirt water creek that I will give it to you. You are owed the truth of things so I will try to give you this though it makes me heartsore & shameful to write it.

The guard is changing now outside my

cell. I pray it is one of the Irish boys so that I will have a hot meal at least. I can hardly feel my hands to hold the pen & the ink is thick as strap molasses in the bottle. Forgive —

19

For two days, Kohn has done nothing. He has passed his time visiting Molloy and hoping to speak again with the surgeon but has been unable find a time when the man is not busy tending to wounded men. And the surgeon has not appeared anxious to speak with him. Molloy is improving, an orderly told him, but needs rest and is dosed heavily with laudanum. He is rarely conscious when Kohn visits.

Kohn has called on Rawson in his quarters, a barracks room behind the horse stables he shares with other visiting enlisted men, and is concerned that Rawson has little work to do each day besides tending to their mounts, the Virginia private's idleness a danger to his safety and the personal goods and monies of other men. Kohn takes him for a saunter around the stockade walls

243

and warns him off the thievery that has landed him on their mission.

"You don't got to tell me, Corp . . . *Sergeant* Kohn. I be a reformed man. *Re*-formed. Been to church on Sunday. I did not see you there." Rawson smiles, his face all innocence.

Kohn stares at him until the smile dims and Rawson looks away. He thinks he may volunteer him for the woodtrain guard but, despite Rawson's misdemeanors, Kohn does not wish to be responsible for his scalping. The woodcutting is done, Kohn has learned, in a forest six miles from the fort and the train of wagons that goes out in the morning — as he witnessed from the viewing platform with Colonel Carrington — and returns each evening is attacked almost daily. In the week since they arrived at the fort three men have been killed, another six wounded. Several more are missing and it is not thought they have deserted for the gold seams of Virginia City this late in the season.

"Straight as a rail, Rawson, or I will have your head. I will have you riding guard on that goddamn woodtrain every single day until Red Cloud cuts your hair if I hear you've so much as looked at another Bill's purse."

"I hear you, Sergeant. I've a mind to keep

my hair on, pretty as it is."

So Kohn plays cards with the men he bunks with, unassigned or winter-stranded NCOs like himself. Some of these are fine company, and some a burden, the army guaranteeing only close quarters. Kohn visits the sutler's store for tobacco and beer, examining the new proprietor each time, hoping to catch him alone and have a word but unconcerned that he cannot. Molloy will be up and about soon, and will know better how to proceed. Or will know better how not to.

In a fit of boredom Kohn buys whiskey from a timberman in the fort who has brought enough for the winter and sells it at extortionate prices. He drinks some, and then some more, passing two days this way but finds the whiskey makes him weary and sad and prone to thinking of times past; of Cleveland, of his father, his mother, his brothers and sisters he will never see again, the *shul* he will never again visit, the wife he will never have, the bolts of cloth he will never cut and the suits of clothes he will never sew. He joined the army to escape these things. He joined the army so he would not have to think or to remember. Drink and idleness do not suit him. He pours his last pint of whiskey into the snow and walks again to the sutler's store.

There are a few men at the tables in the store drinking beer, as is allowed on most Western posts. On some posts whiskey and rum are sold during certain hours but Kohn has heard that Carrington is a dry commander and has forbidden it. Had he allowed it, perhaps Kinney would not have established his tavern off-post but that is *vaser unter'n brik.* He hears his mother's voice in the Yiddish and his heart stumbles. A woodstove warms the store and Kohn begins to sweat under his coat.

The men at the tables look at him and then back to their weeks-old newspapers. Kohn knocks on the counter and waits as the new sutler enters from a back room. The sutler's store, Kohn notes, is a far grander building than any other on the post, having a duckboard floor and wall boards planed and painted. It is a rarity in that it has more than one room and doors in place of blankets between them. There is a glass window beside the front door and the late afternoon light is weak through it. Lanterns hang from beams high enough that a man must have to stand on a ladder to light them.

"How can I help you?" the young sutler says.

Kohn has heard that he is the son of the

sutler at Fort C. S. Smith and arrived some weeks earlier to take over the concession on the death of Mr. Kinney. Wracked with grief, no doubt, the new sutler. Hapworth is his name, and it is newly painted in fine lettering on a sign outside the front door. His father was a judge in Pennsylvania until he decided to tap his Republican cronies for a far more lucrative concern selling overpriced beer and tobacco, clove candies and woollen socks to soldiers stranded out West.

"Do you know who I am?" Kohn asks.

The sutler frowns and desultory conversations cease.

"I . . . should I? I don't know, no . . ."

"I'm here with Lieutenant Molloy, 7th Cavalry, who is laid up in Company Q and we are sent here to investigate the death of your predecessor, Mr. Kinney. Did you know that?"

"No, I did not." Hapworth is in his twenties, and blushes under Kohn's gaze.

"I have General Cooke's orders and Colonel Carrington's sanction to investigate Mr. and Mrs. Kinney's deaths. Do you understand me, sir?"

"Yes."

"Good, then I will need to see Mr. Kinney's account ledgers for this store."

"His account ledgers?"

"Yes, get them for me please. I will wait here."

The sutler smiles and Kohn takes it to be nervousness rather than spite. The sutler says, "But, well, I can't because they were not here when I arrived. I packed his personal properties to ship back East myself and they were not among them. I would like to have seen them myself for there are many men owing for goods purchased who may not now be held to account but I could not —"

"And if I were to come back in there behind your counter and have a look myself, I wouldn't find them, or anything like them?"

"Why, no, of course not. I am at a loss myself with the ledgers missing. I am out of pocket, Sergeant. The debts accrued by the soldiers on this post will not be honored because of it."

There is laughter from one of the tables and words spoken *sotto voce.*

Kohn turns and walks over to the table, addressing a raw-boned private. "What did you say?"

The laughter stops and now the men stare at Kohn. The soldier says, "We didn't say a thing, only that you must be the only Bill in the whole of the fort who wants to see them

248

books found. There's many a man happy they are gone and hope they stay there."

The private is Irish as are, no doubt, the men at the table with him. A cursed, wandering race, like my own, Kohn thinks. And I am cursed to wander the world alongside so many of them.

"You'd do well to mind your own business, Private," Kohn says.

"And you'd do well to mind yours . . .."

There is one empty chair at the table and Kohn pulls it out as if he will sit and join the men. Instead, he raises the chair over his head and swings it crashing down onto the table top, shattering beer mugs, gouging the table, sending the men scrambling away, falling from their own chairs. He brings the chair down onto the table four times, smashing it until it is kindling. The men at the other table rise.

"Go on," Kohn says to the raw-boned private, holding one of the chair legs by his side. "Unsheath that knife. I want you to do it."

The private leaves his hand on the knife's butt at his belt for a moment and then takes it away, raising the hand up in supplication. "There's no need for that, now, Sergeant, is there? No need at all. I was only jesting.

Just easy talk is all, no need for the Black Flag."

"Stow your 'easy talk,' you fucker. Is this how you speak to ranking men in this fort?"

The men are staring at him but none answer. Kohn turns back to the sutler. "How much for the chair?"

The sutler is too stunned to speak. Finally, "Four . . ." He cannot hold Kohn's eyes. "Three dollars. Three." He looks over to his customers. "It was a good chair."

Kohn takes out the money and lays it on the sutler's counter. Loud enough for all in the store to hear, he says, "There is a reward for those books. Ten dollars, for whoever turns them up."

"It'll be a dead man claiming them ten sheets," one of the standing men mutters.

"Maybe you'll claim it then, pay off whatever it is you owe in Mr. Kinney's books," Kohn says.

"Them books is ash I'd say."

Kohn turns to the sutler. "Make it fifteen dollars. More than a month's wage for most of the men on post, Mr. Hapworth. Easy leaves for some Bill."

"Only thing easy round here is getting kilt, Sergeant," the private says, stuffing his kepi onto his head and wiping the spilled beer from his tunic. "You'd do best to remember that."

Kohn takes a step closer to him. "Pull that knife and I'll show you how easy." When the man just smiles, Kohn says, "I thought so." He turns and passes by the men, close enough to smell the beer soaking their tunics. The transition from the heated store to the icy December wind is breathtaking in the dying daylight.

Later Kohn will curse his lapse, his temper. Now it feels good. He still has the chair leg in his hand as he crosses back to his quarters. He will burn it in the barracks stove. He has paid for it.

20

December 13, 1866 — Fort Phil Kearny,
Dakota Territory

"It's more like a wild Sessioner you're looking each time I see you, Daniel. Your locks are truly rebellious. And I can bathe myself, for the love of God."

"Thank you, sir. I should have them barbered but I am in no mind to trust any man in this fort with a razor to my throat," Kohn says, sponging Molloy's back. He lifts the officer's arm and washes his ribs, his underarms, his shoulders. "You smell something less than sweet, sir, but you are looking better. You'll be back in the saddle before long."

"Please God you're right, Daniel. I am feeling like a right and proper blue mass bummer, you out there unable to have a haircut for your troubles."

"You've been through it, sir, and need to rest. The sawbones says the leg is healing." He dips the sponge into the warm and soapy water and continues to bathe the captain. "Time is the best doctor as my father always said, never wanting to pay for a doctor when time could be had at half the price."

"Yes, yes . . . enough of your Dutch wisdom, Kohn." Molloy swallows and looks away. "A bloody buggering bum of a molly-grubbing malingerer I am, with you whipping yourself with the work on your lonesome. You should stand down from your inquiries, Daniel. Nothing good will come of them. And you are dripping water on my bloody mattress, you damned fool."

Kohn ignores this and roughly washes under the captain's left arm. "A transfer from the 7th, sir, for both of us, is the good that will come of them." Kohn has almost convinced himself that, with a transfer, Molloy will contain his drinking, will wish less for death. A new start. New memories to replace the old ones that plague him. He hopes more than thinks this may happen because he is not certain what he will do if Molloy does not recover, does not cease his slow suicide. He does not allow himself to think about it. He loves no one else on this earth but Molloy and yet much of the time he cannot abide the man. He has only the army and for him, Molloy is the army. He is not certain whether it is the army or Molloy he loves and hates so. *Dos hartz makht fun mentsh a nar.* It is his mother's voice this time. The heart makes a fool of men. He has a flashing image of standing in a tin tub as a small boy while she bathed him, his brothers waiting their turn but their mother smiling at him, taking her time.

As if to mock sentiments Kohn can hardly admit to himself, Molloy says, lowering his voice, "Would you not have a dram on your person, Daniel, for an old warhorse recovering?"

"I most certainly goddamn do not, sir." It is his father's voice he hears now. A fool goes to the bath and forgets to wash his face.

"There is no need to curse your betters, Daniel. It is unbecoming a man of your rank and breeding." Molloy sulks but only for a moment. Not as long as Kohn would have imagined and he takes hope in this.

He says, "My *betters*? You may go and jump, sir, if you think I will aid in your debauch. I need you to speak to the Irish when you are well if we are to discover anything about who killed the sutler and his wife. The fort is full of them and none of them has a mind to bleat to a soreass Jew."

"The Irish . . ." Molloy says. "A filthy, treacherous race of men, the women fit only

254

for the milking shed or brothel. Round heels have the women of Ireland. Keep that in mind, Daniel, when time comes to choose a wife."

"I will, sir." He tosses the sponge into the bucket, dries his hands on a towel and holds out a freshly laundered undershirt for the captain.

"Tell us then, what have you learned on your travels, Daniel?"

Kohn helps Molloy into the shirt, followed by a wool sweater and two pairs of socks. He lifts the captain's legs, one of them locked in thick plaster, from where they rest on the floor back into the bed and covers them with a fresh laundered sheet, several blankets and a heavy buffalo rug. He makes to tie a woollen scarf around Molloy's neck but his captain shoos him away and does it himself. The hospital barracks is warm relative to the common soldiers' barracks, having three wood stoves for heat and a raised floor of planed boards, but the building was hastily constructed and drafts of icy wind find their way through gaps in the planked walls and windows. Kohn can see his breath if he looks carefully.

"Nothing of note, sir. But that every soul on post assumes that it was other than Indians who killed Mr. Kinney and his wife and not one seems to think they did not have it coming. Some of the men I've spoken to appear to be delighted by their demise."

"Death freeing them from debt, no doubt," Molloy says, nodding, smiling as if he too sees the joy a murder can bring. "Give us a cheroot, Daniel, good man."

"Yessir. Though they would *not* be exempt the debt, in fact, since they have signed their names to the monies owed the sutler, whoever that may be, and as such *any* serving sutler has the right to stop their pay up to five dollars a month until it is paid. You know yourself there are men who are never fully clear of a sutler's debt and owe money on their discharge. Of course they might be considered free of their debts if the sutler's account books cannot be found, which according to the new sutler, they cannot."

Molloy smiles again. "As a Jew, you look first for the account books, Daniel. I would have expected nothing less."

Kohn smiles back at him. "I thought that if I could have a peek at them, I might find the man or men with the call to blot out their debts with blood."

"That is a fine, poetic way of putting it. A man of the book, you are, Daniel. But not every action is motivated by money. Some are driven by temperament. You of all people should know that."

Kohn blushes and heat rises to his face. The book has always been a problem for him, as a boy and a man, the Hebrew letters never standing still long enough for him when it was his turn to read them at *Krius ha toire.* Even now words still jumble and rearrange themselves on a page if he is tired or lacking in concentration. He has noted in the past how much longer it takes for him to read an account in a newspaper compared to other reading men and he does not think he has ever handed over a message or drafted a bill of larder without it being blighted with misplaced letters and ill-spelled words. No man of any goddamn book, that is for certain, Danny boy. He does not say this and Molloy has no idea of it.

Instead, Kohn gives Molloy what he has been fishing for. "Certainly, sir, the pleasure a man takes in rash action can be its own motivation. And before you ask, I have been somewhat rash, sir. I yesterday destroyed a chair that had not wronged a single soul. Poor chair."

"You didn't kill anyone, so? I am disappointed to hear it." Molloy smiles. Kohn's furies have ever been a source of delight for

257

him though it is a long time since he has properly relished anything.

Kohn is aware of this and pleased that he has amused Molloy, if only for a moment, with his recklessness. "No sir, I have made valiant efforts to restrain myself, though I have met more than one who could use killing."

"There is a hardly a day goes by in this life that we don't, Daniel. If only we could oblige them. Have you offered a reward for the return of the ledgers? You have said there are more Irish here on post than bedbugs in a whore's mattress. And where there are Pats and Micks in abundance, there are chuck-a-luck debts to be paid and bark juice to be bought. The prospect of windfall will turn the account books up if they are not yet ash and scrap."

Kohn laughs. "I've offered fifteen of your hard-earned greenbacks for their return. We shall see what happens."

"And have the brass hats been welcoming, Daniel?"

"As if we've brought the cholera with us in a bucket. Colonel Carrington thinks we are here as spies sent by General Cooke, with our investigations as mere bluff for the purposes of reporting back just what kind of a no-count show he is commanding here.

He has given me . . . given *us* freedom of the camp of sorts but he is no help otherwise and insists I bring anything I find to his attention. At the same time he doesn't appear to have any interest in encouraging anyone in the camp to speak to me, including his wife. So welcoming, no. We are the least of his worries with his men dying or deserting by the day, but we are a worry to him nonetheless."

"His wife?" Molloy lights his cheroot, filling the air with aromatic smoke. He begins to cough then, a heavy, liquid hack that tells of corruption of the lung, of cold journeys and possible pleurisy. It is the most common sound in every bivouac, camp or fort Kohn has ever set foot in and he is not unduly concerned by it.

When Molloy has finished coughing, Kohn says, "I was told I might want to speak to a serving girl working for the colonel's good wife. An Indian who used to work for Sutler Kinney."

"As?"

"She is a pretty girl, despite her injuries, so you can imagine yourself, sir."

"The colonel's wife with a whore for a serving maid? She would not have her, surely, if she knew."

Kohn shrugs. "I don't know, sir. The

Carrington woman seems a kind soul, a Christian woman." He thinks of a phrase Molloy often uses himself. "There are no flies on her, as you would say. I reckon she knows well what the girl did for Kinney. But she is good to her, you can see that and she did not let me speak to her so there is no point I can see in pursuing it. She said something about 'being held to account for how we treat others,' whatever she meant by it."

Molloy smokes his cheroot and says nothing for some time. Then, "Sometimes the best work is done by doing nothing, Daniel. I was often told this by my schoolmasters."

"I can only imagine, sir."

"I will be fit soon enough to aid you. Hale and hearty as ever I was. Until then do nothing else. There is nothing to be gained from our finding out what everyone here already knows. The man and his wife are not, by your account, sorely missed and not worth losing blood for. Mind yourself, Daniel. I'll have no one to wash my arse for me if you ship a knife in the guts for the sake of a man and his missus already homesteading with the devil."

"The prospect of washing your arse again, sir, is call enough to keep looking into things. A knife in the guts might just be preferable."

21

COL. CARRINGTON'S OVERLAND TRAVELLING CIRCUS & HOW TOM MET HIS SWEETHEART

All that I put down about how yourself & myself once met Sir well that is not important. Your coming was the reason I began to put words to these pages but they are not the reason I continue. I feel now that I am seeing the course of things for myself for the 1st time & by writing it down the twists & turns of how I got from there to here in this icy Guardhouse become clear to me. And so while I did commit to this testament because of you I continue it for to explain to myself how I was brought to this impasse this woeful site of sadness & confinement & guilt. But perhaps it is not the guilt that you imagine.

Anyway it is Tom's girl who I will write about now for she is one cause of all this surely. That cutnose whore well she does be a key in the lock to this sorry tale. For our story is likely no different from the stories of a hundred other Irish Greenhorn veteran soldier boys up til when my brother met her. As I did write before Sir if we were not made horse soldiers well then the brother may of never met her but be ever careful what you wish for in this life as the saying goes.

Of course Tom likely would of seen her or even poked her as that b_____ of a Sutler kept only so many hogs on his ranch & it was the only place for 1000 miles around this fort for a lonely Bill to sojourn of a payday but there is no telling he would of picked her over the other 4 girls. Sure was not one of them a fine fat doll with hair as thick as molasses & most of her teeth in the bargain? She labours for herself now from a tee pee just beyond the stockade with no pimp to take a cut of her earnings & fair wind to her for there be far too many bosses in the world for it to be a fair one. There does be 1 less now I am not sorry to say if I am put to it God Forgive Me.

So Tom may of come to know the cutnose girl or even to like her perchance for it is not rare in this world that a soldier grows fond of a whore & not at all rare that they might marry. But it is not likely in the case of my brother that he might of fell so hard for her if we stayed run of the mill foot soldiers when we set out for the Powder River country from Ft. Caldwell in Nebraska we 2 brothers among the multitudes in what the men came to call Carrington's Overland Travelling Circus.

And God In Heaven what an A Number 1 Circus it was with 2 battalions the 2nd & 3rd nearly 1000 men most of them Sunday Soldiers or <u>fresh fish</u> we did call them though 1/2 again of these would be posted elsewhere along the way & not serve here at Phil K at all. We were maybe 200 of us mounted on horseback with 200 or more wagons & Army ambulances carrying every tool seed barrel or box under the sun & all the civilians the wives & children too of the officers & long-serving NCOs. We even brung with us a broke down saw mill with its boiler in more than one wagon & a grass cutting machine of the like I never seen before & there was the contract timber men & their tools & oxen & drivers & sawyers. There was more than 200 civilians as well as near 500 head of cattle & their tenders if you can imagine for it feels fierce strange that less than a year ago we had all that beef while now we are set to starve for the winter but that is the nature of this forsaken place. The Sioux & Cheyanne have fed mightily on them cattle.

But it was a powerful procession that left Caldwell that day to come up here & build a Ft. going by the name of Phil Kearny after Philip Kearny a fine Irishman I am sure who was killed in the War at Chantilly though it does be something of an insult to his memory to name this cursed place after him. A powerful parade of man & beast all the same it was setting off to tunes from the 25 man regimental band that Carrington did insist on having with him the band being so instrumental (Begging your pardon!) in fighting Indians. Though they <u>can</u> play I will give them that & many of them are grand fellows & welcome company round a fire of an evening. 1 or 2 of them are even fighting men would you believe it?

Tom & myself were horse soldiers by then as I said before. As such we rode rear guard in the main eating the dust of 1000 men wagons & cattle but what of it? It was riding not marching at least & the odd time when someone somewhere did spy an Indian or did think he spied one we were sent forward to ride guard on the herd or the wagons in front of them & that was fine.

On the day Tom laid eyes upon his girl we

were ordered forward riding at a slow walk at either wheel of a wagon loaded with crates & croaker sacks & clanking bottles & bumping barrels. But more inticing to us was to ride behind the next wagon back which was loaded to the rail with Indian & 1/2 breed women. They were goods of a different sort you might say though it is sad to say it.

Says I to Tom as we did clop a lazy pace behind them wagons, "There is nothing wrong with being a mounted soldier if you do not mind the dust Tom I tell you."

"There is worse things in the world than riding picket on wagons full of whiskey one end & doxies the other," he said back to me.

"Far worse brother," says I.

But you know well Sir as an Officer & Veteran Fighting Man that in the War a wagonload of painted dolls privately owned would not of been given the privilege of a mounted guard such as us to protect it but there is so much different in this new Army of ours most of it not any good at all.

The driver of that queer vessel full of Indian doxies well that driver did look to my eye part Indian himself the other part something else & in truth he did not look to be any kind of proper muleteer at all but a whore skinner more like. We came to know him later as the boy to speak Indian to the whores & collect coin off them & keep their furrows running straight but as well to knock about the heads of soldier Bills who might chance a poke with no money in their purses or who got too full of lip when the Sutler's wife lowered herself to come calling to her husband's hog ranch off the post.

As you may of guessed Sir it was the very same blackleg Sutler Kinney from Columbus who was the owner of the doxie wagon we rode guard upon. Yes that same rum swindler who would sell a fool of a raw Depot recruit 2 cleaning kits when 1 does be plenty in connivance with the swindling training Sgts. of the Depot but more in truth with the connivance of the Generals & Politicians & other high hats. For to have a Sutler's contract at a training Depot in a town where goods can be sold for a fair price outside the gates & thus drive down your own you must be the brother of some mere State Senator or Party Boss. But to get your doxie wagon & wares latched onto Carrington's 18th Infantry parade to the most faraway outpost in all Creation where you may charge very well what you f_____ like for anything from stockings to sourmash? Well it is said that you may be the brother to Christ the Lord himself but if you are not the brother to a <u>Washington</u> Senator at least well you will never sell your goods as a Sutler on a Western Army post. Holy Jesus & all His Disciples could not purchase you such a licence to print money but a brother or cousin in Congress could once his Party is in power. And you would think it would be enough for a man & his grasping bitch of a wife to have the sole licence to hock liquor & beer & tobacco to poor soldiers a fair million miles from his nearest rival at prices you would not charge a leper for a sup from your canteen. You would think it would be enough but not for him. Because I tell you Sir that filthy nuck did have the notion that alongside his peppermint sticks & breeches & bolts of cloth well what else would soldier Bills a million miles from home be in want of but a few whores on his off post hog ranch?

Mind you even Little White Chief Carrington (which is what the Indians call him) well even he might note a stew house <u>within</u> the walls of his blessed stockade & throw a conniption but outside of the Ft. belongs to nobody but the man or woman fool enough to brave the Indians without a wall of sharpened logs around them.

And so that b_____ of a Sutler did

transport his whore wagons in Carrington's circus parade while we did mind them & the whiskey under orders from some Officer who along with every other man up the chain of command did be in that Sutler's pocket. A blind eye here a blind eye there & a few bob in your purse for to see nothing & the Sutler's Indian whores ride in the Col.'s parade with Uncle Sam's horse soldiers to guard them from attack by their Indian brothers. I tell you it is a strange f_____ world we live in all the same & I think my brother fits into it just grand for it is stranger he gets by the day since his eye caught a stray smile from that cutnose whore that is no word of a lie. And yet betimes I wonder am I the only one in the camp who notices it for all here are taken with a kind of madness a queer ticking strangeness that comes from living with the fear of death always on you.

But how did he meet her I did not tell you that did I? For we did hardly lay eyes on the whores at all mostly. They travelled the days under Murphy wagon canvas while our Company was most nights camped some distance away from them with our time upon stopping for bivouac much taken with picket duties & tending the horses.

Well it was a week or so into the march &
a squad of us was <u>detailed</u> (yes proper
detailed if you will believe it!) to ride guard
on them wagons up along the East bank of
the Platte River a worthless alkaline torrent
that in spate as it is then in late May from a
long & heavy winter in the mountains does
rush like milk from a tipped churn. Even up
front with the wagon we choked on dust
from the troops & wagons before us & we
wore kerchiefs over our faces against it like
highway men & if our eyes were not so thick
with dust 1 of us might of seen some yds.
ahead of the doxie cart the sidewinding
shape of a rattler crossing the trail between
wagons at the feet of that cart's lead mule.

Well I was a good way back & packing my
pipe with tobacco when it happened so
would not of seen the snake anyway but
who would of thought a snake such a fool
as to wind its way between the hoofs &
wheels of 1000 odd beasts & wagons for it
is said that snakes be fierce shy of any sound
that comes as a drumbeat through the earth
to them. Oh we are told stay clear of shad-
owy rocks or clumps of brush & most
particular the overhanging banks of rivers
where they lie in shelter when the sun beats
down from the heavens. But there is no
counting for the work of the Devil no more

than the ways of Man & that snake had in its mind to cross in front of the whore wagon's mules & cross he did sending them mules into a holy terror I tell you bucking & raring up in their traces & raising panic in more than 1 of our mounts nearby as well though my horse at that time was as steady & stupid as myself & she did only raise her head & wonder at the carry on around her.

My brother's gelding though did buck & shy a bit & let out a whinny but Tom hauled him in & spoke his muddle of imprecations & threats at him in the Gaelic & English (which he did sometimes use telling me that not all American horses could understand the Irish). Tom pulled his horse out of the column to settle him more & as he did he saw at the same time that snake make its blessed way into the shade of a tipped boulder while all hell let rip around them because the whore wagon's bucking mules chose just that moment to bolt all 4 of them together like the finest team of prancers pulling a Princess's barouche jerking the wagon up out of the wheel ruts in the trail with a shot & throwing back onto his arse their driver & heading at a clatter for the banks of the spring swollen Platte.

Now if I tell you the drop off the bank into that rushing torrent of a river is 10 ft.

at least I tell you no word of a lie. It is high enough for the drop alone to kill man & horse never mind the rushing water for to drown them & remember this was 4 mules & a ton weight of wagon whores & driver thundering madlike over rock & brush across 200 yds. (no more than that) of sage & scrub racing toward that drop of a river-bank & pure death with goods & sundries spilling out the back while the whores screamed from inside the poor creatures clinging on for their dear lives. I tell you there was foam at the mules' mouths & eyeballs bulging behind their blinders.

200 yds. in seconds they did hurtle to-wards death Sutler Kinney's whores while 12 horse soldiers including myself settled spooked mounts & watched on like fools. Only 1 of us thought to dig his spurs in & reef his reins towards the river & set off after the runaway wagon. Only 1 of us & that was Tom true as God his horse skipping away from the trail its tail up for the chase. It was a sight to see that gelding's barrelling hind pumping as it rushed over the scrub for the wagon.

And that wagon to my eye was doomed I tell you Sir & heading straight for the river. But did I act? I did not but only looked on as 1 of the poor whores leapt from the back

272

of the wagon to bounce & tumble off the hard ground her neck snapping in the fall God Rest Her In Heaven & causing Tom to veer his speeding mount around her bouncing body to close on that mule team while the other whores & their skinner was thrown about in the back of the wagon under canvas like dice in a cup I tell you as 100 yds. became 50 then 40 then 30.

Says one of the boys beside me, "He won't G_____ D_____ catch em no way Johnnycakes."

"He G_____ D_____ will," says another.

I could not answer as my heart stuck in my throat & I watched as Tom closed his mount on the foaming blind rushing mules pressing his horse close in til it was crowding the beasts pushing them with its side away ever so little bit away from their course towards the river. I watched as Tom did reach out & grab fast to the lead mule's ear guiding his mount away now still at speed though slowing with that mule's ear tight in his fist so that she followed & the team followed her & they all turned together to bounce along in line with the edge of the bank instead of off it til he did finally bring the team to a halt to great rounds of cheering from every man & woman who seen it.

Tom then dismounted himself & hobbled the mules with a stretch of rope before walking to the back of the wagon to inquire on them inside.

It was now that he 1st lay eye on that girl & I do curse that moment I tell you. Out she came from behind the canvas stepping down from that wagon like a Queen & my brother held out his hand to aid her like some Gallant Knight of olden days. But for fate it could of been any of the whores who came out the back of the wagon 1st to take his hand for by the Grace Of God none of them who stayed inside the wagon had much more than lumps & bruises for their troubles.

I tell you <u>any</u> one of them girls could of took Tom's hand & seen him smile at her. His smile is a terrible sight surely him with a face that would make a funeral turn from a main road but it must not of been terrible to this whore who perhaps like many a Veteran Bill has lain eyes on many horrible things & must betimes scare her very self at the looking glass.

I wonder now did she see something in Tom's smile to make her fond of him at that very moment or perhaps she has no fond feelings for him at all beyond what any hardhearted whore might have for any soldier boy who brings fistfuls of prairie flowers & gifts of half drunk jugs of trade whiskey to her when he has the coin to call for a f_____. Or perhaps her fondness for him is but her thanks to him for saving her body from the terrible watery wreckage of wagon & mule but whatever it is she did smile back at him that poor cutnose Indian whore.

A whore's smile of gratitude is all you may think it was Sir & you would be right but for Tom well how long was it since a girl had given him the tilt of her lips in a smile? How long I ask you? There was the Mexican Gal at Leavenworth though she would hardly count or maybe she would but I reckon for Tom it must of seemed a lifetime as even whores did mostly recoil from the sight of his face. To be sure they oft came around & smiled at him when they seen what he had in his purse (when he had anything!) but a true blue smile I ask you how long was it? Well God himself could only tell you for it was rare enough it happened even to me but since Chickamauga you could tick it off on 1 hand the smiles or small kindnesses paid by a woman to my brother. You did see for yourself Sir the terrible state of his mug & also you must of seen the fierce far away gleam of madness in his eyes & this too does drive women & men both across the path to pass him by. (Yes I will call it madness for there is no sense at all in calling it anything else this late in the day.)

And all this is more of a pity for you must remember what a fine handsome fellow my brother was before he ate that ball of lead in Tennessee. He was a boy well used to the girleens & their fond attentions. There was once kindness in him too & this was returned most times though it could be said that even before his wounding Tom could fly to anger quicker than most I suppose. But he was not damaged Sir. He was not back then what you would call truly <u>mad</u>.

But here was the sweet Indian pet with her nose cut down to the bone but a fine strapping girl all the same smiling at him & it did twist his heart. Mr. Bridger the Scout did later tell us it was a custom for the Sioux Brave to carve the nose of his woman if she lay down with another man much like a white man might give his wife a thump or 2 should she be in need of it. But Mr. Bridger did say to me also that he never seen such a terrible scarring as this one with nothing but two holes left in her face her visage now indeed as flat as a ploughed field. Altogether it is a fierce savage price for a strayed wife to pay & altogether too much in my eyes to do that on any woman no matter her sins. Sure no civilised man or woman would begrudge a husband a harsh word or the rare slap upon catching his woman with her heels tipped at the Devil with another boy astride her. But that? There is many the strange custom in the world but some I cannot ponder on much at all.

So maybe too theirs is a love founded on the wounds they share & who am I to say the cutnose girl did not (or _does_ not) share some true love for my brother in the same manner that he does love her?

I do not know & do not reckon I ever will but all I can say to you now is that my life & my brother's have come to this pass perhaps on the back of nothing more than a smile from a whore & whore's smiles are bought far less dearly than we are paying now with me in this Guardhouse cell & Tom Only God Knows Where.

22

December 14, 1866 — Fort Phil Kearny,
Dakota Territory

Kohn is dozing on his bunk in the late afternoon, eight days after arriving at Fort Phil Kearny, when he senses something shift in the quality of the lantern light; something blocking its dim purchase on the silent barracks room. Someone, not something, he knows in his half-lucid state, coming to consciousness but keeping his eyes closed and his breathing regular as if he is still sleeping. He makes to roll over so that he may reach the Remington New Model he sleeps with under the rolled blanket he uses for a pillow.

"You will have a ball in your brain before you reach that iron, Sergeant, so leave it be. You may open your eyes or leave them shut, it makes no mind to us."

More than one man. Eyes still closed he thinks to make a move for the pistol, to take

278

his chances. One man he may kill or at least take with him but two men will have the better of the odds, positioned above him as they are. He wonders where the other men in the barracks have gone and resigns himself. If he is to die today, he will go out fighting. He tenses to spring and senses the men above him do the same. He hesitates, which is unlike him. If they had come to kill him, he thinks, it would've been easier done to slit his throat or smother him in his sleep already. Something else they want? Kohn opens his eyes.

Standing over his bunk are two men in knee-length buffalo coats and tall hats fashioned from a buffalo's hump. Around their faces they have tied blue muffler scarves of the type sanctioned for uniform wear and sold to soldiers in sutlers' stores across America. Woollen mittens with fingers cut away. Only their eyes are exposed, though in the dim lantern light Kohn cannot determine their color. They are like bears standing above him in their thick furs, their human features obscured. Or the Golem, Kohn thinks, remembering how as a boy he was so frightened of one day meeting him. But that beast who once stalked his dreams is not these men.

One of them holds a Springfield carbine

and the other a kindling hatchet. Kohn drops his eyes to their boots. One is wearing standard issue artillery boots but the other, holding the hatchet, wears dragoon boots with the knee flaps turned down to reveal well-balled red leather. The man is proud of the boots. He is no dragoon, Kohn reckons, or he would be holding a Colt instead of a hatchet like a wife in search of a chicken's neck. Won the boots in a card game or took them from a dead man. You will be easy to find, bub, Kohn thinks, if I live long enough to do it.

So not beasts, but not parlor soldiers either. The barrel of the Springfield is not altogether steady but is steady enough to be fatal and neither of the men appears frightened. The speaker's voice has been calm, reasonable almost. Take the rail to the next station, Kohn decides. See what happens. He says, "I asked to be woken for supper, boys. I did not need two of you for that."

One of the men laughs. "You are a fine, jesting Jew fucker, all right. I heard what you done to the boys with that chair in Hapworth's store. A right jester, surely."

Irish, again. One of the men from the sutler's store? Does not matter.

"I wasn't jesting then and I am not jesting now. I'm the dog robber in this barracks

280

tonight and the boys will be sore if I don't have their vittles up promptly."

"Them boys will be back and ready to ate when I tell them and no sooner, so listen you now if you know what's good for you."

"All right," Kohn says. "Can I sit up?"

"No you may not sit up, by fuck," the soldier with the hatchet says. "Listen and don't spake." He says something in the Irish language to the soldier with the Springfield who replies with a calming gesture.

"My pal says we should shoot your bothersome self as a Jew spy. Investigators, agitators and touts. As fair Fenian boys we do not abide them, we don't. Do you understand that?"

"I understand you don't like them. But I'm no English agent come to spoil your revolution. I had high hopes for the Fenians and their invasion of British Canada." Kohn smiles.

"I'll split your head wide open, you —"

Springfield carbine again makes a calming gesture with his free hand and says, "We know why you're here which is why you're drawing breath still."

"Good. So what is your purpose for waking me?"

Again, the hatchet man says something to Springfield in Irish and the man answers

281

him, impatience in his voice this time. His eyes do not leave Kohn's. He knows his business or Kohn would have been upon him by now.

The first man says, "Them ledger books belonging the sutler, Mr. Kinney, the whoremaster. 'Tis true you offer fifteen bucks for them, is it?"

Kohn makes to sit up, no desire to gut or shoot these men now. Dragoon boots raises the hatchet with menace and he lies back.

"It's true. Do you have them?"

For the first time, the soldier with the Springfield looks to his partner. Kohn cannot see the color in his eyes but he can see the doubt in them. Uncertainty on the verge of action. "We don't. But we know who has them." He looks back to Kohn. "And we will tell you this for ten dollars reward and the man who has them be fucked."

Kohn smiles. "I thought you could not abide informers."

The soldier with the hatchet says, "You curly whore's pox. I'll stuff your bashed Jew skull with salt pork —"

Springfield carbine says, "Go easy, Ow . . ." He is about to say the man's name but stops himself. "Go easy, for the love of God. We are here to do business with the bastard."

"You hold a gun on a man and then ask him for ten dollars? That is robbery and not business, Bill," Kohn says but he is still smiling.

"You cannot be trusted, I was told."

"Who told you that?"

"You don't need to know but it does be nearly all who meet you. Now do we have a bargain, soreass?"

"I am going to sit up and discuss it with you but if your pal waves his hatchet at me again I'm going to take it from him and chop his cock off with it, do you understand that?"

Hatchet says something in Irish and takes a step toward the bed. His friend stops him with an arm across the chest and more words in the same language. Kohn does not speak the language but knows without doubt that Springfield has asked his friend if he wants his cut of the reward or not. He sits up on the bed and takes a cheroot from a packet on the crate beside his bunk that serves as a makeshift locker. He asks Springfield carbine for a light and he nods to his friend who grudgingly tosses a tin box of matches to Kohn, who takes his time lighting the small cigar.

Kohn punctuates his words with exhaled smoke. "So tell me who has the books."

"The money first," hatchet says.

"You holding that axe does not make me a fool. If you care to try to take the money from me, then take it and skedaddle as thieves but if you care to bargain, you prove to me you have what you say you have. I will then give you a dollar. When you tell me the rest, what I need to know, I will give you five more."

"Six skins?" hatchet says. "I may sooner kill you and take it from you, boy."

"You may try." Kohn puffs on his cheroot and blows a stream of smoke up at the men.

"Eight," says the soldier with the carbine.

"A reasonable man. Seven and we shake on it, Bill," Kohn says.

Springfield nods and gestures spitting on his left hand, holding the carbine in his right, and mimes a handshake. "Done. Struck like a Jewman. Show me the dollar and I will tell you that there are three books in all with over two thousand odd dollars owing within. I will tell you a fellow here on post has them and is making good use of them and when you give me the other six bucks, I will tell you who he is."

Kohn mummers the spitting on his hand and the handshake. "I am reaching into my pocket for my wallet."

"Go ahead, Bill."

Kohn takes a two-dollar note from the wallet and holds it out to the man with the carbine but the man indicates to the hatchet man to take the money. He switches the hatchet to his left hand and snatches the greenback with his right. Kohn then removes a five-dollar note and folds it around his fingers.

"Now speak up while I check that pot for coffee," Kohn says, rising from the bed and passing between the two men, forcing them to step aside. He crosses the rough board barracks floor to the stove and lifts the boiler pot. He takes a tin mug from a shelf above the stove and pours coffee for himself, sitting down at the barracks' long table. "There's coffee enough for two in the pot boys but I won't vouch for its quality."

"We won't be needing it," Springfield says, taking a seat across from Kohn at the table. His friend crosses to warm himself at the stove but remains standing. "We will be going shortly. But I will tell you that them books you seek are held by a E Company boy who dogs as the fort's smith and farrier. Never hardly been off-post nor fired no shot in anger for his work is valued highly by the brass, so he is left at it to smithy while we fight and die and do picket."

Kohn remembers passing the smith's, one

of the larger structures at the southern end of the post within the quartermaster's stockade and somewhat removed from the other barracks and stables for fear of fire. He cannot recall meeting the blacksmith but he ordered Rawson to have the horses reshod only yesterday. "What is his name?"

"He is called Ezekiel Sweetman, or that is the name he goes by. He's a corporal, and a bull of a man as you would expect of a blacksmith. Sure, you may have met him if you've your horses shod since coming or p'raps you did refuse to pay his going, for he is a mean bastard who will shoe Uncle Sam's horses all right as he is paid for it but will ask a king's ransom for to shoe a civvie's beast or a private-owned mount. So 'tis not like he needs the money as he's his wages and a smithy's special duty pay atop them, but there he is all the same with them ledger books and putting them to ill use for ill gain, the fucker."

"How is he putting them to use?" Kohn asks, sipping his coffee and puffing his cheroot. He has a fair idea but is open to correction.

"Well the bastard is collecting what is owed at a half-rate before blacking a fellow's name from the pages when he is paid up. Sure what else would he be doing with them?"

"Half-rate? How kind of him . . . and are the men paying up?"

"They are, for half is better than the full whack by far, and the smithy has given his word to burn them books once all owed is paid up so the whole of them owing have a bargain made with the devil at half-rate," Springfield says, setting the butt of the carbine on the floor beside him. "And them owing can pay it by-the-by so 'tis never a hardship for them like when they owed the sutler hisself who did dock their wages as owing Uncle Sam."

"That sounds fair enough but why do they pay him at all?"

"Well, he could sell the books back to the new sutler and they would owe the full whack then, surely. For the love of Christ, what kind of a Jew are you at all?"

"Not the kind who would pay another Bill for the privilege of halving debts I do not owe him. Are there any soldiers on this post or only wives with pearl shell combs in hock —"

"— to the Jewman," hatchet says.

"If the Irish could reckon the arithmetic, they would own pawn stores instead of pubs," Kohn says, without looking at him.

"So tell me why don't the men with their names in the books get the ledgers back themselves, or have they even tried to yet? Have you?"

Springfield looks away now. "No, we haven't at all."

"But you are asking me to get them. And what would you have me do with them if I succeed?"

The man looks back and Kohn can see the smile behind his muffler. "Why, burn the bastard books, to fuck. Once you've had your look at them."

"But you haven't answered me. Why haven't you tried to take them yourselves already? Or why has not one Bill in the whole camp gone to his company first sergeant and told him what's become of the books?"

"Tell a company first shirt and have *him* go to the brass about it? That would be a fool thing to do when all would then have to pay full whack if the books was given back to the *new* sutler and he had the power to dock wages for the whole amount each boy owes to Uncle as listed in them books. Sure, touting the bugger to the bosses would only cost you *more* money than you've to pay now, so that makes no sense at all."

He looks at Kohn, as if the cavalryman

has understood nothing of what he has said, before continuing. "As of now we pay half, see, though we don't like that for Mr. Kinney's death should benefit all of us who did owe him, much in the way as if a storm did blow them books away or a fire burn them. 'Twas an act of God — which no man should profit from, even by half — that thieving Mr. Kinney getting his throat cut. So there's fair's fair to consider. Them debts should die with the man who held them and not be run on by another no matter who he does think he is."

"You still have not told me why you have not banded together, you fine Fenian boys, and taken them back."

There is some shame in the man's eyes now. Not as much the stag as Kohn had thought.

"Well, you would have to know the boy you would be taking them from to see that. For he is a bad fellow, a terrible bad egg altogether I'm telling you. A Nativist fucker, a hater of all foreign born soldiers. And he's men about him who are the same, a fair number of American boys who is Protestant and Masons even, 'tis said, but all of them veteran Bills, hard men who do not leave his side for so much as a piss. And 'tis said . . ." The man leans across the table to

Kohn and lowers his voice. ". . . 'tis said that Sweetman is a Missoura reb. One of Quantrill's raiders joined up under a bluff moniker because he did be too cruel even for them slaughtering Ozark boys. And as I did say he and all his boys are fierce wild men who do revile the like of us Irish or you Jews. They do hate all followers of the Roman Catholic Church, whether they is Dutchies or Eye-talians or Portugee. And they specially cannot abide freed niggers but they are not alone in that."

"They galvanized Yankees?" Kohn asks, referring to Confederate prisoners who switched sides during the war and enlisted in the Union army.

"Some is, I imagine. They are all sorts but they are rough and they would have the whole of America, God bless her, full of hale, Protestant, American-born boys and the U.S. army the same, I tell you."

"That would make for a small army," Kohn says, and the two men chuckle under their mufflers, knowing this for truth.

Kohn thinks it unlikely that this Sweetman is a former Missouri bushwhacker but considers only that the man has numbers who support him. He has heard there are factions in this new, regular army who despise immigrants — particularly the

290

Catholic Irish and Germans but Jews and the emancipated blacks as well. And he himself, in his occupation posting with the 7th Cavalry in Louisiana and Texas, rode down on white-robed raiders and unrepentant rebels who thought the way to undermine Republican order in the South was to lynch freed black men and those thought to be land-grabbers and profiteers — who all assumed to be Jews, though they were as likely to be Ohio Lutherans as anything else. He decides he will enjoy paying Ezekiel Sweetman a visit.

"You'd do well to mind yourself around him, Bill," Springfield says to Kohn now.

"Corporal Sweetman may be the one who needs minding if he does not present the ledgers to me when I ask him."

"Oh Jesus, I would like to see it, I would," hatchet says, his eyes gleaming.

"Well you are a fine man, for a Jew, I have to say it," says Springfield. "A fine fucking man altogether."

"A fine man for one man," hatchet says. And then to Springfield carbine he says, "Why do you not ask him, sure, ask him why don't you, boy?"

Kohn smiles, knowing what is coming. He hands the five-dollar note across the table to Springfield who takes it and tips his

291

fingers to his buffalo hat.

"Ask me what?" Kohn says.

"More business, p'raps," says Springfield. "Twenty leaves easy, we could muster up from the men, for you to kill that Ezekiel Sweetman bastard and burn them books. Twenty-five even. Once you've your read of them of course."

Kohn shakes his head. "Four hundred blood-and-guts Indian fighters here on post and not one to be found to kill a man but a wandering Jew looking for a set of account ledgers?"

"Well, things is hard, Bill, and I'd not risk a rope for the small sum I do owe. Others might, sure . . ."

"No one had better try it until I get a look at those books or I'm coming looking for my seven bucks back, never mind your twenty."

"Sure, you will have your work made up to see them, but now you know where to look."

"I am going back to my bunk boys. You will see yourselves out."

"We will, Bill. May God go with you."

"Yours or mine?"

"Well, whichever watches over a body best, I s'pose," says the soldier, standing and lifting his Springfield.

Kohn takes another look at the hatchet man's boots so he will remember them if he sees them again. All in all, he thinks, he has done a fine bit of business this afternoon.

23

A WARNING FROM THE MULESKINNER

As I told you Sir it was the smile that did for Tom. A single smile was all it took & in the days after he 1st met her my brother would visit that girl at the doxie wagon every night. After we grubbed & done our duties Tom would stroll to where the mule-skinner made their camp. (For the whole of the march North we saw nothing of that Sutler or his missus they were likely at the front of the procession with the other bigwigs.) Each time Tom went visiting he brung her small offerings of salt pork & beans or a tin of oysters or once the grounds of our drunk coffee all these things in lieu of money for none of us had been paid for several weeks & there was nothing in Tom's pockets but dirt from the road.

Now take heed Sir when I tell you he did not then be tupping her when he called on the wagon them nights with his gifts. No it was like he was courting a farmer's daughter with his offerings & doffed cap & shy looks.

You will hardly believe it but one evening some days after the runaway wagon incident when I did go fetch him from her company for to stand picket I found him sitting with her on the buckboard of the wagon him holding her hand like 2 summer sweethearts. Now God Himself did only know how far they could go in the way of talking for she is part or wholly Indian & does have but few words of English & though my brother does have fine <u>Bearla</u> in his head it rolls now off the ruins of his tongue like another language altogether. But there they sat him mumbling soft words to her there in the prairie dusk. A dry crackling fire burned & the other whores sat around it with their sinister muleskinner standing just outside that firelight & watching over it all neither in favour nor disfavour of it but taking it all in that boy seeing every D____ thing going on about him. That bucko boy knew the score he did & I will say that even as early as that night on the plain that bucko knew the ill that would come to us all in the end.

And maybe I am something like that 1/2 breed bucko too because though it did all seem fine & calm to the eye that prairie eve round the whore wagon's campfire I thought to myself, "No good will come of this." I cannot say why the feeling came on me & I cannot claim foreknowledge of later events the ones which sent you here to us Sir but that is how I felt.

I made that muleskinner one to watch I tell you & only a day later who did pay a visit to our bivouac at Mad Woman's Creek (where we stopped for several days more while the wagon wheels were retreaded) but that buck whore tender himself. He came up behind me silent as the plague as I staked out our mounts for grazing nearly scaring the very piss from me when I turned to see him standing there like something cut from a tombstone.

Now I do not be an easy sort to get the jump on the War having done me some service there making me start to every crackle of branch or scuff of boot & nor do I shy from any other man though betimes I know when my hand needs be folded like any Bill with his wits about him. I know when to fight & I know when to flicker but this fellow well he put the skin of my back to crawling he did.

I swallowed before speaking so he would not hear the fear in my voice. "You are not to be among the horses by the Colonel's orders," says I.

At this the boy did show a smile his teeth very white in his gob against the tanned hide of his skin. He wore a muleskinner's set of clothes & could pass for a Mex surely with the long plait of black hair that fell from his black stovepipe hat though he spoke like any American fellow you might pass in the road but slow & more carefully as if his mind did gander a peek at each word before they passed his lips. Again I did say to myself, "Watch this boy he is no more a common muleteer than you are."

After some moments of silence says he, "You can tell your brother he ain't to be among the whores anymore. When we gets where we going then he can pay up for a poke like any other soldier. Them is orders too." He shown his white teeth in a smile again & though the fellow did be no older than me there appeared something ancient in it like it was 1000 years since any gentle feeling was in that smile.

I cast a look over my shoulder at the camp. The boys from my Company were there fixing up supper or gathering buffalo chips for a fire & they were but 50 yds. away though it did seem much further. I swallowed again & said to the b_____, "You are giving

297

orders to serving soldiers now are you?"

"Boss's orders not mine," says he.

"And who is the boss when he is at home?" I let my eyes drop for a second to the knife on his belt. 1 second I tell you but he caught it & again gave that grin with no warmth at all in it. The knife at his belt was bigger than Tom's D Bar a fair cutlass it was & I could nearly smell the blood of past murders on it.

"You know rightly who is the Boss & who is the sonofabitch." He set a hand on the butt of that knife.

I did know it but would not let on.

Says I, "My brother does not take kindly to being drove about by any old bucko walking into camp with a songbook full of orders. I would reckon on that if I was you."

"It aint any old bucko doing the ordering. So you just tell him we are obliged for him hauling up the wagon when it got away but he aint to be buzzing about the whores til we all get where we going. You will tell him that if you are smart."

Something in how he spoke made me think this was the most words he used at one time in a long while & that he was not much used to conversing with his fellow man in the ditch.

"I will tell him but promise nothing to

you. The brother does what he wants & there is few who will tell him otherwise," says I wanting to be away from him altogether but not wanting to show fear to him neither.

The dusk took on a fierce chill then & the horses moved away from the muleskinner straining at the ends of their ropes. They bunched together their eyes balled & vexed making a clear wide space about us there in the prairie grass.

"You just tell him," says the skinner before he turned & lost himself in the lowering darkness & the horses again shifted & tugged on their ropes to be as far away from him as ever they could be when he passed.

"Whisht now," says I to the horses my mouth gone dry & stone weariness upon me of a sudden. "Whisht now my pets he is gone away Thank God."

Well I would of wagered agin it but Tom took my message from the muleskinner in grand stead. He did not rage or give voice to what he would do to such a buck who dared tell such a terrifying man as himself what he could or could not do lest he be an officer in the great Army of the United States & even then he might better be a good one. No I would of lost my money betting on Tom. More than once in this sad life I would of.

We were sat about the embers of the cook fire sipping coffee after relief from picket duty the sky fierce sparked with stars like spilt salt on mourning cloth I tell you with our brothers in C Company asleep in their rolls around us the prairie nights cool & dry with no need of dog tents at all. They slept the sleep God intended for us under His heavens with the low licking flames of a warm fire beside them & the laughing yips of Coyotes off in the darkness. Outside the faint light from the fire all was in darkness & though there was many hundreds of folks & hundreds more of beasts that made up Carrington's Overland Circus Parade it seemed that night that Tom & myself were alone to ourselves there on the prairie & this made me feel close to Tom closer than I felt in a long while.

I said to him, "So you will abide by it Tom & not be calling on the whores til we get where we are heading? Or til we are paid out Tom til then at least?"

My brother was quiet for a moment puffing his pipe & staring into the embers before he says to me, "I will heed your message Michael but only as she did tell me herself she did. Not to come back nor to bring no more gifts. She says my gifts will sow trouble for her with the other girls. And the muleskinner may whip her."

He spoke this last part with a smile around his pipe as if the thought of the muleteer putting his whip to the poor girl was a fine sort of joke altogether. As if the fellow would dare put a finger to her knowing what bitter tribulations would befall him in the shape of Tom should he try it.

"Well," says I & said nothing more because betimes with Tom there is nothing more to say.

Tom gave a nod & then removed his boots lacing them tightly up again for to keep the rattlers from making a bed of them. He took off his stockings next hanging them beside the other stockings from the yoke erected above the fire like all the old soldiers among us knowing that clean stockings be best but dry were near as good & that bad stockings make for bad feet & bad feet for bad marching. (Though we were mounted as mock Dragoons we did this out of habits we learnt the hard way in the War for in the Army there is no telling when a body might be marching.)

I did too lace my boots tight & set them beside Tom's. "No snakes back home," says I in the Gaelic just to be saying something.

"Please God none here will find my bed roll warm while I am in it."

Tom lay out his own bed roll bunching his tunic for a pillow. He pulled his blanket up to his chin & lay there with his arms behind his head his eyes up at the stars. After some time he did reply, "There is f_____ snakes everywhere Michaeleen. Every G_____ D_____ place in the world there is snakes of some sort."

He said this in English & I understood it very well.

So he did promise to abide by the skinner's orders but still he laid his eyes & something more upon that girl before we arrived to hammer down stakes here in the Powder River country. It was 5 or so days later when the march hauled up at Ft. Laramie in the Dakota Territory. I will tell you about it but not now. Now I am tired & so cold it is hard to remember the baking heat of them days. It seems so long ago though it is less than a year. A lifetime ago it does feel since there was heat in my bones or sun on my back. So much is come to pass since then.

24

December 15, 1866 — Fort Phil Kearny,
Dakota Territory

Under low, gray skies, Kohn watches the busy blacksmith's shop in the bitter cold on the morning after his meeting with the informants in buffalo coats. It snowed during the night but the heat from the smithy's fires has melted a halo of bare mud around the building. From his place in front of the quieter mechanic's shop, some fifty yards distant, he can hear the hiss of the bellows and the roar of the forge from the smithy's. The clank of a hammer on an anvil.

Kohn has not seen the blacksmith himself but he has seen men whom he assumes to be his protection. Big men with mustaches worn long and upturned like the horns of bulls, they come to the open door of the shop or stand and smoke under the shoeing area outside which is covered by a slanting, wood-shingled roof. The mustaches are uniform and sinister and so similar that they must be worn as a sign of affiliation. Two of the men wear pistols in holsters and the three others, Kohn assumes, have them stuffed in belts beneath their tunics, knives in boots no doubt. One or two of them squat to pare and shoe horses as they are brought in but in their wariness — the way they eye the yard and the passersby, the way they stroll to cover the back and front of the shop — they reveal themselves to be on picket at the smith's, convincing Kohn that his visitors were correct and Sweetman the blacksmith does indeed possess something as valuable and coveted as the ledgers.

Kohn wears two pistols, his Remington in a cavalry holster and a Colt Baby Dragoon in his own belt, but hopes they will not see use. Earlier it occurred to him to consult Molloy about how to proceed but he decided against it. The officer was sleeping that morning when he went to visit him and one of the surgeon's orderlies told Kohn that Molloy had suffered fits in the night and so the surgeon had dosed him once more with laudanum. It was not an unusual thing for drunks drying out to suffer, the orderly told him, and not much harm in the long run just so long as he don't swally his tongue. Hell, the orderly said to Kohn, the lieutenant will dry out fine and dandy and be fit to drink again in no time at all.

The cold riding hard on his impatience, Kohn makes his decision and crosses from the mechanic's to the blacksmith's shop, having seen enough to know that he will be better to go in daylight, with the comings and goings of cavalrymen and civilian drovers alike providing him what safety he will need.

He enters the shop, his eyes taking a moment to adjust to the forge-lit gloom within. The air is superheated by the brick forge and two open, raised fire pits and Kohn begins to sweat under his coat. A big man in a leather apron worn over an undershirt with its sleeves cut away tongs a horseshoe still glowing orange from the forge over to a tub of water. He plunges the shoe into the water and it hisses and steams. The smith then lifts it from the water and tosses it into a wooden bin full of shoes with a loud clank.

The smith's head is shaved tight against lice, like many of the men in the fort. His mustaches are worn long, the same as the men outside, and hang below his chin, glinting with sweat in the forge's firelight. Like fangs, Kohn thinks. He does not look at Kohn when he says, "If you need a beast shod, you talk to one of the boys. Likely to be a wait today as I'm up to my ass in the devil's work."

Kohn sees one of the boys look up from where he is shoveling coal into the forge. He is in uniform trousers and an undershirt, a leather apron and thick leather gloves that extend up his forearms. Noting Kohn's uniform and boots, the man says, "What you need, soreass? You gonna shoe yourself or you gon' wait your turn?"

"Do you know who I am?" Kohn says to the blacksmith, ignoring his man.

The smith looks over to him now and after a moment says, "I know who you are. You the Jew dragoon broke up the sutler's the other day, ain't you?"

"Word gets about a camp fast."

"Every goddamn jack on post heard that five minutes after you done it."

"So you know what I need to see already."

The smith laughs. "I heard you offering fifteen sheets for some books is what I heard."

"You heard right. I have it right now in my billfold. You just get the books and we'll do business together."

The smith's man sets his shovel against the forge's brickwork and takes off his leather apron. He leaves on his gloves. He is younger than the smith but just as big. The

306

same mustaches but straggly like winter grass.

"The Dutchie Jew wanna do business," the blacksmith says to his man and the man smiles and shakes his head. Another of the smith's men, as if summoned, enters the dim shop and stands behind Kohn, blocking the door.

"That's right," Kohn says. "I came to do business because getting my lieutenant or your first sergeant to come here and order you to hand over the books would do no one any good, would it? You or any of the men whose names are in them."

The man in the leather gloves laughs and looks over at the soldier who has just entered. "Well, there's our first sergeant right there. Whyn't you ask him yourself?"

Kohn looks at the figure in the doorway and notes his sergeant's stripes. He looks around the shop and takes in the American flag hanging on one wall. Beneath it, a smaller flag showing a coiled snake and the legend "Don't Tread On Me." In the dim light he can see the blacksmith has extensive tattooing on his massive arms. Not unusual among soldiers who fought in the war, many had their names and hometowns etched in simple lettering under arms or on shoulders in case there was no other means of identifying their remains. Others had skulls and mermaids or eagles underscrolled with the name of their regiments in bold, gothic numbers and letters. Squinting, Kohn reads the legend in bold, black, cursive scrawl on the smith's arm. "America for Americans."

"I'll offer twenty to you to look at those books. That is my final offer."

"Your final offer, hell. Makes a man think, don't it, why you want a look at these books I s'posed to got. What you hope to find in 'em."

"If you know who I am, Corporal, you know I'm here to investigate the killing of the owner of those books along with his wife. Those books may be evidence in our investigation. I could order you to hand them over but here I am, offering you twenty leaves for a look, no questions asked. If I were you, I'd hand them over, but if I were you, you'd have more sense."

Again, the smith laughs and shoves a half-rendered shoe into the forge, his face glowing orange in the firelight. "And if I were you, I'd kill my Jew self before someone else got wits enough to do it for me." He spits tobacco juice into the forge and the spittle hisses and jets steam when it hits. "Anyhow, if them books is so goddamn priceless, you make a fool of yourself offering me twenty, when what's in 'em's worth more than a thousand, or so I hear."

Kohn stares at him for a moment. On a table within reach is a heavy iron mallet. He thinks what he might do with it.

Kohn says, "I heard you were one of Quantrill's raiders."

"You might have heard right."

"I heard Quantrill's boys liked killing kids because it was a sight easier than killing Dutchie farmers. Buggering them, killing them, whichever took your fancy on the day," Kohn says and notes that the three men are no longer smiling.

"You gon' get yourself hurt, Jewman." The smith takes a hot iron poker from the fire and looks over at the gloved apprentice.

"You know, Don, you know what I got a mind to do?"

"What's that, boss?"

The poker's tip glows bright orange and the smith holds it up, hefts the poker as if gauging the balance of a cutlass. "I got a mind to stick this iron in the Jew's eyes. Each eye, one and the other. Then sit the Christ-killing son of a bitch down in front of them books he say I got. Give him a look at what he can't see in front of his own face."

"What books would those be?" the sergeant blocking the door says.

"Oh I don't know. Some books this Jew fucker says I got."

Kohn looks again at the iron mallet on the bench, at the anvil and then at each of the three men. The sergeant in the doorway meets his gaze but the soldier in the gloves will not. The smith smiles at Kohn.

Kohn says, "I have offered good money and you have declined my offer. Your loss, Smithy. You won't be offered it again."

The smith shoves the tip of the poker into the heart of the fire and holds it there for a moment. "I'm a let you leave with your eyesight, Jewman. But I hear you say another goddamn word round camp 'bout any kinda books at all, I'm gonna cook your goddamn heart on my fires. You understand me?"

"You assume I have one, Corporal."

"You a funny boy. A laughing Dutchie Jew dog. You won't be laughing we come for you in the night, boy."

There are voices raised outside the shop and the three men turn to them. Kohn takes the iron mallet from the workbench and slips it into his belt under his tunic.

A young officer enters, shoving the sergeant blocking the door aside. "Corporal, my horse has thrown a shoe and is waiting

310

to be goddamn shod and I am left standing outside with my prick in my hand."

"Yessir, I'll do it myself, pardon the wait, Lieutenant," the smith says. "I been busy as two flies fucking, sir."

"And less of the goddamn cussing, corporal," the lieutenant says. "This fort is not the cock-sucking whorehouse where your sister works."

"Yessir," the smith says, taking four shoes from the bin and a box of shoeing nails from a workbench. He smiles at Kohn as he follows the lieutenant out into the cold.

25

THE FT. LARAMIE PEACE TALKS & 1ST MEETING WITH MR. LO (AS WE DO CALL THE INDIANS)

I will take up the pen again Sir because I cannot sleep for the cold & the terrible thoughts in my head. I do not know what time or day it is now though I suppose it does not matter. It is still today or it is tomorrow but nothing has changed for me since I last wrote here some hours ago.

I was writing before about the march of Col. Carrington's Overland Parade arriving at Ft. Laramie & we soon learnt the reason for our hauling up there. It was the big Pow Wow between the chiefs of the Sioux & Cheyanne & our very own Big Hats of the Army & Government that was called the Laramie Peace Talks.

Well we now do know how much good them talks were at all for you can see how peaceable they made the lot of us both red & white neither side of us giving a penny f_____ for the terms of the treaty signed but preferring the bow & musket all round. But for us back then it did be a rest from the road & we took it as soldiers in any Army would & tore up on a fine old spree.

Sure none of us common Bills knew a thing of the negotiations then only that we were free for a day or 3 with light duties & the Paymaster God Bless Him was due to catch us up there with 2 months back pay & Thank God for that for soldiers do raise a fierce thirst in marching. (You know all this well yourself for I can see it in you no offence Sir. I can smell the whiskey on you when you watch me through the Judas window in my cell door.)

But I will tell you of this time because it has a bearing on events to come though I feel that it is only in writing about it that I will discover how.

Well it was at Ft. Laramie where we did lay eyes on our first proper Indian Braves anyway. Of course we did see Indians before back East even & betimes at Leavenworth come to trade skins or meat but they were common sad fat fellows & no soldier of Uncle Sam's Army would fear them much. And we did see 1 or 2 on the march as well but at some distance. It would happen that one of us Bills would point to a faraway hill where a lone rider or 2 on horseback spied on our dusty parade as it plied the Platte River bank.

"Injins boys," would say the fellow to spot them. "Taking our measure so's he can have our hair for a winter hat."

We would have a fine chuckle at that & point at Buffalo Stu a bald fellow of barely 30 years of age from the great falls of Niagara or the city called Buffalo close by them saying, "Well then you are safe Stu. Your scalp would leave a Brave right f_____ cold come winter."

And Stu would say, "That may be right boys but my ball sack would make a fine hairy hat for an Injin baby."

"An ugly f_____ hat that would be Stu," says another Bill.

"Ugly f_____ babies," says Stu & we did all laugh.

I remember saying, "A fierce strange man you are putting the mockers on us talking of losing the ball sack Stu talking like that God Bless Us."

"Talking like how Paddy Mick? Can you talk like I am talking? In English & all Paddy Mick? Hell them Injins would make a fine pair a boots from that thick Irish tongue of yours."

Stu was a gasbag of a man a fine Yankee Bill altogether & a veteran like myself & Tom. Also like us he was a 2nd time take on man who did freely admit to coming back in the Army under a different name because he put his cousin up the spout while her husband was away in Canada. "A French Canuck," says Stu, "is not the type to be trifled with!" & so Stu took on again with the 18th & kept us mightily entertained. God Keep Him Close for he is dead & gone Buffalo Stu or so we do think as he went out to meet the woodtrain one day in October by himself (a fool thing but done at the time before Carrington put a stop to it with one of his Special Orders) & well poor Stu was never to be seen again.

I tell you Sir on that long march we had a smile most of the days & the ragging between us was mighty. Even Tom took his rags from the boys about the campfire his spirit better by far since he made acquaintance with his darling whore. I did worry betimes when some fellow would crack on about the brother's dinted gob for as I did tell you he was once terrible handsome to look at & it is not easy to go from pretty to what he is like now overnight but in them days Tom just gave a smile or raised an idle fist or shook his head.

But forgive me Sir for it is Laramie I am writing of how it was there at that Pow Wow where we met our first real & proper Indian Braves the ones who will fill you full of arrows & take your scalp or your ball sack if you are not careful. Our first sign of them was near a mile of tee pees along the river outside the Ft. I tell you there must of been 1000 of them & soon we would meet the boys who camped in them.

A fine lot them red boys were & taller than you may think for the Indian Paint horse they raise up as a breed well these are small & betimes bowbacked but the Sioux & Cheyanne lads they are tall men some of them taller than manys the Bill sent to fight them. As well they appear stronger in the arm & shoulders on the whole with fine white teeth & long plaited hair shining with buffalo grease some with Eagle feathers in bands or larriots round their heads & some without & some wearing shirts of cotton or calico. Others their chests are bare & smooth & fat with muscle their necks hung in beads of every colour their fine horse bowed legs breeched in leather with fringes for to take away the rain from their flanks so they may ride in all weathers. And all of them did pure peacock about the Ft. & its surrounds making our own ugly shower of bluecoats feel small & plain as pea hens.

I tell you some even had rifles to make a sad soldier green with envy. One had a Sharps that our 1st Sgt. reckoned could only of been stolen from a dead coachman or prospector so fine a weapon it was. But all did carry skinning knives & bows slung cross their backs & quivers stuffed with arrows which we did soon see up close. Steel tipped & as fatal as any bullet they can run straight through a man if fired from near up enough. We could only guess at this then but know it well enough by now God Bless Us.

But them Braves were not there for scalping or fighting no more than ourselves wanting only for to slake the thirst of a long journey & to fill their bellies full of pies & boilt sweets from the post stores selling them. Most of all they was there to wager what they had on shooting & racing & wrestling or rodeo. Anything by Jove them Braves would bet on. 2 pissing flies I tell you & a wager on which would finish 1st making them much the same as your common soldier Bill. I have heard it said by some English & American boys that the Irish soldier is little better in his manners than the Indian & I have come to blows over this but both the Irishman & the Indian love wagering & fighting & supping so there is some common strain between us I will confess though now I hate the red b_____ as much as the English or more even.

But I did not feel this bitter hatred then & so we did wager agin them & they agin us & ourselves agin ourselves & them agin themselves. Well the bets did fly like winter geese over the two days of rest & recreation & in the betting we did learn a thing or 2 about them Braves.

Every soul in the country has heard of the Sioux & his horse but to see it up close is a wonder I shall thank God or the Devil some day for letting me see it. I lost 25¢ right off on Tom riding a race versus a Cheyanne fellow the 2 of them at speed having to lean off their mounts to snatch horse shoes from atop a barrel & hook them round spears stuck in the ground 200 yds. apart & my brother nearly took it I tell you but he was pipped at the post by that Brave on his short legged Paint. 1/2 a nag that Paint looked but a goer & it swung round them staked lances fast as a wife may change her mind. The Indian paints do not show much of beauty or might when put beside a white

man's Quarterhorse but they do go like
lightning for the steeple & cover the miles
without feed or water as no horse has the
right to & no horse of ours can surely. I do
imagine them Braves will rare up a finer
strain of horse still from all the stock they
thieved from us here in the past months &
soon there will be no catching them.

But this was of no mind to us then for we
saw what they could do & they saw what we
could do & it comes to me now that we did
not much impress them. Instead they perhaps became much boldened by our poor
showing in the games of martial skill between us.

Did you ever see Sir them boys fire their
bows? For most men who see it it is the last
thing ever they see but there in Laramie we
did wager some Braves a buck between 5 of
us if 1 of their number could put a quiver
full of arrows into a target on a tree from a
100 yds. away. Well in the setting of the
wager with one of the Braves speaking
between English & Sioux there did arise
some confusion & the Indian to do the
shooting understood he was to shoot from
horseback when we meant nothing of the
kind never thinking to ask for it. But up he
got on his pony loosing 15 arrows in as
much time as it takes a man to whistle Dixie

keeping 2 or 3 in his fist at a time the bow twanging like a banjo string the next arrow in flight before the first had hit its mark as he galloped up one way & down the other 100 yds. or more from his goal. And all of them May God In Heaven Be My Witness struck home some splitting the shafts of the ones landed before them & deep in the tree they did lodge. I am telling you Sir you would need chop the tree down altogether to get them arrow heads back. I do not recall if this was done that day but it might of for Mr. Lo does not abide losing an arrow tip if he can reclaim it as they are made of iron or steel from melted skillets or the like or flattened & folded tin pales traded for furs & be hard enough to come by. Manys the time since coming to this valley I have seen them reaching down from horseback at full gallop for to reef them from the bodies of dead men on the ground which I now suppose makes the race Tom rode with the Brave to pick up the horseshoes of some use to them as practice surely.

But none of this did we think at Laramie for the days had the fine mood of a Fair. Puck Fair I did think at the time making me smile in a sad way of remembering fine days from Kerry summers past. Or it could be like the Horse Fair you have in Ballinasloe Sir you being a Galway man. It is a fine week out in Ballinasloe I am told & the Pow Wow at Ft. Laramie for 2 or 3 days was the same I tell you it was like the finest day of the finest summer you can picture in your head.

But you know as well as any man Sir that no Fair is a proper Fair without a few whores & Tom did not take long to find where his favourite wagon was set up & because he can betimes act a kind & thoughtful brother to me he asked if I cared to come with him away from the games & wagering for some sport of the softer kind at that very wagon.

Now in all God's truth I had no mind to spend what little I had in the way of wages on such a rabble of whores. You see the Paymaster (God Bless Him!) had not factored on the number of men in camp that week in need of paying & did only issue us all 10$ each against our back pay & this I was happy to piss away on whiskey & gaming & cherry pie from Robber's Row where the Sutlers sell their wares & not on whores at all. But something in my mind said to me that my brother may be in need of minding with him already gut deep in beer & Bust Head which is what we soldiers call trade whiskey stilled to kill them who care to drink it so I did consent to go with him & have a gander at the geese at least.

So we went forth through the Ft. passing the fine white tent they raised up on the parade ground for their talks with the Sioux & Cheyanne chiefs which in the heat they did open wide the flaps of for all the world to see them smoking the peacepipe good & proper while putting all the terrible troubles twixt White & Red to bed. Now you & me & the dog in the road knows it was but a sorry sham the whole lot of it for their Big Bugs in their eagle feathers who sat down with our Big Bugs with their polished brass & hanging braid for the Laramie Treaty talks well they were but a small crowd of peaceable Indians & could not speak for their more War minded brothers who we came to know so well here in this Valley of the Powder River. They could make no agreement them Chiefs no more than our gentleman Officers could speak for the multitudes of prospectors & panners tramping their way to the gold fields without permission or mind to seek it from the Government. What a sham all of it.

But nothing of this did we know then & thought it all a grand fine carnival with squaws in all their coloured beads with black braids thick as hemp ropes & skin as brown & clear as campfire coffee with fine fat babbies bound to their backs. Sure the squaws around Ft. Laramie them few days in their 100s were a different breed altogether from the ones we did be walking down to see in the Sutler's 2nd wagon.

Well I am wandering in my words here & in time we did reach the wagon set a fair piece away from the all the others to the rear of the Ft. in a clearing of cutdown Cottonwoods by a brackish stream.

We would not be the first men there though it was quiet enough & peaceable with the sun still high in the afternoon sky. There was a kind of sail or tent cover strung from the wagon & propped up by 2 lodge poles offering shade to the whores dozing on thick heaps of buffalo hide rugs & the Bills waiting their go up in the bed of the wagon. The whores did flick out at flies now & again with buffalo tail fans while 2 boys from I Company who we did know by sight sat supping whiskey on stumps that served as stools. The mule driver was there as well & this time he did not warn us off for what whoremaster runs off his custom when they have coins in the purse?

"2 bucks," says he as we walked into the shade. Nary a "Fine Day" from him he was as rude as a land agent come for rent.

To spite his rudeness I did say, "2$? Fair steep for what is on offer."

"Well 2 sheets or you can f_____ a gopher hole," says he not looking at me but at the brother as if he did fancy his chances.

I made to reply but Tom put his hand on my chest for to stop me. "2$ will do grand," says he.

Says the skinner still looking at Tom but pointing at me, "2$ each if he wants his own poke. He ain't to share yours."

I did consider it a moment for standing there with money in my pocket nature's hunger came upon me & I took a long look at the whores lounging there about the buffalo rugs. They are fat I will give them that which is the best thing about them with eyes puffed & at 1/2 mast with liquor & they were damp of brow in the dust & heat. One puffed a long stem pipe & another wore a forage cap no doubt forgotten by some drunken Bill. The 3rd whore took note of my looking & she lifted her skirts & tossed open her hams for to show me the thick black thatch about her privates. The two I Company boys on their stumps stared over at her c_____ for a moment before turning back to their whiskey as if they had their fill of such a sight altogether & could not stomach another portion. The hunger I can tell you Sir went off me lickety quick with me thinking terrible thoughts of mercury cures & broke glass piss as sure to come with a visit to these whores as the sun is sure to rise in the morning. My prick did droop to think on it.

Says I, "No you may keep your wares. I will just set with these boys to wait."

The muleskinner said nothing in return & instead turned to the back of the wagon & ordered them inside to put an end to their business. Tom did doff his kepi & made to fix up his hair with a whale ivory comb he won in a card game causing me to smile for it was like tying down lines on a sinking ship my brother trying to put his head right for to spark his whore.

"I will not tell you again," says the muleskinner into the back of the wagon as I took a free stump nearby the I Company boys. Says he, "You button up & get your ass out the wagon."

From inside the wagon came the voice of a man telling the skinner where to take himself & that he did not yet have his shot away & would G_____ D_____ have it as he paid for it.

The muleskinner smiled at this I tell you & cast an eye to my brother as if to say, "Look at this you ugly sonofabitch for here is a message for you."

He then did climb up into the wagon &
soon there was a fierce bellow of voices like
cows in a burning shed it sounded & no
more than a tick after this did a man come
flying down from the back of the wagon to
land in the dirt with an almighty thump his
britches tangled about his boots. Next came
the muleteer climbing from the wagon calm
as a man coming down church steps while
the boy on the ground jerked & wrestled
with his kersey pants cursing the skinner for
a 1/2 breed b_____ who would have the
blood draining from him before the sun hid
behind the mountains.

Well that Bill had his britches part way up
his legs when the skinner without so much
as a Pardon Me let rip a terrible kick into
his guts & up did come that boy's breakfast
like a cannon spewing grapeshot.

At this the two I Company boys sitting by
me on the stumps took to their feet &
moved for the skinner though one of them
was so drunk he did skew wide & go for a
gambol off in the scrub grass forgetting I
reckon why he took to his feet in the 1st
place & shortly he too was puking over a
bush in fair contentment. The 2nd boy well
I sat watching as he hove toward the skinner with his whiskey bottle held by the neck

& glinting in the sun. Now this boy he did remember the reason for taking to his feet but remembering does not mean able & I made a small prayer for him to stop as he was unsteady on his feet & no match for an old aunt's scolding never mind a proper scrap.

Well the skinner drew his knife from its scabbard & like the bottle in the drunk's hand it too set to glinting in the sun & I got the feeling that he had fierce pride in that knife & kept it buffed up like a chalice on an altar & when the drunk saw it well Thanks Be To God he did get 2nd thoughts altogether about bashing that whore minder with the whiskey bottle & instead changed his tack to aid his retching friends 1st the one who took the kick & then the other.

The muleskinner looked at Tom & then to me & then back to Tom & I saw again there would be troubles to come between them. They are 2 boys cut from the same swatch of cloth with no fear of pain or dying 2 boys who would not shirk from anything God could bring upon them in light or darkness. Terrible troubles surely & well you & me know Sir whence them troubles did come & know too that they had their start as I told you Sir back in the Depot in Columbus when that clam tight c_____ of a Sutler tried to ruse us into buying 2 cleaning kits when all we ever would need was 1.

But here I am driving the cart before the mule in my tale for that hot day there was no trouble just a far off rumble of it like thunder in a blue sky as happens here betimes in this valley. Fair warning like of a storm to come.

"2 bucks," says the skinner to Tom again & Tom went to his pocket for the money his eyes locked tight on the skinner's eyes like only sweethearts & killers do in this world.

"Sure you did tell us that already," says my brother & his words were clear as a ringing church bell clear & as easy to reckon & did sound to my ears like a true American soldier sounds. To spite the trouble to come I did be proud of the way Tom sounded with his intentions to that mule-skinning whore beater made right & clear for all to hear.

As Tom spoke the cutnose girl climbed down from the wagon causing my brother to break his eyes at last from the skinner & to raise his cap in salutation. She did not see this or did not care for it but instead walked behind the wagon & hiked her skirts for to wash herself. We turned away from seeing this even the muleskinner. My brother handed the skinner the money.

"There is 4 bucks there," says Tom surprising me. "I will bide awhile with the girl. And my brother will have a bottle."

"You just finish up when I call you," says the skinner pocketing the bills & sheathing his blade. "And all will be hunky dorey."

I sat on my stump & waited & gave the whores on the rugs no heed at all while the sound of sloshing water & wet rags was loud in the heat. The muleteer brought me a bottle of Bust Head from the front of the wagon & I did not thank him for it.

Shortly the cutnose girl finished her ablutions as is the saying & came round the wagon to take my brother by the hand & this time she did smile at Tom & he paid her back a smile such as none I seen him give another since that day at Chickamauga.

Trouble says I to myself then. Terrible troubles are coming & that did prove to be the truth of things as you can see.

2 days later we broke camp & departed Laramie sore headed & sour breathed our souls aching with shame the way a fellow does oft feel after a skite.

Carrington's parade again forged North away from the last bit we might ever see of civilisation so it did seem then. From this time of the march there is 1 strange thing I will always remember 1 thing that is stuck fast in my head & will not shake from it. That is when we passed the death scaffold (a <u>pyre</u> one boy called it) built for the daughter of one of the chiefs of the Sioux or Cheyanne I do not know which but he was called Spotted Tail this Chief.

Well in the way of the Indians he put his poor dead daughter (may her own God Rest Her) on a log frame & did not bury her in the earth at all but left her body there under the mighty blue bowl of the western sky atop this lodge pole frame for all the birds of the air to pick at & spread her bones about the place. Fierce strange it was this custom & myself & my brother could not take our eyes from it as we passed slowly by her in silence the black ugly vultures perched upon her poor body their gobs besmirched with gore & not a sign of our Christian God anywhere around us. The horses were quiet too though they did show miscomfort with the blinking of their eyes. The silence was broke when Tom said to me, "What is that fool doing?"

He pointed as one of our boys rode his horse over to the pyre making the black birds take wing. That Bill (I will not tell you his name for he is no longer with us & I will not speak ill of the dead) well that fool of a soldier reached up to the pyre & pinched a beaded necklace that was hanging from the poles & put it round his horse's ears. His horse did not like the reek of death upon it & begun to buck & whinny & so he hung it from his own neck laughing all the while the blaggard. He then reached up upon the scaffold & took down the poor dead girl's hand & made to wave it at us in terrible jest with her hand of bone & only a small bit of meat upon it.

"Put that down you shit for brains!" roared Sgt. Nevin riding up & seeing this rotten jape all of us starting at his voice as if at a father's & the soldier seeing the Company 1st Sgt. did drop the hand to the ground in a fright & gallop his mount back into formation.

"And take off them f_____ bangles," says Nevin. "You break out of step again I will put you in a f_____ coffin do you hear me?"

"Yes Sgt. sorry Sgt.," says that cursed Bill & sorry he soon was but he was smiling when he said it & though he took off them beads he did not put them back with their owner but instead stowed them in his saddle bag.

Says the brother to me in the Gaelic so he would not be understood by the others, "Do not ride near him now not after what he just done. Stay a piece away from him. The Indians will not take kindly to such carry on & there will be wigs on the green for it. Keep a horse or 2 tween yourself & that f_____."

That is all & I do not know why I remember it. There is much you forget about a time & strange wild things you recall. This is one of them things.

26

*December 15, 1866 — Fort Phil Kearny,
Dakota Territory*

"Why, that is a court martial offense, Corp
—"

"Sergeant."

"Sergeant. I can't get myself caught up in
no —"

"Rawson?"

"Yes, Sergeant." Rawson will not look
Kohn in the eye.

"You've been gaming again, haven't you?"

Rawson says nothing. He glances up at
Jonathan, the Pawnee scout standing still
and quiet in the corner of the stall.

"I can see it in your eyes, Rawson. You are
as easy to read as a French postcard."

"One or two games is all and I ain't
pinched or a stole a thing from nobody."

"First the chicken, then the egg, Rawson,
you mush-brain. What did I tell you I'd do
to you if I found out you were gaming or

333

thieving?" Kohn holds up his Colt Baby Dragoon and with a flourish cocks the gun, then uncocks it.

A horse in a neighboring stall snorts and shifts.

"I don't remember, Sergeant, 'xactly what you said but it was bad."

"It was."

He hands Rawson the pistol by the barrel. "Will I remind you?"

"No, Sergeant."

"What hour on the clock, Rawson?"

"Eleven?"

"Not a second earlier, not a second later, Private." Kohn takes out his watch.

"I ain't got a timepiece, Sergeant."

"Take mine, here. And if you try to sell it —"

"What do you take me for, Sergeant, Christ almighty —"

"Rawson . . ."

"Yes, Sergeant."

"Eleven sharp. Make a ruckus like you've never done before. And if you are hauled up, Rawson, what are you going to say?"

Rawson looks at Kohn for the first time since Kohn found him mucking out the cavalry stables. "Not a goddamn thing, is what I'll say."

Kohn pats him on the shoulder. "You'll

make a fine soldier one day, Rawson."

"No, Sergeant. No I won't."

"You're right, Rawson. You won't."

Eleven o'clock, give or take a minute, and Kohn and Jonathan stand in the darkness with their backs against the rough logs of the mechanic's shop when they hear Rawson's first shot. They hear a second shot and raised voices brought to them on the wind but from too far away to understand the words. They do not need to understand them because they know who is shouting and what is being shouted and before long, men begin to exit barracks throughout the fort carrying muskets, some in shirtsleeves, unlaced boots, repeating the cry that started with the two shots. *Indians. Indians inside the palisade.*

The door to the mechanic's shop opens, throwing out a bolus of lantern light from inside, and Kohn and Jonathan retreat to the shadows at the side of the structure. They watch one of the civilian mechanics run out of the shop holding a Henry repeater rifle and listen as he shouts over to the men now pouring out of the blacksmith's and the wagon shop. A timber contractor's barracks at the far side of the quartermaster's yard empties of men shouting and carrying rifles. *Where are they, god-dammit? Where? They inside the fence, boys?*

"You see anything?" the mechanic shouts over to the men gathered in front of the blacksmith's.

"No. You seen anything?"

The wind brings more voices from the north end of the fort. Another shot, this one nearer.

"They close!" shouts one of the men standing in front of the smith's and he and three others with him begin to jog to the gate wicket leading into the military stockade, one carrying a storm lantern like a beacon. They pass within ten feet of Kohn and Jonathan. Men clop up onto the rough boards of the sentry stands along the palisade. Orders are barked in high-pitched panic.

Kohn says to Jonathan, "Two, maybe three." He pauses to think. "Maybe four but I don't think so."

Jonathan nods, his face blank in the shadows.

"No killing, Jonathan . . . if we can help it. If we don't need to."

Again, Jonathan nods and Kohn imagines that if he told the Pawnee there were ten men in the shop and they were going in to kill every one of them he would respond the

336

same. Kohn nods back and when the mechanic rushes past to follow the smith's men, he and Jonathan make their way across the yard to stop in front of the smith's. They stand to either side of the door and Kohn signals that it is time to begin. He raps hard on the door with his gloved fist and waits.

They hear movement from inside and can feel the heat of the forge's fires through the walls. The smell of iron and wood and coal smoke. The door opens and orange light from inside the shop stretches out across the mud in front of the shop. "What —"

Kohn grabs the man by the shirtfront and jerks him outside. Recognition flashes in his mind as he acts. The private working the bellows. The smiling boy not smiling now. All this in an instant and Kohn swings the mallet he took from the shop earlier. The sound of it against the soldier's skull is like that of a melon dropped on cobbles and Kohn wonders briefly if he has killed the boy but does not stop because Jonathan is in through the open door now carrying a small, thick shield in his left hand and a war club studded with bear's teeth in his right.

Inside are two men and one of them, the first sergeant from earlier, raises a revolver. His left hand is coming down to draw back the hammer when Jonathan smashes the pistol from his hand with the club, driving the shield into the sergeant's face, knocking him over a workbench. Jonathan looks back at Kohn briefly before leaping onto the bench and down to the earthen floor on the other side of it. As he moves for the other man, Kohn sees the war club rise and fall, rise and fall, and he hears the dull, wet thud of the blows.

But this is all in an instant because Kohn is moving for Sweetman the blacksmith at speed while the smith frantically searches for a weapon, tin mug and dinner plate crashing to the floor as he stands and pulls a poker from the resting fire and turns to Kohn. Recognition comes into Sweetman's eyes and he swings the poker at Kohn in a wild, glowing arc. Kohn can feel the heat of the poker's tip as it passes his face. An instant later it comes back but Kohn is inside the arc now and the smith is forced to adjust his swing and as he does, Kohn swings the mallet, bringing it down on the smith's collarbone in full bludgeon. At contact there is a sharp snap and Sweetman drops the poker and throws a punch with his left hand. Kohn swings the mallet again and the blow catches the blacksmith in the ribs and again there is the snapping of bones and the smith doubles over, the breath knocked out of him. Kohn forces himself to cease his attack lest he kill the man. He would like to. You have it coming you fucker, he thinks. You have it coming. He steps back and kicks Sweetman in his broken ribs instead and watches as the smith collapses to the ground.

Kohn becomes aware of a voice now and he turns to it. Jonathan stands over the first sergeant and the sergeant is begging the scout to stop, his face and neck coated with blood, his eyes stark and terrified white against the gleaming red, teeth missing from his mouth. Jonathan's face is stoical but his eyes are alive and Kohn knows he has enjoyed this work. Too much time on his back. Too much whiskey and the attentions of his winter wife. All of it a dull repose before returning to this. Kohn realizes how similar are he and the Indian. Sloth and debauch suit them both less than the fray. A good war is better than a bad peace. Born assways up, Kohn thinks. Things skewed inside men like me and the Pawnee. He watches as Jonathan sets his club on the workbench and draws his skinning knife from the beaded sheath at his belt.

"No, Jonathan. He is done. Leave him."

The scout turns to look at Kohn, the light dying in his eyes. He sheaths the knife. He does not appear angry at the loss of the sergeant's scalp. A soldier, Kohn thinks, taking what he can, whenever he can, but expecting nothing.

"Watch the door, Jonathan, while I talk to our friend." Kohn watches Jonathan cross to the door and close it most of the way. It would not be a good thing, after all, for an actual Indian to be seen within the palisade, friendly or hostile. Kohn can hear musket fire and raised voices from outside. He hopes his ruse does not result in any needless deaths but does not dwell on this. He has seen too many to care about one or two more.

"Now you," he says to the blacksmith. "You are going to show me those goat-fucking ledgers or you're going into the forge one piece at a time. Do you understand me?"

The smith works himself up to sitting with his back against a heavy press holding tools and iron scrap. He spits on the packed earth floor. "Fuck your mother, Jew. You are a dead —"

Kohn again kicks him in the ribs where he struck the mallet blow and Sweetman's eyes bulge with pain and a feral whine emanates from low in his throat. Kohn then leans down and takes the smith's wrist, limp and

340

useless under the shattered collarbone. The smith roars with pain. He raises Sweetman's hand and pins it under his own on the surface of the workbench, forcing the smith to contort himself so that he is now on his knees, pressing his good hand to his collarbone. Tears have sprung in his eyes and shine in the firelight from the idling forge. Kohn raises the mallet and the smith makes a loose fist.

"Open your fingers or I'll smash your whole hand. And then I'll start on the other and work my way down until there's nothing on you that's not broken."

The smith resists and Kohn leans down, inches from the man's face, and roars, "Open it!"

Jonathan looks at Kohn without expression and then continues his watch at the door. Kohn raises the mallet higher and begins to swing it down.

"Behind the forge, behind the forge, you bastard, behind the . . ."

Kohn stops his swing half a foot above Sweetman's knuckles. "Get up and show me." He drops the mallet onto the workbench and takes his Remington from its holster. "And if you give me reason to, I'll put your brains on that wall, do you understand me?"

"Let go of my hand."

"Get up," Kohn says, dragging the smith up by his bad arm. The smith grunts with the pain and Kohn thinks that he may pass out with it. "Get the books."

The smith cradles his bad arm with his good one and moves to the side of the forge. "There, third brick down, pull the brick out."

Kohn says, "You get back over and sit on that bench."

Sweetman does what he is told and Kohn pulls at the loose brick with his fingertips. The brick comes away after some tugging and in a larger hollow behind are three ledger books. Kohn removes them and walks over to the bench. The interior of the shop is gloomy, lit only by the open door of the main forge and the two low-burning open fires. Kohn gets up and takes a lamp hanging from one of the roof beams and shakes it to check it for oil. Satisfied, he strikes a match and lights it and sets it on the workbench between himself and the smith.

He sits down and opens the first ledger. "Keep your hands on the table," he says.

"The boys gon' be back, you know. Your Injun won't be no use for you against them. You're a dead man."

Kohn ignores the smith as he scans down the columns at the names and the amounts owed. In this first ledger are notes of purchases made by individual soldiers and the amounts owed for various items.

Sweetman spits on the floor and flinches at the pain this causes him. "One more dead fuckin' scallawag Jew like they stringin' up all over the South . . ."

The letters in the columns — blessedly not the numbers; numbers have never given Kohn difficulty — begin to drift out of line, rearranging themselves on the page and Kohn forces himself to concentrate. Because he recognizes most of the words already, he is able to quickly determine that most of the money owed in the ledger is for common items purchased by soldiers on posts all over America. Socks, shirts, boots. Tobacco, beer, canned peaches and decks of cards. Books, bolts of dressmaking fabric. Kohn notes that the same names appear more than once in this ledger. It occurs to him that the debts may be tabulated and recorded in the second or third ledger.

Kohn smiles without looking at Sweetman. "Considering I have not yet decided whether to kill you or not, I'd reckon you're a sight farther down death's road than I am, bub."

He opens the second ledger and is pleased to discover that his assumptions are correct. The soldiers are listed by name and the debt owed recorded along with a payment schedule of monies to be deducted from wages over future months. At an active, frontier post like this one extending such credit, Kohn imagines, could be a risk for the sutler. Men are killed or die by accident with some frequency and the sutler, thus, would take a loss on the debts of dead men but no robbing sutler worth his salt would do it if it were not profitable and Kohn sees debts of more than a month's salary owed in the ledger. This seems startling to him at first and his pulse rises with the possible discovery but soon he realizes there is little to his theory to be found in these pages. He continues to scan the columns, flipping through the pages. The largest debt he sees is sixteen dollars, though this is only a dollar and a half more than the next largest. There are eight or nine soldiers owing thirteen odd and many more owing ten or less. He realizes that the fort has not been established long enough for the soldiers to have accrued debts so large as to be a motive for murder.

From the doorway, Jonathan says, "Things stop outside. They are standing down now."

Kohn curses under his breath.

"The boys on they way back, Jewman. They gonna string you and the Injun up and feed you to the wolves, you black-hearted sonofabitch."

"Shut your mouth or I'll stuff that god-damned mallet in it," Kohn says, opening the last ledger now. He looks over to Jonathan. "How long?"

"Not long. Or we fight again." There is something in his voice that tells Kohn he would relish the chance.

Kohn quickly scans the names and the pages in the third ledger and is confused at first. Like the first book, this ledger lists individual purchases but they are almost always the same. He recognizes one name from the two previous ledgers and traces his finger along the lines to discover that the debtor had bought on the 19th of August: *Whiskey and 1 hr, Martha.* On another date: *Whiskey x 2 jugs, 1/2 hour Martha, $14 total.* Kohn realizes that before him is the debt ledger from the sutler's off-post brothel. The debts here are, in many cases, larger than in the first two books. He smiles.

"I'll be taking this one," he says, closing it and slipping it into his tunic.

"I can't collect out that one any goddamn way. They ain't official owings. The rest I can collect."

"These?" Kohn asks, standing, holstering his revolver, picking up the first two ledgers.

"Yeah, them. You gon' go now or you gon' stay and meet the boys?"

"Oh, I'd like to meet them, I would. Jonathan would especially, though none of you nativists have much in the way of scalps worth taking."

"I'll be seeing you again, Jewman."

"I'll be expecting it. You just get yourself better first and then we'll have a fine old time. A dandy scrap."

"You just leave them books there. And we'll set a time and a place for you to meet your Jew god."

"Sadly, we share the same god, smithy. And He does not give a penny fuck for you or me."

"You just leave down them books or —"

"These books?" Kohn says again, holding them up.

"Yeah . . ." There is fear now on Sweetman's face. Genuine worry for the first time since Kohn and Jonathan entered the shop. The smith knows what is coming.

"Here?" Kohn says. "Leave them here? Or what about here, bub?"

Kohn nods at the forge and smiles at the smith. From the doorway, Jonathan says,

"They are coming now. Through the gate. His men."

The smith says, "No, there ain't no need for . . . you seen what you need to see. Just set them two books down and take the other. You —"

"Growing up, you know, Corporal, books brought me nothing but rum consternation. And now look at what they've brought you . . ." Kohn turns and works the forge's bellows, bringing the fire to a roar. He then tosses the two ledgers into the flames and almost immediately they begin to smolder and then, in an instant, ignite in the intense heat.

"You fucker. You pig-fucker, I'll —"

"You should have shown them to me like I asked, you fool. You'd be twenty sheets richer and still have the books. Live and learn, *mein fraynd*. Live and learn."

Kohn resists the urge to knock the smith off the bench with his fist and instead moves to the door to follow Jonathan out into the darkness. If the smith's returning men see them, they do not pursue. Kohn imagines they will have less motivation for violence on Sweetman's behalf once they discover they will receive no more income from the collection of their comrades' debts. The first man whom Kohn hit with the mallet stirs on the ground as they pass him and Kohn notes that, at least, he has not killed him.

27

HOW WE 1ST MET DEAR RIDGEWAY GLOVER (MAY GOD GIVE HIM REST)

It is now that I must write of Ridgeway though it breaks my heart to do it. That poor boy May He Rest At The Right Hand Of God well he had no business being with us that night or any other. Pure innocent was that Quaker boy & I never learnt in full how he come to be attached to us in the 18th here at Ft. Phil K but that he must of had a high up Big Bug of a pal somewheres or maybe his father did & this Big Bug drafted perhaps a letter to Col. Carrington asking for Ridgeway be taken on for to make pictures of the West for newspapers back East & for the museums of Washington as he told us. It must have been something like this & be careful what you do wish for in this life.

For he was not cut out to live among

soldiers such as us. He was not cut out for this world <u>at all</u> you could say & you would know it from the moment you lay your eyes upon him with his long fair hair & smooth face & bright eyes. He was a sight I tell you with his bow back saddle mule to ride & his rebellious pack mules weighed down with his picture making kit & tent & sundries. This world is too rough & ugly a place for the like of that boy & I did love him because of it.

This page is wet with my tears thinking that if we just left him be he would be still with us walking the Earth & making his lovely pictures. But soldiers never leave a thing alone that can be messed up or mocked or may offer something new & rare to cut through the drudge that does be a soldier's life & poor Ridgeway was just such a rare thing as to draw our attention.

We had a fire up & smoking & the dog robber brewing coffee & fixing his pot for grub some few days after we left the talks at Laramie (a day or 2 after laying eyes on Chief Spotted Tail's dead daughter on her funeral frame with the carrion birds about her) & one of the boys spied Ridgeway a short piece away from us lighting down from his mule.

Franzy Hegland I think it was who spot-

350

ted Ridgeway. Poor Franzy who lays under the hard ground now his body 1/2 ate by wolves before we claimed what was left of him after the woodtrain was ambushed back in October. A fine lug of an Ohio German boy we do miss him. <u>Dutch</u> we called him as we did many Germans in the same way the Germans call us Mick or Pat.

Well when he spied the Picture Maker he said, "Looky boys at the fair doll on the malty." Turning to one of his Dutchy pals he did say something else in their language & though none but the German lads could understand it we all took his meaning as the <u>fair doll</u> was at the time bent down afixing one of the straps on his box of tricks. Well we did all giggle like soldiers are wont & one of the boys grabbed hold of his mate by the shoulders for to show us all what he would do to that yellow haired pet who of course we all did recognise to be a fellow with fine long fair hair & no woman at all. But the locks on him could throw a lonely soldier in the wrong direction I suppose. In truth I hardly ever did see hair like it on any girl & this was likely Ridgeway's curse in the end. There is not a single savage in the whole of the Dakotas who would not of coveted such locks hanging from his shield or saddle. But that does come later.

351

Aside from his hair well Ridgeway's face did be as plain as any fellow's as you did see yourself neither handsome nor ugly but normal though it was different from a regular soldier's mug for you could spy the innocence in it or in his blue eyes maybe.

Of course innocence to a soldier is oft like a red rag to a bull as you know Sir but such was the picture maker's manner that when he became better known to the boys of our Company well the boys did scarcely rag or ruse him at all & were altogether fond of him & considerate of his needs as a maker of photographic pictures & fine gentleman to have around the fire. This was the case until the end when the boys did catch him speaking to you & your terrible Jew. They did shun him then as an informer. I heard they did though I was not there to see it & I do not blame you Sir for this but only blame myself who should of done better by him & Tom who ——

Well I will write no more of this now but will do it later God Help Me.

But that first evening Ridgeway set his camp up fair near C Company bivouack he surely must of heard our laughing at his expense & he did finally look over to us seeing with his own eyes the sight of Sandy Abe making a show of riding young Gianni

Naps or Napoli John as we did call him. Well Ridgeway saw all this & surely did know it was he inspired it but did he curse us or wave his angry fist at the implication that because he had such a handsome head of locks he must be some queer kind of fore & after? No he did not & this does show his innocence for he only stood up & smiled & waved Howdy. He was pure innocent I tell you & it is them who life creases first & not the rum b_____ the blaggards & hard-shaws & jackanape f_____ from the front of the saloon. No for God in his wisdom sees fit to take from us the kind & good & the makers of beautiful things instead of the bad articles. He takes boys like Ridgeway who seek to show the world a prettier place than it is in truth. God takes them as if there is not enough of them in Heaven already.

I tell you Sir it would be better we shunned him like a leper & he might still be walking the Earth & fabricating his pictures of mountains & old tame Indians & serious soldier Bills who think for the time it takes to expose a picture that they are Grant or Sherman for the day instead of some worth-less body sent to die in the wilds of the Dakotas with no hair on his head nor nuts tween his legs. It shames me that we did

353

not shun him when we could of but how could we know then what we know now? Only God Himself could know it & in His wisdom He did nothing to stop what was coming.

So we did not shun him when he took to riding with us the next morning Ridgeway afraid maybe his mules would again give up the ghost & leave him adrift & sucking the dust of the march in Sioux country though I never once heard him say one word agin the savages from the 1st day we met. It was trotting beside us that we came to know the boy & over time brung him tight into our fold. He came to be like a member of C Company which is a thing hard to do for a civilian lad & he did it in no time at all.

It is strange & wonderful how we came to speak to him as we rode the parched trail along the banks of the North Platte. There was 103 degrees of heat & dust upon us with him following close by us all morning stopping when we stopped & riding when we rode & I did say in Gaelic to Tom, "That fellow with his mules is like little Eoin Tom God Rest Him. Do you remember Tom? How he was ever following in our wake little Eoin?"

Says Tom, "Bound to make a priest that boy."

Just low chat like that in the language of home low & melancholy talk of past days we will never see again of memories of that small beloved boy who we did not dote upon 1/2 enough when he lived our poor mite of a brother taken from us by the famine fever that took our father as well.

"Like a pup," says I a hard knot raising up in my throat right there in the baking desert heat a sadness coming on me from nowhere as it does betimes. I think it is a pining for a place & for faces you will never see again in this world & likely not in the next for the faces you mourn will likely be in the One Place while Tom & myself well we will likely be in Another.

But I tell you of this because it is then that Ridgeway the innocent Quaker Picture Maker clopping with his mules behind did pipe right up & break into chat with us. Says he, "A brother of yours boys?"

"He was," says I. "Not 4 years of age when God did take him from us —"

I did stop then & watched Tom twist round in his saddle to stare back at the Quaker boy.

"Where did you get your Irish Sir?" asks my brother & only then did I catch it. Ridgeway the son of Pennsylvania Quakers people of wealth & fine manners was after understanding & speaking the Gaelic of our home country. I did open a space between my brother & myself for the Picture Maker & his mules.

Says he in Irish that was cracked & ill fitting & childish but no matter because it was Irish says he, "My nurse from a baby was from the hills of Achill. She was like a mother to me. She does work still for my family minding my sister's children in Philadelphia alongside her own. I —" He did say the word imagine in English as he did not know the word in our language. Says he, "I imagine she scolds my nephews in the Gaelic as she did me."

I could hear the Mayo in his words now the Connacht Irish in them which is only a small bit different than the Irish of Munster that we speak. His was much like the Galway Irish you speak Sir if you would speak it to me.

Says I in English back to him, "Well don't that just beat the Dutch. I did not mean to call you a puppy Sir. It was our small brother God Rest Him who I meant."

"Of course I never took it another way Sir. You must forgive me as well. I have forgotten most of my Irish but can understand some still. I have trouble understanding yourself Tom please forgive me." He seemed happy to talk now in English as it was easier for him of course.

Says Tom, "And I am better in Irish than English Sir!" And he laughed.

Says Ridgeway in his innocent way which allowed him to speak of Tom's damaged face & his muddy words when no one else dared to, "But I will try my best to understand you Tom because I do love to hear Irish spoken & think you have many fine things to say."

"I will try to speak as clearly as my mouth allows me Sir," says Tom.

"Call me Ridgeway please. Ridgeway Glover of Philadelphia Pennsylvania," says he again in the Gaelic. "My friends call me Ridgeway & I pray we may now call ourselves friends?"

"We may of course," says Tom holding out his hand. "And I pray you will ride with us when we are not riding to orders & we will see you right talking the old talk all the while."

"That would be just fine boys I thank you," says he. "At least we may then ensure the forward motion of my mules for they have taken a shine to your mounts. They think they are after joining a cavalry troop! Would you like a smoke boys?"

He was like that dear Ridgeway innocent

& never taking offence at things always free & generous with anything he owned. In truth he was the sort of fellow who would make yourself more innocent & kindly just by being with him. He did this for me & how did I repay it?

I will tell you again Sir that it is not the crime you accuse me of that I feel any guilt for but only for how poor Ridgeway did get caught up in it. That poor boy was like a fly in a spider's web & it was Tom & myself the creeping black spiders to weave that web. My heart breaks to think of it.

I am sorry but I cannot write more now for if I do I think I will die here in this cell from the shame & guilt of what came to befall that boy.

God Forgive Us. (But I do not think He will.)

28

Kohn sits in a chair at Molloy's bedside and hands him a packet of cheroots and the ledger book. He strikes a match and lights the captain's smoke.

"How are you feeling today, sir?"

"Grand as a pasha, Kohn. Fit as a fatted calf. My leg, the good surgeon has reassured me, shall remain attached to my body. I'll be riding again in no time . . ."

Molloy winks and Kohn smiles.

"That is capital, sir. I'm glad to hear it and so will be the ladies of the Mountain District, I'm certain."

Molloy examines the ledger, front and back. "So, good Daniel, were you compelled to kill the poor bastard in possession of this book before you took it?"

Kohn smiles. "I didn't have to kill a single soul, sir. Though, as you said yourself, some

359

may have deserved it. And I destroyed the other ledgers, the ones with the debts listed from the post sutler's store."

"You have taken bread from Uncle Sam's gob, Daniel, shame on you. Render unto God what is His; unto Uncle give nothing."

"It has done marvelous things for my standing with the men of the fort. I am a hail fellow well met."

"Father Christmas with a snipped prick."

"A present of a bottle of whiskey was left for me in my quarters with a note reading only 'Thanks a bunch Soreass.' And I believe it was not poisoned."

Molloy's nostrils flare as if scenting the sourmash and Kohn wishes he hadn't mentioned it.

"No better way to express one's gratitude than a bottle," Molloy says. "Did you bring it?"

"Here." Kohn takes the ledger back from the officer, ignoring his question. "Let me show you what I've found."

He flicks through the pages and waits for Molloy's disappointment to fade.

"You see here," Kohn says. "O'Driscoll, Thomas. Private, C Company."

Molloy scans down the columns to where Kohn indicates with his finger, the whiskey forgotten. "Twenty-nine dollars."

"Yes. More than twice what the man with the next highest debt owes. And that is a civilian timberman. A sawyer, it says, owing . . . fourteen dollars twenty cents. And I've discovered that those boys, most of them, the civilian contractors, they're on near a dollar a day, making that fellow's debt smaller again."

"You've been busy, Kohn. Why in God's name did you take on with the army for if you planned on working for a living?"

Kohn laughs and lights a cigar. "My mother always said that if you're going to eat pork, let it be good and fat, sir."

Molloy traces his fingers over the entries and smokes his cheroot. After some moments he says, "Most of the debt appears to be for assignations" — he smiles at Kohn — "with one Sarah. Or *Sara* as it is sometimes spelled. The same girl, I would imagine. Herself a bargain, this Sarah, at three bucks per hour or one dollar and seventy-five cents for fifteen minutes. There is a fine lot a man can accomplish in the company of a good woman in fifteen minutes. And here," Molloy says, pointing with his cheroot. "Five dollars for 'rest of the night.' There is true love underlying these raw sums, Daniel."

"Three dollars and a quarter for whiskey

and tobacco and all the rest of it on this 'Sarah.' " The name again sparks in Kohn's memory, as it did the first time he saw it, but just as quickly is extinguished.

"And here," Kohn says, dragging his finger down the page to another name. "Michael O'Driscoll, Private, also of C Company. His brother, this Thomas, do you think, sir?"

"Could be, Dan, though it is a common enough name in Cork and parts of Waterford. Not unusual. Eight dollars he owes, for time passed with one 'Two Doves' and the rest for whiskey. A man after my own heart, this Michael O'Driscoll. A countryman surely."

"Yessir," Kohn says. "I've been told Two Doves still plies. In a tipi just outside the stockade. Near the loafer Indians but apart from them."

"A whore in a tipi. I have heard everything now, Daniel, I have."

"Of the other whores who worked the hog ranch, there is no sign. Though . . . ." And now he remembers. Sarah. The maidservant he met hanging the colonel's laundry.

"Sir, I know who Sarah is. She is the girl working for the Colonel."

Molloy smiles. "Well done, Kohn. You are a true, stinking Pinkerton."

"We should arrest him, sir, this Thomas O'Driscoll. We can report to Colonel Carrington and get him to provide us with an escort. O'Driscoll is an Irish name, no offense, sir, and C Company a strongly Irish company. We will need men with us to arrest him without violence, sir."

"Arrest him? Without violence?" Molloy says, handing the ledger back to Kohn and smoothing his bedclothes. "For what, pray tell me?"

"He has a clear motive for killing Mr. Kinney, sir. His affections for the girl and the amount he owed the man."

"Both of which can be seen clearly in this ledger of yours?"

"Yessir."

"Making him the one who killed the sutler, robbing bastard that he was, and his poor lady wife?"

"Of course, sir."

"We can prove this? With this list of sums owed for bottles drunk and whores fucked in a murdered man's kip?"

"It's clear as day, sir. Everyone in the camp knows that it was not Indians who killed the sutler and his wife. It has to be this O'Driscoll, sir. The guilt is there in ink on the page."

"Guilt? Many's the thing written in ink by

363

scoundrels of innocent men, Daniel. You as a Jew should know this. Do you not suppose that the presumption of innocence applies to the man?"

For once, Kohn can detect no cynicism in the captain's voice. No wheedling facetiousness.

"This is the army, sir. I don't imagine the same rules apply as do in the world outside."

"A place that will accept the likes of yourself and myself in its ranks is surely a place where all civil standards have been abandoned but that does not make this O'Driscoll fellow guilty of a crime. Not without the weight of an accumulation of evidence to back the claim. Or a witness. A witness would help our cause, Kohn, if our cause is to have a man hanged who did all in camp a great service by gutting the sutler." Molloy smiles. "May he rest at the right hand of God in Paradise, of course."

There, Kohn thinks, Molloy is returned to himself again. "Sir, no man in this camp is without guilt for something."

"That may be true, dear Daniel, but there is every possibility that no man in this camp is guilty of carving up the sutler and his wife."

"Sir, the sooner we have a man in irons, the sooner we can select a new regiment.

The sooner we can be away from this place."

Molloy shakes his head. "Kohn, you realize you are condemning any man you arrest to the rope, don't you? Cooke wants a man for it, whether he is guilty of the crime or not. I, for one, will not supply the good general with an innocent one."

"Sir —"

"Help me up, for the love of God. I am sick to my teeth of this bed and that queer surgeon and his drams and potions and soft talk. Help me up, by God, and we shall go and pay a visit to Miss Two Doves and see what she can tell us."

"Sir, you shouldn't —"

"Should and shouldn't be damned, Kohn. You shouldn't be so eager to see your fellow soldiers hang for your own convenience. We will talk to your whore in her tipi and if she can place young O'Driscoll in the hog ranch when its owner and his mistress met their demise, well, then we will have a quiet word with him," Molloy says.

Kohn is stung but does not show this. He helps Molloy to his feet and into his uniform, his muffler scarf and his buffalo coat. He props the crutches under Molloy's arms and leads him to the door of the hospital barracks.

"Are you sure you are fit for this, sir? It is

bitter cold."

"Damn you, Kohn, if I didn't think you were so dangerous to your fellow man, I would have stayed in bed. Stop fussing for the love of God."

"Yessir."

They pass through the camp, crossing the parade ground in front of the headquarters barracks. The sky is a leaden roil of snow-bloated cloud. A cutting wind swipes down from the north. Late afternoon and the light of day is slowly dying.

"Will we pay our respects to the colonel, sir? You haven't met him."

"Jesus in heaven, no, Kohn. You are full to the brim with terrible ideas today. Hang this man at once. Visit the goat-buggering colonel. Visit a *colonel,* Kohn, of our own free will? Can you hear yourself at all when you talk such balls?"

"No sir, only I thought —"

"Stop thinking, Daniel. You'll do yourself an injury."

They exit the fort at the main, north-facing gate. Sentries stand picket on the palisade and a sergeant and several men glass the hills from a raised bastion in anticipation of the returning woodtrain. Beside them, an artillery crew loads and chocks the mountain howitzer.

A worn path takes them from the front of the fort along its western palisade, past the steam-powered sawmill and to the collection of tipis on the Little Piney River that is the fort's source of water. The ground is frozen in places, thawing mud in others, and is hard going for Molloy on his crutches. As they make their way toward the loafer camp, Kohn scans the hills and grazing fields, the woods at the riverside. He does not like being exposed, outside the fort with the captain in his state of limited mobility. It is odd, he thinks. He feels exposed and diminished without his horse in the way another man might without his clothes.

Coming to the loafer camp, Kohn stops at a tipi somewhat removed from the others. A large dog lounges in front of the dwelling and opens its eyes at their approach but does not rise. The tipi flap is closed but opens as if their approach has been observed from a distance and Jonathan steps out into the cold.

"Brave scout, my left leg has come to thank you, sir," Molloy says.

Jonathan nods.

"We are in need of your services, Jonathan. Come with us, good man."

Again, Jonathan nods. He turns and re-enters the tipi, speaks to someone inside,

367

then steps out to rejoin them.

"And who is that, my Pawnee friend? A visitor perhaps?" Molloy says, winking at the scout. He smells the whiskey on Jonathan's breath and his stomach knots with yearning.

"My woman," Jonathan says, walking ahead of Kohn and Molloy, passing the tipis of the few friendly Northern Cheyenne families wintering in the shadow of the fort. Dogs bark and nip at their heels and Molloy swings a crutch good-naturedly at one.

"Your wife has joined you? What luck," he says.

"It's not his proper wife, sir. It's his 'winter wife' he calls her," Kohn says.

"Ah yes, if only we foolish Christians were allowed such an option, the sum of our marital happiness would be greatly increased. Jews, Daniel, I believe to be similarly proscribed in their preference for seasonal wives?"

"Yessir," Kohn says. Then, "Jonathan, we need to speak Indian to the whore . . . the squaw, Two Doves. Can you speak her tongue?"

Jonathan nods and continues walking. They reach the end of the small collection of Cheyenne tipis and follow the narrow river, sheened with a thin layer of ice, around a bend that takes them from view of the fort. Some fifty yards around the bend, in a rough clearing littered with the detritus of past floods, is a solitary tipi. It is smaller than the others they have passed, its buffalo hide coverings dulled gray with age, rotting and fire-scorched and holed in places. In front of the tipi, extending out from its entry flap, an awning constructed of lodgepoles and more tattered hides provides meager shelter from the elements for those outside the tipi. A fire smolders under the awning, a rusting, battered pot half-buried in its ashes. Next to this fire, on a pile of thick buffalo rugs, sits a woman staring into the fire, her eyes watering with the cold or the smoke.

"Two Doves?" Kohn says as they step under the awning. "Are you Miss Two Doves?"

Jonathan says something to her and gestures with his hands. Kohn knows there is a universal sign language that the disparate Indian tribes use to communicate and that there are common words to many of the tribes, much in the way of French and Italian or German and Yiddish.

To nobody she says, "My cookpot is here because the bluecoats no like sniff of dog stew when they in tipi. Two Doves cook out in the cold."

Jonathan squats on his haunches close to the woman and gestures at Molloy and Kohn. He speaks to her, slowly, clearly, while signing with his hands, but the woman does not — will not — look at him.

Staring into the fire, she is silent for a long moment. When it comes, her English is broken but clear. "I no speak to Pawnee snake. I speak to bluecoats or anybody but no Pawnee. Pawnee snakes kill my baby kids, girl and boy. Kill my man and my people. Kill my life, all my life, so Two Doves is whore now. I no speak to Pawnee snake."

The woman spits into the fire. Her bare feet are cracked and filthy. She wears a matted buffalo rug about her shoulders and a blue gingham skirt. Her hair is black and braided. There are the last vestiges of her pride in the care she has taken with her hair, Molloy thinks. She must once have been a beauty. She smokes a clay pipe and the pipe smoke and her breath mingle with smoke from the fire. Her eyes are small cuts in a drink-swollen face and in them Molloy sees great sadness. He wonders has she whiskey for the sadness. It is one certain cure for it. Death is another. He can smell it on the woman. Whiskey. Death. He has a flashing memory of a mother in Tennessee, wailing over the bloodied body of her son.

He says, "May I sit with you, ma'am?"

"Pay money or pay something to eat, to drink. Then sit with Two Doves. One dollar for fucking. One hand of coffee for Two Dove mouth. Fresh bean. One —"

"Kohn, pay the woman," Molloy says, lowering himself onto the buffalo hides and setting his crutches to the side. He pats the woman's arm. "Just talking, missus. Just some easy words between us."

Kohn begins to rummage under his great-coat for his purse but before he can find it Jonathan hands Molloy a bottle of amber liquid. "I will go back now," the scout says.

Molloy says, "Jonathan, you are a fine man. As fine a man as any I've met on my travels. The good lady will be much inclined to forgive the depredations served upon her people by yours, in exchange for what is behind the glass of this bottle, God bless you."

"Sir —" Kohn says.

"— *whisht,* Daniel." Molloy hands the bottle of whiskey to the woman. "I'll have a small chat with the woman while you wait over there by the river. Stand picket so that we are not bushwhacked by her cousins, for the love of Christ. Make yourself useful."

Kohn watches Jonathan return the way

they came. "Sir, I'm begging you, sir."

Molloy whispers something to Two Doves and the woman laughs.

"It will be dark soon, sir," Kohn says. He stalks over to the river's edge, the bank a steep drop of several feet. Across the narrow, winter-sparse waters, across the grazing land that ends in the nearby hills, he can see the procession of horses, men and wagons that comprise the woodtrain. From behind him he can hear voices. In the woman's voice is laughter, occasionally, and the give and take of conversation, and Kohn wonders idly on the impression that Molloy has upon all those who meet him. From the most depraved and desperate of whores and alcoholics to generals and lawyers and men of means, all take to the captain. All laugh with him, dip their heads to him in confidence. It is a gift he has.

The cloud cover thins briefly, as if in anticipation of night, and over the distant Big Horns the sky flares orange and pink, the clouds painted and washed with dying sunlight, and Kohn watches them. It will be dark soon. They should not be this far from the fort without horses, so lightly armed and immobile.

"Daniel," Molloy calls over to him. "Come help me up, please. I cannot manage on my own steam."

Kohn hears the Indian woman laugh as he turns around and walks to the awning. He lifts Molloy to his feet and hands him his crutches. Molloy stinks of whiskey but Kohn notes that Two Doves is holding the bottle and it is two-thirds full. It does not matter, he thinks. One drop is enough to start him.

"You may thank Miss Two Doves, Kohn," Molloy says, more heat in his jesting now, in his bonhomie. "She has been a most helpful witness. There is little a bottle won't buy a man in this life, Kohn. Very little. You'd do well to remember that."

As they begin to walk, gingerly, over the half-buried river stones to the path, Kohn says, "Well, was Private O'Driscoll there that night? Was he there when the sutler was killed?"

"She didn't know. She does not know the names of the men she meets, and I can understand that as well as anybody," Molloy says, merrily. "But she did know a man who will know a man . . ."

"Goddammit, sir, will you tell me what she told you or not?" Kohn says, stopping as they reach the bend in the river in sight of the loafer camp.

Molloy smiles. "Now now Daniel, there is

no need to be vexed. You are sad I've taken a sup and well you should be. But I am not sad, by fuck. I am happy and I mean to continue this evening. In the morning, dear heart, we will go see the 'man who makes pictures.' You have seen his work already I believe."

"Yes, but what does he have to do with anything? I already —"

"He was there, good Daniel. The night when the blades flashed and blood spilled and all was lost for the Secretary of the Treasury's brother-in-law and his wife and the other poor bastard who happened to be present. The photographer was there. By God he might as well have photographed the murders, according to my good friend Miss Two Doves. So let us celebrate, Danny boy. There are few enough things in this life worth celebrating."

"Yessir," Kohn says, walking on ahead of Molloy, almost beyond caring whether or not he follows.

■ ■ ■ ■

III
CITY OF LOGS

■ ■ ■ ■

The founders of a new colony, whatever Utopia of human virtue and happiness they might originally project, have invariably recognized it among their earliest practical necessities to allot a portion of the virgin soil as a cemetery, and another portion as the site of a prison.
— NATHANIEL HAWTHORNE,
THE SCARLET LETTER

29

A BAD SPOT FOR A FORT

— *December 20, 1866* — Well in mid July we did at last haul up & end our march in this Valley but Mr. Bridger & a few of the others (the old hand scouts & Indian fighters in buckskin & the like) well they did not like at all this spot Carrington finally chose to build his fort.

At the time we did think this objection queer but we are just lowly Bills & not much are we in the way of strategising or tactical thinking. We are paid from the neck down is the saying & there is truth to it. But to look at this place in summer it does appear a grand fine spot for building. It is as pretty as a painted picture on the banks of a creek or river called the Little Piney which is a small branch of the Powder River that gives this Valley its name. There are miles of buffalo grass meadows about it which rise up to hills that become the mighty Big Horns which are said to be 15 odd miles away. As well there is ample forests of timber nearby for constructing this grand stockade we now call Ft. Phil Kearny & from where it sits there is a fair view some miles each way of the Bozeman Trail to be defended.

I am told this is the A–No. 1 reason for us being here. It is to build an outpost of civilisation in the wilderness so that we may protect them headed up the Bozeman for the gold fields of Montana. This is a strange thing of course because our arrival here in the Valley has spurred the Sioux & Cheyanne to take a sterner line altogether with the pilgrims. Where before it is said that they would leave the pilgrims pass through & even aid them betimes on their journeys or trade goods & game with them well now they harry & molest & collect pilgrim scalps. No man or beast on that trail is safe from Chief Red Cloud's predations.

But we did not know or much fear the Indian then at all & our commander Col. Henry Carrington chose to build his Ft. in the very heart of the Sioux's home in this Valley surrounded by its grassy sloping hills so that Mr. Lo may peer down upon our every action.

I tell you Sir the savage does know everything about us. He knows when we leave the Ft. & when we return to it. He knows how far we must travel for timber & how many men we need for to guard the wagons to carry it. <u>This</u> is the reason why this spot is no good at all for a Ft. It is only 5 miles to the timber we need for building & though we ran a road over the hills out to the stand of trees we call the Piney Island we must come down from the hilltop road in the end for a long flat stretch & this is where they descend upon us every day to harry our woodtrain so that every day we lose men & mules & horses & wagons.

So I say to you Sir as I sit here in this bitter hell of a freezing winter Guardhouse that this is a cursed spot to spite its beauty. Bridger & the scouts knew it well from the start & now Carrington The Carpenter must know it too but we have come too far for turning.

That very 1st evening we set up camp here in this Valley you would not believe it but on the grassy rise we now call Pilot Hill 2 or 3 Indians on horseback set up watching us as we did corral the wagons & picket the horses & roll out the canvas under which we would live until we raised up proper barracks of logs. Well them Indians just sat

379

there watching us stake a claim to the fine long grass where their buffalo once grazed & they were like harbingers of death coming I tell you. Betimes I wonder now did we seem harbingers of something terrible for them too our band of wandering white faces like the first fat drops of rain to the fore of a coming storm.

But mostly I do think now that if Col. Carrington was a more bloody minded type of up & at them officer & had of loaded up the Mountain Howizter that 1st night & fired a hell of canister at them Indians on Pilot Hill well maybe Red Cloud & his Braves would imagine us to be a hot & terrible consort of soldiery & think to keep a safe distance from us. They maybe would of thought us not worth the loss of Indian blood for a mere patch of land or safe passage on a trail. But Carrington is not such a man & still has no notion of our true business here in the Valley at all & for this indecision the common soldier Bill does suffer greatly. Is it to protect the Bozeman Trail for travellers to the gold fields in Virginia City he wonders as he frets over his building plans? Establish a forceful presence in the territory we hear other officers say? Pacify the savages? Distract the Indians while the railroad is rammed through farther

South? All this is thought by the soldiers but I wonder could even Carrington tell you the truth. He could not tell you is my best guess.

The one thing Carrington <u>did</u> know is that he was to build his great Ft. in the wilderness his City Of Logs as the Sioux call it & start this we did the very day after arriving. For to be fair to him a finer man for getting forts built you will not meet. He is a great man for the planning & building & constructing of things but he is just not a fighting man when a fighting man is what is needed for a War such as we do find ourselves in.

So we set to building our home in this Valley. Well I do not need to tell you it was fatigue details from the cock crow. It was clearing & levelling the ground & chambermaiding the horses & livestock & standing picket over them for though the Indians did nothing as yet their reputation for coveting beef cattle & horse flesh did well proceed them.

And we did scout some Tom & myself (which does be another fine advantage to being a horse soldier) even riding out with Jim Bridger once or twice. Though he is a reknowned man I will say that we saw him to be some fierce kind of a blowhard &

canard spinner as we rode the valleys &
forests at the foothills of the Big Horns at
his side. Up & down the Tongue River we
rode too searching for sign of Indian camps
or war parties in our cabbage patch. We
found none of this though later we would
do when it was too late to be any good to
us which did not much recommend Mr.
Bridger as a scout. But Lord Save Us that
fellow could talk the meat from a chicken
bone he could. A blatherer I tell you though
not a bad sort he was more clown than cat
as is the saying but what he did tell rings
true enough now so maybe he is less a fool
than I thought him.

For he did regale us from horseback as we
rode with tall tales that do not seem so tall
now. He yarned of savages taking the scalps
of men still alive them victims surviving to
walk about the place with their skulls shining in the sun like billiard balls. Stories of
men standing talking to you one moment &
gagging on an arrow to the throat the next.
Stories made for to scare a man into vigilance I see now but I did think them only
nonsense then. Such is the way of soldiers
everywhere I reckon. They learn nothing
until blood is spilt.

And learn we did because of Carrington
choosing such a rum spot for to build his

City of Logs. For though in summer it may appear to be Eden itself it is a rum & cursed place I tell you Sir & I pray you will leave it as soon as your business here with me is done.

For the ground is now too hard for grave digging & the bodies be stacked like cord wood in the Q.M.'s cold cellar & soon that cellar will be full I reckon full up altogether with the bodies of men who did not see Mr. Lo coming with his hatchets bared & arrows strung & knives out for all of us who would choose to build a mighty Ft. in the heart of his Valley.

30

Molloy is not in his sickbed and Kohn is not surprised.

"Never came back," says one of the surgeon's orderlies. "Found what he been looking for I reckon, Sergeant. You might try the junior officers' kip. There was a time had there last night or so the scuttle says."

Kohn sighs.

He crosses the parade ground and knocks at the door to the junior officers' barracks and waits some time for his knock to be answered. The morning air is sharp and still and numbing cold under an almost turquoise tub of sky. A man can see that the sky is a round, bowled thing out here in the empty expanses, Kohn thinks. He has heard it is the same at sea. He waits for another minute and knocks again until the door is opened by a bleary-eyed man in his under-

384

shirt, unshaven, snarling.

"What in God's goddamn name —"

"I'm looking for Captain Molloy, sir," Kohn says, knowing how to broach a drunk and angry officer. It is his lot in life, his cross, Molloy would say, to bear. "The colonel wants a word. Colonel Carrington." Kohn also knows to invoke higher powers when negotiating higher powers than himself. In truth he has neither seen nor heard from Carrington since his original meeting with the man.

"I know who the goddamn colonel is. You don't have to tell me." The officer rubs his face, squinting in the harsh winter daylight. "Who does he want? Does he want to see me?"

Kohn remains impassive. "No, sir. It's Molloy, 7th Cav, he wants to see."

The officer wipes a dried paste of spittle from his mustache. "Well, there is a hobbled cav lieutenant asleep in front of the stove if that's who you mean. I never did get his name."

The officer turns away, leaving the door ajar for Kohn to follow. Inside the barracks two bunks hold sleeping men. The other four are empty, bedclothes in disarray. The air is cold and rank, the stove door gaping, cold ashes in its belly. There is something

385

chaotic and unkempt about the barracks. Officers are under less scrutiny from their seniors than that in which they themselves hold their men but in Kohn's experience, their quarters are generally well squared away. They have men to do it for them after all. Perhaps here at Phil K., things being stretched as they are, the men of the fort are needed for things other than cleaning the officers' billets.

"Sir," Kohn says. Molloy is snoring fitfully, wrapped in a buffalo coat on the floor in front of the stove, his breath visible in the stale, morning-after air. Kohn nudges his shoulder with his boot. "Sir, where are your crutches?"

The officer who answered the door swallows the remains of a glass of whiskey from a long table littered with bottles, mugs, empty peach cans and herring tins. Cigar stubs stud the floorboards. The officer winces and says, "He burned them, last night, when we ran short of firewood. Capital man, the lieutenant." The officer smiles. There are dark circles under his eyes, a haunted look about him. Spooked, Kohn thinks. Like a dog beaten too many times. "Capital man."

"Sir, you have to wake yourself, sir," Kohn continues, knowing how long it will take.

The day will be half over, he thinks, by the time he is able to attend to the investigation, whether or not Molloy will insist on attending to it with him. He thinks to leave him asleep and then worries that to do so will worsen Molloy's pneumonia and he will not be responsible for the captain's death from pleurisy, not after all they have been through together. He will preside over it but he will not be responsible. In his heart is a roil of disgust and sadness, regret for the weakness of man and his wretched, wicked wars and what they do to the good men who fight them. Men like Molloy. Like himself. *Gott sol undz helfn.* God help us.

He slings his officer over his shoulders, noting how light Molloy has become. There is less of the man now than once there was.

In the hospital barracks, Kohn is thankful the surgeon is detained with a patient, a logger with a crushed ankle. Another amputation, Kohn imagines, settling in for half an hour of Molloy vomiting up stringy gluts of yellow bile into a pail before he can run a bath for him.

Two hours later Kohn returns to the hospital barracks and he does not care if the surgeon sees him or not.

Kohn stands over Molloy's bed and

387

watches him. The officer's eyes are closed but they clench and flutter, in thrall to terrible memory in the form of nightmare. Standing there, Kohn wonders if Molloy is dreaming of a Tennessee river town; of how in victory those in Union blue are raging, famished and spoiled to loot, putting fire to what will burn. Papers and smoke spilling from the courthouse windows, flames licking at the redbrick and Molloy has told the remains of the cavalry company he commands that he will not tolerate the harassment of women. He has warned them that, Confederate women though they may be, they are still American women and he will shoot or hang any man who lays a finger on one. He can do nothing about the infantry or artillery troops roaming the town. There is a distillery and it was emptied before being set alight. Darkness will see some hell in the town but Molloy has his own bottle in his haversack and has drunk some from it. The fierce thirst of a five-day siege. The air stinking of rot and char. Bodies bloating in the sun. Molloy and his men ride a sweep for holdout rebels; for raiders or snipers or the just plain suicidal.

The house is set back from the road out of town and appears untouched. Out of range of the shells that rained on the riverfront. Abandoned? No. There are cows in a side field, a horse harnessed to a buggy and tied off to a porch rail. No wind, tall oaks and a willow hang heavy about the property in high summer green. The house is too quiet to be abandoned. Molloy and Kohn, both, have seen it before often enough. The owners are inside, maybe in the root cellar or the hayloft but they are there, praying they will remain undiscovered, as if such a thing were possible. More fearful of losing their stock and possessions than careful with their lives. Poor fools. Molloy is not without pity for them. He would, he imagines, be the same if the situation were reversed. No matter. The cows will be beefsteaks quick as dickens and the horse requisitioned along with the buggy. Molloy will take one of the cows for his men and the horse and buggy to trade for supplies or to hand over to the medicals, though it is a fine buggy and will more likely end up the personal possession of a higher-ranking officer than himself before the medicals ever get it. Such is the way of war but this is not why they have approached the house. The grass is beaten down in the cow pasture, signalling that rebel troops have likely passed through here in their retreat from the town, entering the forest behind the field.

Molloy and Kohn and two other riders thunder down the path to the front of the house, the rumbling hoof beat oft-times enough to convince those in a house that surrender is the best option available to them. They pull up outside, horses excited, snorting, pleased with the gallop and the distant smell of powder, the random popping of musket fire from town like corn in a hot covered pot. War horses. Molloy's mare rears her head and peers with disdain upon the horse harnessed to the buggy.

In his dream Molloy hails the owners of the house. "Come on out. The town has fallen. You will not be harmed if you —"

The front door to the house opens.

Molloy sees it is a boy but the Remington is in his hand already — has hardly left it for the past God knows how many days — and he fires without thinking while at the same time his mind screams at him that it is a *boy* there on the porch. A tow-haired boy with a rifle twice as tall as he is, a danger to slow, low-flying birds with that musket and a danger to nothing much else, but Molloy has fired and a bolt is blown out of the boy's skull the size of the boy's own little fist. Molloy hears the mother keening in his sleep. The boy left the man of the house with his father's musket, protecting his mother from the great rape of the South by Grant's Army of the Tennessee. The mother ever keening in his sleep.

Molloy bolts upright and Kohn reaches out and touches his shoulder. "Sir? You were dreaming, sir. Are you all right?"

Molloy rubs angrily at his face, the hospital barracks coming into focus. He shrugs off Kohn's hand. "I will be fine, Kohn, for the love of God. Just give me the goddamned, poxing bottle, you simpering hen, you fucking nursemaid."

Tears well in Kohn's eyes as he mixes the whiskey he has bought from a contract sawyer into a cup of fresh milk. He swallows rage and hands the draught to the captain.

Molloy drinks, drinks again and closes his eyes. He burps and holds a hand to his stomach and Kohn holds out a filthy pail but after a moment the captain opens his eyes and smiles and the smile is as abject as anything that Kohn has ever seen.

"The very milk of human joy, Kohn."

"I don't think it's the milk, sir."

Molloy takes another draft and waits for it to settle within him. Then he says, "Now, Daniel. This picture maker . . ."

Kohn looks at him. "I'll have to pay one

of the surgeon's dogs for new crutches, sir
—"

"Well bloody do it, Kohn, for the love of
Christ on His cross. The day is half-wasted
already with your fiddling."

Kohn smiles because if he does not he
might knock the captain off his bed and
smash the hospital barracks to pieces with
his fists.

31

OUR FRIEND RIDGEWAY GLOVER & A PICTURE IN A MEADOW

As I did write before I think I began this testament for to tell the truth of events Sir because you are owed the truth. I once had the idea to keep a record of the events in my life but I never did do it & so this is my chance my very last chance perhaps. But as I write I find I do it now for another reason & that reason is the Picture Maker Ridgeway Glover & what happened to him. I feel that it is guilt over this that drives my pen along the pages the ink thick & slow with the cold my eyes stung with squinting in the dim lamplight. The oil for the lamp is corrupted like everything else the Army would have its men use.

As I told you we first met that lovely boy called Ridgeway on the march after we left the Laramie Peace Talks & he became our friend & as such it did be our duty to protect & guide him & before everything went sour for us we did this I swear to you as God Is My Witness we did.

But since we came upon that poor dear Ridgeway's butchered body in the long grass & your terrible Jew brought me to this Guardhouse more than 1 of the boys detailed as guards did ask me (because they too were fond of Ridgeway like all who knew him) <u>Why did he leave the safe harbour of the Ft. on his lonesome?</u> & in the silence of this cell I asked myself the same question 100 times & can halt on only 1 single answer. That poor Quaker boy was troubled over what he was witness to. His heart was blackened by it & then Tom had his words with him & then you Sir went to him & pressed him & not long after that he was seen packing his mules for the road. Oh I do not blame you Sir but I do blame Tom. I told Tom to leave Ridgeway out of it all that he had nothing to do with what happened but Tom said that he did. Tom said that he was there & that did make him a part of it. You will be wondering a part of what?

I do tell myself betimes perhaps our friend would of left the Ft. without escort anyway. He often did in the early days for to spite the danger well known to all in the Ft. well Ridgeway did not fear the world the way yourself & myself might. He did not look out into the forest & see the dark parts of it or the shadows but saw instead the fair side of things the way the heavens carve up the spaces tween the branches with their light or the way dew does sparkle in the morning grass in a sunlit meadow. He would see the world like this & he would want to make one of his pictures of it.

Many is the time we tried telling him that behind all the fine & pretty spots where he might like to make his photographs well the Powder River country is a place of rough peril & that in a sunny meadow may stalk Sioux Braves who would like nothing more than to claim a fair haired scalp such as his. But he would only smile & tell us that if a man did not think ill of others then he could only hope that others would not think ill of himself & that as a Quaker he would not raise a hand agin another man. This he did believe would keep another man from raising a hand agin himself more fool that Quaker boy May God Keep Him. Over time we became accustomed to him being here 1 minute & gone from us the next for to make his pictures of some natural wonder or Indian squaw.

So it oft happened that my brother or myself or even little Addy Metzger (a long time veteran Bill like ourselves a Dutchy bugler who does be a boon companion & liked by boys of all nations in C Company) well him or we would up & say nearly once or twice a week, "Ho boys where did Ridgeway get to now?" And we would set about to find him.

I do recall a time late in August when he did accompany a troop of us sent as the Paymaster's guard to Ft. Smith. Well we made camp the 1st night aside the upper Powder River in a clearing where there was the black remains of old camp fires Indian or trapper or Army or what we did not know but never mind it was a grand place for a bivouack & as pretty as one of Ridgeway's pictures. We caught 7 trout between us in the clear running river for to eat with our beans & pilot bread. That meal by the fire is a fine memory I will always keep with me. It was a happy time & there are not many I can recall since we came here.

Once we felt that this Valley was as close to Eden as any on Earth with its rivers & grass & mountains & clean air & plenteous game. Even now in the dead of winter you can see why the Indians fight us for to keep it. Of course if you stop long enough to wonder on it you may question the sense of losing your hair or your balls God Bless Them to a Sioux skinning knife for the taking of another fellow's country. You might wonder is it right at all to be barging in & taking it. But there is little enough time for a soldier to wonder on things & the Army does not encourage it. The Indians do nothing with this land anyway neither grazing nor farming on it so I reckon they have no right to keep it but there is them that would argue the toss over this.

But none of this did I think the next morning on that Paymaster's escort up to Ft. Smith when Tom & I woke after a good sleep to find the Quaker boy missing from his bedroll by the fire pit the embers burnt down to ashes & the morning air cool enough to see your breath with all around us but for the sentries on picket fast asleep still.

"Where's Ridgeway got to then?" says I to Tom.

"See is his picture making things —" Tom did not know yet the word for <u>camera</u> & not in the Gaelic anyway. Says he, "See if the yokes are where he left them."

"They are not," says I.

Tom heft himself up from his blankets. He is not a Hail The Sweet New Day sort of fellow at all in the mornings. Says he, "For all that is holy that boy is like a G_____ D_____ tinker travelling here & there with no cares in the world for anything but where the road does take him."

Rubbing sleep from my eyes I took myself over to one of the sentries a Swede with no English at all on him. "Did you see the picture maker Henrik?" I made with my hands the shapes of long hair & a box. "Ridgeway," says I. The Swede did catch on at last & point me to a deer trail that led away from the clearing into the woods. I suppose I wondered why he did not stop Ridgeway from leaving the bivouack as was our orders but in truth there is always trouble tween civilians & the Army for oft times no man knows who is in charge of another so mostly a soldier will say nothing for fear of saying the wrong thing to the wrong man.

So Tom & myself took up our rifles & made to follow the deer trail into the woods & I tell you in no time at all we could not hear the running of the river & night shadows still hung heavy in the trees. We kept silence between us as we walked not daring to speak or call out to the picture maker for there is something of the woods that puts fear on a man no matter his age or experience of them.

Well Thanks Be To God but shortly the trees begun to thin & the morning sun strained to shine through the branches & soon we could see another clearing. We came to it after a moment & leaving the forest & our fears behind us in the wooded shadows we found ourselves in a meadow of fine long grass & wild flowers. It was maybe 200 yds. across & it dipped down in the middle to rise up on the far side to another wood. A layer of mist was afloat in the chill air at our knees & sunlight lit the water in it making it like a swathe of shining silver cloth above the grass. And across that meadow where the ground begun to rise into the far stand of forest my eye caught a thing moving & the sound of something did break the morning meadow's silence & this sound was the low growling of a beast. More than 1 beast my eyes could now see & I tapped Tom's shoulder & pointed for him to look.

"Wolves," I did whisper to Tom in English first then in Irish too I do not know why. "Mac tire."

"And there is Ridgeway," says Tom raising his Springfield & using it to point some yds. to the right of what we now saw to be the carcass of a great deer or elk I did not know the difference then. Well it was lain out there in the wet grass that carcass the ribs of it white & bloody red & poking up like the beams of a shipwreck on a beach & 1 wolf had that dead elk's guts in his teeth like a looter at the ship's cargo. 2 other of the beasts did be at the hind of the elk snouts stained red but one was not at all at the elk's body but instead in the long grass on his belly like a snake with his hackles up & his teeth unsheathed at the figure of our friend Ridgeway whose head & shoulders were under the camera's drape with only his hand out of it for to open the lid of the camera's eye or <u>aperture</u> I did later learn to call it.

I made to say to Tom that from under the drape Ridgeway could not see the great stalking wolf at all but before I could speak Tom flicked up the leaf sight on his rifle found his range & fired on that skulking beast for Tom is a man to act before he speaks or thinks. This is good betimes & terrible others. It was good that day for the other wolves did yelp & scatter at the shot & from 200 yds. away I could see Tom's ball strike home to raise a puff of bloody fur & then bring the stillness of death to that marauder. The camera's drape was flung up then & out came Ridgeway not knowing a thing of what just happened.

Well I cast a wave of my arm to show him he was safe & that it was only us boys come to save him & he looked to me as if he could not reckon who we were at all. We trotted then over with the grass wetting our kerseys. I went to Ridgeway & Tom went to his wolf & it was only now did the Quaker boy put $2+2$ together to make 4.

"Oh I never saw that one," says he. "Did Tom shoot it Michael did he?"

"He did. That wolf would of liked you for his breakfast. You know you only need ask & Tom or myself will escort you on your picture making. You should not be off on your lonesome here in the woods & meadows boy. Sure it is not only wolves about this place & we would hate for you to lose them fair pretty locks of yours."

Ridgeway gave me a smile like he always did. Says he, "I have no fight with the Indians Michael & I do expect they will take little notice of me armed only with a camera apparatus. Wolves however may not understand my intentions or the lack of sustenance I would prove to be in any meal. So I thank you gentlemen but I just had to try for that picture. The elk & the morning light & the mist. The wolves. Do you see what I am saying? Of course they would not keep still for the exposure but —"

On & on he did rattle about the framing & exposure & composition & I did not understand all of Ridgeway's words but I looked over at the dead elk with its guts reefed from inside it. The grass about the carcass was tramped down & red with blood the flies already skirmishing & for a moment all I could see was the carnage laid down upon the elk by the wolves. In truth the sight took my mind back to the War to bodies blown to very bits chewed by grape & canister dead men in the grass & mud with their guts like the elk's strewn out as if they were ribbons tugged from a sweetheart's hair. And all of it just a matter of Good Luck John or Bad Luck Jim. God snaps his fingers & the Devil snaps your neck. For a moment this was all I could think of & all I could see there in the meadow.

Ridgeway did perhaps see my confusion. He said, "Look at it. Let your eyes see it the way they would see a picture without the smells of it without the sound or even the colours. Just look at it Michael."

And so I did & I begun to see the sun burning off the mist & the elk's ribs appeared to me now like the ribbing of an accordion & I could see the flies' wings flashing in the sunlight & the dew clinging to the grass like tiny diamonds in a queen's cloak. I <u>could</u> near see what that Quaker boy was getting at even after what the wolves done to the elk I could see it & this made me proud & happy with myself.

"And did you catch the picture Ridge-way?" says I hoping now that he did.

"No. I did not have the time needed to expose it & there was too much movement. I thought maybe the wolves might sit still for me to get my picture." He smiled at this joke.

Tom spoke up then from where he stood with his kill. "Make my picture Ridgeway. Will you make it with my shot wolf will you? I never did have a picture made of me." Tom's words in English were muddy & I did repeat them to Ridgeway.

"Why of course," says Ridgeway. "Of course I will. I am sorry I never thought to ask before."

Across the clearing came some boys from the camp breathless & drawn to the meadow by the sound of Tom's shot. I waved down at them. "All OK," says my wave.

"Tom shot a wolf," I shouted across the meadow to them forgetting my fear of Indians for the moment. Or maybe I reckoned that if the shot did not bring them to us then my shouting would not.

The boys relaxed & strolled up to us. It was Metzger Napoli Jackson Henrik the Swede & Corp. Phillips who plugged two Sioux on a passage from Laramie a few weeks after ours. My brother gave a smile to this mob & held up his wolf under the forelegs.

"I shot this big f_____ of a wolf boys. Ridgeway is going to make a picture of it. Will you be in my picture will you boys?"

Says Jackson to me, "What did he say Mick?"

"He says Ridgeway will make his photograph with the wolf & would ye care to be in it?"

All the boys perked up at the prospect. It was common enough in the War to have a tin type picture made but by chance none of us there took the time or paid the money or had the sweetheart or mother at home for to get one made. I tell you it made the boys happy now the notion of a photograph taken here in the wilds of the West in a meadow with flowers & lifting mist & a dead elk & a dead wolf & a fellow's mates around him.

Well Napoli brung out a comb from his tunic & all of us made use of it wiping down the tunics of our mates each man making like a mirror for another all of us getting

404

shipshape & arguing should we sport kepis or bare heads & tipping canteen water into kerchiefs to wipe dirt from each other's faces like mothers with their children before Mass.

"You should comb your wolf Tom," says Jackson.

"He has a finer head of hair than you have," says Tom back & when I repeated it the boys did laugh.

"And a prettier face than yours by a long piece," says Jackson & he could say it because Tom was very fond of him for Jackson was not afraid of my brother with his Rebel ball scoured mouth & his terrible rages. He did not fear Tom like some of the boys in the Company & so Tom took his rags in good sport.

"Gentlemen," says Ridgeway. "If you please."

He arranged us about Tom & his wolf making sure to get the morning light behind him as did be best. He told me things like this later for I did yearn back then to become perhaps a maker of pictures myself though I am ashamed to say it because there is not much in this world I am good at besides killing & all such dreams for the likes of me are folly in the end. But they were different days so there was no harm in it maybe.

"Now boys you will need to hold yourselves still as statues while the picture forms."

"Shame it aint a dead Injin instead of an old wolf," says Jackson & we all laughed though you could say the Indians had the last laugh at Jackson in the end.

"No smiling gentlemen please," says Ridgeway.

So we held the pose still & silent & unsmiling for our friend the picture maker Ridgeway Glover & in our stillness it came to me how queer it was the 7 of us boys from all the ends of the Earth standing there together holding stony faces like statues of marble you might see in a church but instead in a meadow of grass & yellow & purple flowers where maybe no white man ever stood before. How queer it is I reckoned that day as the morning sun burnt off the mist & warmed our bones no sound but that of birds singing & fizzing flies at the carcass & buzzing bees at the wild flowers & a strange kind of Quaker boy hiding his head beneath a drape with his hand held out on the camera's eye to let the light inside the camera box to catch it there.

And as soon as I felt this well my heart did shift & things of a sudden turned queer

& dreadful & fear came upon me & fierce terrible loneliness seized my heart. It was like the dead wolf had my heart in his teeth & I wonder now can you see this fear in my eyes in the picture though I did my mighty best not to show it then.

After some minutes the picture was done & later back at the Ft. when he cured it Ridgeway gave us each one for ourselves on paper card which made us all very happy even me with my strange heart.

Our journey back from Ft. Smith for all our prickling rifles & skittish mounts did pass quietly but there was happenings galore here in the Valley in the week we were away. Red Cloud's boys made a start attacking the woodtrain on its way to & fro Piney Island running the mules & killing two A Company boys & a civilian timberman whose body never was found God Rest Them All.

Tom skinned his wolf of course & was of a mind to give it to his sweetheart whore as a gift but she did not want it & instead he took lend of 2 dollars from me & put that with 1$ & 80¢ he won at Faro for to buy her a dress of calico with flowers on it much like them in that meadow where he shot his wolf.

In the end Tom stuck that wolf pelt to the

inside of the door to our barracks with shoeing nails. All the boys loved it & would
touch its head for luck when they went out
for back then we thought ourselves true &
proper beasts much like that wolf with his
yellow eyes & dagger teeth but this was only
foolishness & there is no fool like a soldier I
tell you.

32

OUR 1ST VISIT TO THE HOG RANCH

Upon our return from escorting the Paymaster to Ft. Smith my brother was fair flaming to see his girl but because of our duties & details & such it was a long day & night before Tom finally got down to the hog ranch to meet her & that night was the 1st time Ridgeway came with us to Sutler Kinney's rough shebeen. God Forgive Us for bringing him he never should of come but there was no keeping us Bills from the place because where there is whores so the soldiers will go once they have a spare hour & greenbacks to burn.

You see Sir we were paid our wages before leaving on the escort to Ft. Smith & because of the short pay at Laramie the month previous we all had for once fair salad in our pockets. Some of this I did bank away with the Paymaster as Tom & I agreed while the rest I kept.

Of course my brother had his wages spent already. It was owed in Faro debt & such & Tom does not bank his cut of our savings at all except for what is put aside by Uncle Sam as discharge payment. In his own defence he will claim that he has his girl to be spending money on now & he may never even live to see the day after tomorrow let alone next year so it is only right that we drink now & be merry. It was not long before he run up a fine whack of debt to the Sutler for whiskey & time passed with his sweetheart.

When we all heard about the attack on the woodtrain & the dead A Company boys it did not seem so wild Tom's way of thinking. And though this kind of thinking would never buy us a single head of cattle or a plot of land if we <u>did</u> live through this War God Willing well I did of course decide to join Tom & the boys on their skite. For prudent planning is 1 thing while a fierce thirst from the trail is another.

So we gussied ourselves up to go & as we did Ridgeway came in asked could he accompany us to which I did feel some reservation but I consented for I did not want to be the one to say No! after he took our picture so kindly in the meadow with the

410

wolf. I did try to talk him out of coming but by Carrington's orders it was in truth <u>soldiers</u> who were not permitted to venture outside the now finished stockade after darkness while Ridgeway was the only man among us who <u>could</u> freely attend the hog ranch off post without fear of sanction.

Says I to him, "You may not like it Ridgeway. The dolls are terrible rough & the whiskey is worse."

"Well if you boys would prefer I not go with you I shall take no offence Michael."

It took me a moment to work out Ridgeway's meaning. You did oft need a pause to reckon up what that Quaker boy meant when he spoke. Says I when I got it, "Of course you will be very welcome Ridgeway. The more the merrier as goes the saying. But it is a lowly place for low born men Sir."

"All men are born the same in the eyes of the Lord Michael. And you perhaps forget that I passed some time with the Army during the War making photographs. Rough whiskey is well known to me Sir," says the Quaker boy making me smile by calling me <u>Sir</u> even if it was only a way of calling attention to my using it to him.

Says Tom with his hair wet & run through with his comb him smelling all of soap his boots gleaming with saddle soap, "Well

411

come if you are coming boys. Daly does be on the livestock gate wicket for another while but we cannot be sure of silence from the next guard detailed."

Says Addy Metzger our little Dutchy pal, "What did he say Mick?"

"He says you are a short & ugly f_____ of a German hornblower Metzy & you may buy the first jug," I said because spirits were high.

"Ugly?" says Metzger turning to Tom. "You cannot call another man ugly when you can near take your dinner from either side of your face yah?"

I was a small bit fearful of such talk but Tom only smiled & shook his head at Metzy for he is very fond of that small fellow. And Addy served as a bugler in the war as well & if you lived through such a thing as that well you earned the right to call a fellow veteran Bill ugly.

And so we passed out of the stockade with Daly on gate guard turning a blind eye to us & we made our way down to Sutler Kinney's hog ranch.

Once there I soon forgot my worries & Tom did forget his & little Addy Metzger his own Dutch German worries which maybe are more worrisome than ours because he has a wife & child back home in

Ohio. To my surprise Ridgeway did not appear affronted by what he came upon in that shebeen conversing freely with the whores & even with the dark muleskinner who did so exercise my brother. I tell you Sir that Quaker supped his whiskey & stood his shout of it like the rest of us & maybe he even bought more of it than we did because he was such a generous sort. I am not certain Quakers be even allowed to take drink but Ridgeway drank his same as the rest of us & to spite what a man might think he did not succumb to its effects but merely smiled more than usual.

But of the lot of us it was Tom smiling most of all for he had his girl on his knee & did be pouring for her fine drafts of trade whiskey which she mixed with strap molasses & boiled water from a jug for the night had some chill in it though we did not feel it for long. And soon Tom began to sing which was the 1st time in a very long time. In truth I could not remember him doing it since his wounding & it was hard to understand the words of the song he sung but he could carry the tune. His voice was low & sweet & the sweetness of the tune came not from the song's words but from the low & hollow places in Tom's body where music does reside. It is in his heart maybe & before

413

long Metzy set to bending the strings of a warped fiddle from behind the bar that some Bill paid out in lieu of coin for a poke. For Addie Metzger though a bugle boy could turn his hand to any instrument of music you could find for him.

Well I sang the chorus & told Ridgeway the words in Irish so he could sing it with us. It was the song <u>Trasna Da Tonta</u> which does of course mean Across The Waves & I tell you Sir before Tom sung the last note there were tears in my eyes & in Addy's as well though he could not know what the lyric meant. But anyone with a soul in his breast could understand the lamentation of the tune & Addy did carve it out lovely with that warped fiddle. It was a canted 1/2 tuned fiddle to accompany my brother's canted mouth & maybe Addy was thinking of his long lost Bremen or Berlin or wherever he hailed from I do forget. And maybe Ridgeway was pining on a girl he left behind in Pennsylvania or for his mother or his Mayo nurse as I was thinking of home & my mother as that song would have you do.

Well we did then drink & sing the night away & danced now & again with the whores & for those hours a fellow might of got to thinking there was nothing on the Earth that could touch him wrongly or bring sadness

414

upon him unless it was a song sung to bring sweet sadness on you of the kind that in drink feels like happiness at the same time. My brother's darling whore fell asleep in his lap & such was his feelings for the girl he did not even seek to poke her but was happy for her to sit & sip Redeye with him & listen to his muddled songs. We did take the best hours of the night & grip them in both fists I tell you.

It was the cuckoo clock that ended it driving out the sweetness of the songs & the whiskey that cuckoo popping out its hole to announce that our time paid for was up & it was the hour when the darkness starts to fade into morning & the fire is ash & all the songs are sung. This is the same in every tavern the whole world over & all of us sat there in silence finishing our whiskey the joy going sour inside of us. My eyes tipped closed for a minute or I do not know for how long.

Breaking the silence Kinney the Sutler piped up saying, "Pay your bill boys or buy another bottle but you cannot sleep here."

The cuckoo lashed again from his hole 4 more times like a bullwhip to the evening's end. The Sutler's demands & the whores stirring on our laps & the stink of sweat & soiled clothes & rancid perfume did further

415

remind us the night was finished & that we were no better but probably worse than stinking whores ourselves. Says Kinney, "Pay up now & go. Those last jugs need to be paid for."

Kinney when he spoke cast a look to his muleskinner as if to make sure he was ready to collect what was owed & when I saw this such a hatred arose in my breast for that cuckoo clock & then for that man Kinney the Sutler. There was something about him that I cannot explain to you.

Oh that muleskinner may of been a bad article a rough centurion & whore beater but probably no worse than Tom or myself & likely in his life did kill far fewer men than us. But that Sutler well you got to feeling there was infection in his heart put there by the Devil though he likely never kilt a man at all. And I tell you as God Is My Witness his wife did be worse but this I will tell you more of later Sir for you must hear it.

But God Forgive Me as I shooed the fat whore from my lap with the night's cold settling down where she no longer was the notion came to me that the Sutler wanted killing. It comes to me now that this was much the same as Tom once believed the Chillicoth farmer Harris needed it for taking back our calf. I thought it the way I might think about brewing coffee like it was a simple task that wanted doing. But I am sure it was the whiskey doing the thinking for me & I am ashamed to write it now because of what happened later but I will stand by it. There was something spoilt about that man & the world is a better place without him in it.

Says I standing up, "We will pay you when we are good & ready & not 1 moment before. What way is this to mind your custom you grasping b_____?"

Well Addy Metz did tweak at the fiddle all his attention upon it as if of a sudden we did not be at table with him in that lowly log cabin of a hog ranch. For he did not like ill words or bad feelings between men. He was a happy sort who would sooner pay a bill not owed than fall out with another fellow.

Tom stood up with me then & he was not steady on his feet but he took now his girl by the hand & made toward the back of the room where a low doorway was cut into the logs & hung with a sheet. Behind that sheet was the whores' beds in another room of logs that braced the dug out earth. Its roof was also covered with rough boards & a thatching of reeds & branches & moss turf with no window at all in it & only an iron stove for warmth with an ill fitting flue & guttering oil lamps for light. I tell you it was like a cave in there for them poor girls to take their custom.

"Your time is up Bill," says the Sutler to Tom. "You paid for 3 hours of time with Sarah. You did not choose to poke her in that time. That was your choice but you aint poking her now."

Says I with anger in my voice, "How much did we spend here tonight the lot of us that you can talk to my brother like that?"

I tell you I did hate that b_____ though I could not tell you why for there is many the greedy guts round the world & I do not hate all of them but I did f_____ hate him God Forgive Me & I do get sometimes roused & angry of a sudden with drink on me.

Ridgeway stood now & put his hand on my arm. "Leave it go," says he & I am ashamed to write that I shrugged off his hand & pointed my finger at the proprietor of that mean establishment. "How dare you take his coin & then forbid him what he paid for?"

"He paid for 3 hours & 3 hours is up." The Sutler looked again to his skinner & the skinner stood up from his stool. He did not put his hand on his blade because if he did I do not know what I might of done but in the end it was the cutnose girl to bring peace to us all for she did whisper something in Tom's ear something in English maybe or something in her Indian tongue perhaps but Tom took its meaning & let go her hand saying his piece back to her. I never did ask what he said but she gave Tom a small tired whore's smile & he gave a smile back to her.

Just then a pair of drovers came in with money won at the Faro bank in E Company's barracks. They wanted whores & the cutnose girl gave welcome to them & set them at the table we just abandoned. Our seats were not yet cold & Tom's face took on a terrible scowl at the notion that he did not get to lay down with his girl yet one of these two civilian boys would. Of a sudden I saw the wild mad Tom again the one the War made of him & for a moment I felt that he would loose terrible violence upon the shebeen & all within it & in truth (though it does shame me to say it in my sobriety) it would of made me glad at the time to join him in it.

"Go now," says Tom's girl & Tom to my surprise took heed of her.

"Daly will be off picket soon boys," my brother said but looking at the Sutler who would not look at him & then turning his dead eyes at the Sutler's whore skinner. His words in drink can be hard to reckon but Ridgeway & Metzger took their general meaning & made to leave. In Irish says Tom to me, "And pay the b_____ for the last jugs brother. I will take my leave before I make wreckage of this place."

As Tom turned to leave the cuckoo sprung from his hole again some minutes passing since his last visit & says Tom to me, "And before we leave this Valley I will have that clock for kindling."

A queer look the skinner did give me while I paid him & Kinney snapped at the sleepy whores to parade before the drovers so they could make their pick.

It was a sad & quiet walk back to the Ft. & if any Indians were about they might of made mince of us. Later that morning as I rode guard on the woodtrain with the sun boiling the whiskey in my head I swore to myself I would never go back to that low shebeen but of course you know Sir I did not keep this promise.

33

December 17, 1866 — Fort Phil Kearny, Dakota Territory

Kohn has inquired and been told where to find the picture-maker and if Molloy thinks there is anything odd about the photographer's tent being pitched behind C Company's barracks, within the military stockade, rather than with the civilians outside the fort, or at very least within the Quartermaster's adjoining yard, he says nothing.

Halfway across the parade ground to the enlisted barracks, Molloy halts on his crutches and takes what he feels to be a discreet sup from his bottle. "Kentucky mash," he mumbles. "Not trade. Trade whiskey. They distill it in an effort to exterminate the Indian I have no doubt of this. It is this century's small pox blanket."

"Yessir." Kohn cannot look at him.

Several C Company men are in front of the barracks as they arrive, two of them

421

stuffing mattresses from a pile of hay on the frozen ground, three more sitting on a bench with their faces to the low winter sun like pagans worshipping a fickle god. The two soldiers stuffing mattresses turn to Kohn and Molloy.

"The picture-maker's tent," Kohn says. The men on the bench open their eyes.

Molloy smiles blankly at the men. After a long moment of silence, Kohn says, "Well, do you pig-fucking infantry not salute an officer when you see one?"

"How's we supposed to know he's an officer at all, him cloaked in buffalo hide, Sergeant?" says one of the mattress stuffers. The men stand up from the bench and languidly salute. Half-assed, insolent. Irish, Kohn notes.

Molloy says to the men, "Sergeant Kohn has a hardened ass, gentlemen, as you can see. Too long in the saddle, not enough in the sack, you might say." There is something idiotic and ingratiating about his tone. An Irishman playing the Mick for his fellows, Kohn thinks. The fool. The low-born Paddy savages sniffing around each other like dogs.

"Don't know no picture-maker, sir," one of the mattress stuffers says, throwing idle fingers at his kepi brim by way of a salute. Kohn would have had him lashed to a barrel in the war for such slackness, never mind the outright lie. Molloy's pal-and-buddy show has failed. Serves him right, Kohn thinks, making his way around the barracks, not caring whether the officer follows or not.

At the back of the log building there is a wood-frame tent of heavy sail canvas, its entrance flaps unlashed and hanging becalmed in the still morning air. Kohn does not hail but throws the flaps aside and enters the tent. Inside he finds the floor of the tent to be a raised, rough board platform. He is mildly surprised by this as the enlisted barracks still have packed earth or flat stone for floors. To one side of the tent is a table laid with tin tubs of liquid, piled high and randomly with square glass plates, and above these, hung with clothes pegs on a length of thin rope strung between tent poles, are a number of photographs printed to paper from the glass plates. Drying, curing, Kohn thinks. Stacks of paper-thin tintypes next to the tubs. In the corner farthest from the flap is a cot piled high with buffalo rugs and miner blankets. A figure rises up from the mass of bedclothes, a young man, his skin pale and sheened with the sweat of fear or illness; tousled long, blond hair. Like a woman's, Kohn thinks, a whore's head of hair when she wakes.

"You're the picture-maker," Kohn says, not looking at the man but stepping over to the line of hanging pictures. "What name do you go by?"

"I am, sir. Glover. Ridgeway Glover. Might I ask —"

Kohn unpegs one of the photographs and examines it. It is of an Indian girl, naked from the waist up, her back to the camera, half of a pale breast exposed, her head turned to look into the camera's eye, a thick black braid down her back. There is a jug and a basin on a table beside the bed and the walls of the room where the photograph was taken are of dark, barked logs though the woman's smooth, muscular back is lit and cut with shadow. Light gleams in the Indian woman's eyes as if sourced there, though Kohn knows this must be a reflection of an artificial illumination. Despite her nakedness, there is nothing sexual about the photograph, Kohn realizes, thinking at first that the picture was a sort of French postcard. No, it is more than that and Kohn is, for a moment, mesmerized by it. There is something about the image. He cannot see the whole of the face but nonetheless recognizes the Indian woman he saw hanging laundry with the colonel's wife. Sarah. His heartbeat quickens in his chest and sweat breaks under his arms despite the cold.

"You made this in the hog ranch?" Kohn holds the picture up for the photographer to see. "The sutler's tavern off-post?"

"Why, yes . . ."

"She's the whore Sarah, isn't she?"

The tent flaps ruffle and Molloy enters before the young man can answer.

"For all that's holy, Kohn, let the man up and dress himself," Molloy says, resting on his crutches as if he has traveled a great distance. "How terribly rude. Forgive the sergeant, kind sir. You will come to find him a fair man but he can be short in the social graces."

The air in the tent is suffused with whiskey fumes. As if aware of this and to mask the odor of his weakness, Molloy fumbles under his coat and comes out with a cheroot and box of matches. Kohn sees that the captain's hands are steady as he lights the cigar.

Glover shoves off the weight of hides and blankets and stands. He is dressed already in woollen trousers, a bulky knitted sweater, several pairs of woollen socks, the under-pairs showing through holes in the outer layers, and Kohn thinks that the young man may have been several days in his bed without undressing. He is frail and thin under the layers of clothing, his pale hands delicate, knuckles round and raised like the rivets on a lady's hatbox.

"My boots," the photographer says. "I'll just put on my boots." He sits on a milking stool and pulls on a pair of boots that to Kohn's eye must once have cost a cavalry sergeant's monthly wage. They are scuffed and ragged now, carelessly worn and never once burnished. He takes an instant dislike to the young man, his wealth worn so carelessly as to speak of a life of ease. His life, from here out, will not be so easy.

"Is this the whore called Sarah?" Kohn says again.

"Sarah," Glover says from the milking stool, looking up at the photograph. "Sarah . . ."

"Is it her name or not?"

"It may be. I forget. I asked some of them their names. There was more than one I photographed. You can see if you look." He points up to the other pictures hanging from the line. "I didn't really know them."

"You spent a good amount of time among them, making pictures of them and whatever else you did, not to know their names."

"I —"

"This is Sarah. You know her and you know what happened when the sutler was

426

murdered. You were there and you are going to tell me what happened. Do you understand me?"

"Wait. I don't know —"

"You know." Kohn steps forward, looming over the young man. There is a ferocity in his eyes and even in his drunkenness Molloy can see the terror on the young photographer's face.

"Please, sir. I don't know anything."

"Kohn, let the man up. Jesus wept but you are a hard man. A hard, cold man." Molloy turns his attention to the photographer. "Stand up, sir. And then help me to sit down on the bed there like a good fellow."

Kohn turns his eyes to Molloy, the rage not leaving them. Molloy smiles around his cheroot and, standing on his good leg, takes up his crutches in one hand and holds them out to Glover.

The photographer looks up to Molloy as if to a safe harbor and stands and takes the officer's crutches and taking his arm around his shoulder he supports Molloy as far as his bed and eases him down to sit upon the pile of hides and blankets. "Much better," Molloy says. "Thank you, sir. Sit. Sit with me here."

The young man sits down beside Molloy on the cot. His eyes dart from the officer to

Kohn and back. Molloy again goes under his coat and this time comes out with his half-full bottle of whiskey. "Take a sup, sir," he says to Glover. "A balm for the senses."

"I am not fit for a drink, sir."

"Take one." Molloy smiles, beatific, kindness embodied. A smile that saps Kohn's sudden rage. How can he hate the man? Because he loves him. Like a father. Shallow, wicked and weak. Damned. Like a father. Curse him. *Zol er krenken un gedenken.*

"Leave us, Kohn. We will only be a moment. A small sup and some easy words between us." Molloy pats the photographer on the knee.

Kohn throws back the tent flaps and leaves. *Zol er krenken un gedenken.* Let him suffer and remember. He is unsure himself whether he means Molloy or the photographer. Both, most probably, goddamn them.

34

OUR 1ST PROPER SCRAP WITH MR. LO

It was the next day after our 1st visit to Kinney's hog ranch in August or maybe the day after when we did ride out in chase of some Indians under the command of Mad Capt. Brown the Q.M. & chief scalp hunter among us here at Ft. Phil. It does be important I reckon to tell you about it Sir for it gives you maybe some notion of what our days were like. For bloody days did have their sway on our conduct in the night especially the night we will come to soon in this testament.

Well this day had its start after a cutting detail in the Pinery as we returned to the Ft. in escort to the woodtrain. The mountains were purple with the late afternoon light upon them & the Little Piney creek was burbling joyous & everclear & sweet the grasses of the Valley bending to the breeze when out came the Q.M. thundering from the main gate with 8 or 10 other boys in saddle. Seeing the brace of us O'Driscoll brothers he let out a roar for us to follow him & follow him we did for we would follow that fellow to Hell just to see what he might do there.

One of the boys told us as we rode that Red Cloud's Braves just some minutes before cut down a civilian drover & his mate & ran their oxen from the grazing south of the Ft. He is a fierce clever b_____ Mr. Lo I recall thinking. We put our main guard to the woodtrain & while we did he blaggarded us & took the oxen instead from the unguarded grazing.

We did double back along the hilltop road whence we just came & I was glad to have my rifle & my pistols primed & readied. We carried two Navy Colts & already we were of a mind to save a last bullet for ourselves in case the jig was up & we were to be taken captive by the Sioux for it is said there is no worse fate on this Earth for a white man than to be taken alive by the savages. It was only talk then but we did see it with our own eyes since but Mr. Lo will do things to you for sport that the Devil would not do in a day's work.

But none of this we were picturing as we

rode in pursuit of the Indians them having a good head start on us. Instead we were thinking only, "Thank God we did not miss the chance for to go out on this old rumble!" Never did it come to my mind as we galloped across the grass & up higher into the Western hills that I might be struck down dead or scalped or gelded by the red savages we chased for soldiers do not think in such a way when the blood is hot. They think only of doing that which they are paid for & that which will give a jump to his black soldier's heart & that is scrapping. For though my brother & myself did come to rue the War Between The States at its end (my brother especially & no wonder with his injuries) well there was something in us still that was joyful for the chance to fight. Perhaps it is in all men or perhaps more so in Irishmen but every American boy or Olive Oiler or Dutchy German I ever met in Union blue or Sesesh grey well every D_____ one of them nearly did come alive in his body & very soul to the prospect of a bashing combat or dusty punch up & it is all the more to relish if you are ordered to do it.

In our blood lust I was not thinking of them 2 civilian ox drivers flayed out & butchered in the grazing grass back by the

431

Ft. nor did I think of the 3 boys who got theirs on the woodtrain 2 days before our return from Ft. Smith & nor did I know that them deaths was the start of many more to come or that I would soon loathe battle & its sister Death & see her skulking in every shadow & behind every tree & keeping the very dark of night as her own. I did not know I would come to live in fear & that it would make my hands shake & dreams of Death would drive me dry mouthed from my bed the same as it did at the end of the War. I did not know any of this then but I know it now & wish I had the forethought to imagine it back when we had the chance to flee from this place to Virginia City as once we planned. But the blood does heat up in a chase & truth be told I could not think of anything but killing an Indian or 2 that day.

So we rode with our shadows stretching longer in the grass beside us & soon a scout with us (his name is Beckworth I learnt later & he has a whole flock of Crow women as wives & claims to be a Chief of mighty standing among them Crows) well this Beckworth came riding back to tell us he found the trail took by the savages & 1 of the rustled oxen was laying dead upon it. He told us it appeared the other 9 or 10 oxen were still in stampede with the Indians driving them & that we could catch them but the Indians would be game for a tussle if we wanted one.

Our horses were pulled up around him as he said this their heads bobbing at the reins the chase hot in their horse blood too. Says he, "You can make chase or bow out now but the going is hard in the hills & you got a pack of chances for a ambush on you."

Well Mad Capt. Brown did not like this one bit. "<u>Bow out</u>?" says he. "Beckworth what kind of c_____ s_____ coward are you? Did I hear you say <u>bow out</u>? Did I hear him say that boys?"

Our loonie Q.M. who by rights should be back with his woodtrain & his cut logs looked to Tom when he said this knowing well what Tom would think.

"You did Sir," says Tom & his words was clear in his mouth but by this time Brown was no longer listening. He was already turning his horse for them steeper hills after the oxen thieving savages.

"You may bow out yourself Beckworth," says Brown as he lay his spurs into his mount the mount that Tom roped & broke to the gun for him back in Nebraska. "You are not obliged to do the work of the Army of the United States but these boys are."

Though I could not see Capt. Brown's face I knew he was smiling & myself & Tom & all the boys were smiling ourselves too as all of us put the spurs to our mounts & followed with cries of Hup Hup & Heea Heea.

Of course Beckworth joined us as well for far from bowed out did he want to be when there was a chance for the taking of a Sioux or Cheyanne scalp or 2 for his wives who being Crows do hate the Sioux far worse & fierce longer than us & after some 10 or 15 minutes of hard riding Beckworth pointed & shouted & we all caught sight of Mr. Lo & our oxen being drove up a steep trail some 300 yds. ahead.

"Time to take our oxen back boys," says Brown waving his wide brim sloucher hat like a cattle man might & we again lay in the spurs & the eyeballs of our horses went wide & their nostrils flaring with ears pegged back like they knew what lay ahead of them & were eager to join it.

So we lashed our mounts cross a wide meadow of wild hay to fetch the trail rising up to where the Indians were trying to drive the oxen into the mountains & we could see they were now in 2 minds should they fight or flicker. To my eye there looked to be no more than 15 of them but there could of been more or less I did not know only that there would be fewer again when we finished with them.

100 yds. we galloped hooves thundering beneath us the lot of us roaring & hollering like Johnny Reb in the War. 1 or 2 of the Indians drove their ponies on up the trail the whole time bashing the backs of the oxen with their spears & bows but a goodly number of them did turn back to give us a fight. It was 50 yds. uphill for us & 50 down for them with their wolf & coyote cries loosing arrows at us as they did descend.

Closer & closer they came & an arrow cut the air next to my head & I fired my Springfield at the Brave coming closest to me while all of us began to bunch up in a pack with guns banging & men shouting for the trail was narrow at the point where we met with rocks rising up on one side & the trail dropping off steep enough to toss you from your horse on the other.

Everything was lost to my eyes for a moment in the gunsmoke but I did hear Tom shouting, "Swing the gun Michael swing it!" & as he said this two arrows struck my mount in the rear right flanks not six inches from my leg them arrows coming from where I could not see & my horse that gallant girl she gave a pitiful whinny & turned & kicked out her back legs the arrows like the teeth of some lion of the plains at her hind & she did fierce buck & turn in a full circle 1/2 thrashing me from my saddle while I could do nothing but grip tight with my legs my rifle near falling from my hand with the force of her wild bucking & turning.

But with a fierce jerk of the reins she came back to me a fine mount she was I gripped the barrel of my rifle in my two hands & gave her spurs to turn her back downhill to the battle & as I did I swung that rifle at the first thing coming at me from the din & by luck it was an Indian lowering his bow to loose an arrow at me. Thank God but when I struck his forearms a blow his arrow sprung for the sky & not my throat & before I pulled up & swung the rifle again from the other side that Brave did have another arrow strung & was about to shoot when Tom's pale horse crushed by mine & Tom fired his revolver at the Brave putting a hole under the arm holding the bow.

Well I could not swing the rifle with Tom's mount up agin me on the trail & Tom swung his revolver & caught its barrel in the eye of the Brave's pony & tore that beast's eyeball from its socket causing it to buck back & throw his rider & I spurred my horse for to tramp that Indian into the ground with her hooves while Tom shouted something I could not understand but took to mean that he could not get a shot at the Brave. I jerked the reins & danced my horse away & when I looked back that Brave was gone meaning his horse throwing him was the thing to save him though Tom's ball hit him for I saw it with my own eyes.

But I did not stop to think on this & there was more shots as men fired pistols & swung their Springfields like bludgeons & smoke hung on that trail making the men seem as spirits in sea fog & that fog was aswirl with the tumult of savagery red & white. I swear the din of our small battle did echo in the mountains like a stampede of buffalo. There was much screaming & roaring some of it born of terrible pain & fear & in the throws of this Tom lashed his mount up the trail & I did follow & in a flash we were clear of the smoke & could see the hinds of the oxen in the dust ahead with 2 Braves driving them.

Seeing the pair of us one of the Braves did turn & charge at us with a war hatchet raised high up for to split our skulls 1 or the other of us & in this moment as betimes occurs in battle I did for a second pause to wonder what to do with my rifle or if I should go for one of my Colts & just as I decided to cast away my rifle my brother pulled up his mount & aimed & thumbed back the hammer of his own Colt to fire a ball into that Brave who slumped forward & passed between us with no harm from him before falling to the ground heavy & dead. Well his comrade did see this & decide it was the high road for him may the oxen be f_____ for he did turn his pony down the slope beside the trail & make for the cover of the cottonwoods lining a creek at the bottom of this hill.

We turned back then & as we did saw the other Sioux following their pal down the slope 1 or 2 loosing final arrows as they fled. We watched as a Brave stopped & using his horse for cover he dropped down to scoop 1 of their dead from the ground. This was done with such speed & skill you would not of believed it Sir.

After this we saw on the trail before us an Indian & a soldier wrestling with knives drawn in the dust with no sight of anything else in the world but each other's eyes like two lovers abed for the 1st time & I pulled up to see Mad Capt. Brown prance his mount over to them & dismount with his sloucher hat gone missing in battle & his bald head white to the sky.

He stood over the grim struggle for a moment like a spectator at a dog fight or music hall show but when the Indian gave our boy a flip & freed his knife well the Q.M. drew his cutlass from its scabbard swung it down into the Brave's neck like he was chopping wood that sword lodging there with Brown trying to unfix it with his boot on the fellow's back wrenching the cutlass back & forward until he freed it that poor Brave dropping his knife his eyes gone wide & white with the surprise of death in them. The fighting soldier did then shove the Indian from him the Indian's blood gouting from the wound in his neck & from his mouth now & the soldier was covered in it & standing now & swatting & wiping the blood off him like it was burning oil. Our Q.M. then flicked the blood from the runnels of his cutlass & the gore did splay from the blade in a pretty fan shape in the last of the day's sun.

The Q.M. then brung the blade down again for to sever the Brave's spine with a sound like an axe drove into a pine trunk & it came to my mind then that this was the first time I ever heard the noise of a cutlass lopping through a man's backbone & while I was thinking this the wrestling soldier seized up a large rock from the trail side. It was a rock you would think too heavy for him to lift so big was it but there can be no accounting for a man's strength when the fear of Death is on him & well that Bill brung the rock above his head & with a roar that was 1/2 a woman's scream & 1/2 the shriek of a terrible bird or banshee he hurled down that rock upon the Brave's back & it did splash blood & bounce from the body & roll down the slope. Still wailing his queer cry of rage & fear he scoured the dust around the trail for another stone & Sgt. Nevin did then dismount & take him in his arms & peacify him after some minutes of talking quietly to him & holding him in his arms shrieking & crying.

I tell you it was hard to look upon because in the pit of every soldier's mind is the certainty that fear & terror could crack you like a frozen jug with boiled water thrown in it just like that blathering Bill. So we looked away & instead watched as our Q.M. knelt down & rent the scalp from the dead Brave's head with his knife. It made the sound of tearing cloth when it came free from the skull & though it is a terrible thing to write on a page it was an easier thing to look at altogether than Sgt. Nevin with that broken soldier in his arms I never did learn his name.

Turning to me Capt. Brown did say, "Are

you jealous Michael? Look at this f_____ scalp!"

Well that wild Capt. did look like a kid holding a fresh orange on Christmas morning he did.

Horses & men circled now coming back from the fray men laughing & shouting loud with the deafness of gunfire asking where did be so & so & Johnny this & where was Bill that & Bill is here & Oh No Johnny caught his train look at Johnny G_____ D_____ to Hell. Oh not poor John.

And so we all went to Johnny though I did not know him & would not ever know him now for he had an arrow in his neck & a spear through his body & his blood was drained out on the grass. His hair was still upon his head perhaps the b_____ did have no time for scalping & this was some consolation to us.

Some minutes later there came the sound of hooves on the trail & Beckworth & another 2 Bills rode back down from the hilltop with 5 of the oxen which was not a bad return at all for the price of one man dead & 2 more wounded 2 horses dead with one more missing. We could be certain of killing 2 of their Braves & maybe more if you believed every Bill there who told of dropping 1 with his rifle or pistol though there was only 1 Indian body here among us to show for it with no hair on him it being now hung from Mad Fred's saddle. I will not lie the sight of it gave us some cheer.

And as we did gather together & settle the oxen & find our caps in the dust for the return journey to the fort a queer feeling came upon me. I busied myself trying to pull the arrows from my horse's flank & got 1 out but decided to leave the other for the surgeon but I could not shake this feeling. It was like I felt that day in the meadow when Ridgeway made our picture.

I mounted my horse then & took a look around at the sun setting over the hills the shadows below each hill like spaces in the world left dark. On top of the Big Horns the snow was a glory of pinking dusk & going to near red & I could not help think what an odd spot for myself & my brother to be. What a strange & faraway place for an Irishman to come to & maybe die so far from the green hills & salt sea air of home. I got to thinking this as I watched some of his pals put poor Johnny over the back of a horse & I wondered if he was Irish like Tom & myself. I then came to think how far from any white man's home this was German or Yankee or Swede or Italian. What a far & lonely place it was to come & die I reckoned.

It was place perhaps we had no business being & goose flesh sparked up my back & I felt cold though that could of been the fight leaving my blood like it always did after a scrap or battle. I shivered & Tom put his horse tight up to mine & put an arm round me like he knew the feelings in my heart.

Says he in Irish, "You got that first red boy you fired on."

"I suppose," says I liking the feel of my brother's arm round my shoulders in the dying daylight. For more than a year it was myself minding Tom tending to his wounds & his humours & such but here on this bloody hill trail it was him looking out for me. I sound a terrible woman for to say this but I promised you the truth in this testament Sir & this is the truth of my sentiments on that day.

"They are good about taking their dead from the field," says Tom as if to get me thinking of other things. "Likely better than we are."

This was a grand compliment coming from my brother. "I will give that to the b____ Tom. They fight like Devils."

He gave my shoulder a pat & rode away from me then to herd an ox back into our fold & my shoulders did feel cold with his arm no more around them.

35

"Show me some of your tintypes, sir," Molloy says to the photographer, noticing now, sitting beside him on the cot, that Ridgeway Glover is not as young as he had thought. In his thirties, most likely, but there is something innocent, youthful about him. Or once there was. The innocence has been washed from his features, Molloy thinks, taking a sup from the bottle of whiskey. Recently, he reckons, so that only up close can one witness its absence.

"Mostly they are not tintypes," the photographer replies. "Tin is too heavy to transport without a wagon. I put the glass ambrotypes to paper card. It's easier for me to carry. And to send back East. Glass breaks. The images are lost. Tin would be best . . ."

"Men about the camp speak highly of

your work. I've heard tell you worked for Mr. Brady in the war."

"Yessir, I did."

"A fine Irishman, Mr. Brady. I met him once. That man and his camera showed the world what that war was, what it could do to a body or a town. I imagine his pictures may have helped put an end to the fighting. Yours as well, sir. What service to mankind."

The young man smiles sadly. "Few of my photographs were printed in the papers, sir. No paper would print a picture of a hundred amputated legs in the bed of a wagon. They were . . ." The photographer pauses as if reckoning something in his head. "I never could think of it all beyond the light and shadow. How the image transferred to glass or tin or paper. I made pictures of terrible things but I only now remember the pictures, the process of making them. As if the things that happened in the war — the bodies, the ruination and wreckage — didn't exist until I captured their essence on glass. But I only look at the pictures and see the faults, the imperfections in the image, not the thing itself. I try to decide if it was myself or the solutions or the light that was at fault. I don't see, sometimes, what is happening in front of my lens."

"The world needs such men, sir."

Glover shrugs and remains silent, as if self-conscious suddenly, as if he has said too much.

"May I see your work?"

The photographer gets up from the cot and takes a handful of prints from the table. He hands them to Molloy and sits back down beside him.

"I will take a sip of your whiskey now, sir."

"Of course you will," Molloy says, handing him the bottle.

He studies each picture. Most are taken at what appears to be a conference or meeting, officers, white officials and Indians in headdress posed together.

"Laramie. The Laramie treaty," Glover says. "I was asked by the Smithsonian to record it and I attempted to remain true to my mission. I tried to let the camera be a witness, a recording device. Some of the pictures are fine, I think, and would have served the historical record, though I don't imagine they will have much relevance now, considering how both sides have so dishonored all agreements made there. You have perhaps seen how . . ." Glover sips from the bottle, winces and takes a bigger sup.

"Oh I have seen it," Molloy says, leafing through more photographs. Indian women in various poses Molloy vaguely recognizes as classical. In various states of undress, turned this way and that. Like nymphs or Greek goddesses in old paintings. Their poses strike Molloy in his drunkenness as ham-fisted, almost comical. And yet they are strikingly beautiful in a way. They are whores, he knows, and yet something else emerges in this man's photographs. Humanity. Nobility. It's in their eyes, Molloy thinks, a maudlin tide washing through him. What would show in my eyes? It has been several years since anyone has taken his photograph. They would be photographing a different person now, he thinks. He blinks and accepts the bottle, drinks and hands it back to the photographer.

"Your work is beautiful, sir," he says, and he means it.

"Thank you."

"This one . . ." Molloy holds out a photograph of a group of soldiers. They are outdoors, in a field of long grass and wildflowers. In the center of the group one soldier holds a dead wolf up under its front legs and the wolf, held upright, tongue lolling in death, is nearly as large as the man holding it. A big wolf. A bigger man, his face scarred and damaged. Unbidden, memory comes to Molloy of Miss Two Doves and the man she described as having a broken face.

He taps the picture. "These men, Ridgeway. May I call you by your name? You don't mind do you? These men. What are their names, Ridgeway, can you tell me?"

Glover is silent for a moment. He takes a sip from the bottle and clears his throat. "I don't know all the names, sir. Not all of them of course."

"Just the ones you do know, Ridgeway. Can you do that for me?"

The photographer takes the picture, its surface glossy, minor blots of aberration at the margins of the print but otherwise perfect. The men are proud, clearly rendered, the light in that clearing allowing for a short exposure, the humid, dew-laden air in early morning perfect for treating and fixing the print in the portable tent he used as a darkroom in the field. His paper stock and curing solutions, those months ago when he made the print, fresh and plentiful.

"This is Private Napoli," Glover says, pointing to soldier with a thin black mustache who is not smiling but is on the verge of it. "He is dead now. And this one, he is Jackson, I think. This one they called Henrik the Swede but I don't know if that is his real name either. He is also dead. The others . . ." He takes a swig from the bottle. "I don't know the others. I . . ."

Molloy taps the photograph, his cheroot smoldering between his index and middle fingers. "This fine fellow, holding the wolf. You remember his name surely."

The photographer takes another drink and stares at the canvas wall of the tent, pale daylight flaring and dimming inside the flimsy structure as clouds mask and unmask the winter sun far above them. The weather is turning and the loose entrance flaps of the tent stir in the harbinger wind.

"I don't remember . . ."

Molloy puts a hand on Glover's knee. "You may not believe it but I've no mind to have a man hang for anything that has passed before my coming here. I know how things come to happen. Things no man wants to happen but they happen, and God in the heavens lets them happen and, it's said, He stands to forgive those things that are not intended. At least that is what I'm told and I am inclined to believe it. I pray it is true, sir, though it makes no odds for some of us. But I won't stand in judgment over what a man's done that he's not meant to do. I won't see a man swing, not on my word. Nor on your word, Ridgeway."

"I don't . . ." Glover takes another drink

and tears now shine in his eyes.

"This is Thomas O'Driscoll, isn't it? And this, this boy here is his brother." Molloy points to another soldier in the picture standing to the right of the one holding the wolf. Despite the damage to the big man's face, there is a clear resemblance between the two. "His name is Michael."

The photographer blinks and the tears tilt under his lashes and run down his cheeks. The tears make the man look younger again, Molloy thinks, and sadness fills his heart. He squeezes the young man's knee gently.

"They were there that night. They and maybe some others, when the sutler was done for, weren't they?"

The tears flow freely now but Glover sits in silence.

"They are friends to you aren't they, sir? Good men, I imagine."

Glover nods so slightly, it is barely perceptible to Molloy.

"I don't wish to see any man swing for the sutler, a man who kept women as little better than slaves. Do you trust me when I say that?"

The photographer nods.

"Help me to my feet, sir."

Glover wipes the tears from his face with

a rough swipe of his hand and stands, helping Molloy to rise, handing him his crutches.

"You are good friend, sir. A fine friend to those men and you will not be sorry for it," Molloy says, crutching himself to the tent flaps. "Rest easy, sir. You have told me nothing I did not know before."

Ridgeway holds out the bottle to Molloy, nearly three-quarters empty now. "Keep it, sir," Molloy tells him. "I will find another soon enough."

"Well, what did he tell you? Was it Private O'Driscoll and his brother there in the hog ranch?" Kohn asks.

Molloy continues past him on his crutches, making for the gate wicket to pass into the quartermaster's stockade. Kohn follows him. "Captain, was it O'Driscoll who killed the sutler and his wife, sir?"

"For the love of all that's holy in the world, Daniel, leave it go. You are a full chisel bastard every waking hour of the day and it is not becoming of a friend, much less a soldier. Has the army taught you nothing?"

"He was there, wasn't he? And his brother?"

Molloy crutches on in silence, sweat running from beneath his Hardee hat. They reach the gate wicket, unmanned in the daylight, and pass through.

"Sir, what did the picture-maker tell you?"

"He told me nothing, Daniel."

"He told you they were there, didn't he, sir?"

Molloy halts his progress. A long-haired billygoat trots up to him and noses his palm. Molloy pats its snout, takes a long, curved horn in his hand and roughs the goat. The goat playfully butts Molloy's thigh. "That's right, billy," Molloy says. He digs under his buffalo coat and comes out with a boiled hard candy, thick with lint and flaked with loose tobacco, and feeds it to the billygoat. "That's right, billy."

"Sir, where are we going? We must arrest the O'Driscoll brothers. We have to find out where they are and put them in irons. You know the men in C Company will tell them we've spoken to the picture-maker. The two of them will be on French leave before we can get to them."

"*We*, Daniel? *I* am going to call on the one-armed sawyer to get another bottle. *We* are going nowhere."

Kohn stares out at the snow-capped peaks of the Big Horns beyond the palisade. He clears his throat, spits. "You are drunk, sir. You have finished already a bottle and it is not even two bells in the afternoon."

"I did not finish the bottle, I gifted it to the good photographer."

"Quakers are not known as to take a drink, sir."

"Because things are not known does not mean they do not happen, Daniel. You know that well enough from the war. And there is not a man on earth of any persuasion who will not bend temperance given the right or wrong circumstance."

"You are drunk goddamn it, sir." Kohn shoves the goat away roughly.

"Not drunk enough, Daniel."

"I'll go and lift them myself, sir. They killed that man and his wife."

Molloy turns to Kohn and there is life, rage, in his features that has not been there for some time. "Cooke sent *me* to do his bidding, Daniel, not you. And not his own bidding, either. Not the bidding of a general officer in time of war but the cess work of a fat, cocoa-sipping fucker back in Washington with no more manners or care for a soldier's lot than this goat. A politician, for the love of God. No, a politician's *wife*'s bidding, Daniel. I am not inclined to carry some politician's nightsoil nor his wife's. Nor will I be Cooke's executioner so that he may receive a posting more suited to his glorious and wholly blinkered view of his abilities as a fighting man. Damn Cooke and damn the Secretary of the Treasury's wife. I will see no man, no soldier hanged for them."

"They are murderers, sir, not soldiers. The picture-maker, Glover. He told you as much."

"What do you know of them, Daniel?"

"I know they were there when Kinney and his wife — a woman, sir — harmless, unarmed, were cut down in cold blood. That's not soldier's work. Soldiers don't kill unarmed women, children. It is not a soldier's work . . ."

Kohn realizes his mistake and goes silent. Part of him wonders if he is glad to have said it, if only to hurt Molloy.

Molloy smiles sadly at Kohn and shakes his head. "It is not soldier's work. You are right about that, Daniel. Neither is being a stinking constable, a filthy Pinkerton man turning over stones to read trails of snail shit beneath. That man told me nothing, Daniel. Nothing. A good friend to them and no informer. A fine friend." Molloy's words are beginning to slur.

"What will we do then, sir?" He has difficulty keeping the disgust from his voice.

"I will get a bottle and so should you. We will wait out the winter and when the thaw comes and my leg heals, we will decide what we are to do but no one will hang on account of my word." He heaves his crutches into motion in the direction of the timber contractor's workshop.

"I am going after them, sir. I'll go to Carrington if you forbid it. I'll go to Cooke himself."

Molloy stops and turns back to Kohn. "You are a terrible man, Daniel. There is nothing to be gained from it."

"There is justice. Justice will be —"

"Justice? Did you ever stop to think that justice may have been done already?"

"You don't know that, sir. We have been assigned —"

"Fuck Cooke's assignations and fuck his promises, Kohn. Can you not see we are nothing to Cooke? Nothing to anyone. For the love of God all of this will be forgotten by spring. Another few deaths among many. Can you not just do *nothing*? Can you not just wait for the thaw?"

"You will be dead by then, sir."

Molloy turns away. "Better me than any other man."

"They are guilty of murder, sir."

"So am I, Daniel. Would you have me hanged, would you?"

"I'm going after them."

"Do what you will, Daniel. I find it hard to care any further, what you or anyone else sees fit to do . . ." Molloy begins to crutch toward the timber contractor's workshop across the yard.

Kohn watches him for a moment and spits again into the half-frozen mud. The goat dips his head to investigate the spittle, then follows Kohn to the gate wicket, staring after the sergeant as he passes through into the military stockade, heading with purpose for the stables and his horse.

36

CONVERSING ON A BASTION WITH RIDGEWAY & 1ST SGT. NEVIN

And so the weather turned cool & we came to see more & more of Mr. Lo.

Day in & day out he did attack the wood-train & so it was that Tom & I begun to do more guarding of the train & the cutters than we did cutting or sawing ourselves & this was fine & lively work at first as August ran into September & the leaves of the Cottonwoods turned from green to yellow in the cold nights with the dying off season coming early in this Valley.

It was at this time when we too like the trees began to change from regular soldier Bills to proper Indian fighters. Mad Capt. Brown our Master Of The Hunt did form us up as his Praetorian Guard his terrible contingent of Berserkers. So while he accounted for his logs & beams & nails & bails all of us were praying for Red Cloud to engage us & our prayers were oft answered for the scalps fairly collected about Brown's saddle the sleek black hair of dead Braves bounding up & down as the Capt. raced 1/2 to death that mare Tom once broke for him. Some sight he was that Mad Capt. & a fearful sight were we all his special few with our cavalry cutlasses issued by the Q.M. himself God only knows how he got them. Carrington was agin us carrying them I do not know why. Perhaps because we are only pretend Dragoons & not proper horse soldiers like yourself Sir & he did not like it but as I told you Carpenter Carrington is no fighting man at all & will defer to those who are. Brown must of told him we had need of them so the Col. allowed it & we further turned into a rightly mob of marauders with our prickling array of arms & our faces burnt bright red or brown by wind & sun with beards or mustaches bleached fair & yellow & with locks near as long as Custer's. We looked like white savages I tell you & no different did we act. Some of the boys collected scalps about their saddles in honour of Capt. Brown though I did not do it but all of us howled & hollered as we closed to battle so that you might see us as less men than beasts.

There was a part of all of us changing to suit the seasons going from the bright days of Summer to the rough cold of Autumn from peaceable days spent cutting trees & yarning to days of fizzing arrows & bloody business. And Mr. Lo too grew bolder as the days shortened. By night he danced round signal fires on the hills about the Ft. like Hell's demons awaiting our arrival there only to be scattered by the bark of the mountain Howizter packed with exploding shot.

And though we did come to <u>look</u> fearful & savage like the Sioux & the Cheyanne & the Arap well the truth is we also came to live a sad & fearful life for as you well know a soldier's Company does be like his family & nearly every day someone of our family got creased or wounded terribly & without Sgt. Nevin for to hold us together like a Company of soldiers well there would of been much more of the drinking & carousing & waking our dead than there was. 8 men of our C Company's 65 struck down dead or disappeared & another 12 wounded tween August & September if I recall rightly & still the fort did rise up from the grass. It was safer we would feel (so we did tell ourselves) when it was complete.

I tell you many of our number began to

wake with the roaring & shouting of foul dreams in the night. By daylight some of them started & cringed like dogs at the sound of a rifle shot or a harsh word & we were forced for to comfort them & to show them pity & not the contempt a soldier may feel (to spite himself) for fellows who will be no good to him should he get in a tight spot. It did fall to Sgt. Nevin in the main to calm them. A good man our 1st Shirt Sgt. Nevin though not agin the wrangling of a soldier's wages if he could manage it but that is a privilege that comes with rank as you well know Sir & I did not blame him for it.

I passed a night with himself & Ridgeway on picket in 1 of the bastions which rose up above the gates of the finished stockade wall. 1 of our men Teddy Van Rick was shot through a loop hole with an arrow & killed while on picket within the walls some weeks before this God Rest Him after an Indian cloaked himself in a wolf skin & crept up to the Ft. in ambush so that even <u>inside</u> the finished stockade we did not feel safe & Nevin could get no sleep thinking about it. He would visit every picket posting when C Company was detailed telling us to beware & to keep the head down & that he would flay the skin off any man he caught napping.

And Ridgeway well he did oft just come for a natter when we stood guard for Tom & myself did not see as much of him now that we passed most of our days as Mad Fred's Marauders.

That night he came to share out some of his tobacco & brung coffee in a pail because he was a proper sort of gentleman like that & I recall the night now because both of them are gone West never more of the Earth & I do miss them terribly May God Keep Them.

I recall that at the time the bastion had no roof yet on it but only beams of wood awaiting planks & shingles & we put a brazier to burning cow & buffalo chips for heat with the stars spangling above us in the Heavens in a way no man can tire of seeing. The air was cool & calm September mountain air & we smoked our pipes saying nothing for a long time.

It might of been lovely such a night under the stars of the Powder River Valley 3 pals sharing a puff & a pail of coffee but from the hospital barracks soon came the sound of a man screaming. The 3 of us knew that the keening came from a civilian timber man who took an arrow in his thigh some days before & was now surely in a state of terrible gangrene of that leg. Manys the time I heard screaming like it here in the Ft. & on battlefields & from the infirmary tents in the War but you never get used to it & as if in reply to that keening the coyotes of the Valley did take to yipping & the wolves howling from distant hills & though we are well accustomed by now to the songs of wolves it does always put the goose flesh on me. For the wolves do nightly wait for the moon to set so that they may come to scavenge the Ft.'s slaughter yard for offal & marrow bones & Carrington well he will not let us shoot the beasts any more for it does disturb Her Ladyship's sleep. This angered the men greatly & many of them say this is why Van Rick bought his ticket West. I tell you if I did not hate the red b_____ so much I would call that ambush a fierce clever one but I cannot because Van Rick was a soft fellow never meaning any harm to any man least of all the Indians. That boy did not know which end of a rifle to shoot with God Rest Him.

So I do hate the wolves & I do hate Mr. Lo & I tell you the wolf cries do sometimes fill the whole Valley from one side to the other as one pack answers another & there on the bastion with Nevin & Ridgeway I imagined they might stop it if the surgeon's victim ceased his screaming but in truth I knew this was not the case at all. The wolves do not need a reason to howl no more than the Indian needs a reason to cut us down though if I am honest the Indian has every reason to do it & part of me cannot hardly blame him.

"Sounds like the surgeon's got his saw out," Sgt. Nevin said to be saying something to block out the noise of the poor fellow's cries.

Says I feeling low & melancholy, "God Preserve that wood cutter. He will be no more cutting this season with 1 leg."

Ridgeway said nothing at first & the terrible wailing & wolf howling continued til it all came to be like fingernails against a schoolboy's slate a terrible sound that will twist a fellow's blood making him vexed & anxious. I wondered how any man or woman in the whole Ft. could sleep with the din of it & why did the Surgeon not give the poor man a draft for to make him senseless under the saw & why did we not shoot every f_____ wolf & yipping coyote in the territories as well. I would do it if I gave the orders round here.

After some more of this Ridgeway looking up at the stars says, "Is it worth it Sgt.?"

"Is what all worth it?" says Sgt. Nevin in a peeved manner for he did not know what to make of the Quaker boy & as a rule did not abide questions that did not have ready answers. Also he could not employ the usual threats a 1st Sgt. will use to silence a soldier. But truth be told I did want to hear the answer myself for oft times I had no notion what Ridgeway's questions meant at the time only to find myself later in agreement or thinking & pondering on his words in my bunk.

Says Ridgeway, "This fort. The precious Bozeman trail & those who travel it to the gold fields. The gold itself which is mere metal & no good of its own accord for anything but the harvesting of avarice & the fostering of greed. Is any of it worth the lives of the men here? The lives of the people dying out there on the trail? The lives of the Sioux & Cheyanne?"

There did be times when Ridgeway's words sounded to my ears like words from a book but this time in his voice I could hear something like anger or weariness or both in his words & this was not like him.

Nevin puffed at his pipe & I could see the cut of his frown in the orange light of the brazier. Says he, "The lives of the Sioux & Cheyanne well I do not give a G_____

D_____ about them. The deader they are the better we are but after that I care not a good G_____ D_____ neither if anything is worth anything else. Soldiers get told where to go & what to do & they G_____ D_____ do it. <u>Worth it</u> does not figure at all for a soldier Sir."

"That man is not a soldier Sgt.," Ridgeway did reply. "Those killed on the road to Virginia City are not soldiers. And the men telling soldiers where to go are quite comfortable in their beds back in Washington or Ft. Riley."

Nevin pointed his pipe stem at the Quaker. "We are here to protect them folks on the road & that wood cutter is paid a fair wage to cut wood in Indian country. He is no slave & chose to come here. You will have to ask him was losing a leg worth it."

I grew nervous for I could sense by his words & by the sound of them in his mouth that the 1st Sgt. had it up to his eyeballs with Ridgeway & his queer manner & his questions & because I am fond of both men I did not want a row to start.

Says I to them, "Well it would be worth something I think to God above but what only He can tell. Otherwise the Sgt. may be right Ridgeway. We Bills just do what is ordered & do not think much on it. I am

465

told protect the road & build a Ft. so I guard the road & build the Ft. If someone does order me chase & kill the Indians well then I do that as well. No one above me ever asks do I think it worth anything & I never in truth ask it myself. For a body has to eat & soldiering is as fine a way of getting your grub as any." I stopped myself for a moment realising I was thinking while speaking which can be a dangerous proposition for a lowly soldier but I decided I could speak my mind to the 2 of them without fear of judgement.

I went on, "Sgt. Nevin is right as well Ridgeway to say that poor chap hollering down the heavens well God Help him but no one did order <u>him</u> to come here & take 10 times the wages a wood cutter in Maine or Massachusetts would get. But I agree with you that it is fierce sad all the same to hear a man in pain & my prayers go with him & his lost leg Ridgeway."

The Quaker boy smiled at this. "You make yourself out to be a simpler man than you are Michael. But I take your point & meant no offence by my question Sgt."

"None taken," says Nevin sounding less mithered by young Ridgeway now.

He stood up then taking one last long look above him at the stars. The keening did quieten down a little & the poor patient was saying something along with his wailing perhaps praying for mercy or perhaps cursing the sawbones for a butcher.

Says Nevin to me in a peevish manner as if it was myself asking the odd questions, "You keep your eyes wide Pvt. & sing out if you see anything strange. Mind not to let your attention be tied up by the Picture Maker's wonderings or I will feed your G_____ D_____ corpse to the wolves out there."

"Wide I will keep them Sgt.," says I hoping that Ridgeway would not take offence but he never did.

In truth I think only Sgt. Nevin in the whole of the Ft. could be angered by that Quaker boy. You never met such a peaceable & generous & untroubled fellow until the things that came to happen later the things which brought you here Sir God Forgive Us. Poor Ridgeway. Poor fellow he was cursed to know us.

37

December 18, 1866 — Wood Road — The Pinery,
Dakota Territory

The hard, dry winter cold has given way to dark skies and sleet-fall. Buffalo coats matted wet and dripping, heavy about their shoulders, Kohn and Jonathan ride the crest of Sullivant Hill, northwest of the fort en route to the Pinery.

Kohn has not gone to Carrington for permission to ride out. Nor would he draft a letter to Cooke. He will see this through himself. Molloy has not forbidden it and would hardly remember if he had. When this is over, he thinks, he will ask for his transfer out of the 7th. If Molloy wants to join him then all the better but he will not wait for him. He will no longer help him if he does not want to be helped.

To the west, clouds gather in their winter masses about the peaks of the Big Horns.

In the dips between hills there is week-old snow. Jonathan pulls up his horse and points down into a small valley, to the banks of a creek that runs through it.

"Sioux," he says, and it takes Kohn some moments before he sees them, three, no, four, their horses dipping their heads to drink from the stream. The North Piney Creek he has heard it called. The Indians see them too, silhouettes against the gray skies above them, and wave for them to come down and fight, calling out challenges lost to the wind and distance.

"There will be more about, I imagine," Kohn says.

Jonathan nods and digs his heels into his horse. "More," the scout says.

They come down out of the hills and follow the trail across a vast meadow of winter grass. Beyond this is a stand of pine forest where the fort's timber is cut. Several hundred yards away a herd of antelope turn their heads to the pair and then bound away. Approaching the stand of forest known as the Pinery, they are stopped by sentries on picket at a circle of upturned wagon boxes acting as a corral for the wood-train's grazing mules and oxen.

"Ain't no Indians 'llowed in the cut, Sergeant," one of the sentries says.

"He is with me, Private, as a scout."

"Suit yourself, Sergeant, but I aim to tell you they get mighty spooked in them woods on seeing Mr. Lo. They's like to shoot him first and ask you later who the hell he is."

"I would not like to be the man to take a shot at Jonathan here," Kohn says.

"Well, I wouldn't neither but that's the way it goes, Sergeant."

"There are hostiles on the other side of that ridgeline, Private."

"Oh, there be hostiles every-damn-where. Hell, we had a picket out yonder, out in a dug-in post just a hunnert, two hunnert yards that ways, there. But he ain't there now. A little bit of his blood and hair is all they left of him and not a one a us seen nor heard a damn thing. We abandon that picket post and graze the beasts hereabouts now though the grass ain't no good. Hell, you ain't telling us nothing we don't know. They everywhere, the hostiles and there ain't no goddamn fucking thing we can do about it nohow."

"Look alive then, Private," Kohn says, scanning the plain, the grass caressed by the cold wind. In the distance, at the foot of the hills leading west to the Big Horns, the antelope have reassembled.

"Better than looking dead, Sergeant, I tell

you what."

Kohn spurs his mount and Jonathan this time follows him. If the Pawnee has understood the sentry's words he gives no indication and soon they enter the stand of forest. The high whine of the horse-driven sawmill can be heard over the hack of axes, the rasp of handsaws. All around are the stumps of cut trees. The trail is mud and there is dirty snow on the denuded, north-facing side of the hill rising up from the creek that runs through the stand of forest.

They are met by a young lieutenant on a hungry piebald, the officer's filthy greatcoat hanging open, two Navy special revolvers in his belt, a cavalry carbine in an open scabbard on what appears to be a civilian's saddle. There is stubble on his jaw, his eyes are bloodshot. The officers of this posting, Kohn thinks, are some of the worst he has seen in his time in the army. To a man, they are slovenly and drunk. He has experience in such matters. Even during the thick of the bloodletting between the states, most officers at least attempted to appear in command of their faculties. Many couldn't manage it but in this place it is as if, much like Captain Molloy, they have given themselves up to ruination. Their men, Kohn knows, are only happy to join them in this. He salutes the lieutenant.

"Sir," he says, handing the officer the oilskin wallet containing Molloy's orders from General Cooke. "I am under orders from General Cooke and have the run of the fort and its surrounds, sir, by orders of Colonel Carrington. I am here to arrest two men from C Company, sir. Privates Thomas and Michael O'Driscoll."

The lieutenant stares at Kohn and Jonathan with dead eyes. "Who's the Indian?"

"He's our scout, sir, out of Omaha. He's Pawnee. Friendly, sir. Hates the Sioux as much as we do, if not more."

"Oh, I don't think that's possible. We do fairly hate them here."

"The two men, sir. Where can I find them?"

The lieutenant shakes his head as if coming out of a dream. "Arrest them? What men are these?" He opens the oilskin and removes the paper orders, glancing at them before shoving them back into the wallet. "You mean to arrest these men, for what, Sergeant, goddamn it all? You are a cavalry man, I can see from your boots and the way you hold yourself in the saddle like God gave you the buggered earth and a horse for you to survey it from, damn your eyes, and look down on us poor, haversack-humping infantrymen, but I cannot have . . . who did you say you wanted to arrest again?"

The lieutenant blinks and blinks again as if attempting to focus.

"Privates Thomas and Michael O'Driscoll, sir."

"You and this goddamn, son-of-a-bitch Injun?"

"Yessir."

"Well, fuck your sister, Sergeant, but we haven't enough men here to fight off this stinking savage's wife and children let alone a war party. They took our picket from his post and we have still not found his body. Yesterday. Or today I cannot remember. I don't imagine Captain Brown will allow —"

"Where can I find Captain Brown, sir?"

"Why he is in the blockhouse, you blockhead. Where else would you expect the man to be?"

Kohn does not answer but moves on, his horse's hooves sucking in the cold mud. Sawing and chopping men, civilian and army alike, stop their work to watch Kohn and the Pawnee.

"Sergeant!" the lieutenant shouts after him and Kohn pulls up and turns his mount to face him.

"You salute an officer when you depart his company, goddamn your soreass heart."

Jonathan does not turn his horse but waits, baiting the watching sawyers and soldiers to hold his eyes for more than a second. Kohn salutes, crisply.

"That will be all," the lieutenant says, as if he has lost interest in them already.

Several hundred yards away, following a muddy trail through the wreckage of stumps, passing more soldiers and timbermen who stop their work to watch them, they come to the sawmill on the stream. Beside it is a fortified blockhouse, a long, deep pit dug four feet into the earth with walls of stacked stones rising several feet up from the banks of the pit. One half of the pit is roofed over with logs, thick mud and moss covering, for insulation and protection from fire. A chimney pipe rises up from this roof and there is a fire roaring in the long, open end of the pit around which are seated several men drinking from steaming tin mugs. Muskets rest against the walls, and crates of cartridges are stacked at convenient locations in the pit. Kohn notices loopholes built into the dry stone fortifications from which the men in the blockhouse can direct fire. A formidable defense, Kohn thinks, if they can access the stream for water. A half-company of men could hold out for days here if they had the ammunition.

From his horse, he calls down to the men around the open fire. The whine from the sawmill and the hack of axes force him to shout. "Captain Brown — is he here?"

All the men stare — with hatred, and some fear, Kohn thinks — at Jonathan, and Jonathan stares back. Kohn rests his hand on the butt of his revolver under his buffalo coat and repeats his question. One of the men looks over to him and nods to the roofed end of the blockhouse.

"That fucking redskin stays where he is," the private says, looking back to Jonathan now. "He climbs down we're likely to gut and skin him, like his friend in there . . ." Smoke from cook fires and wood dust from the mill hangs dense and low in the air, enshrouding the few remaining trees around the mill and stream bank.

Kohn says, "This Indian is a scout serving the United States Army, under command of General Cooke. If he is bothered in any way, there will be broken bones here. Is that understood?"

The men around the fire cough and go back to their mugs, taking their eyes from the Pawnee and ignoring Kohn, who climbs down a ladder into the blockhouse pit before crossing to the rough pine door of the shelter.

He knocks and calls out. Some moments later, he is given leave to enter. Inside, his eyes wince from the heavy smoke of tallow candles and an orange-glowing woodstove and he must duck his head under the low, log beams of the roof. Moss and earth hang between the logs and Kohn brushes them away from his face.

Two privates lounge on cut log stools in front of the woodstove. They are smoking pipes and drinking from tin mugs like the men outside, though no steam rises from their mugs and there is a smell of strong spirits in the cramped bunker. As Kohn's eyes adjust, he notices an Indian lying on the earthen floor, his hands and feet hogtied behind his back. The captive's eyes are closed, whether in sleep or death or swollen injury, Kohn does not know. The Indian wears no shirt and his torso is coated in something dark and dried that Kohn knows is blood. Even inside this smoke-filled shelter, the temperature is not far above freezing. He would be surprised if the Indian's eyes ever opened again. At a table of offcut boards sits an officer.

"Captain Brown?" Kohn says, saluting. "Sergeant Kohn, 7th Cavalry, we have met once before." Above the seated officer is a line of twine festooned with scragged, black

476

swatches, some with feathers in, others without. It takes Kohn a moment to recognize them as scalps.

The captain smiles at Kohn and he is missing several teeth, his own face swollen, a patchwork of scarring on his forehead, a black eye, fresh stitches across his cheek thick as bootlaces.

"I know who I am and I know who you are, Sergeant. You have come to arrest my boys. Boys," Brown says to the seated soldiers, "this fine fellow is here to arrest you."

Kohn turns to the men, his hand on the butt of his gun. He feels as if he has had it there since he entered the logging camp. He says, "You are the O'Driscoll brothers, aren't you? We have also met before. You were with the captain when I met him about our horses and you were at the hog ranch when the sutler and his wife were done in. You will come with me and answer my questions or I will have you up for their murders."

The brothers say nothing but look to the officer.

"Those are scurrilous accusations, Sergeant." There is amusement in the captain's voice.

"They are backed by witnesses, sir."

"Witnesses? Who would that be? Witnesses? Have you been out interviewing the Sioux and the Cheyenne?"

"I am not at liberty to say who at the moment, sir. But I will question these two men. I have orders giving me the power —"

"Show them to me again and I'll piss on them. General Cooke and his 'investigations' may rot in hell for all I care. I'll be dead and so most likely will you, long before he or any other bastard stands in front of any court martial or hanging judge. Do you see that red fucker on the ground there?" the captain says, rising now from the table.

He crosses the short space in front of the woodstove to the Indian and kicks him in the ribs. The Indian grunts but does not open his eyes. "This red bastard is your murderer, Sergeant. You may tell that to General Cooke. This mutilator, this savage" — he kicks the Indian twice more — "you may string him up when we return to the fort if it pleases you, but you will not arrest any of my men."

Kohn is silent for a moment. He turns his eyes to the seated men, who look from the captain to Kohn and back again. The silence of guilty men, Kohn thinks. Or dumb beasts. "You men were there. I know you were there and I know one of you or both of you killed the sutler and his wife and the other fellow who was with them."

"You know damn all about anything, Sergeant," Brown says. "Now get out of my camp before I have you shot for . . . for something, I don't need a goddamn reason. You and that red beast waiting outside. Pawnee or Crow I will still have his guts hung in the branches."

"You are refusing me leave to arrest these men, sir?"

"Get on your horse, Sergeant," the captain says, drawing a pistol from his belt and pointing it at Kohn.

38

THE BAWD OF THE HOG RANCH
SHOWS HER TRUE COLOURS

I did only go with my brother 1 more time to the hog ranch before the night you want to hear of. We will come to that night Sir as I promised but only when I am ready to write of it.

After we took our September wages it was & our blood was hot that is the reason I went I think. A mob of Red Cloud's Braves were after taking a clatter of beef cattle from the far grazing & well we did have a lively chase lasting near a whole day & a fair dust up at the end of it with none of ours hurt & none or maybe 1 of theirs hurt but most of the cattle got back & so on returning well out the livestock gate wicket we went under Pvt. Daly's watch a dollar in his trousers for his troubles.

And though it does not make for pretty

reading I will write of this for maybe it is on this night that some of the things to come was decided concerning the Madam of that rough house who was wife to the Sutler of course. For you could say that she was married to a rum & evil man but that she was as bad if not worse herself.

It is this I will try to show you though you will not want to read it for it is a terrible thing done by a terrible woman altogether. I tell you Sir since the War I am not oft shocked by things in this life but I was shocked by what I saw that night by the cruelty of it. Such shame I felt I tell you Sir that Ridgeway not only bared witness to it but it was he who had to stop it & maybe only he who could. It does shock my memory to recall it.

I say it was perhaps only that lovely Quaker boy who could bring peace to that house because he knew that whore kip better than we did in a fashion. For he did pass his time there by day making photographs of the whores & I do not know why but he did also make photographs of the Sutler's wife but this does be neither here nor there.

You should not think the worse of Ridgeway for this Sir because I did see the pictures he made of them whores & they are full of beauty & well composed though

481

you might not think it possible. He made them look like ladies every one of them & less like whores altogether. He put them in finery & dresses like ladies & not just in shifts & corsets like in picture cards you see of whores now & again. These dresses he put the whores in he bought from the Sutler's store himself & gave them as gifts to the whores after so you can see why Kinney & his wife could tolerate him loafing about the place with his apparatus & keeping the girls awake by day for to make pictures of them. They did great business selling the dresses & such to Ridgeway.

And Ridgeway was a gentle soul who did not vex the girls for gratis pokes so that they let him make his pictures happily & did treat him like a fond relation when he came with us to the shebeen in the evenings. He paid them money to pose for him as well which is always a help in getting a whore to do your bidding but in Ridgeway there was no badness or no lustful intentions I may tell you truthfully. Perhaps he had a sweetheart back at home but if he did he did not speak of her.

He even made a picture of Tom's sweetheart too & this I could not imagine until I saw it for she did cloak her face with a shawl or blanket whenever she could & you would not think she would show her terrible injuries to a photographer but she did & this picture she then gave to Tom for a gift. Well this nigh moved my brother to tears & I had to look away when she gave it to him for his love for her at that moment did be like the sun. You could not look directly at it for the harm it would do you.

But that night I did not know that Ridgeway had the lay of the land in the shebeen or that he was no stranger to its ways. It was much the same sort of night as any in such a place with drink & some songs though with the Madam of the house there tending instead of her husband things were maybe a mite more quiet in truth. But we were in fine spirits altogether laughing at one thing or another & jibbed up on the edge of wildness in the way that men who live in fear can be betimes.

All the bloody business of the Army was forgotten with the whiskey. Tom had his girl on his lap & I played Pontoon with Henrik the Swede but even I could see the sour gob on the woman of the house. She did scowl when asked for more drink & would leave it on the bar for a fellow or the whores to collect rather than bring it down & serve it up like a proper landlady might. But this meant nothing to me at all til the poor fat girleen who sat on Metzger's lap rose up for to use the jakes out of doors. That girl had a jug of Trade Sap in her guts already & she was unsteady on her feet & I do not know how it came to be or why she did it but before the Devil could say Boo! that whore did have her skirts up & was soon pissing into the fire steam hissing up from the logs & souring the air. Well 1/2 way to finished with her piss she did tumble from her hunkers with it running down her legs & great farting winds came from her arse & being soldiers we set to laughing. Like yipping coyotes we did sound & she was laughing too her face squeezed tight with joy for there was something of the clowning harlequin about it all & even with a gallon or more inside her she could see it. In truth we thought her a harmless simple creature. Even the mostly silent muleskinner smiled from his stool in the corner & all of us were thinking Oh what a wild jape! But that wife of the Sutler well she was a demon if you did ever see one walking.

For when she saw this she came belting round the bar & took up one of the iron fire pokers herself the whole time roaring, "You filthy bitch who do think you are? Who do you think you are doing that? What kind of establishment do you think this is you filthy

484

whore you filthy sloughing whore!"

Well we did laugh harder at this for what sort of establishment did the Madam herself think it was? But the laughing soon stopped short as Mrs. Kinney took the poker to the girl in wild reefing swings knocking bark from the roof beams every time she swung it while that poor whore was not able rise to her feet & only covered her head wailing & pleading in her Indian tongue. I do not think any of us knew rightly what to do for we were so shocked by the suddenness of it & only when blood begun to leap from the poker with each blow did we see that something needed doing or the girl would perish under that witch's battering. But before this thought passed from one end of my drunken mind to the other Ridgeway was on his feet to catch the poker in his hand as the terrible slut brung it back for another swipe & our brave Quaker friend then snatched it from her. Ridgeway was soft & quick at the same time & before you knew it he had an arm round the Sutler's wife leading her away from the poor girl who now the other whores tended to.

Well blood did pour down that girl's face as blood from a head wound is want to & she did commence to weeping & wailing & cursing God & Mrs. Kinney in her language until the other whores took her back behind the curtain to tend her while Ridgeway sat up at the bar beside the Sutler's wife.

He sat there beside her telling her what I do not know but she did not take agin him nor curse him nor cast him out as barred from her husband's rough saloon. No I tell you in no time did she be pouring out glasses of good & proper whiskey for them both & soon after this that awful woman took to weeping herself maybe in shame or maybe in the pity the wicked oft feel for themselves but whichever it was Ridgeway was there for to give her consolation.

Well the 3 of us soldiers did not know what to do. I felt sick to my stomach the whiskey bitter in my mouth & Metzy was white as fresh linen with shame & fear & no doubt wondering would he get back the money he paid to poke the girl who was now in no fit state for it.

As for my brother well you can guess how Tom's face was cut with rage agin that woman & when his girl came back to his knee she too was quiet & sullen & cursed the back of that Sutler's wife with her eyes until the muleskinner said something in her Indian tongue & she looked away. Tom did then lay his gaze down upon the skinner but his sweetheart whispered something to him & after a time Tom broke his stare & looked back to her & she made to smile though in truth it looked to me like her heart was not in it.

Myself I did grow sad & ashamed. "How did I come to such a lowly place?" says I to myself. There are shebeens & whores the world over but of all of them I never did see a worse place than this one. Such a sink ditch for such low borne men as us. I felt ashamed to be there & yet perfectly made for such a place. I was an abject creature. I am one still now.

Finally Ridgeway stroked the arm of the Sutler's wife & said his last piece to her & came back to our table. Just then did the Sutler Kinney himself return to his tavern bringing the cold of Autumn in with him smoke coughing from the fire with the open door. He took but one look about the place & knew that something was wrong & the muleskinner gave him a look so he went to his wife for a whisper & then disappeared behind the sheet into the whores' quarters.

Tom's girl raised her head from his shoulder & spoke to all of us. "You go now. You come back the morrow."

Tom I could see did not want to leave but I think there was nothing he would of not done for her & he slowly stood & so we all did. But the whole time he kept his eyes on the muleskinner & Kinney's wife. It was like he was warning them without words to mind how they treated his girl. Ridgeway saw this & thought the same thing & said to my brother, "It will be fine, Thomas. She will be fine."

Tom turned to him his eyes dark with poison. "You would do well to keep your whisht Sir. This is not your affair."

"Tom!" says I sharply. "He is only being a friend. Mind your tongue."

Tom turned his eyes to me.

"You go now," his girl said to him & stroked his arm.

Says Tom, "I am sorry Ridgeway. I did not mean it. You will forgive me?"

"Of course I will Tom," says the Picture Maker gentle as always. And I will say to you now that to spite the night's terrible beatings & the fierce trembling violence in Tom's mind there was something about his apology to Ridgeway that was so regular & common & heartfelt that I saw in it the old Tom the one from before the War. Truly it came to me that the cutnose girl & Ridgeway both were a healing balm to my brother.

So we left the shebeen all of us & it was not the morrow but some weeks later when I went back to that pit again. Of course my brother went regular any night he could & even some days when he was not detailed though I hardly know how he did manage it. I think he took credit from Kinney God Only Knows how much. But I know his love for that girl grew stronger. It was blooming by the day & with it came Tom's yearning to protect his sweetheart to keep her from harm & someday to have her always with him so that when everything that I will tell you came to pass it was almost like a thing destined. It was like cards that are dealt & must be played.

It is said that God gives us the will to choose the right or the wrong thing & His Son came down to forgive us for oft picking the wrong one but I wonder about this. I do think betimes there are no choices for the poor of the Earth at all & if there is any choice to be had it sits part way between 1 wrong thing & another. I oft wonder does a right thing even exist in such a place as this for such men as us to choose. In truth I do not think so.

39

*December 18, 1866 — The Pinery,
Dakota Territory*

Kohn and Jonathan wait hidden in the trees at the streambank, the damp cold making Kohn's feet ache in his stirrups. He considers riding back to the blockhouse and having it out with Captain Brown and the two O'Driscolls. He would like to. There would be shooting and some of them would die but at least it would all be over.

Why am I doing this? Kohn asks himself. Because once he has started something he cannot stop? Because he cannot abide the thought of men going about their business in the world untroubled by bloody murder? He had thought that by bringing the sutler and his wife's killers to justice he and Molloy would have their transfer out of the 7th and away from Custer; that for Molloy such a change might act as a spur to cure himself of his affliction but in his heart Kohn has known all along that whatever happens, it will not matter. Nothing matters to Molloy now but his memories and the drink he uses to quell them. So it is pure stubbornness mainly, Kohn concludes. And because it is the right thing to do. Men should not profit from murder. Or is that too simple? He puts the question from his mind. It doesn't matter.

He decides he and Jonathan will stand down for now and return to the fort and as he moves to speak the scout points to the corral of upturned wagon boxes several hundred yards away in the winter meadow.

"Sioux," he says.

Kohn takes his spyglass from a saddlebag and peers through it. Three Indians on horseback are riding full bore at the corral, behind which the sentries have retreated. He sees the puffs of smoke as they fire on the Indians and a second later he hears the sound of the shots. The Indians break ranks to ride in a frenzied circle about the corral and through the glass Kohn can see one of them holding aloft a streamer or red and flailing banner of sorts. The Indians appear to be oddly dressed in white cotton shirts open over their leather jerkins and one of them is wearing a wide brim black hat. On the wind Kohn can hear their war cries and the frantic blast of a picket's whistle announcing the attack.

Some moments later the dull of thundering hooves, five riders coming from the Pinery. Though Kohn cannot see their faces he knows who three of them are already and spurs his mount to pursue. As they ride, Kohn draws his Remington and watches as one of the attacking Indians vaults a wagon box with his horse and rides across the corral, scattering livestock. He swings what appears to be a club at one of the sentries and then vaults his horse back out of the corral.

A final volley of arrows and amid much whooping the Indians turn their horses for the hills as Kohn and Jonathan reach the trail some fifty yards behind the five riders from the Pinery.

The five fire rifles and pistols but the Indians are too far in front to catch and the group slows to a canter as the Indians top the rise of a hill and disappear behind it. The group of riders comes to a halt at the corral and are assured that the livestock is accounted for and the sentries unhurt. At Kohn and Jonathan's approach, the five riders turn and again Captain Brown raises his pistol.

"You —"

"Sir," one of the riders says, "there is

something on the trail, sir. Ahead there."

The captain holds Kohn's gaze for a moment and then turns his horse and follows one of the men farther down the trail. The O'Driscoll brothers and two other mounted soldiers hold their gaze on Jonathan and Kohn.

"You have some steam in you, soreass," one of the other soldiers says. "I'd put a hole in you right here if I was one of these boys you stand accusing."

"You would not be the first who tried, Private," Kohn says.

The quartermaster hails the men forward and they turn their attention from Kohn and begin up the trail to the captain. The winter grass bends in the breeze across the vast meadow.

"Can we fight the five of them, Jonathan?" Kohn says but he knows the answer.

"We can kill some," Jonathan says.

"Some will not be enough."

Jonathan does not reply. Kohn watches as the men reach the quartermaster and whatever it is that has drawn his attention. One of the O'Driscoll brothers dismounts and kneels to something on the ground. There is shouting and consternation.

"Come on," Kohn says. "Let's see what it is."

"I know what it is," Jonathan says.

When they arrive at the group, no one challenges them at first. Kohn and Jonathan watch as the younger O'Driscoll brother embraces the bloody, naked body of a man. Steam rises from the body, from the fresh and bloody wounds. Kohn can see an arrow protruding from the victim's anus, gaping injury where his privates would be. There is an open wound to the abdomen and the intestines have been pulled through it and unspooled onto the grass. The dead man has been scalped, his skull bashed and broken. There are red and white fragments of bone in the grass around the body.

A mule lies dead and bleeding some yards away and the load it carried is strewn about like the flotsam from a sunken ship, sheets of heavy paper catching the wind, glass plates smashed, a camera and tripod askew and broken, a shredded tent canvas like a cast-off sail in a heap on the muddy trail-side.

"Ridgeway," Michael O'Driscoll says, weeping. "Ridgeway . . ."

All of the men watch this for a moment and then look away except for the man's brother, Thomas O'Driscoll. There is rage in his eyes as he turns them on Kohn.

"You did this," Thomas O'Driscoll says,

the words unclear in his war-damaged mouth. "You and that bastard of a Galway man with you." He raises his revolver and points it at Kohn. Kohn raises his own and points it at him.

"You will pay for it, you fucker. 'Tis you done this, you bastard."

"I did nothing, Private, but follow the trail you left me. A blind man could've followed it," Kohn says, his finger heavy on the trigger of his revolver. A small part of his mind tells him that he will not live long enough to see his own shot strike its target. He will kill Thomas O'Driscoll and Thomas O'Driscoll or one of the other men will kill him and that will be all. Nothing more. Thomas O'Driscoll's knuckle is white with the pressure of his finger on the trigger of his own gun. Kill. Die. The End.

"No! No, Thomas."

The words are shouted and then more words in Irish and the grieving O'Driscoll brother sets the corpse gently on the grass and stands. He takes the pistols from his belt, the cartridge belts from around his shoulders and hands them to one of the soldiers on horseback. He turns to Kohn.

"You take me, Sergeant. For the love of God I am responsible as if I killed the boy myself." Tears run down his face.

Thomas O'Driscoll speaks in Irish to his brother, not lowering his pistol and Kohn has an urge to shoot him now that his attention is taken. He hesitates. Michael O'Driscoll roars at his brother, in a mixture of Irish and English. "You . . ." he roars, spittle spraying from his mouth. "You did this. You put fear in the boy . . ."

Michael O'Driscoll turns to Kohn then and holds out his hands. "Put me in irons, by God, and arrest me. I did this . . ." He falls to his knees, weeping, his hands outstretched to Kohn in as if to God Himself.

Captain Brown appears disgusted with the scene before him and he turns in his saddle to Thomas O'Driscoll. "You and Jones. You go get a wagon and see to the body."

Thomas O'Driscoll turns to the quartermaster as if waking from a trance. "Yessir." He looks down again to his brother.

"Michael," he says.

"Go on, brother," Michael O'Driscoll says. "Go on."

"Private," Captain Brown says, "I gave you an order."

"Yessir," Thomas says, sticking his Colt back into his belt and wiping the tears from his face.

"You go with him, Jones. And Jones . . ."

"Yessir."

"Bring that goddamn Indian from the blockhouse."

"The Indian, sir?"

"Yes, Jones, the goddamn Indian. I aim to show Mr. Lo that he is not the only fucker in this meadow."

Kohn says nothing. He dismounts and ties Michael O'Driscoll's hands behind his back with leather cord and helps him up to his saddle. He is anxious to be away before the men return with their prisoner, and the captain makes no attempt to stop him as he leaves with his own.

40

Later that evening Kohn sits his prisoner in a chair across the table from him in the guardhouse, the prisoner wearing shackles at his wrists and ankles.

Kohn says, "You think you will sit there in silence but you will talk when I make you. Do you understand me, Private?"

Michael O'Driscoll stares at the tabletop. "I will not talk to you. I will talk to the Galway Captain. No one else, by God."

"God will only watch when I start to work on you."

A faint smile comes to the prisoner's lips but there is little defiance in his voice. "You will try it but those boys on guard, they are all C Company boys. They will stand for no wildness with me, Sergeant."

Kohn studies the prisoner, wondering whether he needs a confession or an incriminating admission to move him from here to Fort Reno or Laramie. Of course, if he could move him to Reno or Laramie, he could more easily work on him, get the confession or statement of evidence he feels he has a right to hear.

"The captain is ill again. He cannot attend you."

O'Driscoll considers this for a moment. "Then get me paper and ink and I will write my confessions to him and him alone. My brother and I are in his debt. He will be repaid, not you."

"What debt?"

"That is between myself and my brother and the captain. It does not brook on you, Sergeant."

"I've a mind to hang you now in your cell."

"You have the makings of a fine constable, with talk like that."

Kohn stands. "You will have your paper and ink and I will have a confession before the night is out or you won't see tomorrow."

"Tomorrow is a long way from now, Sergeant. And I couldn't care a fuck if I see it or not. Get me paper and ink and a lamp. I will need light if I am to scratch out my tale for the captain."

41

ALL HALLOW'S EVE & TOM'S PLAN FOR HIS SWEETHEART

September did tip into October & the fort got built to spite 10 or maybe 12 more soldiers & civilians sent West by Mr. Lo & his predations. All souls in this redoubt were afrazzle with the killing & dying even them such as us who was doing a great deal of killing ourselves. But gone was the joy of the chase or the banging of the musket & we went around always with the hackles up on us so that we never felt at rest even in our bunks. At times when my mind was not caught up with scouring the grass & trees for Indians hidden in ambush well it might cast itself back to Ridgeway's question. Is any of this worth it? I did not know the answer & still do not know it of course for I am only a small nail in a tiny corner of God's house & cannot see the whole of anything but more & more of me was coming to think that the Quaker boy may of been right in his thinking.

It was this sort of thinking that made me again begin to wonder should we draw down what money I put by & make a flit for the goldfields like some already done. To be sure I am no fool & know that the boys who deserted here may be shot full of arrows their bones picked clean in a ditch now instead of lords of the gold mines as in their dreams. But some of them must of made it safely. Some of them surely did for you would hear of it from the timbermen or civilian drovers now & again.

But I must confess all was not bad for us. No there must of been good as well as bad. I can remember 1 time as good Sir & I will tell you of it for there is bad to come in these pages I can assure you.

It was the time when Col. Carrington did finally declare Ft. Phil Kearny to be finished & complete. Perhaps he did not know what the day means for the Catholic soldiers especially the Irish but Carpenter Carrington went & chose the last day of October for to celebrate this. Would you believe such a thing?

Now you know well Sir this day is the feast of All Hallows Eve or Halloween or <u>Sowan</u>

as we call it at home. You know it is the time when the spirits do return from death to visit the Earth & bonfires are built for to drive them away or welcome them home if they are loved & mean no harm to the living & glasses are raised & feasting done in their honour. It is done in Ireland & would be done here for there is a fair mob of untethered spirits in this Valley.

Now to make the prospect of a fine day all the better the Paymaster arrived on the 30th with a month's wages for the lot of us him with his armoured wagon boxes & an escort of 20 men from Ft. Laramie like the magi come to see the Christ Child if Christ was in need of his wages for to pay his Faro & Chucka Luck debts or buy Bust Head & whores God Forgive Me. The Paymaster came as part of a supply train of wagons carrying all & sundry such as newspapers & letters from back East bandages & poultices & several hundred bottles of medicinal stout for the surgeon of the Ft. which the escort did liberate & save from breakage so that the surgeon took possession of only 50 odd bottles. Of course we regular Bills was offered the rest at a price for to heal ourselves of an evening the stout being medicinal & us eager invalids! The bandages & poultices by some miracle of course did complete a safe journey unmolested.

Well we did buy trade sap from that thief of a Sutler as well as corn mash from one of the civilian loggers. I tell you C Company made ready for a mighty knees up. Truly it was the last of the fine days we had in this place but my brother well my brother did not enjoy it at all. Gone was the only calm & contented boy in the valley my dear love-struck Tom. For even while the rest of us flinched at every shadow Tom suffered no such petty fears but yet now his humours turned grim & dark again like his blood was aboil at something. Oft times there was no reason for his spirits turning & so I did not wonder on the reason that day but maybe I should of known. Looking back I can see that it must of been the Paymaster's arrival that set my brother stewing for full pockets do cause a right stir of custom at the Hog Ranch. It is the same in any Army post the whole world over.

But that was later & never mind Tom's humours for my spirits were bright how could they not be? The night before the celebrations our Company dog robbers stayed up til cock crow roasting spits of antelope & baking cherry duff & wild blueberry & blacka & raspberry pies with what flour they had that was not gone off.

And one boy from B Company a Belgian or Dutch fellow I never did know which (he is dead now) well he did swop some partridge he shot for 2 tins of oysters in brine & didn't he bake the finest oyster pie you would ever eat & I never ate one before at all! Picture it in your head a fine oyster pie with not a drop of ocean for 1000 miles!

As well as antelope we bought two fat legs of beef from a civilian cattle man & they too turned overnight on spits filling the whole of the Valley with the scent of roasting meat. I tell you Sir it set the wolves howling in the distance & drew Mr. Lo to light his fires on the hilltops about the Ft. where he did whoop & call along with the wolves. One of them Braves with a bellows of a voice begun to rain insults down upon us in the cold autumn air of that night so that we could hear him clearly but he called out a queer kind of English so that we laughed more than trembled at his words.

"Sons of rats in the city of logs you will die tomorrow with your pricks put where you eat your meat!" he shouted & many more things besides.

"Well," says Cpl. Jackson to me as we stood picket at the livestock gate listening to that red fellow barking down at us in his Injin English. "I think my mouth will be too full of beef steak for my prick to fit in there too."

"Your prick would surely fit Jack," says I & he did cuff me one. I tell you we were in high spirits.

In time the wolves did cease their howling & Mr. Lo put himself a bed or shifted back to his tee pees & we came off our picket as the sun rose up in the East forging shadows in the rolling hillocks of the plain that stretched as far as the eye could see. And though they are dry & vast & it is frightening to be lost in them hillocky plains of grass well they do take onto their grassy tops the orange light of the rising sun while mist fills their dips & hollows so that you cannot take your eyes from the beauty of it. It makes you wonder if some day your cattle might graze that grass or will your children make hay from it or will your horse tramp the stream beds in search of wandering calves with the sun on your shoulders & a belly full of a wife's breakfast? It is easy to dream & hard to know a dream will never come true.

But I was telling you about the celebrations Sir & after a short sleep we followed the sun up to heel ball our leather & climb into our clean & flat ironed US Army blues. We did look the very business for the celebrations & the day passed with the firing of the Howizter & the raising of the mighty 10 foot wide hoist of a flag. We then marched in review all the fighting men of the Ft. & after this Col. Carrington made a fine speech telling us how brave & hard grafting boys we were & I will not lie a tear came to my eye when the band struck up the Star Spangled Banner & The Battle Hymn of the Republic & the mountain Howizter banged while all of us both officers & men did snap to salute the raising of Stars & Stripes over this Valley. I will not lie to you for it moved me & many other men felt the same.

Oh we may grouse & piss & moan as men of armies have done down all the days of History but the sight of that flag does turn some lever in my heart & I swelled up with pride seeing it rise up that sky high pole to wave over this Valley as if to declare to every soul white or red who comes in sight of it that the Great & Powerful Army Of The United States is here & within the walls of this Ft. at least a man can find safe harbour & a hot meal & kind word. All this I felt in my heart while in my head I knew it to be all balls but that too is the way of soldiers since Caesar drove his armies into Gaul. Many is the time a fellow feels one thing &

thinks another & just gets on with soldiering for better or worse.

While all this was happening Red Cloud's boys did appear back up on the hills around us for to see what all the ruckus is about & they spent this time signalling each other with mirrors & burnished tin from hilltop to hilltop. At one point 20 or 30 of them made a gallop down Sullivant Hill toward the Ft. But they veered off then around Pilot Hill not to return that day as if they saw all they needed to see & were satisfied with it.

Finally Col. Carrington's beautiful band played us out to Hail Columbia! & we made for tables heaped high with food in front of each Company quarters. Well the clay jugs of Oh Be Joyful & glass bottles of beer & surgeon's stout did not be long in coming out & we did rag & jest & eat like Lords Of The Manor I tell you. And when the eating was done & the drinking just getting up steam Metzger took up his fiddle & another boy a banjo & another a guitar & another a mouth organ & another a squeeze box making up a proper Halloween orchestra.

I joined in myself with a ballad or 2 as the sun took its turn round a sky so blue you felt you could drink it & when it sunk to rest behind the Big Horns we lit the fires of <u>Sowan</u> there being so many Irish boys among us. The others from different lands or America herself just took them for camp fires (for who among us does not love a camp fire?) & they thought it a great waste when we Irish boys in the Company poured a measure of whiskey into a tin mug & left it with some beef by the fireside for the good spirits while we piled wood & buffalo chips onto the fire for to ward off the bad & all of us & some of the Scots boys too toasted the end of the light part of the year while we drank to welcome in the dark part to come blessing ourselves & pouring sups from our mugs onto the ground in offering. The spirits of our fallen brothers in C Company were there that night & supped with us.

It was then the drinking did rightly take off like rockets & the dancing came on a fierce roiling too with all the boys arm in arm with each other tearing up the earth with their clumsy dancing boots. The officers & their wives could be heard dancing & yarning too from Carrington's H.Q. & for 1 day all seemed fine in the camp about us with the dying & killing forgotten. All was fine as we drank & danced & sung us C Company boys. It was like we were closer than brothers that night almost though to spite this it did not take <u>my own brother</u>

508

long to gather up his bile.

1/2 scuppered says I to him in Irish, "Why are you vexed Tom on today of all days?"

For a long time Tom did nothing but stare at the fire like there was something to hate inside the flames.

I let him stew & turned myself to belt out a few bars of Aura Lee a favourite from the war that John Napoli sung in his Italian way so that I could not hardly understand the words but the voice on him was so sweet you did not care & felt he would be better fitted to a music hall than a Ft. in this vast wilderness. I tell you Sir that sweet Italian boy had a throat like an angel's but his hands were the hands of a devil when he welt them in anger at an enemy. A strange world we live in when there are such different aspects in a man I recall thinking but at the time this thinking did not bring sadness with it. It was just the reckonings that come with drink & a smile did be nailed on to my face like the rung of a ladder.

Says Tom at last over the din of the music so that at first I did not hear him, "There will be a battalion of them just waiting their go."

Says I turning back to him, "What's that Tom?"

"There are hundreds down at Kinney's

kip pure hundreds of men & I fear for my Sarah," says he innocent like with no withholding his sentiments.

I told you Sir that the spoiling rage was upon my brother that day & this could be far worse when he had drink taken but now there was a sad weakness to his voice & to the words he spoke to me in the language of our home. But again all of it felt to me like something pitiable & wrong & <u>nought but trouble</u> this love affair with the hog ranch girl.

So I felt heartsore for him but I asked myself too why could he not just relish 1 day with the boys in C Company in this fine Valley in this Elysium at the very ends of the Earth where though we may be dead tomorrow well at least we did get to see such beauty. Why must he ruin all this with his mad love for a girl (a whore no less!) who you & I would not look twice upon except in pity.

Some anger raised up in me & I stumbled at what to say to him for it came to my mind to say, "Well she is a whore so what do you expect brother?" But Thanks Be To God the words stopped at my lips & did not leave them. I took a long sup to drown such thoughts.

Instead says I, "Well there could not be

that many of them Tom. Your heart has your head fooled."

Tom did be silent again staring into the fire. I kept silent company with him though the ragging & singing went on around us like Billy O. He did finally speak. "I was detailed to Mrs. Carrington this morning for to set up her quarters for the celebrations. While you slept after your picket."

"Well that is fine work Tom," I said hoping that such a thing might of been something to relish. For Tom was fond of Mrs. C. & she of him ever since he did warn her off setting her camp chair on a nest of rattlers on the march up from Ft. Caldwell. She oft asks specially for him as stryker & feeds him jam & bread & sugared tea by the gallon as he labours for her. It is a lovely fatigue that is much in difference to the usual bloody business of a soldier here in this Valley.

"She is a fine woman. Kindly & good," says Tom then in a strange manner.

"She is," says I.

Then says he, "When I was done with the work I stepped above my station."

"You did what Tom?" A stab of worry pierced my drunkenness.

"I asked Mrs. Carrington would she take on my Sarah as a servant for she could not have rough soldier Bills making her beds &

511

cooking her grub no more than a lady in any town or city. I had to say it more than once for her to understand it but she took my meaning in the end & told me she would meet her & would see about it. She told me then that no woman should live such a life as the poor girls in the Hog Ranch. When I gave her a look of surprise that she should even know of such a place she told me that it is no secret to anyone at all in this Valley who has ears or eyes & that she did speak of it to her husband more than once."

Well I will tell you Sir I did not expect this & did not know what to say thinking that surely a woman such as Mrs. Carrington even such a fine Christian woman as herself would not abide a fallen woman in her home & around her child who is a boy of 12 or 13 yrs. old. A 1/2 breed Indian of a fallen woman as well I did think to myself but I did not say this. Instead I said, "Well can your girl just up & bolt the shebeen? Can she do that Tom?"

"She will need be bought out & I do aim to do it," says my brother.

"Bought out," I replied knowing already this would be the case for whoremasters did not let their wares leave the store for free not when there was money to be earned off the backs of them. "How much?"

"She does not know only that it will be a lot. More than a soldier has in pay in manys a month but I told her I would pay it whatever the cost."

"Well Tom I will give you what I have saved away for our stake but it does be only 18$. It will be 21$ next wages but I do not reckon that will be enough. Is there no way Mrs. Carrington can get her man to order Kinney to do it? Is he the C.O. of this Ft. or is he not? I'm fair shocked Kinney & his bitch are allowed run the place at all."

Says Tom, "I would not ask you for the money Michael though I would be happy for it. And I would not ask Mrs. Carrington to do such a thing for it would put her husband in a tight spot. Kinney is brother in law to a Big Wig in Washington & it would not go well for a lowly officer such as Carrington to cross the man or his whore madam wife. I would not ask it."

"What will you do then Tom?" I was not sure I would want to hear his answer.

But when it came it was meek & mild though wholly foolish in its conception. Says he, "Sarah will be paid & given board by Mrs. Carrington if she is taken on. Perhaps the 2 of us can buy her freedom from Kinney in small doses from her wages & my own."

Says I, "Do you think that hungry c_____
of a Sutler & his wife will allow for that?
Sure she is the fairest by far of their whores
never mind her —" I did not know how to
put it to him. "Never mind her misfortune.
She would earn more than the others for
the Kinneys."

Tom looked at me now & I took a drink
so I would not meet his eyes but I could
feel the heat of his bothered heart none the
less.

"Certain things you do not need remind
a man of," says he. "I will find the money
or I will take her out of there by hook or
crook & may the Sutler & his wife & the
grim muleskinner who looks over them be
f_____."

"I am sorry Tom. I only want to tell you
how things are."

"I do not need telling Michael not from
you nor from anyone else."

"I am sorry Tom. I will help you whatever
you decide to do."

"It's all right Michael. I know you would."

He did look at me then. "We will be for
the hills perhaps. It will be the end of the
Army for us. You do not mind that?"

"We are brothers Tom. I will do whatever
it is you need of me as you would do the
same for me surely."

A smile came to his terrible face then & it was a sad thing to see I tell you. Says he in the Gaelic to me, "I know I am a hard man to have for a brother Michael. You are cursed with me."

"Of course not Tom," says I sad myself & filled with dread even as full of beer & mash as I was. "You have another sup Tom & think no more about it. Tomorrow will come with its own sorrows. Leave todays in the bottom of this jug."

Tom took the whiskey but did not drink from it. The fire cracked & popped while Metzy played a slow lament on his fiddle & some soldier who did not know how to play it plucked a queer & ugly tune on the banjo. One of the German boys sung along with Metzger in his Dutchy tongue & it sounded like he had a mouth stuffed with cabbage & all the boys round the fire laughed & made to sing like him.

But I could not join this larking for some of the joy was gone out of the night & I supped more & more whiskey so that I might get it back but of course I never did. Tom is the sort who can rob the good from a day. God Forgive Me for writing it but it is true.

42

Kohn stands beside Molloy's sickbed, the hospital barracks' stoves fighting in vain against the bitter cold outside. Kohn can see his breath. Molloy is yellow, his skin the color of whiskey piss, his breathing labored, eyes twitching and rolling under their lids in troubled, laudanum-induced sleep.

"He is in a bad way, Sergeant," the surgeon says to Kohn.

"Yessir. Yes, he is."

"You have a man in the guardhouse for the killings I hear."

"Yessir. He has done something and was there when it all happened but I am not certain he is the sole killer."

The surgeon looks as if he is considering something. "Look," he says. "When you first came here it seemed important, somehow, that justice be served for the killing of the

516

sutler and his wife and their man. It seemed necessary . . ."

"But?" Kohn says, turning to the surgeon now.

"But since then . . . I have seen twelve more dead men. Nine men are missing. Twenty odd maimed and injured. Look around you."

Kohn has seen the beds full of wounded men. Some are septic and will not live out the week. One man has the broken shaft of an arrow protruding from where his left eye once was. He does not need to look at this again.

"Killed in action and killed in a tavern are different things, sir."

Again the surgeon is silent for a long moment. Then, "You have heard what kind of man the sutler was. What kind of woman was his wife?"

"I have heard but I don't think that should matter, do you?"

"I didn't once but now I am not so certain. You seem a good soldier, Sergeant. Kinney and his wife are not worth your dying for."

"I will keep it in mind, sir."

"I think you should."

43

A TERRIBLE DAY IN THE PINERY

It is now we arrive at it the day & the night you wish to learn about & because my brother & myself do owe you as much Sir I will tell you the truth of things. But part of me wishes to God now I never put ink to paper for the lie comes far easier to the tongue than it does to the pen. It is like the page demands truth in the way spoken words do not.

Well the next day was the 1st of November & I will never forget it. Our heads were like they had mules kicking inside them & the boys who passed their revels at Kinney's Hog Ranch the night before did be feeling already the sting of whore's vengeance in their waters. I tell you Sir it was a sluggish muster for parade & the forming of work details. You have seen the like of it before I am sure with the desperate din of coughing

& retching ringing from one end of the Ft. to the other & more than one Bill swaying in formation that morning with a face as green as marsh grass.

That morning my brother stood behind me at muster & because 1st Sgt. Nevin was speaking to Lt. Grummond (who looked not sick like the rest of us but was surely still drunk as always) I turned to look at Tom & though his face was set as haunted & pale he did not appear the worse for drink like the rest of us but was the worse for something else by far for as I told you Sir he was sick with love for a woman he could not have but all others could for a price. Seeing me looking at him Tom did say to me, "Will we up for the Pinery today Michael? I cannot bear to be around this place."

I tell you my head was a muddle & my guts like eels were swimming in them. Truly I did not care where we passed our day's work for I would feel as poorly here as there.

"Tell Nevin so," says I to him & he did. In return Nevin ordered the pair of us to make sure the horses were saddled & watered for we would be riding guard on the woodtrain & standing picket rather than cutting today.

"The best mounts," says Nevin to us as we turned to the stables. "We will take 8 men on horseback & the rest of the boys will be a foot & will double as timbermen. With the civilians we will have 35 men all told."

"8 of the best Sgt.," says I though it hurt my head to say it.

Well that woodtrain did take some time for to get moving each morning & this morning of All Soul's was no different for there was always some loose yoked oxen or objecting mules or a cracked wagon axle & since the train set off all together or not at all it was proper morning before we made for the trail a top of Sullivant Hill. This was the same hill where Red Cloud's boys lit their fires by night to terrify us & there was fresh sign of them there as we climbed to the summit trail overlooking the Valley. There was sooty ashes in a ring & moccasin & hoof prints in the dirt & flattened down grass.

Nevin pulled his horse up beside me & together we did gaze over the Valley seeing from that hilltop what the Indians spied when they looked down upon us.

Says he, "The whole place looks awful small from here."

I gave a shrug & said nothing. Truth be told my mouth was dry & I did not feel up to talking much. I felt I might spew up my coffee.

Says Nevin then, "Keep your eyes open today. Them red f_____ just wanted a looksee yesterday. They are still around & we need to be sharp to them."

"Sharp as an Arkansaw toothpick," says I & watched Nevin trot off to the fore of the woodtrain where he led the wagons from the front for he did be that sort of soldier.

I rode up beside one of the wagons on the West side of the trail & kept pace with it relaxing some while we rolled over the summit trail for I did not think Mr. Lo would harass us on high ground. I would be <u>sharp</u> I told myself when the time came to start down from the hilltop trail into the meadows that bordered the Pine forest but until then I would let the gentle stepping of my mount ease my head & stomach & just as I was thinking this the 1st arrow sang over my head. For a moment I did not know what it was I took it for a bird or a bug or some other whistling thing I do not know what when the 2nd one came & this dart landed with a whack behind the driver in the empty bed of the wagon I escorted. 2 more arrows sailed over me & some fellow cried <u>Hostiles</u>! & another shouted, "Where are they G_____ D_____ it all?"

Well we did turn our horses & eyed the shallows to both sides of the trail which was atop the hills as I told you. After a moment of this the driver of the wagon I rode beside cried, "Down there!" pointing down the hill on the other side of the trail from me. A shot was fired & then another 2 or 3 more from behind me & I steered my mount to that side of the trail where she scuffed & danced til I could make her steady & take aim with my Springfield.

Before I could shoot I heard Nevin's voice shouting for to hold fire that the Indians were on the run now. I could see them scarpering away down the hillside to the cover of the cottonwoods by a stream bank & crossing the stream. Some of them were mounted & some leading their mounts by the reins all of them giving hoots & hollers & Rebel Yells back at us but they did not appear to want a fight to which I gave thanks to God In Heaven for my head was thumping I tell you & the sound of musket fire would surely only make it worse. I felt that if some Brave did take my scalp that morning it would only make him sore to carry it & any savage who stopped to drink my blood would surely drop down dead so rank with poison was it.

"Stand down & keep moving," says Nevin

riding back along the train of wagons asking if everyone was all right. One driver took an arrow through the brim of his hat & he was laughing like a lunatic at this saying, "Look at my hat! Look at my G_____ D_____ hat boys!"

When it came time we rode vigilant & sharp descending from the hilltop trail & Mr. Lo made no appearance though my senses were sparking & small things such as a rabbit in the grass or a bolting herd of antelope in the distance served to fray my nerves further.

Tom came up to me. "Stay close by brother," says he. "You do not look well at all."

Well I did not feel well at all & it was nothing I had not done to myself before but I <u>did</u> feel a strong love for my elder brother then for he would look out for me I knew he would. And at this moment I felt sorry for thinking him a wrong headed fool for loving his girl & for being melancholy in drink about her & how she could not be freed from that b_____ Kinney's bondage.

My spirits did swing towards the gloomy then & the land & sky made like to match them. I watched the grass wash & flow like ocean waves to the wind in the vast meadow where we would corral the oxen & mules with the wagon boxes. The great grey clouds were like fists in the Heavens shifting in the sky above as if to beat into us the notion that our celebrations were finished & the dark 1/2 of the year was now upon us & of a sudden I had a feeling that we should not be here at all. None of us should be here I thought with our wagons & oxen & soldiers & timber men with their sawmill & fancy store bought repeating rifles. We are not welcome here I could not help but feeling & I could not take my eyes from the grass as it shifted & flowed in the wind that Valley grass seeming to whisper & hiss to me, "Go away Go away Go away" & I did thank God again that I had my brother with me.

"I will stay close to you brother," says I. "And I am sorry about your girl." I must of sounded a fool saying it but I did anyway.

"Thank you Michael," said my brother.

"Stay sharp will you Tom?"

He gave me a nod & we entered into the Pinery crossing a waste of naked stumps to the rising wooded hill side the timber men were cutting that week. It was some weeks since I was in this lower stake of the Pinery & so much of it was cleared since my last visit that the sight of it now cast my mind back to battle grounds in the War with trees stumped & shredded by cannon shot or cut down to offer clean lines of fire to the infantry.

"Shall we take the ridge line Sgt.?" says Tom to Nevin.

"What is he asking Mick?" says Nevin to me.

"Will we picket the top of the hill or down here Sgt.?" says I.

Says Nevin, "You boys head on up & remember to keep watch over the back side of the hill. That aint cleared yet & it is easy for any f_____ to creep up in them trees. I will be up to spell you in 2 bells." From his tunic he took out a watch on a chain. "Maybe by then you will be able to take some grub without throwing it up."

We both did nod our heads & I smiled at him though it hurt my head. A finer soldier you would not meet in this life than our 1st Sgt. God Be With Him wherever he has gone.

So up the hill side we climbed Tom & myself & so steep was it betimes we did dismount & lead the horses round stumps & parties of men working saws & axes. The men worked to the low side of the trees so that when they fell they would slide some of the ways down the hill where they could be shorn of branches & chained to oxen to be drug away for planing in the mule powered mill. The very air of the Pinery was filled with the sound of men sawing & chopping & even laughing for somebody no doubt brung a bottle. I reckon the civilian timber men were many of them already 1/2 jugged which I did not reckon wise with towering pines crashing down around you but wise is not a word you would use to describe timber men at all.

All of it was the noise & racket of a normal days work & a body might get to thinking it was just like any stand of forest in America. My head was thumping like an apprentice drummer & as we passed the highest up group of cutters I asked Tom if we could halt our climb for a moment. "I may be sick Tom," I recall saying to my brother & he gave me a small smile that all men fair love to give to them that are more hung over than they be themselves. I spat a few times & with the cool air working on me at last I felt well enough to continue. I tell you all was normal as you can imagine Sir so that when from the top of the hill there came a terrible din a crashing of hooves & cracking of branches & terrible yipping & howling well it was a fierce shock to me. The Indians did rarely attack the Pinery but rather preferred to attack the woodtrain itself but now coming down the hill at us was a mob of them. It did not seem real to me it seemed like something out of a fever dream.

Tom & I sat as if frozen for a moment watching as the marauders barrelled in & out of the trees like dancers at a fair not one of them dismounting but passing tween the trees like fog or mist leaning aft on their queer saddles for balance as their ponies descended upon us. They were 50 yds. from us & coming strong down that hill.

Tom broke our spell. Says he, "Dismount Michael." He said it calm as could be & it was like he shook me awake. My heart begun thumping in earnest fear now but I followed Tom & we swung down from our saddles & stood down hill with our horses as cover holding the reins & aiming & letting fire with our muskets over the horses' backs. Two arrows struck Tom's mount in his flank & shoulder & he did whinny but stood his ground as if knowing he was there for to cover Tom & myself. My horse she was not as staunch after her wounding some weeks before & she spooked at the onslaught as I fired & I did not hit a thing other than trees but Tom caught one of them Braves square in the bread basket knocking him back off his mount to come crashing & bouncing down the hill to smash up agin a tree beside us his back broken along with the ball inside him. Though I am shamed to say it I thought to myself that this dead Brave had a fine head of long black hair & I should like to return & scalp it when the shooting was done. Even a fool can speak the truth if he is let.

But I did only think it for a second for the Indians kept coming a bloody howling terror some 20 odd of them though they did not stop for Tom or myself which surprised me. I did not reload but turned my Springfield round & held it by the barrel swinging & missing as one Indian passed but he could not shoot now neither as he was too far back in his saddle for balance down the hill so we were both unwounded that Brave & myself.

I saw then what they were up to & Tom & myself did not feature in it for they sought to split the wood cutters & their guard into 2 parties to have at the one 1st & then chase down the other if it did not stay & fight. They did also want to cut out the route to the block house where we could gather & defend ourselves.

I let drop my rifle & drew my Colt to fire down at them & my horse did again spook & jerk the reins this time from my grasp. That sonofabitch horse then fled leaving me to share Tom's mount for cover which I did not need as the raiders kept pace on down the hill into the cutters where they engaged in battle tomahawk agin tree axe. Some of the gunless men took off running down the hill with some of the Indians in pursuit. I did watch one cutter holding his end of a 2 man saw & just staring up at the Indians like he did not believe they existed at all let alone be coming down upon him. His mouth was agog & well the last thing he ever looked upon in this World was the fall of a club & I did flinch for that poor man's head burst open under that warclub like an egg hit with a spoon. I will never forget that sight I tell you.

After that I could hardly make out anything for the hill side did go off like a banging cannon & gun smoke from the timber men & from the soldiers & the Indians did bloat the air. There was terrible screaming from the cutters & soldiers & howling from the Indians & before we knew it fire from the timber men & the soldiers came a flying up at Tom & myself splintering the pine trunks about us & we did be forced take cover from our own side instead of rushing down the hill to aid them.

And just like that before we could get a grip of the fight & before Tom & myself could join it in truth it was over for the Indians skitted their ponies across the pine stumped waste & out into the meadow where they cut down one man on picket & chased another & ran the mules & oxen off in the direction of the Big Horns.

"The mules! The mules!" some fellow was shouting & I mounted the back of Tom's horse & held tight as Tom spurred that horse down the hill to the bottom. There we came up on Capt. Brown who I did not know to be with us. He must of rode up after the train with a section of the new Cavalry boys arrived at the Ft. under Capt. Fetterman.

There was my horse bucking about with the eyes rolling round her head with her reins held in a Cavalry man's hand & I jumped down from Tom's mount to take the reins from him. I gave the beast a good pelt in the jaw with my fist for desertion & mounted that high blooded horse. She was not a bad horse but not the best either.

Brown was in high spirits with the horse Tom broke for him dancing & tugging at his reins. "After them men! After them!" cries Brown. "I want every G_____ D_____ mule back & scalps for every one of our dead."

This did give me cause to wonder how

many dead he meant & later heard it was only 5 but 1 of them was worth 100 men. I will come to who in a minute.

Well we did hare out after our mad quartermaster across the stretch of stumps & into the meadow grass after the Indians. They had maybe a 2 minute start ahead of us but their flight was hindered by the mules & oxen & I thought we would catch them up if they did not shed their booty of livestock. I tell you Sir that chase was a lively one 10 or 15 of us full belting across the meadows of grass with white foam ruffing our horses' mouths firing our Colts as we rode wild down on them raiders. They were 10 or so it looked with some of them turning their ponies to the hills in hope that we might follow but no we stayed together in pursuit of the main body driving the stolen mules but before we could ride them down they began firing arrows & 1 or 2 bullets into some of the mules before making for the shelter of the mountains knowing our mounts were spent & that their ponies could run beyond death itself. They had our number & I suspect they were laughing as they rode away in victory up into the foothills of the Big Horns.

At last I fired a final shot after them though I know it did no harm for they were too far away to hit with a pistol bullet by then & I pulled up my horse for he was 1/2 dead with the running long lines of spittle hanging down from the bit in his mouth & heat rising up through his saddle like a stove burning wood. "There there now," says I forgiving her for her panic on the hill side because she ran well in pursuit as if to make up for deserting me before. The other Bills & Dragoons did also pull up now all of us fearing that if Mr. Lo decided to turn back on us there was nothing left in our horses to run or fight but only for to drag them down & use them as cover.

Brown was in a rage shouting, "The b_____ those f_____ red b_____ !" but he was smiling behind it for the Mad Capt. is not like regular men at all & does not care too much how many white men get mustered out by the Indians only for it gave him excuse to chase them. But that day even he was not smiling for long.

It took us almost 1 hour to walk our horses back to the Cut with stopping off at the Little Piney to water them & when we got back well we came upon something that will never leave my eyes no matter how long I live & nor will it ever leave my heart. It is fierce hard to recount on the page but I will because it might show you how things to happen later perhaps were forged by it so. I will brace myself & just write it here without pause or reflection.

On our return we found Sgt. Nevin laid out in the bed of a wagon box with a white haired timber man & a Bill from another Company tending him cleaning & bandaging him with torn shirts best they could while the driver & others gathered what mules they could to put them in harness.

In tatters was our dear 1st Sgt. & I felt like spewing my guts up at the very sight of him. The broken shafts of many arrows at least 8 of them pierced his body which was stripped of his clothes. He lay there naked as the day he came into the world & his head was soaked red with blood the whole of it like he was dipped in crimson paint & under this blood his skull shone through to the bone where the savage b_____ lifted his scalp with their skinning knives & our dear Sgt. Nevin still living while they done it. This they did before filling him full of arrows like a lady's pin cushion.

And through all of this Sgt. Nevin must of suffered terribly for there in the wagon bed he was yet alive if you can imagine. You may think it a miracle Sir that breath was still in him after all that but if you could see his lower parts & what them f_____ savages done to them well you might think poor Nevin better off dead surely. For they did rend his balls off altogether & the Sgt.'s legs were red washed with blood & gummed in dirt & pine needles from how he crawled some 100s of yds. through the forest where he was ambushed to make it back to the lower blockhouse where our men found him. His prick was barely hanging 1/2 on him & 1/2 off him like the b_____ did not care to finish the job they started or were disturbed in the work of it. It was terrible Sir. Even in the War I never saw such a thing.

Another of our men Linders a quiet gentle Swede was found dead too with his throat cut & with no scalp but his trousers on him in the same spot where we reckoned Nevin had his horrors for there was blood on the ground & even on the pine trees & in the branches. One of Nevin's boots was found too but his & Linders' horses were gone no doubt stolen away by the savages God's Curse Upon Them. I tell you when I think of it I would kill every 1 of them in this whole black country women & children all. I am not the only one to think this as you will see.

Well Tom did turn his mount away from

the sight of Nevin steering him this way & that among the stumps like he was searching for something he might strike down or kill & some other of the men were the same while many of the boys from our C Company had tears cutting ditches down their faces their very eyes gleaming with them. And tears came to my eyes too for our 1st Sgt. his chest rising & falling with the labour of taking breath & the broken arrow shafts rising & falling too with blood leaking from their wounds with each breath.

I made a prayer to God In Heaven. "Please Holy God Take Sgt. Nevin from here & keep him now beside You for the Devil has already done his filthy work. Seat him with You in Heaven Holy God because this place is no more for him & he is no longer fit for it." But God as He is want did not listen to me at all.

With the mules at last harnessed we made an escort around the wagon as the timber man & the soldier in the wagon bed with him tried to pour water through Nevin's lips but I could not see if he could take it.

All I can tell you now is that the 5 mile journey back to the Ft. felt a life time & again I prayed that our Sgt. would die & be free from his terrors & his torment but he did not pass on yet but instead lived for 10 more hours. A harder man to kill you will never in your life meet but this quality does not always be a blessing.

If my prayers were answered & he did pass on in that wagon bed then all that was to happen later that night might not of happened. If one thing was different or if God ever listened to a single prayer I made —

44

December 20, 1866 — Fort Phil Kearny, Dakota Territory

Pale light flares as the guardhouse door opens.

"Daniel, my dear Daniel." Molloy is propped on his new crutches.

"Captain, you should not be out of your bed."

Molloy laughs and begins to cough. He holds a handkerchief to his mouth and hacks, heavy and liquid into it. Kohn sees blood in the kerchief as the captain wipes his lips.

"I have come to see your prisoner, Dan. I hear he has a testament of sorts for my eyes only."

Kohn notes how weak is Molloy's voice — the officer's skin yellow, malign shadows under his eyes — as he guides him to the woodstove to warm himself. "It is near a book now, sir. He wants to see his brother, he says, before he can finish it."

"A book . . . fine thing. I will sit with him and read it but he won't be seeing his brother any time soon I don't imagine. The surgeon's dog has told me he's skedaddled."

Kohn shakes his head. "I could have told you it would happen, sir."

"Daniel, you make me weary with your hard charging."

There is a stirring behind the cell door and then a banging on the door. "What is that, sir? What did you say of my brother?"

Molloy crutches over to the door and opens the Judas hole. "You should not take it as gospel, my friend. It is said he has deserted but that may be false. There is worse news you could hear of him around this valley I would imagine."

Michael O'Driscoll says, "He would not run without me, sir."

"I can only tell you what is said, Private. I'm sorry for your troubles."

Michael O'Driscoll curses under his breath in Irish.

Molloy smiles and says, "If your brother is a bastard, Private, pray what does that make yourself?"

The prisoner does not smile. "I did forget you can speak in the Gaelic, sir."

"Would it have changed the sentiment if

you remembered?"

"No, sir." Michael turns away from the Judas hole and goes back to the open ledger on his desk. "It would not change a thing for either of us." He begins to write, scratching hard at the page, and the officer watches for a moment.

Molloy then hobbles back to the table and sits. "Boil that kettle, Kohn, and we will have coffee. And pour a mug for Mr. O'Driscoll, hard at his labors."

"He's had his grub, sir."

"He will need it to go on, Kohn, if he is to finish his tome. And paint the three mugs with this," Molloy says, placing a half-empty bottle of whiskey on the table.

Kohn turns away from Molloy. "It is cold in here, sir. You will catch your death."

Molloy smiles at Kohn. "Daniel, my friend, I caught that some years ago, as you well know."

45

THE NIGHT YOU WISH TO HEAR ABOUT & THE END OF THIS TESTAMENT

You have said my brother is in the wind now so there is no reason for me to go on or there does be every reason. In truth I do not know which but I feel I am come this far so must finish now. And you are owed it I suppose. I cannot forget what you did for us once that day at Chickamauga though it does seem another lifetime ago. It is strange to think of the War as a simpler time for us but put agin the spot you find me in now it does. Was it a simpler time for you too Sir? But that is by the by.

Anyway I need not tell you that when we returned to the Ft. & word went round of poor Sgt. Nevin's torture at the hands of the savages well all of us not on picket or fatigue went for to stand vigil outside the hospital barracks & we did stand there until the Surgeon came out & ordered us away telling us that he & his nurses would do all they could for the 1st Sgt. but that prayers was what he needed not men standing round waiting. He told us that our vigilance would be better served watching for another raiding party such as the one who did for our beloved 1st Shirt Nevin.

And so we all did mope back to barracks to light the stoves as normal though not many were in mind to take food. But as you might imagine Sir all were of a particular mind to take a drink & as dusk turned to darkness the whiskey it became like tinder to the fires of fury in the camp.

It was late when a fellow coming off picket let us all know that the good Sgt. was dead finally & Thank God for that. There was a long silence then with men just sitting & thinking I can only imagine what. The silence was finally broke by my fine Italian friend. "Red b_____," Johnny Napoli said aloud in his Italian way & Pvt. Rogers from Cincinnati said he would like to gut every living last red skinned c_____ on the plains of America & more boys said the same & jugs did be tipped & drunk while lo & behold someone of us did know where to find some Indians G_____ D_____ It All & we did decide right then we would send them straight to Hell we would.

Though none of us could see it from inside the stockade we all knew of the loafer camp just outside the Ft. for we passed it or looked down upon its pointed tee pees from the sentry stands nigh every day. Living in this camp is the so called friendly Cheyanne who are not joined up with Red Cloud & his Bad Face mob to fight agin the U.S. Army. They claim to want peace & carry letters of safe passage signed by Carrington the Carpenter himself. They are not our enemy in that camp & truly they are a harmless rabble of old folk & women & babbies & some men who be more fond of trade sap than hunting. But it did not matter to us were they friend or foe only that they were f_____ Indians.

What we would not do to them I tell you Sir such was our terrible thirst for blood & like one man the raging bitter gang of us got up & made for the livestock gate wicket which is closest to the riverbank by which the friendlies make their camp. It was a terrible sight this wild herd of men some of us hefting pistols & others muskets & skinning knives. In my own belt was my pistols & my brother had his too & of course his mighty D Bar knife & I am now brim full of shame

542

to say I joined that mob with murderous intent in my heart.

The pickets on the livestock gate did nothing to halt us they just swung it right open for us for they fully approved of our action & we did maraud in silence from the Ft. with not one of us thinking that aside from them <u>friendly</u> Indians in the camp there perhaps might be proper hostiles in the grass or in the cottonwoods along the Little Piney bank. No we did not think this & only for the night's blackness to keep us from running we walked slowly towards that camp like snake's venom working its way up a man's arm.

I tell you Sir a man could hear the grass swish about his legs as he walked & the rasp of sabres & knives as boys drew them from scabbards. Rounding the bend in the riverbank I could see the Indians now in the light from their fires & their dogs took to barking upon seeing or smelling us. In scarce a minute we would be upon them & as we closed on that camp some 50 yds. away 1 or 2 stood up to look into the darkness while others just sat on like it was their fate that such a horde be coming for them in the black of night & they did not seem to fear what was coming for that thing was already there & it was us.

It brings shame upon me to write it but as we neared the camp I picked out the Indian I would shoot down 1st for all the rage & fear of the weeks & months in this Valley was in me that night. It was a rage for all the dead comrades & timber men & stolen horses & cattle surely but mostly it was for Sgt. Nevin who we all loved. I thought again of him in that wagon bed with his body pierced by arrows & his balls & hair cut clean off. That man did not deserve to die in such a way. Well all of this came rising up in my breast & it was like I had no control at all of what was inside me.

Closer we got & I could hear a babby crying from one of the tee pees & 1 of the Indians by a cook fire held out his letter from Carrington of safe passage & by God you would not wipe your arse with that paper or mop up blood with it & though we did try to be quiet about things there is no way for 50 men with drink & rage upon them to be quiet about anything in the world. Every one of us had a weapon drawn. My heart beat hard in my breast harder than it did any other time I met an enemy in battle.

I raised my Colt & began to run towards that camp of Indians when of a sudden there came the rumble of hooves & I did halt fearing attack. It was not Indians on them horses though for someone must of gone informing Carrington of what was afoot because he & Capt. Van Eyke & a whole body of officers & some of the new cavalry men came from the main gate riding like Hell's raiders & as one our whole mob turned to the sound of their coming & their terrible shouting to Stop! & Halt! & What did we think we were at? & Back to the Ft. for you lousy f_____ no good b_____ or you will be strung up like game birds!

Well we were all like a man woken from a terrible dream & the officers & soreasses rode in rings about us some of them splashing in the shallow river lashing out with their reins & others batting at us with the flat of their cutlass blades while our mob took to running. I went myself one way & my brother another until he turned back & took hold of my arm.

"This way!" says Tom to me. "Tell Metzy to come this way!"

So finding a gap in the furious circle of cavalry we 3 did run opposite the direction of most boys who tried to make for the Ft. We instead ran away from the stockade into the darkness of the cottonwood trees on the banks of the river just below the Indian camp & for a moment I did think that my brother was circling back on the loafer camp to wage his terrible vengeance for our poor 1st Sgt. come hell or high water. But now I did not want this for that babby's cry was still fresh in my ears but Tom was not thinking this Thank God. Maybe in his heart he could not bring his own self to cut down kids & squaws for even <u>he</u> is not so mad or bad or wild as that but I am not sure of this.

"Wait," says he there in the darkness of the trees so we stopped to watch as Carrington & the cavalry boys rounded up many of the mob & drove them like beasts back through the livestock gate some jogging & some walking with heads held low like they were caught at something filthy in the night.

"They will be f_____ rightly," says Tom.

"And so will we Tom," says I. Metzy leant over with his hands on his knees sucking wind.

I will confess that part of me rose up in respect for the Carpenter Carrington but another part of me did hate him there in his saddle lashing boys with his reins & roaring orders for them to return to post. If only he could be so fierce & bloody minded in the face of the Sioux & Cheyanne b_____ who kilt Nevin as he was <u>in defence of them</u>

he might be some sort of officer finally but I was not thinking straight that night you surely can see that I was not.

"Well what will we do now brother?" says I to Tom in Irish & then again in English for the sake of Metzger.

"We will go to Kinney's," says he.

"Is all you can think about for the love of God?" says I back to him.

"No," says he. "We will be hauled up for quitting the post if we are caught at the shebeen but that is a lesser crime than trying to kill them friendly Indians. We will take a rotten detail or 2 for whoring against Carrington's orders but them boys will be for it far worse. Do you see it brother?"

I did see it though I did also see it would give him fair chance to meet his girl either way but I did not mind. For the day had been hard & I could not think of anything else to do then. I felt only a fierce sadness for Sgt. Nevin & a sudden terrible fear standing there in the shadows of the trees on the river bank even if I could see the Ft. only 100 yds. away. I tell you I felt the fear of death there in the cottonwoods. I felt so far far away from my home in Ireland as far away from it as I could be & all alone in the world at that minute as if my brother was not with me at all & in a way he was not for his head was in other places altogether.

Well this fear took the place of the rage I felt before. Cold goose flesh came out on my back & all I could want was for to be inside some place warm any old place at all that would let me think that I was not in this Godforsaken pit this horrible dark Valley of Absaraka. Such guilt & fear I felt there I could of wept bitter tears for what I was just then. Nearly a butcher of babbies & women. A lost soul with no home at all in the world. I was a black hearted thing as black as a crow altogether.

I know now I should of gone back to the Ft. & took my medicine like a man but what a fellow knows now means nothing to what he did then.

Instead of returning to the Ft. my brother said for us to follow him & we did crossing the Little Piney stumbling over rocks & stones at a shallow point. Our boots were soaked through but we were afraid to take them off lest we crack an ankle in the dark rushing water that covered only our shins but was still treacherous to us in our state of agitation & with the drink upon us.

So with wet boots we followed the opposite bank of the river around the back end of the Ft. some time later leaving the river bank to tramp through the long grass making 3 dark shadows tween Pilot Hill & the palisade. Well we could of been wolves there in the darkness & chill night air of autumn. Such was the labours of our silent march we broke a sweat by the time of reaching Kinney's hog ranch & we brought the cold of the air into that low rank dugout with us.

My brother did be smiling as we went inside because there his girl was sat in the corner though she was not smiling I tell you. Says Tom, "Whiskey Mr. Kinney & keep it coming & if you are asked we were here all evening for there is malice afoot outside & we should not be caught up in it."

I repeated Tom's words to the Sutler for they were muddled in his mouth with the whiskey already on him & the cold of our journey. 1 of the whores came up to Metzy now it was his favourite the 1/2 mad squaw girl who was beaten with the fire iron by the mistress of the ranch as I told you before. Well this hen says to Metzy, "Take off your boots & sit here by the fire Metzy my little Metzy." So he did & we all took off our wet boots & socks & hung them there about the fire & before long they did set to steaming on the pot irons above the flames while we took our jugs of red eye & set to drink it.

I did not tell you that Ridgeway was already there on our arrival. I wish to God he was not. But there he was sitting at the bar with his picture making kit in its trunk against the wall near where the mule-skinner sat.

Now it does pain me to say it but I felt a stab of spite for Ridgeway him there all the time in the kip house making his pictures of the whores & playing at or indeed <u>being</u> a great friend to Kinney & his wife who were nothing to me but scheming greedy Devils far below the likes of our Ridgeway. But in truth that Quaker boy did be better in <u>all</u> ways than the low borne likes of myself & my brother too for he did not judge anybody roughly but instead had a kind word for everyone. But spite did rise in my breast all the same.

Says Ridgeway, "Michael I am terribly sorry to hear of Sgt. Nevin's misfortune. A terrible day for him. A terrible day for us all."

I gave a nod but did not go over to him because of my spite. Instead I set by the fire & held my toes out to it like I might take some joy in the heat but there was no joy in me then not even in a whorehouse with a jug of whiskey to warm me & more coming.

No there was no joy in such a place on such a day.

"To Sgt. Nevin!" said my brother out of the silence. "May God Keep Him." We all raised our glasses to his memory not hardly able to say his name. 1st Sgt. Nevin. William Nevin. And as if God could hear us in the Heavens or the Devil down below the wind began to blow like a bellows & smoke choked back down the chimney & our eyes & the eyes of all the whores & the mule-skinner on his seat in the corner did sting red.

Tom had his arm around his girl & he alone was smiling. I did not know if it was the smoke or just the thought of Sgt. Nevin but tears began to run down my face & down Metzy's face too & Ridgeway came over to us & set on a stool but just outside our little circle of whores & soldiers saying nothing.

I tipped some of my whiskey into the fire & the flames did flare up & it was like Nevin's spirit ascending or maybe I was just dolted with drink to think such a thing.

Says Metzy now, "Will I play us a tune boys?" And though I did not feel like singing it was the proper thing to do for Nevin did always like a sing song & so I said this.

"Nevin would not have us acting like kids

with no cake about the place boys. He would want us to raise a glass & wake him with a song or 2 well would he not?"

"He would," says my brother.

"Then get us that fiddle that f_____ plank of wood that sounds like a strangling cat Mr. Kinney," says Metzy to the Sutler who did not smile but did not object for joy in a hog ranch meant more coin in his trousers & he fetched the fiddle with its warp you could see across the room so a boy would nearly have to play it arsewise. "And another shoulder of Bust Head there too," says my brother & the Sutler went back to the bar like he did not hear him but still came back with the whiskey.

Well the singing & playing did start up rightly then. Even one of the whores sung a song for Sgt. Nevin in her own tongue & though her song was an Indian lament it did not bother the lot of us because it was well intended & soon the stools & chairs got moved back & we begun to dance with the whores & with each other with only Tom's girl to stay sitting for she did not look well. And as always (I will never forget it as long as I live which may not be long) but that G_____ D_____ cuckoo clock did set to cooing & ringing in the hour of 2 in the morning & Tom's girl started at the sound like she knew that clock was counting down to something.

"Take a drink," says Tom to her sweetly. "Take one & you will feel better."

But she did only push his glass away & left the room for her quarters behind the curtain with Tom following. Tom did always worry after her so I gave it no more thought then for we were whirling & dancing & singing now about the place with our bare feet on the cool packed dirt of the floor all the time pouring more whiskey into us & singing songs for the soul of the good Sgt. May He Rest At The Right Hand Of God. I sang The Vacant Chair & Hardtimes & Metzger played sad airs betimes & wild tunes for dancing as well & the clock ran on but it felt like no time was passing at all.

Everything was just grand I tell you Sir. It was just the wake Nevin would of wanted but things took a turn with the Sutler's wife arriving at the shebeen. God Himself only knows what she wanted with coming there at such an hour. Likely it was to make sure her husband was not drinking away their profits as was his way but no matter. She came & if she hadn't well things might of been different altogether.

Says Ridgeway to her, "Good evening Madam."

Says she back to him with a face like the plague, "Good what's good about it? The Ft.'s been locked up for good now. The Col. issued an order for courts martial of any soldier found outside the walls after taps. It will cost us pretty." And then she looked to her husband like it did all be his fault. "It will cost us a pretty f_____ penny," says she with a mouth like a deckhand on a whaler.

Says the Sutler back to her, "Well these boys were never allowed off post without orders before tonight but they still came. Do not get vexed about it Clara." But Clara was vexed & spat a string of tobacco juice into the fire. She did think herself high borne but was just as low as the rest of us.

Well it is hard to write it but now Tom came back into the room through the curtain to take up a water bucket. Seeing this Mrs. Kinney with no Fare Thee Well at all did light upon Tom for no reason we could see. Metzy stopped his sawing of the fiddle & Ridgeway let go the hand of the girl he danced with. Says the Mistress of the house, "You! Did you pay for your poke or are you still rutting around that bitch for free?"

I think it took Tom a moment to get her meaning & when he did a darkness came on him you could see it in his face. Says he,

"Well I did not poke her at all. The poor thing is unwell & in no state. She is resting."

"Resting?" says the Mistress nearly screaming it at my brother & Ridgeway made to soothe her like Tom might soothe a spooked mare. "There there Mrs. Kinney. There there the poor girl is sick as Tom says."

"Sick? Resting?" says the woman & then she did something that I would not believe for she began to mumble & blubber in a mockery of how Tom does talk saying again & again, "Sick? Resting? Unwell?"

Even her husband that rum b_____ came around the bar now for to catch her on & Tom only stood there taking her malice for what else could he do?

"Now Clara," says the Sutler to his wife & she did light on him in turn. "Now Clara? You can f_____ a horse for all it matters."

It was then that Tom's girl came out from the whores' quarters through the curtain with her voice so faint I could not make out what she said but the Mistress could.

Says Mrs. Kinney, "You will be fine & all right for poking & drinking & any other thing I tell you. There will be no malingering —"

But the poor girl did not hear her because she just then begun to spew up her guts & though Tom made to catch her flow of sick in the bucket some of it splashed the hems of the Madam's skirts. It is no lie to say that all in that kip went silent on seeing this all of us waiting with our breath held like time was stopped.

It seemed an hour but was only seconds before time started back up & that Madam did lash out & struck Tom's girl across her cheek so hard you might of heard that slap all the way back in Kansas & before the sound of that slap fled the air Tom did seize that woman by the throat & raise her up off her feet as if to throttle her & it came to me that instant (that very second I tell you!) that this would be the end of 1 thing & the start of something else.

For it does pain me to say it & I am ashamed of its happening but that woman's face did go right blue with Tom's grip about her neck & Tom's poor cutnose girl did turn & spew some more & all of this seemed like a terrible dream at 1st until that muleskinner stood up from his stool & drew his knife.

Well yes this is where everything came a cropper. All of it was a mistake I swear to you it was not meant to happen even though that Sutler's wife was a low borne evil

woman & probably deserved her come up-
pance or maybe she did not. But that mule
driver had enough blood on his hands so I
do not feel so heart sick to say that before
he could cross the room with his blade I
drew my Colt & though I was deep in my
cups I was so accustomed to shooting I
could do it in my sleep & I did thumb back
the hammer & fire & put a ball in the chest
of that fellow where he stood. My 2nd shot
missed but my third did not & the skinner
fell back to sitting on his stool with 2 bloody
holes in him & no change at all in his face
but maybe a look in his eyes that did say,
"What is this? I have been shot."

Well the smoke from my Colt filled the air
of that foul tavern & Tom did release the
Kinney woman who took a mighty gasp of
air & then fell to the ground in a fit with
froth about her mouth & her eyes rolling
back in her head & her body shaking.

True as God Sir I did almost go to her
aid but her husband well he should of gone
to her & not for the Henry rifle kept above
the bar on the wall in case of an Indian raid.
If Kinney went to his wife instead of for
that rifle well then he might be living still &
my brother & I both hanged from short
ropes but he did reach for it in the end.

He did not get it of course for Tom

stretched an arm across the bar-top to grab a fistful of Kinney's shirt & then he did drag him back & lay his D Bar knife up into the back of that Sutler's head like I saw him do several times in the war so that the Sutler was stone dead before my brother dropped him & he hit the floor with the blood gouting out of his mouth in one final surge.

And all the while I must tell you Ridgeway did be shouting, "Stop! Please stop this!"

But we could not stop what that woman started & though many things may of happened tween the time my brother met his sweetheart whore & the time he lifted that Madam by the neck for striking her well nothing did happen that may of stopped it all from coming to pass. It is like God did ordain it to happen & well I am sorry that it did but more so for Ridgeway who had nothing to do with it & is dead now & died with such a thing blackening his soul. If there is any mercy in Heaven I am sure God will understand this & take pity on him.

For there was worse to come yet in that dugout tavern I tell you. Not knowing what to do I sent the other 2 away saying to them, "Metzy & Ridgeway you go back to the Ft. & speak not a word to anyone or we will all hang I tell you. Not a word."

Well Ridgeway he did not move at 1st & though he must of seen a good piece of dying & dead men when he made pictures in the War I do not think he was ever in such close quarters to bloody murder as this. Well like I did say I was sorry & <u>am</u> sorry but done is done & already I was angry at the Sutler & his witch of a wife for making all this murder happen.

"Away with ye both. And not a word," says I & finally they did leave.

"What will we do brother?" says I then.

In Irish Tom said to me, "The woman still breathes." Like that he did say it like he was surprised by this.

"We will have to run for it," says I.

"We will get nowhere without horses Michael. They would be on us in no time. And the woman still —"

I cut in on him.

"I know she is still alive for the Love Of God Tom! And now what? Now f_____ what?"

A rage came upon me for I did also blame Tom for all this. Every bloody bit of it. We could of hung in Ireland & been buried in the earth of our home next to our father & mother & their fathers & mothers before them but instead we had to come to America to kill & suffer & tremble before the

Rebs & now the Indians & all of it just to hang for the honour of a slapped whore? God In Heaven it was a rum scene & the vanity of it did twist my heart. "Why brother?" I begged him in my head. "Why did you never ever do the right thing? Why did I always follow you brother? Because you are my brother? Or because I am such a fool?"

But as I was thinking these angry questions Tom's girl crossed the room to the muleskinner & took up his knife & before you knew it she did set to carving the scalp right off that dead boy before bringing it over to me. Well I did not want it & could not believe my eyes & she seemed to understand so she put the bloody pelt of long black hair down onto the bar. Then with the knife she went to the Sutler's wife who lay there in the dirt agin the dugout wall. In truth this does be hard to write but I knew well what Tom's girl would do before she did it & I will confess to you I did nothing to stop it & nor did my brother.

For the Sutler's wife ceased her fitting now & was taking in big gulps of air & she opened her eyes in a state of terrible confusion like she did not know where she was or how she came to be there. Tom's girl standing over her said something in her Indian tongue & through the curtain came the other whores from their quarters where they were sheltering from the shooting & terrible doings & they went over to stand around the Madam all 5 of them.

When they were all gathered there Tom's girl did hand the muleteer's blade to Metzy's girl with the wide innocent face the one who Mrs. Kinney beat with the fire poker. I swear to you that girl smiled such a smile of sweetness you would think she just seen the Light Of Heaven before her & this did appear to stir something in the Sutler's wife for she started to weep then saying, "No no no no."

Well I do not need to tell you Sir but that whore did reach down & grab that woman's hair & pulled her head back & with a swipe did cut clean through her throat. One of the other whores took the knife from the fat one then & she stabbed the woman some times before she passed the knife on to the others who did the same & blood flowed & sprayed about the place so that myself & my brother were forced take a step back. And as they did be stabbing & killing that woman stone dead well that cuckoo leapt out of its hole in the clock there on the back bar & well didn't Tom's girl stand up from her terrible labours & go over to it & take it

561

& smash it to bits on the bar with wood & pieces of it flying about like the clock had done her the same great wrong as that dead & bloody woman on the floor.

I tell you Sir I did wonder what kind of God in the Heavens would look down on such a slaughter of blood & rage & murder & not do a thing about it. But maybe He <u>did</u> do something & <u>you</u> are that thing. Perhaps you are his Angel sent to claim justice for the murdered whore master & whore madam & their 1/2 breed sentinel & though I cannot say we do not deserve such justice I must ask the question <u>Are these the best of those I've kilt?</u>

I do not think so. I know I did lay to rest far better men white Rebel Sesesh boys & Indian Braves alike & no one sought to hang me for doing it. So it is a strange world where you can kill fine men with no consequences & then be arrested & strung up for killing the rum & no good of the world like that Sutler & his terrible wife & their skinner God Forgive Me but that is the way I feel.

After the whores stopped their butchery Tom & myself decided then to make it look like hostiles did raid the tavern & do the killing which in a way is true though not true at all. We took the liquor out from behind the bar & threw the bottles into the river & we took the safe box where that Sutler kept his takings & the key from his body to open it but we did not take the money in the end for we could not decide if Indians would thieve paper money or even would know what it is. You may think we took it but we did not I promise you Sir. Maybe the whores took it & if so I wish them well for it was hard earned by them.

I do not remember what else we did to leave it look like Indians attacked that hog ranch but Tom told his girl to say this to anyone who asked & she said she & the other girls would say this.

Them girls I do not need tell you did not stay about to say anything to anyone & took to their heels before the sun shown the next day over the Valley. They are in the wind now maybe gone back to their tribes or maybe to new kips under new names & wherever they went you will never find them. Of course Tom's girl did stay as I told you but she & my brother are now gone too. Only the slow fat doll remains the girl once beaten with the fire poker by Mrs. Kinney the one who works now for herself from a tepee by the river. I did hear you & your terrible Jew paid her a visit & so you surely know she is away in the head from her mistreatment & so can hardly be blamed for any crime. Though to save her own skin I think she may of turned Turk & informed you about Tom & myself but for this I do not blame her. She is only a poor beat down creature.

In the end Sir I beg you not to judge them poor whores harshly for they did have a terrible time of it from that woman. For though they killed her that Madam did be killing them slowly every day by cruelty & enslavement & I think a skilled barrister may argue that they did for her in self defence or in a bout of madness & thus be not so culpable but you will likely never find them & I will be dead before then anyway.

It now comes to me to state that Pvt. Daly who was picket on the gate did know nothing of our part in the crimes at the hog ranch & only let us through the livestock gate because we forced him to do it. He is in no way guilty of any crime but silence & should not suffer for it. If his testimony did help land us in this gaol then so be it I do not hold it against him & do not think him an informer. Also Addy Metzger is innocent of all crimes he did nothing & had only the misfortune to be there when they happened. I would burn these pages if I thought you would have him up over something he had no part of.

And though I betimes feel it should be Tom sat here in this cell waiting the noose instead of myself & though I curse him for abandoning me when I would of never done the same on him well if you should find him I pray that you will take account of how my brother has not been right in the head from the time of his wounding at Chickamauga. You know well Sir that my brother took his wounds in the service of the Nation so maybe you can show <u>him</u> some mercy if not myself.

As for me I am sorriest of all that Ridgeway is dead more sorry than you can know & I feel that it is mine & Tom's fault that he is gone & we will pay for it in the Next Place we are bound for when we are dead. But as for the Sutler & his wife well you reap what you sow in this world. I put to you Sir they had it coming.

This is the end of my testament.

God's Will Be Done.

46

*December 20, 1866 — The Pinery,
Dakota Territory*
Dusk descends on the Pinery and with it a
stillness unnatural to a forest but not to this
one that is razed to a field of stumps and
frozen mud for hundreds of yards about the
blockhouse. The only sound Thomas
O'Driscoll can hear is the ticking of cooling
blades from the mule-driven sawmill shed,
some fifty yards away from the fortification
that will serve as his billet for the night. Tom
has often wondered why the Indians did not
destroy the mill shed or the blockhouse in
the night but they never had. He himself
would have done it, if only out of badness,
but that is the way he has come to see the
world and he knows there is no turning back
from it.

The woodtrain has since departed, taking
Ridgeway Glover's remains with it, and Tom
stands now over the fading embers of the

566

blockhouse pit fire. The stone embankments with their loopholes rise a foot above his line of sight and he has retracted the ladder deep into the trenched seam of earth. Not that anything will help him, he knows, if Indians come for him. They will come in numbers and though he may take one or two of them to hell with him, they will have his hair in the end. But he will put a bullet in his own head rather than be captured. Death he does not fear but Tom has seen what Red Cloud's warriors did to those they took alive. And he has heard from a Crow who passed the woodtrain one day that the Sioux know well about him and what he has done to so many of their own. The Crow told them that the Sioux call him Broken Face. That they call Carrington the Little White Chief and Captain Brown Burning Face. They would love to get their hands on Broken Face, the Crow said, pointing to Tom.

So if they come, they come and some of them will regret it. Better by far to die fighting than skinned and boiled. Better a bullet in the brain than a hangman's rope for that matter. Poor Michael, he thinks. Poor brother. He squats over the fire to take the last of its dying warmth. Let them come.

But if they do not come? There are decisions to be made, he thinks. *And I will make them on the morrow if I am still alive and walking.* He has hardtack and cooked bacon and a tin of cherries in juice given to him by Captain Brown himself when the officer told him to stay in the blockhouse until things with the brother cooled down at the fort. Out of sight, out of mind, Captain Brown said. And you need to stay out of that Jew bastard's mind now that he has your brother in irons.

Tom rests his Springfield against the stone wall. When it becomes too cold outside, he will retreat into the blockhouse itself. There is no doubt the dregs of the captain's whiskey inside and that will keep him warm.

Dusk becomes darkness and the wind works the trees on the hillsides where they have yet to cut. A bird or beast, he does not know which, screeches from someplace nearby and Tom thinks of the banshee but she does not scare him anymore. He thinks of Ridgeway. Michael was right, he thinks. He shouldn't have gone to Ridgeway and threatened him to silence. It would not have mattered at all in the end, for the Jew and the drunken lieutenant came anyway. Someone somewhere had talked and likely it was not the poor Quaker boy, God give him rest. Too many about the fort knew about what happened, though most thought it a fine end to their debts to the thieving sutler. Two can keep a secret, Tom thinks, if one is dead. Ridgeway was a friend and Tom is sorry for his passing and how hard a death the Indians gave him, but with the way he often wandered off on his own it might have happened anyway. God rest him, but he was too soft for this world. He should have stayed back East making pictures of ladies and gentlemen in their homes of redbrick and lawns of green grass. He had no business here because the only business here is cutting trees and killing and Ridgeway was opposed to both. A kind and decent man, Ridgeway, but too soft for the world altogether.

The creature, a fox, Tom decides, screeches again, yips. A coyote maybe. Later he will hear wolves but he does not fear them. There is nothing left to fear but a hard death. If wolves come, he will take one or two of them with him same as if they were Indians. Poor Michael, he thinks. Poor, poor Michael, will I ever see you again? Another man too soft for this world in the end, Tom thinks, with his notions of a farm or becoming a picture-maker like Ridgeway. There is no farm of land or pretty pictures in a poor man's future. Only sweat or blood or the rope. Tom spits into the dead fire. There is no luck for the poor man in this world at all.

He stands to take himself into the blockhouse and as he does he hears footsteps, the frozen mud sucking and crunching in turn and Tom lifts his Springfield, then sets it down and takes from its sheath his Bowie knife, pressing his back against the wall, using the shadows there. He cranes his neck to peer out of a loophole in the stone wall but through it sees only darkness. The footsteps stop some feet down the pit from where Tom waits in shadow and then there is the sound of scrabbling and a figure comes over the stonework, feet feeling among the set stones for purchase. A leap then of several feet and the figure is in the pit eight feet from Tom and Tom comes from the shadows with his knife drawn back. He swings the knife.

"Tom."

The knife is a foot from the throat of the figure when it stops.

"Thomas?"

"Sarah?" Tom says, a shudder running through him. "Sarah?" His voice is loud and thick in the darkness, as if he has shouted. Joy and terror surge through him. He has a desire to roar into the darkness and the joy and terror lodge in his throat as a sob and he knows that for a moment he will not be able to speak. He fumbles his knife back into its sheath in the darkness and steps forward to take the girl into his arms. The girl pulls away.

"I have horse. We go now," she says.

He swallows and the sob dies in his throat and joy wells in its place. It is the first time she has ever called him by his name.

"Come now. We must go," she says.

"But it's no good, girl. The Sioux will be out. We will be got by the Indians, Sarah."

Sarah turns and begins climbing back up the stone bulwark. "No Indians tonight," she says. "Indians fight the morrow. We must go now."

Tom grabs his rifle and meagre supplies. He is smiling as he follows his woman up the stonework. The wind has stilled itself and the stars above the Pinery are sharp and clear in the night black sky.

47

At the table in front of the guardhouse
woodstove, Molloy sits with Michael
O'Driscoll. In front of him is a quartermaster's ledger, its pages thick and swollen with
damp.

"I'm told it is true that your brother has
run to the hills, Private, and he has taken
his Sarah with him and the colonel's missus
is without a parlormaid this morning."

The prisoner smiles. "I am only sorry I
am not with him but one of us free is better
than none all the same, God go with them.
I have made my choices in this life."

"You chose this guardhouse, didn't you?
There was no call for it. There is little
enough in the way of evidence, Private, little
enough to point to your guilt."

"There is enough of it inside me, sir."

"Guilt is a hard thing on a man. I know

it. But you overestimate the choices you have in life, Private, I imagine."

After some moments of silence, Michael O'Driscoll says to Molloy, "We met, sir, once in the war. You did save the brother and myself and we are in your debt."

"Kohn has told me this but I am ashamed to say, Míceál, that I do not remember it." Molloy pronounces Michael as an Irish speaker would and the prisoner smiles.

"I did write of it in this." The prisoner gently pushes the ledger across the table in front of the captain.

"Of course you did."

"I am no scholar, sir."

"You are wise enough to know the truth, Míceál, I can see it in you."

"I have tried to know it and to write it, sir. My story, and Tom's, well, it is there as best as I could put it. What happened to them in the shebeen —"

"What your brother did, perhaps, Míceál?"

"It's not my brother," Michael says. "He — I did tell you all of it in them pages in front of you."

"You've told me some of it, Private, but not the whole of it."

"Sure, when does any man get the whole of any story? We take what we do get and use what we need and go on about things from there, sure. There does be no whole story, sir, only the one we do choose to tell."

"And you have chosen to tell me that you are guilty of the killings in the tavern."

"It is there on the page, sir. You may hang me now and be done with it but the truth is that them three are dead but so is Ridgeway and the guilt I feel is for that. He was my friend and I did fail him and my neck will fit the noose for it, I tell you."

"*Whisht,* Míceál," Molloy says. "*Whisht* and fetch me a light from the stove for this cheroot."

Michael returns from the stove with the lit cigar and hands it to Molloy, who puffs the tip to burning orange. "Tell me this, Míceál. Your friend, the picture-maker. Would he see you hanged for what you claim you did? For what your brother did?"

"For what I did, sir."

"Would he see you hanged? A friend?"

The prisoner is silent for a long moment. "I don't know, sir."

"And if the situation were reversed? If you were dead and some blame could be attached to the action or inaction of a friend in its cause, would you have your friend hanged for it?"

"I would not. Of course not, sir. But there is what I want and what is right in the eyes of God and —"

"God's eyes are not on this place, Private. He is looking the other way if He's not blinded altogether by what we get up to down here."

The guardhouse door opens and a breathless private enters. "The woodtrain is under a big attack, sir, bigger than any before, and Colonel Carrington has ordered all men here released to defend it, sir."

The private carries a ring of keys and begins to unlock the large cell at the far end of the room where seven men are held for various offenses.

"All men here, Private?"

"Yessir, but he didn't say nothing about your prisoner. I don't know what that means you is to do with him. I'm only a dog private, sir. Uncle don't pay me for what's 'bove my shoulders, sir."

"Nor does he any of us, Private. Think not another moment about it but go about your business," Molloy says, pulling on his cheroot. The racking cough recommences and when it stops Molloy wipes a ribbon of blood and spittle from his chin with his coat sleeve. He then takes a bottle from under his coat and pours out two measures into tin coffee mugs on the table.

"You will share a sup with me before you

go, Míceál? *Céard a déarfá le deoch an do-rais?*"

Michael O'Driscoll says back to him, "*An dorais,* sir?"

"The woodtrain is under attack, Private. All hands are needed. Any man who can hold a gun. You can hold a gun I have been told."

"But sir —"

"I have made a choice, Private. It is time for you to make yours. *Deoch an dorais, Míceál?*"

Michael O'Driscoll watches as the men from the cell emerge blinking into the light of the open guardhouse door. One or two of them are refusing to leave the cell and the private remonstrates with them in the cell's doorway, a winter's incarceration preferable to what awaits them outside the palisade.

"Thank you, sir. *Deoch an dorais.*" A drink for the door. O'Driscoll raises his mug to the officer. "For friends dead before us."

"And those soon to be dead," says Brevet Captain Martin Molloy, raising the tin mug to his lips. He pauses before drinking. "And take your story with you when you go. I know well what is in it already."

48

December 21, 1866 — Fort Phil Kearny —
Sullivant Hill — Lodge Trail Ridge

There is the sound of hooves on frozen mud and the rough footsteps of hurrying men and Kohn thinks to wake but sleep binds him. He has sat up watching his prisoner draft his confessions for the past several nights, and now he turns and hugs himself under his buffalo coat, the grass ticking in the mattress holding him in its warm embrace.

Molloy is dying and even in sleep Kohn's body is thick and slow with the sadness of it. He dreams of the captain smiling. Or perhaps it is not a dream but a memory from a long time ago.

Private Rawson bursts into the visiting NCO quarters where Kohn sleeps and Kohn reaches for the pistol under his pillow.

"All up," Rawson shouts, as Kohn's hand

reaches the walnut grip of the gun. "Colonel's orders. All up to defend the woodtrain or stand picket. Every man who can hold a rifle. I got your horse saddled and ready outside. Hup, hup, Sergeant Kohn. Rise and shine, sweetheart."

Kohn relaxes at the sound of Rawson's voice and rolls over.

"All up and fall out, goddammit, Sergeant," Rawson shouts, relishing his opportunity to let roar at Kohn, to rouse him from his sleep. "This attack ain't like others. Bigger, fuckin' big as they come's the word. All hands to guns. Every damn body on post from chaplain to Guardhouse Charlie, says the colonel, and that means you too, Sergeant, so you may get your ass outta that rack and —"

One word sears through Kohn's stupor and he throws off the weight of buffalo coat and blankets. *Guardhouse.* He jerks on his boots, shoves his pistols into his belt and holster. His gloves, his cutlass, the Spencer repeater he takes up from the corner beside his bunk.

"You tell me, Rawson, you tell me that guardhouse still has my prisoner in it."

"Hell, Sergeant, I can't tell you that but every man in the fort is called to defend it or the woodtrain so —"

"Where's Captain Molloy?"

"Well how in a month of fucking Sundays could I know that, Sergeant?"

Kohn leaves the barracks and mounts his horse. He gallops her halfway to the guard-house and stops on the parade ground, not needing to proceed farther. Molloy is standing in the guardhouse doorway.

"I was only following orders, Daniel," Molloy shouts and Kohn has to strain to hear him over the commotion of horses, clattering kit on running men, barked orders and men mounting the sentry stands around the palisade. Molloy is smiling as he shouts and then begins to cough, a deep and malignant hacking that Kohn can hear clearly above the mounting din of readiness around him. God damn you, Kohn thinks. God damn you to hell, Captain. He turns his mount for the main gate and assembling troops without looking back at Molloy. He is not sure he could face the man if he had to.

Horses drag at reins, nipping those around them, riders jerking them to order with gloved fists as the main gates to the fort are hauled open with a shriek of frozen hinges, the popping of winter-solid pine sap, and Kohn scans the horse soldiers gathered and waiting to leave the fort. Over the noise he can hear the faint crackle of rifle fire from some distance away but this is not what concerns him. He scans briefly the orderly files of the newly arrived company of cavalry out of Fort Laramie and disregards them, focusing on the loose rabble of mounted infantry, many in scarves and buffalo hats, several in buffalo coats that Kohn knows will make any fighting that may need to be done difficult and unwieldy. As he notes this, he sees him, one of the coated men. No hat but the heavy hide coat and a blanket roll strapped to the back of his saddle. *God damn him!* Kohn barges his mount through the rabble as the mass of horsemen begin to move out the gates. Somewhere behind him he hears an officer say to somebody that they are not to pursue the Indians, under no circumstances are they to pursue them.

"You will be back in that cell by day's end, Private. Do you hear me?" Kohn says, coming as close as he can to O'Driscoll amid the mass of horseflesh and riders.

There are four men around O'Driscoll and they close ranks about him. Hard men. Scarred faces. Wide-eyed mounts keyed for the chase. One of the men speaks in German to him, blond hair spilling from under his kepi, a bugle on a strap around his shoulders, short in the saddle. "You will do better to stay here, Sergeant. No one knows where a ball will find its home once it is fired."

Kohn says back to the bugler, in English, "I know mine will find a home in your head if you so much as look cross-eyed at me, Private."

Someone shouts, "Heeya, move out." O'Driscoll and the men around them spur their mounts and tug reins and they are away at a gallop out the gates. Keeping one eye on O'Driscoll, Kohn follows the pack of riders out onto the plain of winter-dead meadows that lead from the fort to the foothills from where the snapping of muskets has become so rapid that it sounds like a fire catching in dry grass.

Michael O'Driscoll rides alongside Metzger and Daly and several others from C Company and these men form a phalanx around him. They will not see him taken by the terrible Jew but O'Driscoll knows as he rides that the cavalryman is behind him. He can feel the weight of his eyes on his shoulders, the burn of them, and he knows that if not the Jew cavalryman it will be someone else. Always someone behind him as it has been since his brother felled and killed that boy on the Kilorglin Road back in Ireland. The hot breath of the hunter, the guilt rousing him from sleep ever onward. He shakes these thoughts away. The gallows rope would have ended all this for him. Better the rope maybe, than living with one eye forever cast behind you. They crest Sullivant Hill, the thundering of several dozens of horses, and all such thoughts are banished by what Michael sees before him.

The woodtrain has halted some fifty yards over the lip of the hill, gunsmoke smearing the air around it, and a number of Indians charge the train, loosing arrows, one or two firing rifles, before taking their mounts down the slope of the hill and around a stand of trees at the bottom, as if making for open country. Michael and the pack of mounted infantry climb the trail, closing on the woodtrain, and as they do the Indians appear to see them and flee from their muster point at the top of the road above the train and at this the mounted infantry steer their mounts down the hill in pursuit.

Michael turns down the hill with the other riders, leaning back in his saddle as they descend, focusing on the frozen ground under the grass, the hidden furrows and rabbit holes that will shatter a horse's leg and kill you on a hill like this as quick as a minié ball or arrow.

They reach the bottom and the ground levels out by a stream in the crux of two hills. Here the air is clear of gunsmoke and Michael can see the first of the fort's contingent of cavalrymen under Captain Fetterman rounding the stand of trees to their right. A half company of infantry soldiers on foot come down into the stream-bed next at a jog, never having made it to the top of Sullivant Hill, and they too round the stand of trees, a winding blue snake against the snow-clad ground, and Michael and the other mounted infantry follow. Around this stand of trees there is a beaten path leading to Lodge Trail Ridge and then the undulating open plains where the Indians will lose them. He spurs his mount and pulls away from Metzger and his friends. Better to hunt than be hunted.

Kohn follows O'Driscoll down the hillside into the creekbed, riding alongside mounted infantry sloppy in their saddles, civilians, timbermen equally awkward in theirs, some of these carrying modern repeater rifles like his own. All hands to the guns. He notes arrows now, flashing from the tree line in stinging flurries, and sees a rider ahead of him fall. An arrow passes between him and another rider. The sound of musket fire again now from around the stand of trees and Kohn senses what is coming even as he knows he will not stop despite it, will not cease until he once again has Michael O'Driscoll in irons or sees him bleeding out on the frozen ground.

Kohn sweats under his tunic despite the bitter cold and he rounds the stand of trees and splashes through the shallows of another stream, the ground rising up from it on the other side to form a small ridgeline. It is more gully than valley here and in the tight suck of streambed between the tree line and rising ground uniformed riders have broken ranks and are riding in a chaos of directions. A rider with terror in his eyes barrels back across the stream and Kohn is forced up the bank to avoid a collision with him. As he does this, his mount slipping and clawing at the frozen mud of the bank for purchase, he loses sight of O'Driscoll, clamps his thighs around his mount as he senses her tense beneath him to leap up from the streambed onto flatter ground.

Kohn's horse lands and skips awkwardly and Kohn thinks she has broken something or slipped a shoe and as he looks down to check there is a raking pain across the back of his neck, an arrow snagging at his skin and lashing his scarf out behind him in its lethal flight. If I hadn't looked down, he thinks, then looks up and he hears it now, above the smattering of gunfire and through the gathering smoke in the gully where they have followed the Indians; where, as he sensed and now knows, the Indians wanted them to follow all along.

The sound is high-pitched and terrible, goose pimples washing up Kohn's back as they did in the war when he heard a similar noise coming from rebel lines. Howling, yipping, barking, laughing. Like the rebel yell but not like it. Kohn forgets about his horse's leg and spurs her up the incline toward the top, following any number of others who have done the same as Indians pour from the tree line, splashing through the stream, firing arrows, hacking, stabbing, howling. Kohn spurs his mount harder and can feel her fear beneath him as she can feel his. Still he searches for his prisoner.

O'Driscoll leads Metzger and the others as they round the tree line into the gully, their horses splashing, smashing through the thin sheen of ice on the stream. He sees the mass of cavalry ahead of them turning, firing into the tree line, flashes of fire followed by billows of smoke, and the cavalrymen turning in their saddles, pistols pointing into the wood. Whatever they are firing at is obscured suddenly in all the smoke and like Kohn, some thirty yards behind him on the upper bank of the stream, Michael hears the gathering howl from the cottonwoods and sees the ambushers emerging from the trees, the vague shapes of them coming, fifty, a hundred, in the swirling gunsmoke, and terror sparks down his spine and through his legs and his horse feels it too and lurches for the high ground and he lets her.

"Metzy," he shouts. "This way, Metz." His breath is barged from him as he is thrown back in the saddle, gripping tight to the reins as his mount eats yards of frozen hillside, kicking snow behind her as she climbs and then reaches the top of the low hill, bounding over it and into a raised and frozen meadow onto which, from all sides, hundreds more Indians come, howling, howling, some on foot, many more on horseback and what seems but a handful of blue-coated soldiers in a frenzy of terror. Horses are jerked this way and then, bolting for one side of the meadow only to find more Indians there, turned back and more Indians are coming. An arrow passes so close by Michael's ear from behind him he can hear its hiss, feel it carve the air.

"Michael!" It is Metzger's voice and his friend now comes thundering up to him, his mount's eyes wide and white with terror. "They are everywhere coming behind us."

A bugle sounds from across the meadow above the howling, a weak and incoherent bleating, a panicked cavalry bugler attempting to blow some sense of order to the fight or to the retreat and without waiting for an answer from O'Driscoll, Metzger raises his own bugle and sounds the order to retreat, loud and sharp in the icy air. He does not wait to be ordered to do it, in essence taking command of the fort's riders, mustering them to flee behind the blaring of his bugle.

Michael scans the meadow — flailing tumult, pistols and rifles firing, smoke beginning to cloud the field — and then spurs his mount forward, north, away from the fort. There appear to be fewer Indians to the north of the meadow. He has his Colt in one hand and fires as he rides. Around him there is slaughter, the snow churned to mud and blood and Metzger is behind him and then is not. Michael sees an arrow strike Daly in the throat, another in the chest and Daly falls and Michael lashes his mount with his reins, horse and man thundering through the storm of ambush.

As he rides, long reins lashing, his senses are alive to flashing aspects of the battle. There is powder smoke in the air — he can taste it now and knows the taste well — and the heat of the beast beneath him; there is blood and glinting steel and bodies battered to the frozen ground. Most of all there are Indians and in their hands are every manner of swinging blade and bludgeon, gun and bow, spear and scalping knife. Michael has a flashing view of a bluecoat crumpling to the ground, an ambusher upon him before the soldier has hit it.

He is nearly clear of the tumult, more than halfway across the frozen meadow, when an arrow strikes his thigh with a force that feels as if he has been hit with a hammer, the arrow driving through muscle, deflecting off bone and emerging partly from his leg to enter his horse, pinning his leg to the beast as the horse bucks and turns and then continues on, riding, riding. Another arrow strikes his mount and she stumbles nearly to the edge of the meadow, to the decline there, the shelter that might be had in the cottonwood trees if he could make them.

Another arrow strikes Michael's horse now and she falls and he is thrown, his fall tearing the arrow from the side of his horse. The breath bursts from his lungs as he hits the frozen ground and he gasps, bright lights like fireworks exploding in his eyes. He lies on his back, his mouth yawing for air and it comes finally, a deep relished breath that brings back with it the sound of the slaughter around him. Above him there is a brief respite of blue sky between the clouds. Around him there is smoke and blood and howling. He feels the approaching footsteps through the ground on his back.

Kohn hears the bugle call to retreat as he crests the rise into the meadow and his eyes are drawn to the bugler and next to him is O'Driscoll who spurs his horse and begins to race across the meadow as if straight into the heart of the fighting, firing his pistol as he goes, and Kohn follows.

He is closing on O'Driscoll when he sees his quarry's horse fall and watches as O'Driscoll is thrown. Watching this Kohn feels but does not see his own horse stumble as she crushes someone or something beneath her hooves, and from his left comes a rider, an Indian on a pony painted in bright shades of ocher, tomahawk raised, and this Indian closes suddenly, faster than Kohn imagined possible, the tomahawk coming down.

Kohn twists in his saddle and fires his pistol and the hatchet glances off his shoulder with a thud and lodges itself in the thick leather of his saddle and for a galloping moment he and the Indian are riding side by side, the Indian trying to wrench the tomahawk from the saddle and Kohn trying to thumb back the hammer of his Remington and finding his arm paralyzed by the axe blow and, as if sensing this, his horse turns abruptly away, pulling the Indian still gripping the tomahawk from the back of his own horse to the frozen ground. A fine horse, Kohn thinks. A wonderful beast. He scans the meadow as he rides, his eyes passing over the battle around him, looking for the fallen O'Driscoll.

Before Kohn has put forty yards between them, the Indian is back on his feet and he draws an arrow from the quiver at his back and strings it to his bow. He looses the arrow at Kohn and the arrow flies true and straight.

49

December 21, 1866 — Little Piney Creek
  Bank,
Dakota Territory

Jonathan sits outside his tipi on a log at a small fire and listens to the distant sounds of battle. The scout sees the lieutenant coming along the riverbank on his crutches.

"Jonathan, I would have thought you might join in the hurly burly, my friend," the officer says. His face is pale, his eyes yellow.

Jonathan motions with his hand. "Too many to fight. Only them who want death today choose to fight."

Molloy coughs and the coughing continues for some time. He holds a kerchief to his mouth and when he is finished coughing, he does not check it for blood because he can taste the blood in his mouth.

"The wisest among us, Jonathan. Where is your winter wife?"

The Pawnee nods up stream, towards the mountains. "She went away with the other Cheyenne. They are afraid. Of what is coming."

Molloy notes that many of the tipis that were along the riverbank on their last visit are gone. A few remain but are silent, void of life, their fires cold. "You're not fighting but you're not afraid."

"I will go when you pay my wages."

Molloy smiles. "Of course. Here you are, my friend." Molloy takes his billfold from inside his tunic and counts out thirty dollars. He hands the money to Jonathan who takes it without speaking and puts it into a leather purse worn on a thong around his neck.

"And tell me this," Molloy says. "Our friend Two Doves. Is she gone away as well?"

"She is there where she always is."

"She's not afraid like the others?" Molloy smiles.

Jonathan notices that the distant firing has all but ceased, the battle drawing to a close in the foothills beyond the fort. He says, "If you have nothing in life, you do not fear death."

Molloy laughs and begins coughing. When he is finished, he wipes his mouth with his sleeve. "No, Jonathan. No you do not. God speed to you, sir. We will not be requiring your services any further."

The Pawnee nods to Molloy. There is nothing more for him to say.

HISTORICAL NOTE

Wolves of Eden is set during Red Cloud's War (1866–68) — an uprising of Sioux, Northern Cheyenne and Arapahoe Indians against the encroachment of migrants to the gold fields of Montana. In response to Indian attacks on travelers, the U.S. Army sent several companies of infantry to protect white "pilgrims" and establish a fort on the Bozeman Trail in the isolated Powder River country in the Dakota Territories. Nearly half the soldiers manning Fort Phil Kearny — and thirty-odd of the eighty-one killed in the ensuing Fetterman Massacre of the fort's troops by Indians, the Battle of One Hundred in the Hand, as it is known to the Lakota Sioux — were native-born Irish immigrants or first generation Irish-Americans.

As such, Fort Phil Kearny as seen in this novel was a real place. It *is* a real place and you can visit a wonderful recreation of the fort — the original was abandoned in 1868 and burned by Red Cloud's warriors — just outside of Storey, Wyoming.

To spare the reader the same confusion I experienced during my research, I have changed the name of another fort which features in the novel — Fort Kearney, in present-day Nebraska — to Fort Caldwell.

Many of the events in the novel are as true to the historical record as I could render them within the bounds of fiction. The crime for which the brothers stand accused is fictional, though based on similar incidents in other Western forts. The crimes perpetrated by the government and army of the United States on the indigenous peoples of the American West are real. Fiction has nothing on them.

Kevin McCarthy
November 2017
Dublin, Ireland

BIBLIOGRAPHY

I read upwards of fifty books — or parts of them — when researching this novel, some better than others but all useful in their own way. The first of these, and the text that drove me to further investigate the role the immigrant Irish played as soldiers in the genocidal conquest of the American West, was Nathaniel Philbrick's *The Last Stand: Custer, Sitting Bull, and the Battle of the Little Bighorn*. Set ten years after the events in my novel, it is nonetheless an invaluable and gripping examination of the Battle of Little Big Horn — the Battle of the Greasy Grass. As in Fort Phil Kearny and the Fetterman Massacre, a disproportionate number of the government soldiers killed in that battle were Irish-born, and reading of this in Philbrick's brilliant book inspired my initial researches into the subject.

The Fetterman Massacre by Dee Brown is a very readable, popular account of the building of Fort Phil Kearny and the events leading up to — and the aftermath of — the Battle of One Hundred in the Hand as seen in this novel. The definitive account of these events, however, is *Where a Hundred Soldiers Were Killed: The Struggle for the Powder River Country in 1866 and the Making of the Fetterman Myth* by John H. Monnett, not least because Monnett gives equal weight in his account to the testimony of the Indians who fought in Red Cloud's War.

For a first-hand account of life at Fort Phil Kearny, *Absaraka: Home of the Crows* by Margaret Irvin Carrington is a wonderfully written — if sanitized and obfuscating in relation to her husband's responsibility for the deaths of his troops in the Fetterman Fight — memoir of life as the wife of the commander of a frontier outpost.

ACKNOWLEDGMENTS

The author would like to thank the following: my agent, Jonathan Williams, for his expert representation and editing; Starling Lawrence, Emma Hitchcock and the staff of W. W. Norton for their faith in, and tireless work on behalf of, *Wolves of Eden;* Allegra Huston for her expert copyediting and editorial suggestions; Bernard Wassertzug for his expert help with the Yiddish spoken by Kohn in the novel; Moya Nolan for her photographs; my mother and first reader, Juliet McCarthy, and novelist Ed O'Loughlin for their vital, occasionally brutal, professional edits; Colin McCarthy, Susannah McCarthy, Niall Hogan, and Diarmuid O'Dochartaigh, who read and offered valuable feedback on late drafts of the novel; Andy Connolly and Cynthia Olson for so generously lodging and feeding me on my trip to New York; Giles Steele-Perkins and Marty McGlynn for their amazing hospitality on my trip to Boston; Suzanne Matson of Boston College for her inspiration and advice, literary and academic; the staff and patrons of the Wagon Box Inn, Storey, Wyoming, for their hospitality and generously-shared knowledge of the Powder River Valley; the staff at Fort Phil Kearny, Wyoming, for their help with my research; all my colleagues and staff at ODC — particularly my jobshare partner, Carmel Hogan — for their support and tolerance; Breda Dunne, Mary McCarthy and Sergo Gabunya, Geoffrey "Jefe" McCarthy and Karen Fullencamp, Jonathan Grimes, Gina Pavlovic–McCarthy, Seamus Dunne, Eamonn Dunne and Susan Dunne for their support and encouragement; likewise my good friends Dennis Carolan, Alex Connolly, Giovanna Tallarico, Julie Cruikshank, Georg Ulrich, Niall and Natasha Mahon and Kieran and Teresa Roe; most especially, the author would like to thank Regina, Áine and Eibhlin, without whom this novel could not have been written.

ABOUT THE AUTHOR

Kevin McCarthy is the author of the highly acclaimed historical crime novel *Peeler,* selected by the *Irish Times* as one of its top ten thrillers of 2010. He lives in Dublin, Ireland.